THE WAY TO THE CATS

the
way
to
the
cats

❋

yehoshua
kenaz

translated from the hebrew by dalya bilu

STEERFORTH PRESS

SOUTH ROYALTON, VERMONT

Library of Congress Cataloging-in-Publication Data
Kenaz, Yehoshua, 1937–
[Ba-derekh el ha-̣hatulim. English]
The way to the cats / Yehoshu'a Kenaz; translated by Dalya Bilu.
p.   cm.
ISBN 1–883642–20–5
1. Title
PJ5054.K36B313 1994
892.4'36—dc20   93–49577 CIP

ISBN 1–883642–48–5
(Paperback Edition)

Manufactured in the United States of America

First North American Edition

chapter one

From the side entrance Mrs. Moscowitz could see a lawn and standing in the middle of it a lofty, broad-boughed tree with big, dark green leaves. A cement path crossed the garden, separating the lawn from an area paved with large, square flagstones and dotted with white chairs and tables standing in the shade of bright umbrellas. A few visitors sat there with patients talking quietly. Evidently patients from a more elegant ward, secret and privileged, she said to herself, people with connections for whose use this garden was exclusively meant. Even the clothes these patients wore seemed to her more attractive than those worn by the patients in her own ward. The visitors' appearance, clothes, and behavior all testified to their elevated status.

The atmosphere of the place seemed more suitable to the garden of a European café or a grand hotel in a spa rather than a hospital. The people spoke pleasantly and politely, and a restful, respectful quiet reigned over the garden. There were no noisy children like those constantly running up and down the corridors in her own ward, laughing, shouting, and quarreling, even during the afternoon rest period, sneaking into the patients' rooms and stepping right up to their beds, with their inquisitive, malevolent stares.

In order to get into this garden Mrs. Moscowitz would have to pass through a narrow doorway and go up one step to the landing that gave onto the sloping cement path. There were flowering shrubs with orange blooms on either side of the path. She tried to turn the wheels of her chair and force them up the step, again and again she tried, in vain. She was about to give up in despair, turn around and go back to her own wing, when suddenly she felt someone behind her raising the chair and gradually hoisting it onto the top of the step. By the time she realized what was happening, and turned her head to see who it was and thank him for his help, she felt her chair begin rolling down the slope of the path, at first slowly and then with terrible speed. The path did not look long at all, but the downward rush went on for suspiciously long seconds, until the chair overturned at the end of the path and she lost consciousness. There was no telling how long she had lain there before she came to. She labored to push the wheel-chair off her body, but it was too heavy. She shouted for help, but she didn't know if her voice could be heard. A long time passed before the wheelchair was lifted from her back, two strong hands raised her, seated her on the chair and pushed her up the path. She opened her eyes. The garden was empty. There was nobody on the paved terrace, the white tables were deserted and the umbrellas were furled. She passed alone there now, with the hated nurse Satana pushing her wheelchair and scolding her behind her back in her coarse voice, which scratched the nape of her neck like fingernails: "What were you doing here? If you died it would have served you right. This is no place for the likes of you, it's for different people here. If you lived seven more lives you still wouldn't get here." There was so much hatred in the head nurse's voice. No doubt was left in Mrs. Moscowitz's heart that it was Satana who had previously pushed her to the death from which only a miracle had saved her. And she had no doubt that Satana would try to kill her again.

A long time passed before this event surfaced in her memory. She had already risen from her wheelchair by then and was getting about with the help of a walker. Every evening after supper Mrs. Moscowitz would sit with her friends on the chairs lined up against the wall in the long corridor of their ward in G. Hospital, keeping one eye on the Arabic programs on television. One evening she told them about Satana's cruel attempt to assassinate her. She spoke in a whisper, scanning the corridor in case Satana, who knew their native language, should appear and overhear her. Her friends reacted skeptically. Mrs. Moscowitz stuck to her guns and would not back down from her story.

Frieda boomed in her deep male voice: "If that really happened to you the first week you arrived here, why did you wait all these months, why haven't we heard a word about it from you before now?"

Mrs. Moscowitz didn't know why. Why had the event been forgotten for so long? Why only last night, when she woke from her sleep, had the memory come back, sharp and vivid as new? But she knew that it had really happened to her, it wasn't a dream or a fantasy, it was alive in her memory as if it had happened yesterday. Why didn't they believe her?

Clara said: "It sounds like a TV movie," and laughed silently.

"Perhaps you dreamed it," thundered Frieda.

"No, it was true, it really happened. It was in winter, I was still in a wheelchair. It's as alive to me as if it happened yesterday."

"Supposing it really happened," said Allegra in her soft, hoarse voice, "how do you know it was Satana? You said yourself that it happened before you had time to turn around?"

Mrs. Moscowitz gave her an astonished, angry look: how dared she! What did she mean, "supposing?" Did she think she was a liar? She would never have expected this from Allegra, whom she loved for being a "simple soul." She wouldn't tolerate it, not from her of all people. The ingratitude of it made her blood boil—when she, Mrs. Moscowitz, supported her! True, not with the kind of money people

3

were accustomed to nowadays, but then she herself wasn't rich either and had nothing but her pension to live on (she had been a French teacher in a school in one of the rough neighborhoods on the city outskirts). Considering the modesty of Allegra's needs and her straitened circumstances, a few shekels a day were not to be sneezed at. And the assistance required of her in exchange was insignificant, fetching some little thing and returning it to its place, especially in view of the fact that Allegra was always wandering about aimlessly anyway. As for laundering her underwear, Allegra had offered to do it of her own free will, after seeing how difficult it was for Mrs. Moscowitz to bend down. Allegra had once found her in the bathroom, crouching over the basin they used for doing their laundry, groaning in pain. And she had knelt down beside her, taken the laundry from her hands, and finished the job without saying a word. Ever since then she had washed Mrs. Moscowitz's underwear regularly and received her reward: the dry, cracked skin of her hands suffered from the harsh soap, and Mrs. Moscowitz paid her the price of a good hand cream. Allegra used this cream frequently and liberally, after doing her own laundry too, and even sometimes without any particular reason— and Mrs. Moscowitz had never once made a remark about it. And now Allegra said: "Supposing it happened ... "

"And even if it was true," Frieda persisted in expressing her doubts, "who gets killed falling out of a wheelchair? At the most you can get hurt. But the whole story never happened anyway!"

Frieda had a family. Her son and daughter and their children came to visit her every day. The doctors and nurses were very friendly to them, listened to their requests and did their best to satisfy them. Every complaint of Frieda's found an attentive ear among the staff. She never said anything to her friends about what her family did for a living or their material circumstances, and when they asked her she avoided answering their questions. Mrs. Moscowitz guessed that they were very rich and well connected.

"What's the matter with you, Yolanda? What kind of tales are you telling us?" said Allegra.

A new note of self-confidence was evident in her voice, the tone of an equal speaking to equals. There was a smell of conspiracy in the air. The insult of Allegra's betrayal stirred in Mrs. Moscowitz's heart like an irritating insect, but she said nothing.

Mrs. Moscowitz was a big, heavy woman, her face was very raddled, and between the drooping flesh of her eyelids and the pink, wrinkled pouches below, strips of surprising blue peeped out through narrow slits, a pristine blue, clear and bright, like scraps of a lost, distant sky. Above her flabby, haggard face her hair, dyed a dull brown, lusterless and lifeless, rolled and puffed with exaggerated care, looked more like a wig than natural hair. She treated her hair almost as if it were an object of worship, as if it possessed some magic power to protect her; it was not merely for the sake of her appearance that she was so dedicated to its care, but out of some inner duty for which there was no reasonable explanation. For years her ailing legs had made it difficult for her to leave her fourth-floor apartment. Her few needs were supplied by her neighbors or by the delivery boys from the shops to which she telephoned her orders. But the hairdresser who had taken care of her hair as long as she had been able to go to the hairdressing salon, a hard-hearted and avaricious woman, would not agree to come to her house when the state of her legs worsened, despite the tempting remuneration she offered her and in spite of all her pleas and attempts to arouse her pity. And still Mrs. Moscowitz did not dare entrust her crowning glory to any other hands. Her only excursions were thus the agonizing journeys on behalf of the cruel Moloch on her head, journeys that grew more and more difficult as the years went by.

Every two weeks she would laboriously force her tortured legs down the four flights of stairs to the taxi, which was waiting outside the house to take her to the hairdressing salon on the corner of the next street. And when the neighbors heard the moaning and groaning and puffing and panting on the stairs they knew that Mrs. Moscowitz was going to the hairdresser. And they would bring a chair out to the landing for her to rest and recover her strength and offer her a drink of water to revive her spirits, and someone would volunteer to go out and calm the taxi-driver impatiently blowing his horn. And she, sitting on the chair, pale and panting, her large handbag hanging from her arm, full of various lotions and sprays for the care of her hair, would point to her thick, heavy thighs, and murmur faintly, perhaps to herself, perhaps to the neighbors standing beside her: "It's like knives inside, like a thousand knives."

On one of these expeditions Mrs. Moscowitz slipped and fell and broke her leg.

When she woke up after the operation, as soon as she regained consciousness, her first thought was: If only she had listened to the hairdresser's advice and had a permanent on her last visit, she wouldn't have had to worry about her hair now, at least not for the first weeks of her stay at the hospital. Salvation arrived only at G., the hospital to which she was transferred several weeks after the surgery, for a period of recovery and rehabilitation. Every week a hairdresser came from the little town nearby, equipped with all the necessary implements and supplies, and did the rounds of all the wards, shaving, cutting and setting, and giving manicures and pedicures as well. From the other patients Mrs. Moscowitz heard that it was the head nurse, Rosa, who had brought the hairdresser to the hospital, where she jealously guarded her monopoly. Some even said that Rosa got a cut of the hairdresser's fees. These rumors, however, only strengthened Mrs. Moscowitz's faith in Pnina the hairdresser, and after she had experienced her skills at first hand, she was so satisfied that she asked her if she would come to her apartment in Tel Aviv to do her hair after she recovered and went home. There were not many patients interested in Pnina's services in Mrs. Moscowitz's wing. Some of the women there were paralyzed, some had had their legs amputated, and most of them were either completely senile, or their looks were so devastated that hairdos were the last thing on their minds. Every week, therefore, Pnina spent a couple of hours attending to Mrs. Moscowitz, who entrusted her with her most precious possession, her hair, and rewarded her handsomely for her pains.

The next night she again remembered careening down the path of the elegant garden in the wheelchair. The sound of Leon's laughter in the corridor roused her from her slumbers. With a sense of relief she realized that nothing was happening to her now, that the event in the garden had taken place long ago, and only the shards of the memory remained to haunt her. She tried to ignore the noise coming from the corridor and fall asleep, but the voices grew louder. Mrs. Moscowitz could recognize each of them. Next to the duty nurse's station, facing the doors to the rooms, a few of the staff had gathered to watch television, to laugh and enjoy themselves. Leon's voice growled something, and the nurses responded with loud laughter. It wasn't hard to guess that he was using foul language, making lewd, suggestive remarks or telling dirty jokes. Mrs. Moscowitz had often regretted placing her trust in Leon and, in illusory moments of intimacy, even confiding her life story to him. He was a clumsy, ageless man, round-faced and balding, his eyes were big and bulging, with an unfocused look, his complexion was swarthy, and there was a lot of power in his thick, hairy hands. She imagined that like her, the nurses too were attracted in an evil way to the dark, the dubious, and the brutish in him.

She had already changed her mind about Leon a number of times. She recoiled from his coarseness and feared the suppressed violence in him, but whenever he came to help her up, held out his strong hands to her, gripped her elbows and with a grunt of encouragement raised her up until she was standing on her feet and leaning on the walker, her heart filled with warmth towards him, she regretted her hasty condemnations, felt guilty toward him, was afraid that he would hate her, and gave him his monthly gratuity before it was due. The other women suspected him of being the guilty party in the thefts of money that had taken place in the ward, and she was inclined to believe them, although she had no actual proof. He was a man of volatile moods. Sometimes he was even transformed before her very eyes, changing in a moment from a cheerful, good-natured man into a silent, gloomy one. All the men she had ever known were more or less the same. At first she thought that it was related to the size of the gratuity she gave him, later on she understood that his changing moods were affected not only by this, but also by things stemming from his own soul and from circumstances of his life she knew nothing about.

"I'll kill you, I swear I will! Ooh, you don't know what I'm going to do to you!" shrieked the head nurse Rosa—referred to by Mrs. Moscowitz, when speaking to herself or to her friends, as Satana—in a hoarse, vulgar, wanton shriek. And even the delicate, gentle voice of the little Ethiopian, Shulamith, whom Mrs. Moscowitz regarded as a snow-white soul imprisoned in a black vessel, now cried out, choked with laughter: "Stop it, Leon, stop it!"

At such moments Mrs. Moscowitz decided again, as she had already decided several times before, that from now on she would be more reserved and aloof in her relations with Leon.

In the bed next to hers, her friend Allegra sighed, sat up slowly, shook her head from side to side, and got out of bed to go to the bathroom. Someone in the corridor said: "Shhh ... " and the voices fell silent, who knows why, but in any case certainly not because they had seen Allegra going to the toilet. Mrs. Moscowitz waited for Allegra to return, and when she was on her way back to her bed, she called to her softly, holding out the empty glass on her bedside cupboard. Allegra turned round and went to the bathroom, where she stayed longer than she should have. Suddenly there was a sound of glass shattering and the thud of a fall. Then silence. Mrs Moscowitz was choked with dread. After a long moment she managed to cry out in Hebrew: "Nurse! Nurse! What happened to Allegra in the bathroom! Quick! Quick!"

It was still difficult for her to get out of bed without help. The stumbling block was the transition from sitting to standing. Two loops hanging at her head helped her to sit up, but her knees were too weak to bear the weight of her body. Nobody responded to her cry. The rowdy noise of a few moments before had given way to a suspicious silence. Mrs. Moscowitz called again: "Nurse! Nurse! Allegra fell! Hurry!" She gripped the two loops and sat up in bed, exerted all her strength and tried to stand up. For a moment it seemed to her that she would be able to prevail against the accursed weight, but her body fell back onto the bed. Finally the nurse Suzie came into the room: "What are you screaming about? You'll wake the whole hospital!"

"Allegra fell in the bathroom."

The nurse went into the bathroom and when she came out she was carrying Allegra in her arms. After laying her on her bed, she switched on the bedside lamp, and Mrs. Moscowitz could see her friend lying still on her back with her face bleeding. The nurse left the room and Mrs. Moscowitz burst into tears, of fear but also of pity. For the first time in years, she wept not for herself and her miserable fate, but for somebody else. She wept for love of this woman, who served her for a very meager reward, who lent her her legs to replace her own useless ones. And the tears dissolved all the remains of the resentment she harbored in her heart against Allegra for daring to cast doubt on her story.

The nurse returned, with cotton wool and a bottle of alcohol or some other transparent liquid, and began to wipe the blood off Allegra's face. When she saw Mrs. Moscowitz crying, the nurse said to her: "It's nothing, it's only the glass that broke on her face. Don't worry, she won't die—not of that anyway."

Allegra did not stir when the damp cotton wool touched the cuts on her cheeks and forehead. Her sick blood streamed down her face. With her thin, emaciated body, her head balding from the treatment of her illness, she looked like a young boy suddenly overtaken by old age. Mrs. Moscowitz had never loved her as she loved her now.

The head nurse, Satana, came into the room and examined Allegra. She looked at Mrs. Moscowitz and said in Hebrew: "Are you afraid, Yolanda, that you won't have a servant to fetch and carry for you any more?"

"She isn't a servant," protested Mrs. Moscowitz, raising her voice: "You don't know what you're talking about. We're friends and we help one the other. You don't understand that? You don't know that I'm a woman sick with the legs?"

"And whose glass cut her face, not yours I suppose? I suppose you didn't send her to get you a glass of water?" said the nurse.

"No," said Mrs. Moscowitz, "that's not true."

Allegra began to stir, opened her eyes, put her hand on her forehead and looked with a strange indifference at the bloodstain on her palm. Then she saw Mrs. Moscowitz weeping and she began to turn her bloodstained hand toward her, front and back, and front and back again. In the meantime the duty nurse finished treating her wounds, switched off the light and returned to her post in the corridor.

"It doesn't hurt a bit," Allegra's hoarse voice said in their language. "It's nothing, really it's nothing." And she added immediately, in a tone of astonishment: "I don't know what happened to me. All of a sudden I fell. I must have fainted. There was nothing out of the ordinary. Nothing at all." And when Mrs. Moscowitz failed to react, Allegra continued: "I've already told you a thousand times: I don't mind dying, I don't mind when I die. And I don't mind if it hurts a bit then either. There's only one thing I'm terribly afraid of: that I'll die alone, in the dark, in an empty room, without a single soul next to me. Oh, my sweet God, just don't let me die alone. Not alone. Not alone. Not alone ... " She went on repeating this in the dark, in a whisper completely free of fear. When the subject was death, Allegra would introduce words in Ladino into their language.

In the opinion of the doctors, Allegra had only a few months left to live. She was no longer getting any medical treatment, and the hospital wanted to send her home, since they could no longer help her, and in spite of her weakness she was capable of managing by herself. For this reason she tried as hard as she could to make them feel sorry for her and to postpone the evil day, to put it off from one week to the next, because she wanted to die in the hospital, next to her friends. A woman of about fifty called Adela, who spoke their language, took care of Allegra and helped her when she was still living at home, a room under the stairs in an old apartment block in Ramle. And every two or three days, Adela came to visit Allegra in the hospital, brought her dishes she liked to eat, bought her whatever she needed, handed her a little money from the National Insurance allowance that entered her bank account every month, and then, with indescribable gentleness, massaged her thin, sick body for a long time, and lubricated the dry, rough skin, cracked by disease, with baby oil.

Mrs. Moscowitz often watched Adela at work. Allegra would lie naked as the day she was born, her breasts as small as the breasts of a girl which had only just grown and were already shriveled, her hips as narrow as a boy's, and her skin a strange, dull, faintly brownish color. Mrs. Moscowitz didn't know what made her skin this color, if it came from her disease or from her Sephardic origins. The patient lay with her limbs outspread, her eyes closed, completely passive, her face blank and indifferent, and moved to and fro in time to Adela's hands, gleaming with oil, which turned her from side to side. Adela's fingers annointing her skin sometimes reached the hidden, delicate parts of her body, even lingered there with a special tenderness, since the skin there was more sensitive, more irritated, and more painful. More than once Mrs. Moscowitz had wondered what it must feel like to submit to the gentle, oily, practiced touch of Adela's hands. More than once she had said to herself that according to the state of her legs, she needed a massage no less than Allegra. Maybe even more. Because Allegra's fate was sealed, and her death was only a matter of months, while she, if only her legs would come back to life, if only she could walk, had a lot of good years ahead of her. She had no doubt that this massage would help, she knew that it wasn't like ordinary massages, but what it was exactly she didn't know.

Early in the morning, shortly after she had been helped out of bed, Mrs. Moscowitz saw Allegra carrying the plastic basin with her wrung laundry in it from the bathroom to the back porch, to hang it up to dry on the rope she had stretched from the railing to a pillar. She followed her, and when they were outside she examined her face in the morning light. The scratches on Allegra's nose and forehead looked like cracks in a plate that had been broken and glued together again.

She said to her: "You're doing my laundry today too? Where do you get the strength, after what happened to you last night?"

Allegra answered with a dismissive wave of her hand.

"Does it hurt?" asked Mrs. Moscowitz.

"No," said Allegra, "you don't have to worry about it."

"I'll pay for you to buy rubber gloves," said Mrs. Moscowitz. "They'll protect your hands better. Will you be able to do the laundry with rubber gloves on?"

"How do I know?" said Allegra, "I've never worn gloves like that."

"I'll ask Adela to buy you some rubber gloves, at my expense," said Mrs. Moscowitz. "I got such a fright last night when you fell. I cried so hard for you."

Allegra finished hanging up the washing, put the basin down on the railing, and thrust her hand into the pocket of her gown to bring up the tube of hand cream. Mrs. Moscowitz took her other hand and pressed it warmly. "It was so insulting, what you said to me after I told you what Satana did to me the week after I arrived here. It was all true! It was true, Allegra! I could quite easily have died there."

"I don't want to talk about it," said Allegra and removed her hand from Mrs. Moscowitz's. "She just told me again that they want to send me home." She gave Mrs. Moscowitz a look, as if accusing her of not understanding the gravity of her situation.

"Satana?" asked Mrs. Moscowitz.

Allegra nodded her head, "If only she liked me a little, it might have helped me. But what can I do for her?"

She began smearing her hands with cream, massaging them to make the oiliness penetrate deep into the skin. Then she wiped her oily fingers on her wounded mouth and whispered: "For me to die there alone in that hole, like a rat, that's what they want."

They went to have breakfast in the dining room, and Allegra, whose step was quick, a little nervous, adapted herself to Mrs. Moscowitz's heavy shuffle as she pushed the walker in front of her, bending over it and dragging her feet.

"I'm always nice to you," said Mrs. Moscowitz, "I've never insulted you, right? Tell me, when did I ever insult you?"

At this moment a new patient, a man, came toward them in a wheelchair, and the nurse walking behind him called out to them to move aside and let him pass. As he went by, Mrs. Moscowitz looked at him curiously. His face expressed incomprehension and resentment. For a second their eyes met. She thought that she understood this look. She followed him with her eyes until the wheelchair and the nurse behind it disappeared round the bend in the corridor leading to the physiotherapy room.

As usual, the two friends sat facing each other at the table in the dining room. But Mrs. Moscowitz didn't touch her food, she only took little sips of the tea, her eyes reflective. She didn't look at her friend, or speak to her, she didn't confide the thoughts filling her heart. And Allegra sitting opposite her, with her face which had been broken in the night and temporarily stuck together, with her little black eyes, slanting like a Chinese woman's eyes, out of which stared the quintessence of pain and resignation, was also silent, and she understood.

On their return from the dining room, Mrs. Moscowitz went into the bathroom. There she examined her face in the mirror above the basin. The hair-dye was still holding, but the ends of the hairs in the waves descending from her forehead to her temples, instead of curling in, were rebelliously standing up. She wet her fingers, smoothed the recalcitrant hairs and tucked them back into place, fixing them there with a few little hair pins she took out of the fabric bag hanging on her walker. Then she raised her chin to see if any stray hairs had sprouted up, lifted her upper lip with her tongue and slid it from side to side, until no hidden spot was left unexposed to her observant eyes. After that she turned her face left and right, and with the tips of her fingers, on both sides of her face, she pulled the skin away from her cheekbones and stretched it to straighten out the wrinkles. For hours she could go on gazing like this at the crown of her dull brown hair with its elaborate waves, at her smooth, unwrinkled face, at the strips of clear sky blue looking out of her eyes, at her nostrils flaring sensuously and her jutting cheekbones—as if she were looking at a different woman living inside her, beloved and unattainable.

The sound of the water running in the shower stall disturbed her and she moved over to turn off the faucet. A scream escaped her. A naked body lay on the floor, half in the cubicle and half outside it.

She turned round, pushing her walker as fast as she could, and shouted: "Quick! Quick! Why doesn't anybody see that she fell there!"

Raffy hurried in and soon afterwards he carried the sheet-wrapped body out in his arms, laid her on her bed, and wheeled the bed into the empty room at the end of corridor, the room that was always closed, where there were never any patients. The dead woman was Seniora, a quiet, good-natured old woman, with a smile for everyone, who always got up before everybody else, before the nurses woke them up, and began immediately on her handiwork, which she never put down until she went to bed, right after supper. With a hook and white DMC thread she crocheted tablecloths and doilies of various sizes and patterns, which were universally admired. She would give the products of her labors to the other patients and the nursing staff as presents. She was recovering from surgery performed to mend a fracture in her pelvis, was already getting about with the help of a walker, and was about to be sent home in a week or two. Her two sons, large, embarrassed men, came to visit her almost every day, in the evening, brought her new thread when she needed it, and would sit next to her for half an hour or an hour, sighing and speechless, softly stroking her bony wrists and her white hair. She didn't know how to read or write, she never sat with the other patients to watch television next to the nurses' station, she had no idea of what was going on outside the walls of her ward, but she was very good indeed at crocheting, and she worked at it from dawn to dusk with boundless devotion, and also with a certain urgency, as if she had to finish a certain number of tablecloths in order to be able to depart from this world with a peaceful mind. In Mrs. Moscowitz's bedside cupboard too there was a doily which Seniora had made for her as a gift, an exquisite pattern of netted holes and thread twined into flowers, complicated wreaths of leaves, and triangles whose points met and whose bases formed the circumference of the circle. She intended to put it on top of the television set when she went home.

Although this was not the first time during her stay here that Mrs. Moscowitz had seen dead bodies wrapped in sheets being wheeled into the room at the end of the corridor, it was the first time that somebody she felt close to had died. The only people in the ward now were Allegra and Adela, who had come to visit her, and the two of them were sitting on the edge of the bed and talking quietly. Soon Adela would begin to massage Allegra's body and to anoint her with oil, and Mrs. Moscowitz did not want to see this now.

She collapsed onto one of the chairs lining the corridor walls, removed the fabric bag from her walker, and took out her powder compact. She examined her face closely in the compact mirror, and dabbed a little of the whitish pink powder under her eyes and on the bridge of her nose, over her cheeks and her forehead, smoothed lipstick on her mouth, taking care to keep within the outlines of her lips, took the eyebrow pencil from her bag and underlined the arches of her eyebrows, returned to the rebellious hair-ends and removed the pins, and saw to her delight that they remained where they were, curving smoothly with the rest of the wave. When she had completed her makeup, she wanted to get up, but she couldn't see anyone to help her. The nurses' station was empty, and there was not a nurse or an orderly to be seen in the corridor. Most of the chairs along the walls were low and she couldn't rise from them without help. Again and again she thrust her body forward, with her hands pressing on her thighs, stamped her feet on the floor, as if to wake them up, heaved herself upward and let out a deep, visceral grunt to encourage herself, like Leon when he raised her to her feet—and fell back into the chair, panting and sweating from the effort. Raffy came into the corridor, and at the sound of her grunt he hurried up to her and asked her what was the matter. She wanted to ask him to help her up, but she had just seen him carrying the dead Seniora in his arms and the idea of being touched by him frightened her. He was short and broad-shouldered, only about twenty years old, although his big face looked much older than his years and it seemed that he was even beginning to go bald. His expression was serious and his eyes were small, deep-set and evasive, as if they were trying to hide some shameful guilt. He said little and did not mix with the rest of the staff, even though they treated him almost like one of themselves. Once Mrs. Moscowitz had succeeded in drawing him out and he had told her that he came from a refugee camp in the Gaza Strip. He had passed his matriculation exams and it was his ambition to study medicine at an Arab university. He slept in the hospital and when he wasn't working he spent his time studying, preparing himself to enter the university. He hardly ever went home to visit his parents.

Raffy headed for the physiotherapy room and soon afterwards she saw him again, walking behind a wheelchair with the new man, whose eyes had met hers at the beginning of the morning, sitting in it. She wanted to make them stop for a minute, and so she overcame her previous qualms and called Raffy and asked him to help her up. Raffy stopped the wheelchair and came over to lift her to her feet. The man sitting in the wheelchair turned to look at her. And again her eyes met his.

"Thank you, Raffy, you're a good person," said Mrs. Moscowitz.

There was no change in the serious expression on Raffy's face, and he returned to the wheelchair and pushed it down the corridor.

At lunchtime Mrs. Moscowitz did not go with Allegra and their other two friends to their regular table in the dining room, but stayed in the ward: Seniora's death and the memory of her body lying in the bathroom had spoiled her appetite and weakened her heart—she told them—and she had to rest and recover from the shock. After they had gone, she changed her dressing gown to a blue dress the color of her eyes and went into the bathroom again to examine her face and her hairdo. She dawdled there for a long time, deliberately. When she finally entered the dining room, her eye fell immediately on the new man's table. There were two empty places near him, one beside him and one opposite him. She directed her walker toward the empty seat opposite him, and when she approached him, he gave her a smile of consent, reinforced by a slight nod. Three other people were sitting at his table: opposite him two feeble-minded old women, and next to him, also in a wheelchair, a bald man with both legs amputated, wearing pajamas with the trousers folded underneath him. Mrs. Moscowitz had often seen him in the dining room and shrunk from him. Now his nose was stuck in his soup bowl, and he was rapidly spooning the soup into his mouth with loud slurping sounds.

The new man's face was long and pale, with a grayish tinge, his straight, thick white hair was smoothed against the nape of his neck. His chin was firm, his cheeks were covered with a fair stubble, his eyebrows were thick, white threads mingling with the yellowish hairs, and his beautiful eyes, which had preserved their unusual shape, were a light brown shading into green. She sat down across from him and tried to look indifferent, as if she had chosen this place purely by chance. Impatiently she looked around as if searching for the waitress to bring her her food, even though she wasn't in the least hungry. Suddenly she heard his voice, loud and clear as a young man's, speaking to her, and saw his outstretched hand:

"Lazar Kagan, painter."

She stretched out her hand and smiled at him with a polite, reserved smile:

"Pleased to meet you. Moscowitz, Yolanda, teacher."

"Please also to meet friend of mine, Marcel Fichman," said Kagan. He spoke Hebrew with a marked accent. He was waving toward the man sitting next to him. The man with the amputated legs in the blue pajamas, who up to now had shown no interest in his surroundings, concentrating all his attention on his bowl of soup, heard his name and immediately raised his head, put his spoon down next to his bowl, rapidly unbuttoned his pajama jacket, took it off, laid it on the stumps of his knees, and sat naked from the waist up, stroking his chest with his hand and smiling at her with a gratified expression on his face. Then he looked around to see the effect of this brilliant trick on his audience. Mrs. Moscowitz immediately covered her eyes with her hands and averted her face indignantly. Kagan laughed gleefully but she failed to understand what there was to laugh at. When he stopped laughing, he said:

"Fichman, for shame. In the middle of dining room you take off pajama? This is how gentleman behaves?"

And he helped Fichman to put on his pajama jacket again and fasten the buttons.

"Fichman begs pardon of Mrs. . . . " Kagan began.

"Please, Yolanda, I permit," said Mrs. Moscowitz graciously, with a friendly smile.

Since Fichman was now decent once more, she turned to look at the new man again and examined his beautiful eyes, with their unusual shape and greenish brown color. As she did so she discovered that his lashes were still blond.

"Teacher, what teaching?" inquired Kagan.

"French," said Mrs. Moscowitz, avoiding his eyes in order not to see the blond lashes again.

"What do you think you're doing, coming now when everyone's already finished?" demanded the waitress, coming up and depositing the tray in front of her, "Allegra's keeping a place for you at your table."

Mrs. Moscowitz's heart plummeted in shame. Perspiration broke out all over her body. She stole a glance at her regular table and saw Allegra sitting there, looking straight at her from the other end of the room. Suddenly she heard Kagan's strong, clear youthful voice declaiming with great pathos:

Mon enfant, ma soeur,
Songe à la douceur
D'aller là-bas vivre ensemble!
Aimer à loisir
Aimer et mourir
Au pays qui te ressemble!

And when his voice died away his hand still went on waving for a moment in the air.

In the silence that had fallen Fichman called out from his soup bowl: "Tfu, cholera!"

Kagan burst out laughing. Mrs. Moscowitz wondered what he found so amusing in this Fichman. "Phoo, shame on you, Fichman!" he scolded him again. "You speak like this in front of lady?"

"He's taking off his pajamas again!" said Mrs. Moscowitz, and she averted her face once more.

"Pardon, Madame, pardon!" said Kagan.

"I see that you know French," said Mrs. Moscowitz.

"No," said Kagan. "To speak I never knew. Only little to read, and that too I have forgotten. Today remains only few lines of things I loved. Memory today is not what she was. Once I knew all by heart."

"French," she said, "is the most beautiful language in the world. Nobody can deny."

His nose was slightly hooked, his high forehead gave him an air of nobility. His smooth, thick white hair, drawn back behind the ears, covered the back of his neck, its tips touching his pajama collar. For a few minutes they ate in silence. He polished off everything on his tray, while she ate without appetite. Something pressed on her chest. A feeling of panic took hold of her: everything was happening so quickly, and with her terrible weight, her clumsy movements, her numb legs, she had no chance of keeping up with the pace.

Paula, one of the old women sitting next to her, asked suddenly: "By the way, do you by any chance have the time?"

Mrs. Moscowitz scolded her: "For what do you want to know the time? Anyway you forget it right away and you have to ask again."

"Tomorrow my father's going to come and throw you all out!" said Paula angrily. She tossed her gray head and her eyes, behind the thick spectacles, reviewed the length and breadth of the dining room. "All this belongs to my father," she said, "he's the landlord. Tomorrow he'll come and throw you all out like dogs!"

"Quiet, Paula!" said Mrs. Moscowitz. "Please to stop talking nonsense."

The other old woman clicked her false teeth and moved her lips as if whispering to herself or cursing. Mrs. Moscowitz encountered Kagan's embarrassed look.

"How long you have been here?" she asked him.

"Four days," he said, "but today first time out of bed. Never in my life have I been in hospital before. It was accident in street, from bus. I am healthy man. After R. Hospital, for operation, they say I must stay here for some time or other. Rehabilitation, physiotherapy. I got real shock from this place at first, I can tell you." He looked around and behind himself, as if to confirm the justice of his feeling. "What terrible place!" he exclaimed, with a certain wonder. "At R. Hospital was something more normal. At first when I saw panorama here, I got shock. Depression. I didn't want to get out of bed, to go out of room. I can't see all this. And smell of kaka, excuse me, all the time."

"I was also feeling the same when I came here," said Mrs. Moscowitz, with a veteran's pride, "afterwards you get used. Today there was a dead woman in the bathroom and nobody noticed. . . . "

He interrupted her: "And I, as painter-artist, have strong aesthetic sense. For me it is harder to endure such things, harder than for other people."

A very egotistical man—Mrs. Moscowitz tentatively summed up her first impressions of the new man with the yellow lashes. He thinks only of himself, likes to hear only himself, and isn't interested in listening to anybody else. People have always loved him. He's used to having everybody want to listen to him. People always did whatever he wanted. He had a lot of women in his life and they all spoiled him. And as a result—a grown man acts like a little boy. How far can such a man be relied on?

"For example, this morning you saw me there, how I looked? They dragged me out of room by force. Against my will. First thing I thought: here is Inferno. You know Inferno?" inquired Kagan.

"Here it's worse than Treblinka," said Mrs. Moscowitz, to reinforce his words, "it's not like a Jewish hospital. You shout: 'Nurse! Nurse!' and nobody comes. You don't know what they do at night, when we're sleeping. What kind of behavior and what a noise. And they're so common, common! And today I saw in the bathroom a woman lying dead on the floor and nobody saw her there, nobody came to fetch her, until I shouted. I thought I was getting a heart attack."

He looked at his watch. "Excuse me for looking at watch," he said, "but I have to watch time. In one-half hour I have telephone. My wife rings me up and I have to wait next to booths of telephone."

"Tomorrow my father's coming to kill you, all of you!" cried Paula.

Allegra and her friends sitting at the table at the end of the room got up to leave. Mrs. Moscowitz made a quick calculation. The chairs in the dining room were of the high sort, and she needed no assistance to rise to her feet. She therefore nodded to Kagan with a smile, said, "Pleased to meet you," mustered all her strength, and with one heave rose from her chair. As she pushed the walker away from the table, she heard Lazar Kagan's baritone calling after her:

> O Mort, vieux capitaine, il est temps! levons l'ancre!
> Ce pays nous ennuie, o Mort! Appareillons!
> Si le ciel et la mer sont noirs comme de l'encre,
> Nos coeurs que tu connais sont remplis de rayons!

She looked back at him and saw his hand resting fervently on his heart, as in some pledge of allegiance. His eyes examined her, to see the impression his recitation had made. And she smiled at him with a kind of sad understanding and kept quiet, for fear of saying the wrong thing. Then she turned her walker into the aisle between the tables, walked to the entrance, and waited there for Allegra. But as Allegra approached, she dropped her eyes and avoided looking at Mrs. Moscowitz. She reached the door, walked past, and continued down the corridor. Mrs. Moscowitz called to her and she didn't even turn her head. She didn't go into their room, as she did every day during the rest period, but walked down the corridor and sat on a chair next to the entrance to the lobby. Mrs. Moscowitz stopped at the door to their room, deliberating with herself whether to lie down to rest or go to Allegra and ask her why she was angry with her. While she was standing there, she saw him coming out of the dining room, energetically pushing the wheels of his chair, far more lively than he had been in the morning on his way to the physiotherapy room with Raffy. He smiled and waved to her from the end of the corridor, and his friend Fichman riding behind him followed his example with a triumphant smile on his face. When Kagan passed her he stopped and said: *"Au revoir, Madame!"*

She responded with a polite nod of her head. And he spun the wheels of his chair round and took off evidently eager to reach the telephone and the expected call.

The nurse Satana, who saw that Mrs. Moscowitz was lingering at the door instead of going into her room to lie down for the afternoon rest, called out in her coarse voice: "What's the matter with you today? Why don't you go and rest?"

Like an electric current she felt hatred coursing through her, her hatred for this nurse, who had wished her ill from the day she arrived, who was young enough to be her daughter, and who spoke to her as if she were a little girl on purpose to humiliate her. She wanted to answer her in her own coin, despite the danger involved, but before she could find the right words, Satana disappeared into another of the patients' rooms. Mrs. Moscowitz proceeded along the corridor until she reached the chairs where Allegra was sitting, and dropped into a seat next to her.

"What's wrong? Why aren't you talking to me?"

"Nothing," said Allegra and looked at her with pretended astonishment. The scratches on her forehead and cheeks, the traces of the night before, already more distant than a dream, looked like the evidence of a terrible, unpardonable guilt.

"What have I done to you? " asked Mrs. Moscowitz.

"Nothing," said Allegra. "Nothing. You don't owe me anything."

"Why are you talking to me like this? What's wrong? Is it because I sat down to eat with that man?"

"You can eat with anyone you like. You don't have to ask my permission. But you should know that everyone laughed."

"What did they laugh at?"

Allegra would not tell her. She sat in silence, looking primly and resolutely in front of her. Mrs. Moscowitz had never seen such an expression on her face before. Frieda emerged from the dining room and Allegra immediately stood up, hurried towards her, and pushed her wheelchair into their room. Mrs. Moscowitz was left sitting in the corridor by herself, on a low chair from which she could not get up. In spite of her most strenuous efforts, she was unable to stand. In the end she called the nurse Suzie and asked her to help her up.

"I haven't got the strength to lift you, Yolanda," laughed the nurse, "I'd need a crane. Ask somebody else."

"Where's Leon?"

"Gone to eat."

"And Raffy?"

"Search me."

For a long time she waited. The corridor was empty and silent. Again and again she tried to get up, with all her strength she crouched over, she beat her fists on her knees, she moaned and grunted—and she sank back into the chair again.

"Suzie, please, go and fetch someone to help me get up!" she begged the nurse.

"What's wrong?" said Suzie. "Aren't other people entitled to eat their lunch too? Can't you wait a few minutes? And why aren't you in bed? What did you sit down here for in the first place? You know you can't get up by yourself. If you weren't so fat, you'd be able to get up."

"That's not true, it's only from the low chairs," explained Mrs. Moscowitz, "in the dining room I can get up by myself. These chairs here are for children. Why did they bring them? Maybe on purpose so it should be difficult, some sadist put such low chairs here for people sick with their legs."

"What do you want me to do about it?" asked the nurse.

A great weariness descended on Mrs. Moscowitz. She no longer had the strength to fight. At this hour she was accustomed to lying in bed and taking a nap. Her body was clamoring for its sleep. She closed her eyes, and welcomed the liberating heaviness, all she wanted was to sink deeper and deeper down after her body. She had no idea how long she slept in the chair or what woke her, but when she opened her eyes she saw Kagan coming from the lobby, presumably returning from the public telephones. He stopped his wheelchair in front of her and smiled:

"You were waiting for me?" he asked.

At first she didn't understand his question, perhaps she was still confused from the sudden awakening. Then she asked: "How are things at home, everything's all right?"

"Yes," he smiled, "all right."

She said nothing, and he looked at her as if trying to make up his mind whether to tell her something, and in the end he said: "One day I paint you." And he made her a kind of bow with his head and proceeded on his way. And Fichman, coming up behind him, stared at her with a worried, questioning, incomprehending look in his eyes. She sank back into her slumbers, until she felt the warmth of Leon's body and his familiar smell bathing her face. Then she opened her eyes and saw his big shadow bending over her, his full face, always shining with sweat, smiling at her slyly, his short, thick arms reaching out to grip her elbows.

"What would you do without me?" asked Leon, "Would you sit here for the rest of your life?" And he burst out laughing.

"It's lucky for me you're here," said Mrs. Moscowitz, "Thank you very much, Leon. I'm lucky to have you here. You're a good person. If you like, I'll teach you French."

"I've already told you a thousand times: what good will it do me? Have I got some French girl I can talk to?" said Leon laughing out again. He pulled her elbows, raised her to her feet, and groaned to show how heavy she was, how much of an effort it cost him.

When she was standing and leaning on the walker, she repeated: "You're a good person, Leon."

"Why don't you say right out that you're in love with me? What's the matter, is it a disgrace?" said Leon, and his bulging, unfocused eyes examined her reaction. "Give us a kiss, Yolanda," and he brought his face to her lips. She turned her head away. "On the cheek then, at least," he requested, "like my mother."

The heat of his face on her cheek clouded her vision, as if steam was rising from him into her eyes.

"Really, what's the matter with you!" protested Mrs. Moscowitz and pushed his face away with her hand. "You should be ashamed!"

Her hand was damp with the sweat on his face, and he watched her wiping it on the fabric bag hanging from her walker.

"Do I disgust you?" he whispered in her ear. "Tell me the truth."

"Of course not, Leon. Don't say such things." For a moment she was dismayed by the thought that her reaction had hurt him.

"Why don't you love me? Aren't I handsome? Aren't I a man?"

"You should be ashamed, talking like that to a woman which is old enough to be your mother."

"As far as I'm concerned, you could be old enough to be my grandmother," said Leon, "and I'm twenty-eight for your information. So what? What do I care? Is there a law against it? Some men like older women. Didn't you read in the paper about this guy who. . . "

She silenced him. "I don't want to hear it any more, Leon. Please to be careful how you talk."

"What's wrong? What did I say? Did I say I want to sleep with you or something? All I wanted was a little kiss."

"If you behave yourself, I'll make you a nice present. Don't think I forgot you. I didn't forget. In a few more days my pension comes in the bank."

"What do you think? That I want money from you?" asked Leon. "What am I, a gigolo?"

"Aren't you ashamed to say such a word to me!"

"You can't buy me with money," said Leon. "If you don't really love me, how can I take money from you?"

"I can't make a present? What's wrong with a little present?"

"I thought you really loved me, like a woman loves a man. Now I can see that it was all an act. All this time you were making a fool of me. You don't really love me," he sighed and dropped his eyes.

"If you don't behave yourself, I'll be cross with you," said Mrs. Moscowitz. "Is it nice to laugh at an old woman sick with her legs?"

He turned his face away to hide it, and said again: "You hate me," and his voice choked with laughter, "I love you and you hate me." And then he turned away and hurried off, his shoulders shaking.

In the room Allegra was sitting on the edge of Frieda's bed and when Mrs. Moscowitz came in, they both stopped talking and dropped their eyes, as if they were searching for something on the floor. Mrs. Moscowitz went up to her corner in the wall closet. A number of her dresses and dressing gowns were hanging there on hangers, and she took out one of the dresses, held it up against her chest and looked at it from her chin down, since there was no full-length mirror in the room. Suddenly her hands dropped, the dress slipped to the floor, and her heart contracted inside her. A despairing hatred flooded her, hatred for her body, for her heavy, alien, lonely existence, for the inner voice telling her: It's all useless, everything was over long ago, everything's lost.

Frieda's baritone, whispering in Allegra's ear, rolled like thunder from one end of the room to the other—and for some reason, in Hebrew: "Like a little girl she's playing there with dresses. Who looks at her dress? They only look at her legs."

"You worry about your own legs!" Mrs. Moscowitz threw at her in their language.

"Nurse! Nurse! I need quickly!" cried the bedridden woman, Matilda Franco, in her plaster cast. "Nurse! Quick!" she cried again in despair. When nobody answered she asked Allegra to go and call one of the nurses. Allegra went out to the corridor but did not return immediately. Finally she came back carrying a bedpan. Allegra pulled back Matilda Franco's sheet and tried to push the bedpan in where it was needed, but she didn't have the strength to lift the woman in the cast, who could no longer control herself and soiled her bed. "I've got diarrhea," wailed Matilda Franco, "what can I do, what?"

"Never mind, never mind," said Allegra.

Just then Frieda's family came in to visit her, and the two little grandchildren, as usual, preceded their parents with a race down the corridor. Shouting merrily they rushed in and advanced on their grandmother's bed, and suddenly they stopped. The bad smell spread through the room and the two children stared in embarrassment at Matilda Franco, who quickly covered herself with the sheet to hide her disgrace. "What did they have to come so early today for?" shouted Matilda Franco. "They always come after supper! What's the rush today, I ask you?"

Allegra helped Frieda to roll off her bed into her wheelchair and pushed her into the corridor to her waiting family. They took up their usual positions not far from the nurses' station.

"What do they have to bring children for?" shouted Matilda Franco at Mrs. Moscowitz, who was putting on her dress. "Is this a place for children, I ask you?"

"It's not a place for anyone," said Mrs. Moscowitz and smiled at her sadly. She had already changed for supper and put a bottle of scent and a few cosmetics and hairpins and such into a plastic bag. One of the nurses came to clean Matilda Franco and change her sheets. While Matilda Franco began to rebuke her and set forth her complaints, Mrs. Moscowitz left the room and went to the bathroom. She switched on the light in the perpetually dark room and examined her face in the mirror. The electric light softened its lines. She smiled and at the same time she tried to widen the slits of her blue eyes. The dark blue dress with white spots suited her coloring. She sprayed herself with the good eau de cologne which she kept for special occasions, rubbed cream into her face to revitalize it and dabbed a little orange powder on her forehead, above the bridge of her nose, and on her cheekbones; she smoothed the lipstick carefully over her lips and did her best with her hair, which hadn't been done for a week. For a long time she went on inspecting her face in the mirror, from various angles and with different expressions, stretched her skin until the folds disappeared from her cheeks, let it go again, smiled and looked serious, smiled and looked serious again, as if to examine both possibilities—which of them suited her better.

Today she went to supper early. As she walked down the corridor she saw Allegra sitting next to Clara with Frieda's family, as if she were one of them, taking part in their conversation, sucking up to them. Mrs. Moscowitz walked straight past without greeting them as usual, pushing her walker in front of her, proud and oblivious.

She sat down at one of the tables at the end of the dining room, facing the entrance, her back to the glass wall overlooking the plaza in front of the hospital. After a long time she saw him come in. Next to the entrance he stopped his wheelchair and looked around the hall. She knew that he was looking for her, and lowered her eyes with a pensive expression. She was alone at the table and she very much hoped that no one would sit next to them this time.

"Yolanda!" he called in a loud voice, audible throughout the hall. His wheelchair was at a distance of several tables from her. And he waved at her: "Yolanda!"

There was something wild about him, unpredictable. This upset her and put her off a little, making her fear for the right and proper order of things. But this time at least he was without Fichman, which afforded her a measure of consolation. They exchanged greetings and civilities, he looked straight into her face, smiled and said nothing, as if he had discovered some secret about her, and immediately pushed aside one of the chairs at the table and rolled his wheelchair into the empty space to sit opposite her. His thick, straight hair was wet, with water or perhaps with brilliantine, and combed severely back, exposing his broad, high forehead. His face was shaved and had a faint, fresh flush. His features looked clearer and more definite than they had at noon. The handsomeness of his face was unmarred, only the flabbiness of the neck and the sagging of the cheeks, which blurred the straight, taut lines of the jaw, showed the hand of age. The pallor of his skin emphasized the unusual shape of his eyes and their color, which appeared to change with the hour of the day: for now, at twilight, the greenish tinge had retreated and their color was more brown. She was afraid of looking at the yellow lashes again, but the temptation was stronger than the fear.

"Tomorrow afternoon you sit and I make from you portrait," he said finally, "'Aristocratic Portrait of Yolanda'! This is name of work."

"Oh, really, I'm embarrassed," murmured Mrs. Moscowitz in confusion, in what she considered the becoming manner to react to a proposal at once so flattering and so bold, "why me?"

"You know why," he replied, and fell silent for a long moment, looking straight into her face and smiling. Then he added: "Not to be frightened, please. Nothing difficult. No oil or something like that, only ink on paper." And he drew a fountain pen out of his pajama pocket and displayed it to her. Perhaps he hoped that the innocent appearance of the pen would dispell her fears. "Tomorrow morning, my wife will bring new pad, I told her on phone. Poor woman, she must come here from Beersheba on bus."

"You come from Beersheba?"

"Yes," he answered sadly, "Beersheba is not good place for art. Already I had one exhibition there. Nobody came. Only family and friends and neighbors. Painter must be at least in Tel Aviv. He needs people to know his work. Here nobody knows me. This is Beersheba."

The trays of food were placed before them. *"Bon appetit, Madame!"* he wished her, and she replied in kind. Unconsciously her eyes fell on his hands holding the fork and knife. His fingers were thick and crooked and his nails were warped, thick and humped, a greenish brown color, as if they had rotted, dried, and were about to drop off. How could she have failed to notice them at lunch? His hands dropped the eating utensils and rested motionless on the table. She controlled the horrified shudder running through her body, and raised her eyes to his face to see why he had stopped eating and if he had noticed the effect of his fingernails on her. But she saw that he was looking neither at her nor at his ghastly hands. His eyes were fixed on the glass wall behind her back. He lowered his eyes to her for a moment and said: "Turn around, Yolanda, turn around quick and look outside."

She did as he told her, got up as quickly as she could, leaning on her walker, and turned around.

Through the glass wall of the dining room she saw the plaza in front of the hospital, and beyond it a wood of pine trees sloping down steeply to the wadi, and beyond the grove a few houses and beyond the houses a range of low hills, and above all this a sky red with the summer sunset. This red was poured over the opalescence of the hills on the horizon, and over the dull concrete of the little water tower on top of the highest hill, and over the dark green patches of the orange groves on the plain, over the tiled roofs of the little town, and over the silvery crests of the pines in the wood, over the glass windows and metal curves of the cars parked in the parking lot at the end of the plaza, and over the paving stones of the empty plaza, which was paved like a chess board with checkered grey and wine-colored flagstones. There was not a soul to be seen in this entire landscape, and not a stir of movement. The clarity of the air and the red glow in which it was bathed gave the moment a kind of fatefulness: the world outside seemed to have stopped breathing, every moment that passed now would fade its colors, bring it closer to its end. Mrs. Moscowitz could actually feel Kagan's gaze brushing past her arm as he looked steadily at the glass wall and the landscape suffused in the reddish light beyond it.

She turned around again and resumed her seat. But his eyes were still fixed on the glass wall, and a terrible sadness darkened his face. She looked into his eyes in order to avoid having to look at his hands. When he sensed her looking at him, he said in a low voice: "I expect nothing, for me one second finished everything. I have no illusions. What can there be for me?"

Mrs. Moscowitz hoped very much that only the two of them saw this special sight, that all the twisted, ugly stupid creatures around them had no part in it. As if the two of them had met at some European pension or elegant spa. She hoped that the strange man's sudden sadness would also be a very special, private moment of her own.

"I, when I was dressing myself in the room before, wanted to die." He didn't hear what she said, so absorbed was he in the view in front of him and in his sadness. "My friend," she added, "poor thing, Allegra, she hasn't got a long time left to live, she's so sick. She doesn't mind at all to die, the opposite. But all the time she's afraid she'll be alone when the death comes to take her. She doesn't want to be alone with it in the room, she says, poor thing."

When the women got into bed, Frieda asked Allegra to open one of the windows and let the fresh air into the room. Before this evening she had never asked for such a thing. Mrs. Moscowitz protested immediately, and argued that the air outside was nippy and that she was very susceptible to it. Frieda stood her ground. The other patients didn't interfere; some of them were too muddled in their minds to hear or understand anything, and some didn't care if the window was open or closed. Allegra got up and went to open the window.

"Don't do this to me, Allegra," implored Mrs. Moscowitz, "I know I'll wake up in the morning sick if you do."

"Don't take any notice of her, don't be afraid," Frieda croaked at Allegra, "she won't come to any harm. If she gets sick it won't be from the terrible summer cold, it'll be from the bad air in the closed room."

"It's not the cold I'm afraid of," shouted Mrs. Moscowitz in despair, "I'm afraid of the nip in the night air. There's a nip in summer too. Everyone knows that this nippiness is dangerous, especially for somebody with a sensitive throat."

Frieda's baritone burst into scornful laughter: "Tell me, my dear Allegra, perhaps you know where she heard such rubbish? She couldn't possibly be making it up. You'd have to be a genius to invent such nonsense. Who doesn't know that you should sleep with the window open? It's the ABC of health. Even in the old country, in winter, we always opened the window at night, to have clean air in the house. And here in Israel, in this summer!"

Matilda Franco, who couldn't bear it when people talked in a language she didn't understand, shouted at them: "When are you going to stop with the jabber-jabber already? I can't stand it another minute."

"Maybe I should bring a blanket?" suggested Allegra in their language, in a soft, uncertain voice, either to Mrs. Moscowitz or to Frieda.

Neither of them answered her and Allegra seemed to despair of this compromise. She opened the window on the wall between the room and the back porch, but only a little, hardly more than a crack, and went back to bed.

For a long time Mrs. Moscowitz said nothing. She sneezed four times and blew her nose. Afterwards she began to cough, a harsh, dry, monotonous cough, and she went on so long that a couple of the patients complained that she was preventing them from falling asleep. Allegra asked from the next bed: "Should I get you a glass of water?" but there was no reply. Even if Mrs. Moscowitz had wanted to reply, her voice was choked. She could hardly breathe. In the end she groaned, coughed, cleared her throat, mustered the remnants of her voice and cried: "Nurse! Nurse! Please!"

Nobody answered her. From the nurses' station in the corridor one of the nurses could be heard answering the telephone briskly and briefly in Russian.

"Manya, Manyaleh!" called Mrs. Moscowitz, "Come here please

for a minute. I'm going to die here tonight from the air coming in by the window straight into my throat!"

"Enough! Enough with your nonsense already, enough!" demanded Matilda Franco. "How long is she going to carry on about that window, the whole night long?"

"Allegra, I'm asking you for the last time, go and shut the window," said Mrs. Moscowitz quietly to the thin shadow that had disappeared into the bed next to hers, the sheet up to its chin and only its meager head of hair making a black spot in the middle of the pillow. Allegra did not move. Was she asleep? Had she hardened her heart to Mrs. Moscowitz's pleas?

"Nurse! Nurse! Please to come quick!" cried Mrs. Moscowitz again in the direction of the corridor. The nurse had finished talking on the telephone, but she did not reply to her calls. Mrs. Moscowitz gave up: what good would the nurse do her? She had no chance in this battle of wills. The nurses and doctors would always take Frieda's side, Frieda who had a rich, influential and highly visible family to back her up. A lonely old woman, all alone in the world, couldn't pit herself against the cruel, ruthless power called a family, especially when it was a family like Frieda's.

Although the chill had already spread throughout her body and illness was already making her weak, she decided to gather up the remains of her strength, get out of bed and do something. She gripped the loop hanging over her head and managed to heave herself into a sitting position. In the darkness she made out her slippers at the foot of the bed and pushed her feet into them. The sensation of the cool, solid floor under the soles of her slippers surprised and encouraged her, arousing a hope that this time she would succeed in standing up. Now she bent her torso as much as she could and let out a stifled groan in the effort to raise herself from the edge of the bed, her forearms pressed on her thighs, her chin dug into her chest. Her buttocks rose a little from the bed and it seemed that one more effort would lift her to her feet, but her weight was too much for her. Still she did not despair, she did not stop trying, some power outside herself strengthened her spirit. She felt as if her body was rounding like a ball and when she bent over her thighs, her hips rose and the weight of her body pressed painfully down on her knees. But a kind of frightening balance came into being for a moment between the two halves of her body. Again she groaned, this time a loud, terrible groan into the darkness of the room. Little by little she straightened her knees and stretched out her hands, reaching for the walker next to the head of her bed. Between her bed and Allegra's a bit of the metal bar gleamed in the faint light filtering in from the corridor, but the walker was not standing where she thought it was. Everything began to turn and spin. The feeling of heaviness disappeared from her legs, as if they were standing on the brink of an abyss. All around her the dance of terror whirled. The sensation of weightlessness and the wish to surrender herself to the seductive dance revived an ancient joy inside her. But her body protested against this treachery and called her to order, and she could not withstand its tyranny. She leaned backwards again, her knees slowly bent, and the pain returned and with it the feeling of heaviness and despair. Her hands sought support on the edge of the bed. With a dull thud she fell onto the mattress and teetered there for a few seconds. When she knew that she was sitting securely, and her feet felt once more the cool, solid surface of the floor underneath her slippers, she understood what had happened to her in that fleeting moment, what had been promised her and what she had lost. Her heart beat wildly in her breast. And she tried her voice:

"I could have died," she said quietly, as if speaking to herself. Then she shouted to the dark room: "I could have died!" and pulled her legs up onto the bed, lay down slowly and covered herself. "Frieda'll pay for it all!" she cried, "Now I'm sick. It's all your fault, Frieda. You'll pay for it dearly."

"Believe me, Allegra my dear, I don't know what she wants of me," sighed Frieda, "I didn't do a thing to her. Everybody knows I can't even move by myself."

"Someone's already tried to kill me once," said Mrs. Moscowitz, putting the story of the assassination attempt to the test once more, "and now they're trying again."

"Enough! I can't stand it no more," complained Matilda Franco. "Jabber-jabber-jabber, eshta-beshta-meshta, they never let up. Can't you let a person sleep? My head's dried up already with your jabbering!"

It was late before Mrs. Moscowitz succeeded in falling asleep. Cover herself as she might, she could not protect herself from the outside air constantly coming at her face, tickling her nostrils, being sucked into her nose, penetrating her throat and lungs, wreaking havoc with her body. Again and again the coughing choked her and she hoped that Frieda and Allegra heard and realized what they had done to her and were sorry. But Frieda had been blessed, besides everything else, by the sleep of the just. When she woke up in the morning she never had any idea what had gone on in the room during the night, not even if there had been a terrific racket and commotion. And in any case, the suffering of others was the last thing that would disturb her rest. And Allegra, who had always been so attentive to Mrs. Moscowitz's needs, who had fulfilled her wishes even before she put them into words, had turned her back on her and made friends with her enemies. Was Allegra sorry now? Did she realize what she had done? Had Frieda offered her a higher price for her services, and had the poor wretch, in her desperate poverty, been obliged to agree? Even if she's betrayed me, concluded Mrs. Moscowitz to herself, I'll never hate Allegra.

She was getting sicker and sicker. Her throat was growing hoarser, and however she coughed and hawked, she could not clear it, but only succeeded in making the irritation worse. A dull pain rose from her neck, gripping her nape and temples, and pressed on her solar plexus. The outside air covered her bed and surrounded her like a foul miasma. A new memory came into her heart: something that had happened on her first day here in this hospital. That afternoon, at the command of the head nurse, the Russian nurse had dumped her into a lukewarm bath. With all her meager strength she had fought the nurse, but to no avail. Now her memory told her that the water had been as cold as ice, so freezing cold that the minute it touched her body she had lost consciousness. But before that she had still managed to cry out to the nurse: "Don't touch my hair! Not to touch!" When she regained consciousness her body was numb and frozen. All she could feel was the nurse's fingers on her head, soaping her hair and rinsing it in the cold water. She beat her fists on the nurse's forearms, but she was undeterred, with one hand she gripped both Mrs. Moscowitz's hands and with the other she continued the shampoo. "Nazi!" screamed Mrs. Moscowitz through the bitter streams of soapy water pouring onto her face and stinging her eyes, "Nazi! This isn't a Jewish hospital, it's worse than Treblinka here!" The nurse rinsed her hair for the last time and let go of her hands. And then Mrs. Moscowitz had touched her hair and felt the strangeness of the bedraggled tresses and the cold, dead scalp. Now too she passed her fingers over her hair, to reassure herself that the spectacle shown her by her memory was nothing but a bad dream. Was Allegra still awake? Perhaps Allegra was looking at her in the darkness and feeling sorry for her? And if she cried, would Allegra hear her crying?

chapter two

I n the morning she woke up ill: her throat was inflamed, her head
ached, her eyes burned. At her request, the nurse brought her a
thermometer. Her temperature was a little over normal. But all the
nurse said was: "You'll live."

"I told them!" moaned Mrs. Moscowitz, and explained to the
nurse with the shreds of her broken voice: "It's no good to open the
window at night. I know what I'm talking about. At once it makes me
sick. Now what will I do? Tell me, what will I do?" And she burst into
a fit of harsh coughing that flooded her eyes with tears. "It's all
Frieda's fault!" she continued in a choked voice through her coughing. "If she wants the window open, then the window must be open?
What is this, it's Frieda's house here? The whole world belongs to
Frieda?"

"That's enough, quiet now," said the nurse soothingly, "don't talk
so much, it's bad for your throat."

She turned on her side and looked at Allegra's bed, to see her reaction, but Allegra wasn't in her bed.

"She doesn't know what she's talking about," croaked Frieda's
voice, which was even hoarser that usual when she woke up in the
morning. "A person needs clean air at night. If there's no clean air I
can't sleep."

"A person needs a clean heart," Mrs. Moscowitz called out to her,
and in their own language she continued: "Are you happy now? And

if I die of it, will you be glad? You're such an egoist, you only think of yourself, you don't care about anyone except yourself. As if the whole world was created just for you." Again the harsh coughing broke out of her, and she laid her hand on her heart, as if she feared it would not stand up to the shaking and would burst.

"Now she'll infect us all," thundered the manly woman in Hebrew and pulled the sheet up to cover her mouth and nose, to protect herself from the germs flying from Mrs. Moscowitz's bed. "That's all I need," she said, "for my grandchildren to come and for them to get infected also when I kiss them."

Allegra came in from the bathroom with a little plastic basin full of the underwear she had laundered. When she passed her bed Frieda said to her in their language: "Oy, my angel, my treasure! How can I thank you? How good you are!"

"It's nothing," replied Allegra. "Nothing." And her eyes avoided Mrs. Moscowitz's somber look, a look of rebuke and pain, which followed her as she went out onto the back porch to hang up the washing to dry.

The nurse urged Mrs. Moscowitz to get up and wash and dress for breakfast, but she said: "I can't. Believe me, I feel like a dead woman."

In the meantime Allegra finished hanging up the washing and returned to the room, went up to her bed, bent down next to her locker, and took out the tube of handcream, bought and paid for by Mrs. Moscowitz's money, squeezed out a larger dollop than usual, and began to rub it into her hands. Mrs. Moscowitz watched her all the time but Allegra ignored her look.

Most of the women had already gone to the dining room, and only the bedridden patients, whose meals were served to them in bed, remained in the room.

For a long time Mrs. Moscowitz tried to fall asleep again, with no success. In the end she decided to get up.

In the bathroom she examined the state of her face. Under her eyes the tiny red lines had multiplied, and she knew it was because of her sleepless night, because of the open window. She smeared the appropriate cream onto her face, dabbed it all over with powder, which in her opinion dulled the undesirable shine, added rouge and mascara, and ran the black eyebrow pencil over her eyebrows. Then she did her best to repair her hairdo, which already required the ministrations of the hairdresser. When she returned to the room she felt that her heart was stronger and that she was ready to set out. She opened her corner of the wall closet, deliberated for a moment as to which dress to wear, or whether perhaps it might be better to put on a simple dressing-gown, to show that her appearance was of no concern to her, and in the end she chose her green dress with the long sleeves and the two rows of gold buttons, even though it was too grand, too thick and warm for the summer day.

The friends returned from the dining room. Allegra was carrying a tray with a cup of tea and a plate holding two slices of bread spread with white cheese. For a moment Allegra stopped and stared in astonishment at the elegant winter dress, but immediately she suppressed her curiosity, cleared a space on the locker next to Mrs. Moscowitz's bed, and put the tray down without saying a word.

"Thank you Allegra, how nice of you to take pity on me at last, very nice of you indeed," whispered Mrs. Moscowitz, "now that I'm already sick."

The emaciated woman with the thin hair did not reply. In her small, slanting eyes the shadow of a sober, melancholy smile flickered.

Their hunchbacked friend with the bird face, Clara, came into the room, and when she saw Mrs. Moscowitz all dressed up in her winter party dress, she started back on her walker and began to laugh silently into her sleeve, in her characteristic manner. Perhaps she guessed where Mrs. Moscowitz was going and why she was all dressed up. Other people's affairs and motives were very close to her heart, and owing to the keen interest she took in them she had also developed a special sense for putting two and two together.

The nurse came in too and said: "What's this? Are you going somewhere? All of the sudden you're well again! And why don't you eat what she brought you? Are you on hunger strike?"

Mrs. Moscowitz went to the bathroom to see how the color of the dress—a grass green which she hadn't worn for some time—suited her complexion. But the bathroom was occupied and she went back and sat down on the high chair next to her bed to wait. One by one her friends left for physiotherapy, occupational therapy, and to sit in the long corridor. Only the bedridden patients remained in the room. Hunger began to gnaw at her stomach and her sore throat was thirsty for hot tea. At last she swallowed her pride, took a bite of one of the slices of bread with cheese spread on it and a sip of the tea, which had gone cold. All at once the bread slipped out of her hand and fell onto her thigh, soiling her dress. She stared in horror at the shiny, greasy stain on the green material, and although she had vowed never to hate Allegra, she blamed her now for all her troubles and wished that she would die soon—and alone.

The bathroom became available. There was a terrible smell in it. The previous occupant had forgotten to flush the toilet in the corner. Mrs. Moscowitz held her breath, wet the corner of her towel and hurried out. When she returned to the room, she stood next to her bed and tried to remove the stain from her dress. She rubbed the spot with the wet corner of towel, hoping that the fabric had not had time to absorb the fat, and then she dried the wet stain with the dry corner and put the towel back in its place. With all her might she tried to forget the stain and to feel how the dress fitted her body. When she emerged into the corridor she saw the head nurse, Satana, coming toward her.

"Where are you going now, Yolanda my precious?" inquired Satana, and added with ironic fulsomeness: "Oy! How pretty you look! Is somebody having a party here, now, in the morning? Where? Tell me. I want to dance too. I haven't danced for years. Take me to your party, Yolanda!"

Mrs. Moscowitz whispered to herself: May your legs dance like mine. And she pushed her walker forward and continued on her way, soundlessly muttering a formula she remembered from days gone by, to protect her from the evil eye and turn the curse against the curser. She believed in the head nurse's evil power.

She proceeded down the corridor and stood at the entrance to the men's wing, looking discreetly from side to side but without seeing what she wanted. Then she returned to her own wing, walked to the end of the corridor, and entered the lobby. On her way to the visitors' lounge she had to pass the public telephones, where there was a round table and a number of chairs whose seats were of a height convenient for her, and she intended to sit down there and rest for a while, because her legs were hurting her. But when she approached the corner with the telephones, she saw him sitting there with a woman, and she panicked. She thought that he would be sitting with his wife in the visitors' lounge, and she had planned to walk past them discreetly, keeping out of his sight.

They were sitting facing each other across the round table. In front of her she saw the woman's back and her severe hairstyle, her erect head and long neck. And opposite her, his face. For a split second his eyes met those of Mrs. Moscowitz, and it seemed to her that his expression was now the same as the morning before, an expression of incomprehension and resentment. He immediately looked back at his wife, and as if to stress something, he took her hand in both of his and listened intently to what she was saying. Mrs. Moscowitz pushed her walker as quickly as she could. Would he be angry with her and accuse her of spying on him? Would he snub her from now on? Would he be willing at least to listen to her explanation that she had gone in all innocence to the public telephones in order to make a necessary call, or to buy something at the adjacent canteen, and when she saw him there, to her complete surprise, sitting with his wife, she had turned away tactfully and postponed her phone call, or her purchase, to another time. She advanced as quickly as she could. Her elegant, too-hot green dress, with the two rows of gold buttons, now seemed to her ridiculous and pathetic. Satana's mockery had been justified, Satana whose evil eye was no doubt to blame for this embarrassing incident too.

The woman's voice sounded young and brisk. She caught isolated words and syllables in their language, of which she understood nothing. Before she dropped her eyes, as she passed them, she had time to see that the woman's hair was auburn, combed flat on the temples and braided in a bun on the nape of her neck. Her thin body was clad in a black, sleeveless high-necked dress. There was a considerable difference in age between them, of that she was sure, but she didn't know what to conclude from it.

She continued on her way and went into the visitors' lounge. Next to the entrance she fell into an armchair whose seat was high enough to enable her to stand up again without help. From where she was sitting she could see the corridor branching into her ward and to the stairs leading down to the exit from the hospital. She breathed heavily. Her legs hurt. The ticklish feeling came back to her throat. A faint giddiness overcame her and she felt her temperature rising. The square hall, two of whose walls were made of glass, was flooded with light and deserted. It was furnished with tables and benches and chairs and armchairs, and the walls were hung with paintings and reliefs and various handicrafts, gifts from the patients or their families. Inscriptions expressed gratitude to the institution and its staff. She had never ventured so far before, she had never entered this room and sat down in it, either because she never believed that her legs would carry her so far, or because nobody came to visit her. She felt hot and she began to perspire in the thick, grand green dress. Its collar was wet and there were sweat stains under the arms. Why am I here? Who am I waiting for? she asked herself angrily. I'm sick, I should be lying in bed. And she wanted to go back to her room immediately and lie down to rest. The emptiness all around her made her feel uncomfortable, the space of the hall pressed down on her head like a giant dome. For a moment she deliberated with herself whether to return to the ward or to go on waiting. And then her eyes closed, only for a few minutes, until she recovered her strength. And she fell asleep.

When she awoke the glare from the glass walls told her that it was already late in the morning. She rose from the armchair, and supporting herself on her walker went up to the glass wall of the facade, where she stood and looked outside at the paved plaza, the ornamental shrubs and flowerbeds and the pine grove on the slope of the hill. A cab drove up the road leading from the highway and stopped in front of the entrance. Leon alighted from it carrying a large plastic bag. He waved goodbye to the driver, slammed the door and crossed the plaza with broad strides, until he disappeared from view. She walked along the glass wall to the corner, turned left and walked along the other glass wall. Again she looked outside and saw an elegant garden, a steep concrete path bordered by orange-flowered bushes, and a lawn with a tall tree at its center. Round, white tables and white chairs dotted a paved terrace. There were umbrellas stuck in the middle of the tables. Nobody was there, and the umbrellas were furled.

The more she looked at the garden and examined its details, the more certain she was that she had never been there in her life and that the terrible incident she had related to her friends had not happened to her, but to somebody else, whose memory had been absorbed into hers. The emptiness of the garden and its silent beauty made her long for her forgotten flat in Tel Aviv and for the pleasant solitude it seemed she had known there.

Suddenly she remembered Kagan's fingers, his crooked fingers and their dry nails, the color of a tortoise's shell. He was probably still sitting next to the public telephones with his wife who was so much younger than he, talking to her in their language and holding her hand in both of his, in his terrible fingers. What was there to be jealous of? What was there to expect, to hope for? What illusions could she possibly cherish? More than ever before, she felt in these moments the arrogant, insulting power of this terrible place, which turned all its inhabitants into doomed strangers.

A child riding a bicycle came into the garden, coasting down the concrete path and braking with his bare foot. He dismounted and propped the bicycle against one of the white tables. His thin, dark crooked body was clad in dark gym shorts. His head was shaved, his slender arms were too long, and he walked with a limp. He unloaded a big, green plastic basket from the bicycle, put it down on the ground, and looked for something inside it. He took a package out of the basket and put it on the table. Then he removed a big plastic bottle of some soft drink from the package and took several long gulps from it. He put the bottle back in the basket, loped up the path with his curious hopping gait, and entered the building through the narrow back door. She didn't take her eyes off the garden. No pain or weariness troubled her now, although she had been standing for so long on her sick legs. Gradually her spirits revived, her heart foretold grave danger for them all, and this thought consoled her.

In a little while the boy returned, carrying gardening tools. He dropped them into the basin around the trunk of the tall tree in the center of the lawn, and picked up the hoe. At the edge of the lawn he began to dig a hole. He dug for a long time and the sound of the hoe echoed rhythmically through the glass wall. Mrs. Moscowitz could see the rivulets of sweat running down the boy's back and shoulders.

From time to time he wiped his face with his wrist, and shook his long arm to flick off the sweat. In the end he threw down the hoe, knelt down next to the pit, and thrust his arm into it, as if searching for something inside or measuring its depth. Again the boy stood up and began digging and throwing the loose earth onto the mound rising on the edge of the lawn. A few minutes later he hopped over to the tree, picked up the pail he had thrown there with the gardening implements, went over to the faucet on the other side of the concrete path and filled it with water, returned to the pit and poured the water into it, very slowly, as if taking care not to wet the verges of the pit. For a moment he stood and looked at the pit full of water, and his narrow chest, wet with sweat, rose and fell rhythmically. After a time he returned to the concrete path, limped down to the bottom of the garden, turned left and disappeared behind the hedge. He returned with a lawnmower.

Her knees hurt now, her heavy legs longed to rest, so she pulled up a nearby chair and sat down facing the glass wall. The din of the mower rising from the garden sounded to her as if it were masking some terrible conspiracy, dangerous and seductive at once. For a long time the boy passed to and fro across the lawn, back and forth behind the lawnmower, swath after swath. When he drew near the wall through which she was looking, he disappeared from view, then he reappeared again with his back toward her, receding down the next swath. The noise of the mower began to sound even and monotonous to her. Little by little it filled the inside of her head, and it was no longer a muffled mixture of rattling and creaking and mechanical chugging, no longer a dull, uniform din, but a roar in which she heard voices—the voices of people screaming from a closed place, as if they were being burned alive. At first she flinched back in fear, then she began to listen to the screams filling her head, tried to distinguish them from one another and to hear if there were any words, but she could not separate the voices from the metallic echo that surrounded them.

The din of the lawnmower stopped suddenly and in the silence the boy lifted his gaze to the glass wall behind which she was sitting, as if he sensed her eyes on him. Now she could see his face clearly, and it was ugly and twisted. He too was maimed.

Raffy walked down the concrete path and sat down at the table against which the bicycle was leaning. The child gardener sat down on the chair next to him. Raffy spoke to him and the boy answered him with a nod. For a moment they both laughed. This was the first time she had ever seen Raffy laughing. After that they both stood up. The boy went over to the tap again, bent over it, cupped the water in his hands, and wet his shaved head, his arms and his armpits. Then he straightened up and washed his legs from the feet to the thighs. He limped to the chair where he had left his clothes, picked up his shirt and dried himself with it. From his basket he took another shirt and pulled it over his body, put on his long trousers, and looked at Raffy. The two of them turned toward a narrow strip of shade at the end of the paved terrace, next to the hedge, stood there for a moment in silence, and knelt down to pray.

She watched them, following their movements. The order of the bows, the straightenings and prostrations, seemed to her like a warning of what was about to take place. She felt as if she had joined forces with them in defying the hidden danger that was coming closer all the time. A strange feeling of power filled her and a vengeful glee, but not a trace of anxiety. Only impatience and suspense: how long was it still going to take, how long? Why didn't anything happen? Why prolong the tortures of the damned?

Their prayers lasted for a long time, and she never took her eyes off them. And while she was waiting for the great, redeeming roar to come from outside, she heard a faint sound behind her, from the entrance to the hall. She turned round and saw Kagan coming toward her in his wheelchair.

He reached the glass wall and asked: "What happens there?"

She looked at his smiling face and realized that she had forgotten how handsome it was in its refined pallor, its square chin which spoke of a masterful character and rich experience of life, its unusually shaped eyes, to which the strong light coming through the glass wall now lent a greenish hue, its lashes which still preserved their cruel, yellow color. She looked at his smile and saw in it his happiness in being with her again. And he leaned forward in his wheelchair and pressed his face against the glass wall:

"Arabs praying," he said in disappointment.

"I've never seen it before," said Mrs. Moscowitz, "only perhaps on the television."

"What's to see?" said Kagan and turned the wheelchair toward her. "Poor people, to pray, to believe in God. God is neurosis. It's necessary only to be cured from it."

His words wounded her, and she didn't know why. The two people she had seen praying a moment before now seemed to her like a daydream.

He evidently sensed her distress. "You believe in God?" he asked.

She said: "Good people believe in God."

"I don't believe. I'm not good?"

"What do you believe?" she asked him.

He reflected for a moment. "I only believe in Satan," he said with a grin. "And I pray to him like this," he bowed his head and put his hands together, to demonstrate prayer or supplication: "'*O Satan, prends pitié de ma longue misère!*'"

She looked at him, shocked.

"You don't know this?"

She did not understand his question.

"No matter," he said and looked around him as if seeking something. "Tanya brought me pad. Maybe tomorrow I draw you here?" he asked. "This is good place."

49

"No, please," she said, "this is too far for me. I don't think I can come here again."

"Here is better," he said, "here is fine light and no smell of kaka all the time. And not to see everywhere catastrophes. Believe me, here is good for us, Yolanda."

Her eyes fell on the stain on her dress.

"I'm a little bit sick," she said. "In the night they opened a window in the room and I got a fever from it and a little bit pain in the throat."

"You saw her?" he asked suddenly with a triumphant expression on his face.

She pretended that she didn't know whom he meant.

"I sat together with Tanya and you went past," he said and pointed backwards, in the direction of the public telephones.

"Ah! No. I didn't see . . . I didn't know that you . . . I was only going . . . "

"I told to Tanya about you."

"What's there to tell?" said Mrs. Moscowitz.

They parted at the entrance to the men's wing and she continued on her way to her own wing. She was impatient to take off the thick sweaty dress as quickly as possible, and to put on a light, simple dressing gown. Frieda's thunderous voice reverberated in the corridor: "Nurse! Nurse! Quick! Help!" The shouts and the aggressive tone called up Mrs. Moscowitz's anger: Frieda who was spoiled by her family, who was used to getting whatever she wanted immediately, always exaggerated in everything that concerned herself, her comfort and her needs. One of the nurses went into the room and called the head nurse to come and help her. Rosa hurried into the room, returned to the nurses' station and picked up the phone. By the time Mrs. Moscowitz reached the room, she saw them taking Allegra out in a wheelchair with a high back. Allegra was conscious and her eyes were open, but she looked very tired and gray in the face. When she passed Mrs. Moscowitz, she shook her head slightly and whispered perhaps to her, perhaps to herself: "It's nothing, nothing."

They wheeled Allegra out of the ward.

In the room Frieda told her how Allegra had fainted all of a sudden when she got out of bed. She seemed very alarmed, but Mrs. Moscowitz knew that she was incapable of feeling real love for anyone unless there was something in it for her. Was a woman so spoiled and selfish capable of feeling anyone else's pain? Frieda seemed to Mrs. Moscowitz like a baby with a broken toy. Allegra was only her toy.

Mrs. Moscowitz changed her dress, sat down on the edge of her bed and contemplated the stubborn stain. Leon came into the room and began taking the sheets off Allegra's bed.

"What will happen to her? Will she live?" asked Mrs. Moscowitz.

"They'll do what they can for her there," said Leon, "the doctor said he doesn't give her more than a few days."

$\sim$

She went to lunch with Frieda and Clara. Kagan was nowhere to be seen in the dining room. It's better this way, said Mrs. Moscowitz to herself, with a feeling of relief. The memory of the quarrel with Frieda was forgotten, and the pain in her throat didn't trouble her either. The fear that they would not see Allegra again brought her closer to her friends. She knew that Kagan's absence from the dining room had no special significance. He himself had told her that the nurses sometimes brought meals to his room on a tray. They were eager to fulfill his wishes, giggled with pleasure at his protests and his hints and suggestive remarks, let him do what he liked and didn't bully him like they did the other patients, to get out of bed, to stretch his limbs, and not to pamper himself. He was the kind of man that women enjoy pampering. That was why he was so selfish, so absorbed in himself, he hardly heard what people said to him. But Fichman was in the dining room, sitting at a table near the entrance, opposite an old woman lame in the legs and weak in the head, for whose benefit he was putting on his usual show with his pajama top. After Mrs. Moscowitz's initial relief at Kagan's absence from the dining room, a muffled anxiety began to gnaw at her heart. Perhaps she had done something wrong, perhaps he was already tired of her company. It was a week now since she had had her hair done. She mustn't look like this in front of him, especially since he was accustomed to seeing the face of a woman much younger than he was. And today was the day of the hairdresser's weekly visit.

After lunch she lay down to rest and had a good sleep. At the hour when the hairdresser was due she woke up with a start, but the hairdresser did not appear. The afternoon passed and the evening approached, and still Pnina the hairdresser was nowhere to be seen. In the long corridor, opposite the nurses' station, Mrs. Moscowitz sat on one of the chairs lining the wall with her eyes fixed hopefully on the entrance. Shulamith, the Ethiopian nurse, came past with the tea trolley, pouring out the tea and handing the red cups to the women sitting along the wall.

When she approached and held out the cup of tea, Mrs. Moscowitz to her: "Shulamith, you're the best from them all, you've got a white soul."

The Ethiopian laughed: "Not true! My soul is black too. Black is better. Now black is the most in fashion."

"Of course," said Mrs. Moscowitz, "you're quite right. There are some white people whose hearts are blacker than the hearts of the black people. There are some people like that here too, and I don't want to mention their names."

"But a black heart is good!" laughed the Ethiopian. "What's the matter with you today, Yolanda?"

"Pnina the hairdresser didn't come. And I need her now especially. Maybe you know where they keep her phone number. I can telephone to her to ask what happened. It never happened for her not to come on Thursday on the dot on time."

"I certainly haven't got her phone number," laughed Shulamith again, passing her hand over her frizzy hair.

"Where's Rosa?" asked Mrs. Moscowitz. "She knows, she's her friend. Perhaps you can ask her for the phone number?"

"As soon as I finish serving, I'm going to look for her for you," said the Ethiopian, glancing at Mrs. Moscowitz's glum face, and this time she didn't laugh. "Why do you need a hairdresser? Your hair's lovely and neat, I wish I had straight hair like that, that I could have styled."

"Why? Your hair's lovely, really lovely," said Mrs. Moscowitz, "really it is."

"Would you like to have hair like mine?" asked the Ethiopian and pointed at her hair.

This question was too much for Mrs. Moscowitz and she filled her mouth with tea. "Wonderful, it's hot," she said, "just how I like it. You know, I was never drinking tea in my life, I couldn't stand tea, until I came to the hospital. And now I love tea."

"Tea's healthy," said Shulamith.

"And I'm sick now. In the night I caught a cold, they opened a window in the room, and I got pain in the throat."

"After I serve everybody, I'll bring you another one," said Shulamith, and she pushed the trolley on and continued pouring out the tea.

Satana arrived at the nurses' station. Mrs. Moscowitz had intended speaking to her in an intimate, friendly way, but since she was sitting on one of the chairs that she couldn't get out of unaided, and she didn't want to ask the head nurse to come to her, because she could imagine her spiteful reaction, she called out loud:

"Rosaleh, what happened to our Pnina? Just look what a state I'm in!"

"What state are you in?" asked Rosa. "I can't see any difference from usual."

"My hair," said Mrs. Moscowitz, "look!"

She put her hand on her head and her face fell.

"You can wait a few days. Nothing will happen to your hair," said Satana.

"What?" cried Mrs. Moscowitz in horror. "A few days? She won't come today at all?"

"She's sick. She can't work when she's sick. Do you work when you're sick?" asked Satana.

"But I didn't know that she isn't coming and I waited and waited. Perhaps I can telephone to her? You've got her phone number."

"I'm not giving you any phone number. She's sick. Can't you understand Hebrew?"

"Let her come just for me and I'll pay her taxi fare, special. It's urgent with me, really, like first aid."

"What's the matter? What's so urgent? You can wait a few days with your ridiculous hairdo. You won't die of it, I can promise you as a nurse."

"A few days!" cried Mrs. Moscowitz. "A few days! I can't go on like this!" And again she put her hands to her head to demonstrate the dimensions of the calamity.

"What is it with you and your hair all the time?" inquired Satana, and this time there was a note of curiosity in her question, not just the desire to tease. "You think anybody looks at your hair? They look at your legs, that's what they look at. What else do you think they look at?"

"Why do you talk to me like that?" asked Mrs. Moscowitz. "Why do you hate me so much, what did I do to you?"

Satana began writing on a piece of paper lying on the counter in front of her. She spoke to Mrs. Moscowitz casually, while she was writing. She hardly looked at her. Her voice was calm, indifferent, matter-of-fact, innocent of resentment: "I don't owe you a thing, only what the hospital work demands. That's understood, of course. But no personal favors. It's not my job to bring you a hairdresser. Personal favors I do only for people I like, for people who like me. Not for someone who calls me 'Satana,' not for someone who tells all kinds of ugly stories about me and dirty lies they've sucked out of their thumb. You know, if I wanted to, I could take you to court for telling everybody that I tried to kill you, that I pushed your wheelchair down the path outside so that you'd fall and die. What do you think, they don't put people who say things like that about hospital nurses in jail?"

Mrs. Moscowitz was incapable of uttering a single word. Satana fell silent for a moment, as if she had come across a problem on the sheet of paper in front of her. Then she put down the pen, looked at Mrs. Moscowitz with an inquiring expression and said:

"What did you think? You think I didn't know all that dirt of yours? I know everything, Yolanda, everything, every word that everybody here says about me or anybody else, I know. I know—and I keep quiet. Because I'm a strong woman. And a strong person keeps quiet. Keeps quiet and waits."

"It's not true!" At last Mrs. Moscowitz succeeded in producing an exclamation of protest. "Never in my life was I saying those things. Who told you that? Maybe somebody who hates me. Somebody who wants to harm me. How could anybody say about me that I said things like that? Who told you such a thing?"

"Did Allegra hate you? Did she want to harm you? Was she a dirty person?"

"Allegra?" Mrs. Moscowitz was horrified.

"Yes, may she rest in peace. And I believe every word she said."

"Why do you say may she rest in peace?"

"I don't know. Poor thing, if she's not dead already, she'll die tomorrow or the next day. She wasn't a person who tells lies, she didn't spread dirt like other people. Poor thing, how she suffered in her life, and what kind of a life did she have altogether? At last she'll have a little peace."

Satana tore a page off the pad of notepaper next to her, wrote something down on it, went over to Mrs. Moscowitz, and handed her the paper. "There's Pnina's phone number. What do I care? You can phone her. Let her do what she likes."

"I can't get up," said Mrs. Moscowitz.

"So why don't you stop sitting down in places where you can't get up?" demanded Satana, and this time she raised her voice impatiently. "Leon!" she called down the corridor, "Come here for a minute to help Yolanda out of her chair, I haven't got the strength to lift her."

Leon emerged from one of the rooms and came up to her, reached for her hands with his, and pulled until she was standing on her feet.

"Are you still cross with me?" asked Leon. "Because I have a joke with you now and then?"

"How can I be cross with you? You're such a good person."

"I haven't told you yet that next week I'm getting engaged," said Leon.

"Really?"

"Yes."

"Wonderful, Leon, congratulations. What age are you?"

"Twenty-eight," said Leon.

"Don't worry," said Mrs. Moscowitz, "until thirty it's nothing to worry about."

He looked at least forty to her.

"I'm not worried," he said.

"I'll give you a nice present for your wedding," she promised him.

"No, thanks, really. I don't need anything. I've got all I need. I'm going to stop working here too. Her father's taking me into his business."

"Really?" exclaimed Mrs. Moscowitz. "That's nice for you. I expect you'll get much more money there than you get here. It's a scandal what they're giving you for such hard work. How can you live on it?"

"I'm not complaining," said Leon. "I manage even on the little I get paid here. Up to now I haven't gone short of anything. It was enough for me."

"But now, with a wife, with a family, it's impossible."

"If I had no option, I'd manage then too. We'd both work, and we wouldn't go short. And I like the work in the hospital too. But her father wants me to work with him, to learn his business. She's an only child."

"You're a good person, Leon," she said again, "I wish you'll have a good life and you'll always have enough money and you won't need favors from other people."

The sense of emergency awoke a strength in her that she didn't know she possessed. She set out again all the way to the telephones to call the hairdresser. When she reached the corner where the public telephones were, she saw Fichman sitting in his wheelchair next to the round table, and when he saw her, he began to clap his hands in her honor. Before she understood the meaning of his glee, she saw Kagan's back next to the last telephone booth. He was bending forward and straining to get as close to the phone as his wheelchair would permit. She guessed that he was waiting for a call from his wife, or perhaps he was already in the middle of an intimate conversation with her. But for the fact that it was her hairdo at stake, she would no doubt have withdrawn tactfully. As it was, however, she decided to pretend that she hadn't seen him. Fichman maneuvered his chair rapidly into position and stationed himself opposite the booth where Kagan was sitting, to bar access to his patron. Fichman rolled his eyes at her and mumbled unintelligibly. She went up to the first telephone in the row, undid the string of the bag tied to her walker, took out the purse where she kept her telephone tokens, looked at the note in her hand, and dialed. There was something strange about the way Kagan was sitting squeezed into the booth and in the silence surrounding him. But respect for his privacy and the overriding importance of her own mission overcame her curiosity and her concern.

A man's voice answered her.

"Is it possible to speak to Pnina, please?"

"Who's speaking?" asked the man.

"This is Moscowitz Yolanda from G. Hospital. Pnina's coming every week to do my hair and today she didn't come. I'm so worried about her. . . . Is she healthy?"

"She's not coming any more," said the man.

"Not coming?" Mrs. Moscowitz was sure that she had not understood. "Is it possible to speak to her?"

"She's not at home."

"She's not sick?"

"She's not working there any more."

"When can I speak to her?"

"You can't."

"But I'll pay special for a taxi to come and to go . . . "

The connection was cut off.

She looked for another token to call again, but changed her mind and put the receiver down. Exhausted, she leaned on her walker, as if she had returned from a long journey. Should she phone tomorrow morning and coax her to come anyway? Should she ask her to recommend another hairdresser? A solution had to be found. Why was all this happening to her? Was it happening to her, or to the strange woman who had taken possession of her and her memories and was trying to drag her down the slippery slope to her perdition? A great weariness overcame her and she sat down on a chair next to the round table. When she glanced at the last telephone again, she realized that Kagan was trying to hide. She saw his shoulders and his neck straining to squeeze behind the partition and she even saw his right hand holding the receiver, which was not at his ear but lying on the shelf. Something inside her sent out a warning signal. And something else was alerted to suppress the memories, to dismiss the associations between him and that other man, who had had yellow eyelashes too.

"Kagan?" she called him.

There was no reply from behind the partition. Kagan's shoulders and neck twitched. And she rose from her place and tried to push her walker towards him. Fichman stretched out his hand and took hold of the leg of her walker, to bar her way.

"Kagan! What's the matter with you?" she called. "Come out from there. I can see you!"

He thrust his wheelchair backwards, his bowed back towards her, lunged to the left, and suddenly let out a strange bellow, of laughter or weeping. A brief shriek of alarm escaped Mrs. Moscowitz, followed by silence. He turned his chair toward her. There was a foolish grin on his face, which was even paler than usual. His eyes were red, his neck and shoulders were twitching convulsively. His hands shook. She inspected him and guessed what the matter was.

"Yo-lan-da!" he cried in an unfamiliar voice, pronouncing her name in a strange, special accent, as if he enjoyed rolling each syllable round in his mouth, jokingly or admiringly. "Remember, this isn't last word for us, Yo-lan-da!" He opened his mouth to add something but his voice choked in laughter or in pain, and the words were swallowed. After a moment he overcame the waywardness of his voice and said: "This isn't last word for us, Yo-lan-da, we still have something to say to world!"

"You were drinking," she said.

"A little," he said, "one drop, one teeny little drop."

"You're drunk," she said.

"No!" he protested, and he explained: "It's forbidden for me to drink too much. Wound on my leg is not closing."

"Then why do you drink?"

"I told you, only one little drop. One drop is good. Even doctors say. Yo-lan-da, please to meet Doctor Marcel Fichman, my best friend."

She turned to leave and he called after her: "People must have solidarity to each other, you don't know this? Here is not place in world. Here is Inferno. All is finished, nobody is any more alive, everybody has his punishment, so what remains? A little solidarity, a little love, maybe? What are we, angels, to do everything alone?"

She pushed her walker in front of her to escape from the telephone corner. "Only one minute!" said Kagan. "One little minute please." And Fichman spun his wheels round with astonishing speed, circled to her front and barred her passage again. Kagan burst out laughing: "You see how he loves me? Not like you."

She could no longer hold back her tears.

"Let her go, Fichman. She doesn't love me."

Fichman turned his chair aside and made way for her. She took a tissue out of her gown pocket and wiped her tears.

"You believe in God," said Kagan, "what did he do for you?" From under the flaps of his pajama jacket he extracted a small, flat half-empty bottle, and hugged it to his chest. "She kills me and I love her. *O Satan,*" he cried, *"prends pitié de ma longue misère!"*

"Tfu! Cholera!" exclaimed Fichman in a sorrowful voice.

"Fichman was doctor for children in Tel Aviv," said Kagan. "Who didn't know Dr. Fichman in Tel Aviv? How much money, friends, honor? Now also dead."

On her way back to her wing her tears dried. Everything now appeared surprisingly clear to her, absolutely simple, almost self-evident. She hadn't lived alone for fifty years in order to return at the end of her life to the same misery, the same suffering, the same humiliations. She had to keep away from him. As soon as she had come to this decision, she felt a sense of relief.

⟶

When she entered the room, Frieda's manly voice rebuked her: "Adela was here, she looked for you and she didn't find you. Nobody knew where you were."

A cry of terror and guilt burst from Mrs. Moscowitz: "Allegra!"

"She's still alive," said Frieda.

"How is she?"

"It's apparently the end."

"What did Adela want?"

"She wants the three of us to sign an affidavit for her, saying that we know how she looked after Allegra and everything she did for her. So there won't be any problems later with the inheritance . . . "

"Inheritance?"

"I told her I wouldn't sign anything," said Frieda angrily, "I told her she could forget it. But she said she would come and talk to you, that she was sure you would understand."

"I won't sign," said Mrs. Moscowitz.

"Clara won't sign either," said Frieda.

They went to supper. In the dining room Kagan was already sitting with Fichman and as she passed him with her friends, on their way to their table at the end of the hall, she saw his eyes beckoning her, realizing that she was not going to come and sit next to him, and saying to her: You'll be back.

Clara asked: "Aren't you going to go and sit next to him?"

She did not reply. When they seated themselves at their table Clara and Frieda exchanged meaningful looks. She told them about the telephone call she had made to the hairdresser's house. Frieda said that the man on the phone must have been Pnina's husband, and that she must have run away with her lover. "That explains everything," boomed Frieda, whose voice—simply because it was so deep—always sounded accusing and condemning, even when she didn't intend it to.

Clara the hunchback laughed silently, as usual, crouched like a bird over her plate, pecking rapidly at her food. "I didn't like her from the beginning," she said, "luckily I don't need her, I don't need her favors." Clara's hair was thin and short.

Frieda, however, did require the hairdresser's services, for apart from cutting and setting her hair, Pnina also tweaked the hairs from her chin and her upper lip, and plucked her thick eyebrows. Frieda therefore took it upon herself to exploit her friendly relations with Satana and ask her to find them another hairdresser in the neighboring town.

Mrs. Moscowitz stopped listening to their conversation. She felt increasingly remorseful at not sitting with Kagan. Her place was there, not with these women. Was she going to lose his friendship? Was he going to break off relations with her? From where she was sitting she couldn't see him, but the look in his eyes as she walked past him came back to haunt her and would not let her be. Until she heard the waitress's scolding voice behind her: "Why aren't you eating, Yolanda? Do I have to wait an hour after everyone else is finished just for you? And when am I going to go home, hey? I've got a family, if you don't mind, I've got children, and they want to see me sometimes. Or is that too much to ask?"

When the three friends left the dining room, Kagan and Fichman were no longer there. Frieda's family was sitting in the corridor, waiting for her to return from her meal. In the meantime they were being kept company by Peretz Kabiri, a squat broad-shouldered man with a deeply lined, ashen face and a mane of frizzy gray hair surrounding a bald pate. He was sitting next to them, his crutches leaning against the wall, and pouring a chaotic stream of words into their ears, raising his voice enthusiastically and lowering it again confidentially, about his days in the British army, as a German prisoner of war, and in the struggle against the foreign occupation. When Frieda saw him in the distance, she began turning the wheels of her chair as quickly as she could and thundered: "Go away! Go away! Stop making from yourself a nuisance! We don't want you here! Go to your own people." And Peretz Kabiri looked at her sadly, spread out his arms and slapped his thighs, as if apologizing to his audience for the untoward interruption obliging him to cut short his discourse, thrust his crutches under his armpits, got up from his chair and stood, and as he set out down the corridor to find some other set of visitors to talk to, he broke loudly into his one and only song, which had remained with him from the days of his glory: "*Ama—do mio,* love me for ever!"

Mrs. Moscowitz sat down at a few chairs' distance from the family, as was her habit when she was on good terms with Frieda—far enough so as not to seem to be interfering with them but within hearing range, so as not to seem aloof. She fixed her eyes on the television set, which was showing the Arabic programs, and heard Frieda telling her family about the hairdresser Pnina who had disappeared and about Allegra, who had been sitting here with them only yesterday, fainting, and perhaps no longer in the land of the living, but she didn't hear her say anything about Adela and her suspicious request with regard to the signing of the affidavit. The grandchildren wandered up and down the corridor. First they trailed behind Peretz Kabiri as he hopped about on his crutches singing, and then they went into a room where one of the patients was screaming. Their parents, who were tired of getting up to bring them back, let them run about as they pleased. Clara came and sat down next to Mrs. Moscowitz, and she too stared at the television screen, from time to time stealing shrewd, sidelong looks at the family, as if to note down details in her memory for the conclusions she would draw later.

Satana finished her shift and went home. When she passed them in the corridor Frieda's daughter and son-in-law rose quickly to their feet, to bow and scrape and laugh ingratiatingly, as they did with all the doctors and nurses and the rest of the hospital staff. And Clara, who claimed that they gave members of the staff generous presents of money too, stole a quick look at Mrs. Moscowitz.

It was growing late and she still hadn't heard anything from Kagan. He had definitely said that he was going to paint her portrait tomorrow: had he changed his mind? Frieda's family left, the nurse passed down the row and gave the patients their medications before they went to bed. It was impossible to rely on him—her anger flared against Kagan, who had not come to tell her of his intentions—if he wanted her to sit for him, she had to prepare herself, especially her hair, which hadn't been done for a week. She made up her mind to refuse to pose for him and teach him a lesson.

The three women went into the room and Frieda said: "If she comes tomorrow, tell her that nobody's going to sign for her, that she should leave us alone and go and look for somewhere else to steal money from sick people."

When Mrs. Moscowitz got into bed, Frieda lingered beside her. "Good, let the window be closed," she said in Hebrew, for all the room to hear, "so you won't have anything to complain about that it made you sick." And she went on, talking in their language, as if she wanted to detain her, so that she wouldn't fall asleep, so that she wouldn't plot treachery against her. Mrs. Moscowitz turned her face away and Frieda fell silent but remained where she was and looked at her. Mrs. Moscowitz felt Frieda's eyes moving slowly over her face and her body under the sheet, as if she were seeking something, and then she heard the wheelchair move away.

She closed her eyes. At once heaviness overcame her and she could no longer move. Gradually silence overtook her, and from the heart of the silence, softly at first and then louder and louder rose a high, piercing unmistakable sound, the crying of baby Rosalia, her sister Elvira's daughter. Like a cruel, ancient lullaby, the memory of that crying drew her after it.

"What are you doing now? Are you in bed?" she heard Leon's voice.

She woke up and immediately opened her eyes, thinking that he was talking to her, his voice sounded so close. But he was in the corridor, whiling away the hours of his night shift on telephone conversations from the nurses' station.

"My name's Doron . . . And yours? What's the difference? Someone gave me your number . . . What's on TV now? Am I interrupting anything? . . . Okay, okay, keep your hair on."

Apparently the girl on the other end of the line banged down the phone, for Mrs. Moscowitz heard him dialing again, waiting, putting the phone down and dialing again.

"Are you in bed already? . . . You don't know me . . . I got your number . . . Hang on a minute . . . Doron . . . What's the difference . . . All I want is to talk to you for a bit . . . Why not? . . . What're you doing . . . I'm not phoning from home . . . It's a secret . . . No, not military, security. No, I can't . . . How d'you know, maybe you'd like to meet me, up to now no one's regretted it, take it from me . . . For example, how do you like it . . . You know exactly what I mean . . . What's wrong? . . . Hang on a minute. . . . "

He laughed unpleasantly. And again he dialed and again someone at the other end slammed the phone down and he dialed again and tried different lines in various tones of voice. So it went on, and Mrs.

Moscowitz coughed several times in order to attract his attention, but he didn't hear, so absorbed was he in his telephone game. Then he lowered his voice to give it an intimate tone, but nevertheless she could hear him clearly showering obscenities on his anonymous interlocuter, more patient than her predecessors, who was apparently enjoying the game no less than he.

"Leon, come here, help me please!" cried Mrs. Moscowitz.

He lowered his voice a little and continued his conversation. She allowed him to finish it. Then he entered the room and approached her bed.

"What's up, Yolanda?"

"I have to go to the bathroom and I can't get up."

"I'll bring you a bedpan if you like," offered Leon.

"No, I don't want to. I want to get up."

"Why not? Are you shy of me?"

She sat up in bed, pushed her feet into her slippers and held out her arms to him. He raised her to her feet and she pulled the walker toward herself. When she turned to negotiate the aisle between her bed and Allegra's empty bed, she saw that he was still standing there and watching her. A ray of light from the corridor fell on his face. He smiled at her strangely, as if waiting for her to say something, and in his balding head and his half-illuminated round face, in his bulging eyes with their unfocused look, she saw a certain elusive and surprising beauty that she had never seen there before. He accompanied her, silent and smiling, to the bathroom, and continued up the corridor. When she was inside she remembered that she had left the bag with her purse in it under her pillow.

When she emerged from the bathroom, she hurried as quickly as she could back to her bed, and when her hand encountered the bag under her pillow she felt a measure of relief. Still standing bent over the walker, she pulled it out, removed the purse and began counting her money. The light from the corridor was insufficient for her purpose, and she switched on the little lamp next to her bed. But at once her eyes were drawn to the end of the room where she saw Leon hiding next to the porch door and watching her in the darkness. For a long moment they looked at each other in silence. Finally Leon walked slowly and nonchalantly out of the room, and returned to the nurses' station.

Mrs. Moscowitz didn't know what to do. In the end she put the purse back into the bag without counting her money and thrust it underneath her pillow. Then she made her way into the corridor and went up to him. He was reading a newspaper.

"Leon," she said.

He raised his eyes and looked at her indifferently.

"You're a good person, I know. Better than everybody here. You help me a lot. In the room before, I took the purse to give you something, a little present, so you should know I love you. Just like a mother loves her son."

"Thanks a lot. I don't need your money. Go to bed."

She returned to the room and got into bed. A woman in one of the rooms screamed in pain or from a nightmare. Mrs. Moscowitz heard Leon going to comfort her. Afterward he returned to the nurses' station, where he picked up the phone and resumed his conversations with the anonymous girls. After a while his voice no longer disturbed her. From a distance something touched her, and when the moment of grace and inner sinking began, she called to God in her heart and asked to see Allegra again, even if it were only once.

chapter three

In the morning Leon was in a good mood, as if the memory of the night before had been erased from his mind. After rinsing the last of the shampoo from her hair, she wrapped her head in a towel and emerged from the bathroom. He saw her from the corridor as he was going home from the night shift, and came up to her and said:

"Your boyfriend's looking for you," and burst into laughter.

"Why are you laughing so much?" she asked.

"I don't know," said Leon, "maybe it's exhaustion," and he laughed again.

"I don't understand what you're talking about and what there is to laugh," said Mrs. Moscowitz.

"Why do you want him and not me? Aren't I handsomer than him, younger than him? What's wrong with me that you don't love me?"

"Leon, I don't permit to speak like that to me, you know."

"You don't know what's good for you."

She coiled her hair lock by lock around the rollers she had borowed from one of the patients, wrapped her head in the towel again in order not to catch a cold, and sat down on the edge of her bed.

Frieda thundered: "How long are you going to sit like that for your hair to dry? You could have waited a few days longer for the new hairdresser to come. What's so urgent?"

"You don't have to interfere in everything somebody else does," said Mrs. Moscowitz. "I never tell you what to do."

Frieda turned the wheels of her chair angrily and propelled herself out of the room.

After a while Kagan appeared in the doorway. "Can I come in?" he asked and wheeled himself into the room. Fichman remained in the corridor. Her heart skipped a beat and she didn't know if it was from happiness or embarrassment.

"*Comment allez-vous, Madame?*" cried Kagan.

"You shouldn't see me like this," she said, "I didn't know when you wanted. You never said anything."

"*Au contraire!*" said Kagan. "Like this is very good! I make you exotic portrait with turban!"

"No. Out of the question. I'm not ready yet."

"When?"

She reflected for a moment, and looked at her watch: "One more hour and a half."

"Why?" asked Kagan in surprise. "What are you doing for hour and half?"

She smiled without saying a word, and he submitted.

"I come here," he said.

"Please, with pleasure."

When she removed the rollers from her hair, which was almost dry, and combed it out, she didn't recognize her face in the bathroom mirror. Now I really look like a sick woman, she said to herself. Her head seemed to have shrunk. Her hair was very thin and hung in wisps on her temples, lifeless as the faded face whose features had been swallowed up in a sea of wrinkles. At the roots of her hair the beginning of a grey growth was visible, little gray paths exposing the scalp beneath them. This time she exaggerated her makeup: the red of the lips, the pink of the cheeks, the blue around the eyes, the black of the eyebrows and eyelashes, the white of the powder on the forehead, nose and chin. And when she completed her work, she inspected the face in the mirror and muttered to herself with a strange satisfaction: "Like an old whore after her last chance."

He sat in his wheelchair in the corridor, his back to the wall, not far from the door to her room, with the new drawing pad his wife had brought him from Beersheba lying on his lap. He couldn't see her when she emerged from the bathroom and she scrutinized him before going to change out of her gown into a suitable dress. At that moment he looked to her like a child, an obedient old child, waiting patiently, and she knew that he was interested only in himself and she had nobody to rely on.

"Pity you took off towel," he said when she came out to him, "it was very nice. Like turban."

"And like this isn't nice?" she asked.

"Also," he said halfheartedly, "also."

They went to a little room next to the occupational therapy room. Kagan told her that one of the doctors had heard him saying that he wanted to draw, and given him the key to this room, which nobody used. But when they entered the room they found the bed made and a little table holding several books, newspaper-covered exercise books, and a cup with coffee dregs, two chairs with shirts and trousers thrown onto them, and a number of other items of clothing and personal possessions. The window was closed and the stuffy air inside the room imprisoned the heat and smell of a stranger. Mrs. Moscowitz opened the window and Kagan pulled the clothes off one of the chairs and put them on top of the clothes on the other chair, so that she could sit down. For a moment he contemplated her in silence, examined her posture, the angle of her head, and asked her to tilt it to the left and the right, up and down, until he was satisfied.

Then he asked her if she could hold the pose for a length of time, to which she replied that she was perfectly comfortable.

He rested the pad on his thigh, holding it in his left hand, turned over the cover and a few pages on which he had apparently already drawn, until he reached an empty page and stroked it slowly with the fingers of his right hand, as if he enjoyed feeling the smoothness of its surface. Then he took a fountain pen out of his pajama-top pocket, unscrewed the cap and fitted it onto the other end, looking at her as he did so with his head on one side. In the end he straightened his head, looked at the paper and drew a few long lines on it, looking alternately at her and the paper. The room was silent and she could hear the scratching of the nib on the paper and his rhythmic breathing, soft as the breathing of a sleeping man. Suddenly she felt as if his fingers were touching her face, stroking it as they had stroked the page, and she didn't know which was stronger, her fear and revulsion at the touch or the wish to learn how to give herself up to it. She stole a glance at the fingers of his left hand gripping the edge of the pad, saw his dark, dead, crooked nails, and the possibility of their touching her flesh was as terrible as the sudden, grotesque hope, quickening inside her after so many years, that something would happen to her which had not happened yet.

"Why is face suddenly so sad?" asked Kagan.

"Is it permitted to talk?"

"Of course permitted. Only not to move head."

"I remembered something."

"What did you remember?"

"My friend, poor thing, Allegra, is going to die. All her life she was so afraid to die alone, only of that she was afraid."

He went on drawing, looking alternately at her face and at the page and she didn't know if he was listening to her or not.

"She wanted to be here at the moment when the death comes,"

added Mrs. Moscowitz, not so much out of a need to tell him this, but in order to go on talking, as if she wanted by so doing to put off the pronouncement of a judgment about to be passed. "Only to be beside me, beside her friends in the room. It was so important for her. Only not to be alone when it happens. And now who knows if she'll have someone beside her at the moment when . . . "

"I say," he interrupted her, as he turned over the page of the pad, drew the pen over the paper again in broad strokes and inspected the results, "I say: if to die—then alone, like dog, without sentimental shmaltz. Because, of course, death is biological thing, without beauty, without some secret, just end. Same thing for dog like man."

For a long time he went on drawing, dissatisfied with the results. He turned over another page and began everything again from the beginning. Now he hardly looked at her any more. She was tired of sitting so long in the same position and asked him if she could rest a little.

"Only one more minute," he requested. "Now exactly it comes right. A little longer, please. Few more seconds, please."

She couldn't understand what he needed her sitting opposite him for. He was utterly absorbed in the page in front of him and he had stopped looking at her. He had all he required there, on the paper, everything was decided between him and himself, between him and the page. Her presence there was completely unimportant to him.

Suddenly there was the sound of a key turning in the keyhole, the door opened and revealed the child gardener she had seen through the glass wall of the visitors' lounge. He took a step forward and immediately started back in alarm and stood rooted to the spot, as if too frightened even to run away. His little eyes darted around.

"What's this?" said Kagan angrily. "What do you want?"

The boy was silent. His long arms began to tremble and he held them close to his sides and fiddled with the hems of his short pants with his fingers. He tried to say something, and his face twisted. His ears turned red, his shaven head shrank down between his shoulders. In the end he managed to mumble: "Raffik . . . "

Mrs. Moscowitz said: "Is it Raffy what you're looking for?"

He nodded his head and again he twisted his face and said: "Raffik . . . "

"Are you Raffy's brother?" asked Mrs. Moscowitz.

He nodded his head. His eyes scanned the room, as if searching for something.

"What do you want? " asked Kagan impatiently. "Go away."

"He's Raffy's brother," explained Mrs. Moscowitz. "We saw him down in the garden, with Raffy, when they were praying. Remember?"

The boy recovered, limped to the corner of the room, took a little bundle wrapped in a white cloth and showed it to them, as if asking their permission.

"This is Raffy's room," muttered Kagan and looked around him, making a new and disappointing appraisal of the place. "These things are his. And doctor said room shut, nobody is working here, there is nobody, it can be studio for me," and as proof he took the key out of his pajama pocket.

"This is Raffy's room?" Mrs. Moscowitz asked the boy.

"My brother . . . " said the boy.

"What is here?" asked Kagan.

The boy knelt down and rapidly undid the bundle. It contained some slices of white bread and two smaller bundles, wrapped in white grease-spotted material. The boy began undoing one of these little bundles.

There was a knock at the door, and the boy raised his eyes hopefully. Satana came in smiling sweetly, but when she saw the boy her face grew stern:

"What are you doing here?" she cried angrily.

"He's Raffy's brother," explained Mrs. Moscowitz.

"Thank you very much for the information. I could have told you that myself," said Satana. "Get out and look sharp about it!"

The boy quickly tied up his bundle, tucked it under his arm, and hobbled to the door. On the threshold he stopped and mumbled: "Raffik?"

"Get out! He'll come to you when he's got the time," Satana showed him the door.

"Maybe he needs him?" said Mrs. Moscowitz.

The boy left, and Satana let out her breath in an angry hiss: "He's backward, can't you see? They bring their family here and in the end they'll take the whole place over!" And in an instant her expression changed and she was all smiles and sweetness again: "Well, how are you getting on? The doctor told me you were drawing her picture here. Let's see." She went and stood behind Kagan's wheelchair and looked at the pad on his knees. "Beautiful!" she exclaimed. "Beautiful! And what a likeness! Ha, Yolanda, how lucky you are to have him drawing you, and how beautiful you look in the picture. When are you going to draw my picture too, Lazar? Why only Yolanda, why not me too?"

He turned and smiled politely at the head nurse. Satana stared at Mrs. Moscowitz and cried: "How beautiful you are today, Yolanda! And what an elegant new hair style! Perfect for the picture!"

After Satana left, Kagan turned the pad over on his knees and sighed: "They don't let you work."

"I'll have nothing but trouble from her now," said Mrs. Moscowitz.

"Why?" asked Kagan.

"Didn't you see? She's so jealous from me, that you talk to me, that you draw me. Whenever she can she throws the evil eye on me."

He burst out laughing, hugely amused, and raised the pad from his knees to inspect his work. "It can't be, Yolanda, that you really think this. I don't believe it!"

"Yes, yes! You can laugh but it's nothing to laugh. The ones who suffer from it don't laugh. If you don't want to believe it, you don't have to. I know it from Europe and from Israel too. There are people who know how to throw the evil eye and you can't do anything to them back. How did I fall on the stairs, you think? My neighbor who knows to throw the evil eye saw me going down the stairs, she opened the door and she said, just like Satana said now: You're so beautiful, you look so well! And immediately I fell down the stairs and the leg was broken. They have this power, such people. Where it's coming from I don't know. Maybe from Satan."

He raised his eyes from the pad:

"'*O Satan, prends pitié de ma longue misère!*'"

"Yes," said Mrs. Moscowitz.

"This is Baudelaire," said Kagan.

"It doesn't matter," said Mrs. Moscowitz. "It can happen to everyone. It's nothing to laugh."

"So what will she do to you now?"

"I don't know. But no good will come from it, I promise you."

"Yolanda, I know nothing of your life. Personal questions are permitted?"

"I didn't think you were interested."

"Of course interested. You have family, husband, children?"

"In the old country I had a husband. We were divorced. That was many years ago."

"Why?" asked Kagan.

"In the beginning there was a great love, afterwards he began to hate me. So quickly as it all began, so quickly it was all over. I was young, I had no sense. I had nothing. He wasn't Jewish. He was

French. He came to work there in the consulate. We got married. Less than three years together. After we were married, he began to be drinking very much, all the time cursing, hitting me that I was a Jewess, and saying that he didn't want children from a Jewess. He was handsome, blond, like a star from Hollywood, but his heart was black. He was hating me terribly. Like a madman. I think from the alcohol mainly. It was very hard for me. He had a strong power over me, everything he told me, I did it. All the time I was forgiving him. At the beginning he had the great love for me, the sky and the earth he wanted to give to me. Afterwards he began to hating me terribly, it was becoming like the death for me. Until he wanted to divorce, he made my life a misery. He went back to France, and I never heard from him again. I wanted to begin my life again, but it was hard. They didn't let me. I came to Israel."

"And after?"

"After I am alone. I had enough."

"So many years alone?" said Kagan.

"Yes."

"In Tel Aviv? You own apartment?"

"Yes."

"On teacher's salary?"

"Yes. It wasn't easy."

"Bravo," he said. "How many rooms?"

"Two rooms. But on the fourth floor, without an elevator. For a person sick with the legs, all those stairs, it isn't easy. Impossible to go outside. All the time only in the house. Thank goodness for so much work to do, and the telephone and radio and the television in the evening."

"No family, brother, sister, children of theirs?"

"No."

"No relations?"

"No one. All overseas. No one came here. I wouldn't have come either if I married someone normal over there and made a family for myself. I had a few friends. They died already."

He looked at her in silence.

"And you?" asked Mrs. Moscowitz.

"You saw yesterday."

"She's young," said Mrs. Moscowitz.

"Yes. And I married old. Good woman. But old man and young woman is not simple matter. She was dancer in Russia. Today ballet teacher to little girls in Beersheba. It is hard for her. And I too am not easy man. Sometimes she is a little too much nervous. But she's good woman."

"Children?"

"No," he said. "Children no good for old man. And I am child myself. People say: old men like children."

He showed her the pad and asked with a smile: "You want to see?"

"Why not?"

"She's not finished yet, there's still work to do, but something is already possible to see."

He wheeled his chair toward her, and when he was close, he turned the page with the drawing to face her. What she saw resembled a spider's web. An infinity of fine and thick threads stretching lengthways and sideways and crosswise, straight threads and humped ones, wavy and rounded, creating in their density, as on a map, hollows and peaks, heights and slopes, and among them allusions to the features of a face, blank, empty slits of eyes, eyebrows like black bruises, the shadow of a nose and two pits of nostrils, shriveled lips, the ruins surviving a disaster, shadows gradually being eaten away and obliterated with the death of the flesh.

She averted her face from the drawing and covered her eyes with her hand. He laid the pad on his knees and said in a whisper, in astonishment: "Yolanda, what happened?" His fingers stroked her free hand. She felt their warmth, their softness, their strength, the promise of stability and constancy they held out, and at the same time she couldn't help thinking of their dreadful, repulsive appearance.

"Yolanda," he whispered again, "what happened?"

She took her hand from her eyes and examined his face: "Is that what I look like?"

"That is how I see you. This is not photographic picture, this is drawing. So my subjective eye sees your face."

"Thank you very much," said Mrs. Moscowitz, in pain but not in anger, "a great compliment I must say."

"This is art. You know art?"

She pulled her hand out of his.

"If I want to make photographic portrait, I go to hotel in Eilat and draw for tourists there and make much money. But art is different thing entirely."

"If you could see photographs of me from Europe, when I was young ... " said Mrs. Moscowitz.

"But Yolanda, is not the same thing."

"Of course it isn't. Today everything's full of wrinkles, today everything's like an old rag, you think I don't know? Before I looked in the mirror and I saw it all."

He looked at his drawing, inspected it carefully: "But there is strength here, no? You don't feel strength?"

"Like a witch you made me," she said, "but it's not your fault. That's how you see me."

"Nurse Rosa really made us evil eye," said Kagan sorrowfully.

Mrs. Moscowitz said: "You see?"

His eyes were sad, and the light of the approaching noon coming in at the window of the little room turned them a tender light brown, and his yellow lashes gleamed. He contemplated her face in silence.

From the bag tied to her walker she quickly drew out a tissue and wiped the tears trickling down her cheeks.

He took her hand again and whispered into her ear, like a prayer:

Mon enfant, ma soeur,
Songe à la douceur
D'aller là-bas vivre ensemble!
Aimer à loisir
Aimer et mourir
Au pays qui te ressemble!

"All I ask is for nobody to see it," said Mrs. Moscowitz and pointed to the drawing. "Word of honor."

"Word of honor," said Kagan.

He held out his hand and took the tear-soaked tissue from her, wiped a few places on her cheeks where the makeup had been smudged, repaired the damage with a painter's practiced hand, and in the end he said: "Now everything is fine."

"Don't think I don't know what I'm looking like. If you could have heard the words that I said to myself in the bathroom by the mirror, after I did my face, you wouldn't think I was naive."

⟋

When she reached the corridor, Frieda and Clara greeted her excitedly: "Adela's looking for you."

"What about Allegra?"

"Not dead yet," said Frieda. "That's why Adela's in such a hurry."

The tone of Adela's voice was tearful, and so was her expression when she spoke—in complete contrast to her handsome, confident appearance. She was tall and sturdy, about fifty years old, there were silver threads—not many as yet—in her hair, and she did not dye them; it was also evident that her simple hairstyle was her own work. It was obvious to Mrs. Moscowitz that if she had paid more attention

80

to this aspect of her appearance she would have been far more attractive than she was. She gave off a bad smell of cigarette smoke and sour sweat after the bus journey in the summer heat. She never used deodorants and she changed her clothes infrequently.

No sooner had they exchanged greetings than Adela took two chairs out onto the long balcony, which ran along all the rooms in the wing and overlooked a large lawn, and invited Mrs. Moscowitz to join her there. Mrs. Moscowitz expressed reservations about the wind that was blowing on the balcony and told her about the severe chill that had almost been the death of her. Adela offered to bring her something to cover her shoulders, and by the time Mrs. Moscowitz had finished explaining where to find her shawl, the brisk, efficient woman had already returned, draped the wrap round the sick woman's shoulders and rested her hands on them for a moment with the beneficent and encouraging touch of which only she, perhaps, knew the secret.

Mrs. Moscowitz asked her how Allegra was and Adela responded with a deep sigh and lit a cigarette. She spread out her hands to express uncertainty, despair and helplessness and shook her head as if to say: There's nothing to be done.

"I've just come from there," said Adela and shook the ash from her cigarette over the railing, onto the lawn. "They wouldn't let me stay with her more than a quarter of an hour."

Although she was far younger than Mrs. Moscowitz and her friends and had immigrated to Israel in her youth, she spoke their language without difficulty, and only an occasional hesitation could be heard in the flow of words.

"She was more than half dead already," added Adela, and in the manner of a woman practiced in dealing with the sick, she blew the cigarette smoke sideways, toward the lawn, and away from Mrs. Moscowitz. "They gave her a blood transfusion. Who knows how long that'll keep her going. The doctors themselves can't say. I've got connections there with the doctors and nurses. I did my best to get them to do the maximum for her. If not for me, she would have been dead long ago. Under the circumstances I have to be with her all day long. I haven't got a choice in the matter. Two buses there and two buses back, and a few more kilometers by foot, there and back. And at night I have to do the housework, I don't have time to sleep. God knows how I keep going."

She ground the cigarette out on the iron bannister, held the stub in her hand and looked around for somewhere to put it. In the end she took a tissue out of her pocket, wrapped the stub in it, and returned it to the pocket.

"Today she looked a little better. We spoke a few minutes. She's got the soul of a saint, that woman. Only one thing worries her now, that I'll get what's coming to me for my work. With the last of her strength she asked if everything was arranged according to the agreement between us, everything she herself offered when I began to help her. And I don't do it for money, she knows that very well, but it's important to her that I should get something. Because she knows what I've done for her. She made me swear that I would make all the necessary arrangements. And she asked about you too. She loves you. She thinks about you a lot. She asked for you not to be cross with her, to forgive her. I don't know what she meant. But that's what she asked me to tell you."

"No!" cried Mrs. Moscowitz. "Tell her I'm not cross with her at all, the opposite, only love and prayers in my heart for her to get well and come back to us."

"She won't get well," said Adela. "She knows that these are her last days. And she wants to leave the world with a clean heart, to know that she doesn't owe anyone anything. That's why she sent me to you. And she asked for you to sign these papers. That's her request of you. Perhaps her last request."

"What papers?" asked Mrs. Moscowitz innocently.

"Frieda didn't tell you?"

"She said something but I didn't understand."

Adela opened the leather bag lying at her feet, took out a folded sheet of paper, and handed it to Mrs. Moscowitz. And before Mrs. Moscowitz had a chance to say that she needed her spectacles, the energetic helper stood up, entered the room, went up to her bedside locker, and returned to the porch with the reading glasses in her hand. Her quickness and initiative were truly astonishing. The document was written in their language and Mrs. Moscowitz studied it at length, taking the opportunity to consider what she would say to Adela, and how she would explain her refusal. And why, in fact, should she refuse to sign? She didn't know. Adela lit another cigarette, and watched Mrs. Moscowitz's eyes moving over the document. It said that there were no limits to Adela's devotion to Allegra, that for the past eight years she had taken care of all her needs, visited her at least twice a week at the hospitals where she had been hospitalized, washed her, oiled and massaged her body because of the damage done to her skin by the disease. The document listed all the treatments she had given Allegra in detail, as well as various errands and trips she had undertaken to different places on her behalf. When Mrs. Moscowitz had finished reading it and given it back to Adela, the brisk, efficient woman handed her a document signed by Allegra Levy, in which she acknowledged her gratitude to Adela for her devoted care and for everything she had done for her during the past eight years, while her two brothers had turned their backs on her and refused to lift a finger to help her. This being the case, she had decided to bequeath her apartment and everything it contained to Adela Klein, as well as any money left in her bank account after her death. Attached to this document was an affidavit awaiting the signatures of Frieda Bakal, Clara Hershkowitz, and Yolanda Moscowitz, in which they attested to the fact that Allegra Levy had written what she had written and disposed of her property as she had disposed of it and signed this declaration of her wishes in the presence of the under-signed while of sound mind and in full consciousness and without any pressure, physical, mental or moral, being exerted on her, and without any threats or intent of extortion, open or hidden, and so on and so forth in the tortuous legal terminology of their language that had been dictated to Adela by a lawyer from their country, who had also typed it for her on a typewriter and photograped it on a duplicating machine in a number of copies.

"I can't sign this," said Mrs. Moscowitz.

"Why not?"

"It says here that I was present when Allegra wrote it and signed it, and that's not true."

"You don't understand!" cried Adela. "That's just a formality. It's enough that you know her and you know what she thinks of me and what I do for her. The question of whether you were present or not is of no importance."

"I'm not a lawyer," said Mrs. Moscowitz, "I really don't understand these things, and I can't sign something that's not true."

"If you really loved her, you'd do it—for her, not for me. Because that's what she wants, and you know it's the truth. You know what I do for her. You saw it for yourself. And I don't do it for money."

"What do you do it for then?"

"For love."

"So why do you want the inheritance?"

"I want the inheritance? What are you talking about? What's there to inherit here? Gold, diamonds, crystal? Do you know where she lives? In a room underneath the stairs, two by one and a half meters big. There's barely room for a bed and a refrigerator. How much wealth do you think there is in a place like that? I don't want any inheritance from her, don't make me laugh! It's her who wants me to have it! She doesn't want her darling brothers to have it. I would be happy to give up what she's got there. What do I need it for? But I promised her, as a favor, to see to it that her brothers didn't get their hands on anything of hers. And her wishes are sacred to me. I have to keep my promise. Because breaking a promise to a dead person is the worst sin there is and the most dangerous thing you can do. Everybody knows that."

Mrs. Moscowitz didn't know why she was so determined to refuse Adela and reject her reasonable and persuasive explanations: was it because of the bad smell she gave off, which was also the smell of unfailing energy and tireless hard work? Was it because she was afraid of the trouble of going to court to testify and being questioned there? Perhaps it was because she had been obliged to do her hair herself and she could feel it on her head like a scarf that wasn't part of her body? A kind of desolation was spreading rapidly through her hair, and she could feel it in her scalp. Something was stirring there, separating the hairs from each other, making them grow sparse and lank and wilted. Bald, gray patches would be revealed beneath them, growing bigger all the time, greasy and suffocated, like dead things. And thus she stood before Adela—in all her weakness and humiliation; and Adela, with all the advantage on her side, was trying to get something from her that she wasn't sure she wanted to give.

"I'll have to think about it," said Mrs. Moscowitz with a certain impatience, "it's not the kind of thing you can make up your mind about on the spur of the moment."

"What's there to make up your mind about?" insisted Adela, "I'll simply tell her that you're not prepared to do even this for her, that it's too much for you to sign your name for her. You know she'd do a lot more than that for you. But everybody's got their own ideas. . . . "

Mrs. Moscowitz rose from her seat, leaning on her walker, turned it toward the door and began walking away. Adela watched her intently, and she could sense the determined woman's eyes on her legs, examining their movement.

"Nobody knows what's in store for them, if they might need somebody to help them too one day," said Adela.

Mrs. Moscowitz went on walking.

Adela stood up and asked: "What should I tell Allegra?"

"Tell her I love her with all my heart. That I've never met anyone like her in my life. I'll never forget her." As she said this, the words stabbed her heart like daggers: now she was certain that she would never see Allegra again, never know why she had told Satana what she told her. "And tell her that I know why she thinks I'm cross with her, and it's nothing, nothing at all. I forgave her long ago. I'll never be angry with her."

"I feel sorry for you," said Adela, "you'll regret not wanting to sign—for her and for you, not for me. I only hope that it won't be too late. It doesn't matter to me. I don't know you and I don't care what happens to you. But she loves you, and that's what's important to me."

She folded her papers and put them into her bag, swung it over her shoulder, and came up very close to Mrs. Moscowitz. "Anyone who arrives at a place like this," she whispered, with her mouth reeking of cigarettes close to her face, "anyone who's already in a place like this should know how to behave with more sense and to think of what happens afterwards." And she left without saying goodbye.

＊

At lunch Mrs. Moscowitz sat at Kagan's table. He looked tense and worried. Fichman, who was sitting with them, rolled his eyes merrily at her, devoured everything on his tray voraciously and finished eating before everyone else. Kagan gave him a long, disgusted look, and said: "How are you eating? So fast to eat isn't healthy. Ulcer is possible to get from this. What do you want? You doctor, children's doctor, and you don't know this?"

Fichman's face grew grave and Kagan said to Mrs. Moscowitz: "Sometimes I love him and and sometimes I can't even look at him."

Fichman gave him a questioning look.

"Perhaps he understands what you say to him?" asked Mrs. Moscowitz anxiously.

"Maybe understands, maybe not," said Kagan.

And again he sank into a prolonged silence. She knew that such silences had to be respected—and she knew how to shrink into herself, to disappear, to keep quiet.

"Yolanda," said Kagan in the end, "I have some problem, maybe you can help, but only if truly, truly not difficult."

"What problem?"

"Well, this is very embarrassing. Fifty shekels I need until Sunday. You can help perhaps? But only if it's not difficult for you."

"Yes, yes, of course," she said and reached for the bag on her walker.

"No, not now," snapped Kagan, in a tone she had never heard him use before, "later, after we leave dining room."

Fichman sat with his head lowered and his shoulders slumped. His face looked pained. With his big bald head, his round face, his pointed ears and the brown pajama pants folded at the knees, he suddenly looked to her like a baby in a stroller, as small and helpless as a baby. She felt sorry for him but she didn't dare express her pity, or even smile at him, for fear of arousing Kagan's wrath.

"Drawing I make of you I tore up," he said at last.

"Why?"

"You ask why?"

She was silent.

The three of them left the dining room together. Next to the entrance to the men's wing, she slipped a fifty shekel note into Kagan's hand, and he quickly put it in his pajama pocket. For a moment she stood looking at them, she saw them going into their room in their wheelchairs, Kagan first and Fichman behind him, and she said to

87

herself: if he returned the fifty shekels on Sunday, as he had promised, it would be a sign that he respected her, and if not—she should distance herself from him and spare herself pain and humiliation that would be beyond her powers of endurance. And altogether, when a man asked a woman for money, it meant trouble. What had possessed her to tell him about her life with her husband in the old country, about her misery, about her loneliness in the apartment where she lived like a prisoner? And why had he asked about her apartment, why had he wanted to know if it was hers?

These doubts and fears and her anger at herself would not let her sleep that afternoon. How good her life had been here with Allegra and her women friends, until everything had begun collapsing on top of her. She closed her eyes and tried to distract herself, to pretend that everything was as it used to be. One of the new memories, of things that had never actually happened to her, came into her mind. It wasn't a dream. She was awake, her closed eyes yearning for the sleep that would not come. She even tried to dredge up as many accurate details as possible from the memory she had never remembered before, the memory that was not hers but came from the experience of someone else, and for some unknown reason had been deposited with her for safekeeping.

She was sitting on one of the low chairs in the corridor, one of the chairs she couldn't get out of by herself, and no one would help her. Everyone ignored her cries, as if they couldn't see her, as if they couldn't hear her, as if she wasn't there. Nobody took any notice of her, not even the people who walked past her, their legs brushing the hem of her gown. Hours passed, perhaps days. She wasn't hungry or thirsty, nor did she need to go to the bathroom. All she needed was to bathe. If only they would allow her to sit on the chair in the bathroom, to turn on the shower full strength and let the hard jet of water lash her body, wrap her in a boiling hot blanket, purify her flesh from the dross of the world. But they wouldn't listen to her.

The long corridor emptied and the lights went out. Only the permanent blue light next to the elevators in the lobby went on burning, made dim by the darkness of the corridor. After a long time two people appeared at the end of the corridor. When they approached her she recognized Raffy and Leon but their faces were blank and their eyes didn't look at her. They came up to her, and without saying a word lifted her gently from the chair, and holding her by the armpits carried her along the corridor. Her feet never touched the floor, her body felt weightless and all her pains were taken away. They reached the room at the end of corridor, the empty room with no patients in it. Here they stopped, Leon held her in both his strong arms and Raffy turned the key in the keyhole three times and opened the door. The room was dark and empty, there was nothing in it, neither furniture nor window. At the foot of the wall opposite the door crouched the silhouette of Allegra, and when she saw them she got up and stood naked, emaciated and frightened, pressing her back against the wall, as if she wanted to disappear into it, one hand spread on her chest and the other covering her nakedness. And in the faint light filtering in from the corridor, in the brief moment between the opening and the shutting of the door, Mrs. Moscowitz saw her narrow face crowned by her sparse, cropped hair, the gleam in her slanting eyes, which were dazzled and looked away to the dark end of the room, and her heart broke with longing and love.

In the afternoon Dr. Chen came into the room. He stood next to Mrs. Moscowitz's bed and smiled at her. This young doctor was her favorite of all the doctors and he always treated her patiently and politely. She was sitting on the edge of the bed, rubbing the stain on her beautiful dress with cotton wool soaked in alcohol, which one of the nurses had given her.

"How are you feeling, Yolanda?"

"I was suffering with the throat, now it's better," she said.

"Your walking's improved," said the doctor.

"The physiotherapy doesn't help," said Mrs. Moscowitz, "to the others they give different things and massages, to me just leg up, leg down. Just nothing."

"You have to walk a lot," said Dr. Chen, "that's the most important thing. You'll be going home soon, you know."

"Home?"

"Of course! You don't want to stay here forever."

"How can I?" asked Mrs. Moscowitz.

"What do you mean?" said the doctor in surprise.

"Even one meter I can't walk without the walker. The leg's not yet right."

"That isn't going to change, Yolanda," said the doctor, "I'm afraid it's going to stay like that permanently."

"But they said that after the operation . . . " she tried to dismiss the bad news, as if it were only a misunderstanding.

"Yes," said the doctor, "but the bones didn't set properly, and it's impossible to operate there again."

"Why? Let them operate on the leg again. As long as I can walk."

He put his hand on her shoulder to encourage her. "No, Yolanda, we can't do that. You're not so young any more and you're not strong enough for it."

She dropped the stained dress and the alcohol-soaked cotton wool and her head fell back on the pillow. "All my life I must walk with a walker?"

"Never mind, it's not the end of the world," said the doctor, "you'll learn to live with it."

"Is it possible to send home a woman sick with the legs to live alone on the fourth floor?"

"Do you want to stay here for the rest of your life?" asked Dr. Chen. "Would you like this place to be your home?"

"Here it's better," she said. "I'm all alone, there's nobody to help me."

"Then you should be in an institution. You're only here for rehabilitation, and there's nothing more we can do for you. We'll have to talk to the social worker."

He looked at her dismayed face, bent down to pat her on the shoulder, and added: "Never mind Yolanda, you're a strong, intelligent woman, I know I can rely on you," and then he walked out of the room.

Frieda wheeled herself up to Mrs. Moscowitz's bed, and looked at the heavy woman lying on it with her limbs outspread and her face full of anger.

"What's the matter?" she thundered at her reproachfully: "What have you got to cry about? I'll be in a wheelchair for the rest of my life."

"If I had to spend my life in a wheelchair I'd have killed myself long ago," said Mrs. Moscowitz.

"So why don't I kill myself?" asked Frieda. "Don't I deserve to walk? What makes you better than me?"

Clara came and stood next to Frieda and said: "Anyway you never go out of the house, so what difference does it make if you have to get about in the house with a walker or without one? Nobody sees you."

"Sometimes I used to go out," protested Mrs. Moscowitz.

"You get used to everything, Yolanda. That too. And worse. The main thing is to stay alive," said Clara.

―

Mrs. Moscowitz would not get out of bed, and when supper time came she pulled the sheet over her head and took no notice of the nurses' and her friends' pleas that she should get up and go to eat.

The head nurse came and stood at the head of her bed to give her a pep talk: "Yolanda, this is Satana talking! Aren't you afraid of

Satana? I'm going to kill you—ooooooh!" And she uttered a kind of wolf-howl that was truly terrifying, and dragged the sheet off Mrs. Moscowitz's head.

"Better leave her to stew in her own juice till she calms down," suggested Matilda Franco. "Anyway she'll get up soon enough. First thing off she'll go to the bathroom and stand there for an hour putting on powder and rouge and lipstick and fixing her hair, and then she'll forget everything."

"Thanks for the advice," said Satana and went out to the corridor, accompanied by a long, violent curse which Matilda Franco whispered after her in Ladino.

When Mrs. Moscowitz entered the dining room, she was about to join her friends, who had already received their trays, but Kagan called out to her at the top of his voice: "Yo-lan-da! Yo-lan-da!" stressing every syllable grotesquely, as he did when he was in excessively high spirits, and she was obliged to seat herself at his table.

The waitress, a sour-faced, bad-tempered, shriveled-up woman, Kagan complimented on her looks. Fichman, who was sitting next to him, he addressed as "my brother," Mrs. Moscowitz as "my Yo-lan- da," and Peretz Kabiri, who was sitting at their table and talking to himself, as "commander." He hardly touched his food.

There were candles on the tables in honor of the Sabbath, stuck to little saucers. Into the red plastic mugs from which they drank their tea a little sweet wine was poured for the patients who were allowed it. Mrs. Moscowitz raised her mug and said sadly: "Shabbat shalom." But Kagan did not respond in kind. A mischievous fire was burning in his eyes. He looked around, surveyed the entire dining room, leaned over to Fichman's wheelchair, thrust his hand under a rolled-up sheet in the narrow space between his friend's thigh and the side of his chair, pulled out a flat bottle of alcohol, opened it rapidly, and crouching under the tabletop took a long swig from the bottle.

Then he quickly closed it again and returned it to its place, wiped his mouth on his pajama sleeve, straightened his back, and said: "Lehayyim, my Yo-lan-da, shabbat shalom!"

Fichman smiled complacently, patted the sheet next to his thigh and rolled his eyes at her merrily.

"You want also?" asked Kagan.

"No, thank you," she replied coldly.

The waitress came up, looked at Kagan's plate and said: "Why aren't you eating? You haven't touched a thing."

"Darling," said Kagan, "slowly, slowly I eat. Not to worry, I promise."

The waitress bent down to his face and sniffed. "What have you been drinking?" she cried. "Who gave you wine? Where did you get it?"

"No," said Kagan, "only teeny drop from my Yo-lan-da I take, for taste."

"What are you doing? You musn't give him any," the waitress scolded Mrs. Moscowitz, "he's not allowed to drink wine. The doctors forbid it. What do you think, that I grudge him a bit of wine?"

The waitress went off angrily, and Fichman exclaimed: "Tfu, cholera!" Kagan gave Mrs. Moscowitz a guilty, shamefaced look, and put his hands together as if in prayer: "*Pardon,* Yo-lan-da, *pardon!* Such is life, nobody is angel!"

"Why aren't you allowed?" she asked.

He waved his hand dismissively. "They say with medicines they give me no alcohol permitted. And also from sugar I have, wound is not closing. I know my body better than them. Doctors they know nothing."

"But it's forbidden!" she said impatiently.

"Rubbish, my Yo-lan-da, what are you afraid of? Anyway what is life of man—wound which is never closing? So what?"

"If you bought it with the money I gave you," said Mrs. Moscowitz, pointing to the cache in Fichman's wheelchair, "then I'm sorry I gave it to you."

"Phoo!" said Kagan. "So vulgar about money to talk! And me artist! You don't know this, Madame Yo-lan-da?"

At that moment she knew that he would not return the fifty shekels she had lent him.

"The sergeant-major was like a madman. He couldn't believe it. What we got done in one day," said Peretz Kabiri, "in the evening, 'after-duty.' And you, Lance-Corporal Kabiri, you're in charge of the lot of them. Goddamn him. . . . "

Fichman had already polished off everything on his tray, and when Peretz Kabiri broke into the song *"Amado Mio"* he began taking off his pajama jacket. It no longer bothered her to see him naked. Fichman beat his fists on his chest in time to Peretz Kabiri's singing and Kagan looked at him and laughed loudly in great enjoyment.

"What's there to laugh here?" said Mrs. Moscowitz.

"He's nice man, I love him," said Kagan.

"What's there to love? Even to talk he doesn't know."

"To talk is not important, Madame. Important is to feel, important is heart."

One of the nurses came up to Fichman. "If you take off your pajama once more in the dining room, we won't let you in!" she said. "You hear? And you won't get any food, you'll go hungry!" She put his pajama jacket back on and he offered no resistance. "And you, stop making such a noise!" she said to Kabiri. "Sit quietly and eat."

Peretz Kabiri got up, put his crutches under his armpits and said: "And the girls from the ATS! They all came and applauded, and I sang: *Ama—do mio. . . . "* And he hopped to the doorway, turned to face the room, shouted: "Atten'shun!" and left.

"Yo-lan-da," mumbled Fichman, "Yo-lan-da."

"You see," said Kagan, "if he has something to say, he knows to talk. Say again: Yo-lan-da," he requested.

"Yo-lan-da," said Fichman, "Yo-lan-da."

Kagan laughed. His eyes met hers, which were cold, resentful, and denying. "So, you think I am drunk?" he asked.

"No," said Mrs. Moscowitz, "I happen to know what that is. You're not drunk, you want only to laugh at me."

"I love Fichman. He is my daemon. You know daemon?"

She was silent.

"He looks after me."

"He looks after your bottle," said Mrs. Moscowitz.

"No, no please," said Kagan, "that I have enough from my wife." He covered his ears with his hands. "That I don't want from you. *Pardon,* Yolanda, please!"

She hadn't even managed to tell him that they were going to send her home. Was he interested?

"Tfu, cholera," said Fichman.

She rose to her feet and fled the room, as if from some great danger. Once in the corridor, she breathed a deep sigh of relief. I haven't been on my own for fifty years—she thought—in order to involve myself with the trouble and insults of a sick, drunken egoist. She took a few steps and stopped. There was a sharp pain in her ankle. She bent over a little and leaned more on her walker to lessen the burden of her weight on her legs. She raised her head and surveyed the full length of the corridor. Suddenly it seemed to her that she was standing there for the first time in her life. She had never before been so sensible of the tragic, inhuman beauty of this place. A white fluorescent light shone on the corridor, its white floor gleamed like a mirror, one of its walls was distempered white while the wall opposite it was nothing but a curving glass partition overlooking a long, narrow, interior ornamental garden, roofed and lit up like an aquarium. Behind this was the glass wall of another wing, the men's wing, whose structure was exactly the same as that of the women's wing. And behind the glass wall of the men's wing was the white wall of a long corridor, exactly the same as the corridor of the women's wing, with the doors to the patients' rooms. And at the same time, the glass partition, like a mirror, reflected the white wall of the women's wing, the women sitting along it, the entrances to the patients' rooms, and the paintings and other decorations hanging on the wall, with the plaques in honor of donations made by the patients' families. The corridors of both wings met at one end in the dining room and at the other in the exit from the ward. Both were overlooked by the nurses' station, which was planted halfway down the garden running the length of the corridor, enclosed in its glass walls. It was here that her eyes now came to rest.

Next to the counter a few nurses were sitting, drinking black coffee in tall thick glasses and watching the Friday evening Arabic movie on television. Soon they would begin wheeling the feeble-minded patients into their rooms and carrying them in their arms like babies to their beds. Along the walls sat the patients. Paula, who never remembered where her room was, shuffled with her walker from room to room, looking for an empty bed to lie down on. She was often to be found occupying some other patient's bed, refusing to get up and threatening to tell her father. Only Leon knew how to coax her up: she would stretch out her skinny arms to him, and when his strong hands bore her to her bed, she would promise him that her father would reward him handsomely for his pains. Frieda and Clara had taken up their positions opposite the nurses' station, where Frieda was also keeping a number of seats empty for her family, who would soon arrive to visit her, as they did every day, and refusing to let any of the other patients sit on them. Soon one of the nurses would pass down the row handing out the nightly medications, and giving anyone who wanted it a last cup of tea before they went to bed. When Leon was on duty he would sit with the nurses, teasing them and making them laugh. Even the screams that occasionally rose from the rooms, screams of pain and terror, urgent cries for help, merged into the measured movement of time passing down the long corridor like quiet waves lapping ceaselessly against the shore. Mrs. Moscowitz had never known a truer and more terrible place.

She sat down next to Clara. Frieda's baritone, one of the familiar sounds of the ward, droned on and on: "Why don't they come? They know I'm waiting. And they promised to bring my granddaughter Leora, she hasn't been to see me for ages. When will they let me go home already, to be with my family instead of always waiting for them here. Some people don't know how to appreciate being at home instead of in hospital."

This time, in fact, Frieda's family turned up in force, and there was no room for all of them to sit next to her. They therefore wheeled her to the visitors' lounge, and Clara, who remained sitting next to Mrs. Moscowitz, laughed silently: "Did you see how they ran to her? Mummy! Granny! All over her with their hugging and kissing and sucking-up. But taking her home is something else. She should have been at home long ago. There's no reason for her to be here. But they don't want to take her. Everything they've got they got from her and her husband. And there's still a tidy inheritance waiting for them. But they're prepared to pay any price as long as she stays here and they don't have to take her home to stay with them."

On her way to bed, Mrs. Moscowitz went into the bathroom. In the mirror she saw the strange woman who had begun to invade her thoughts and memories, on her face a close network of fine deep wrinkles, spun out like innumerable spiders' webs. The face of the woman in the mirror was very strange. It was swollen and trembling with effort, as if the woman wanted to say something to her but was unable to do so. She recoiled from the sight and fled from the bathroom. The pain in her ankle came back, hurting her even more than it had outside the dining room. Again she was obliged to stop for a minute, leaning on her walker, trying to relieve the oppressive weight on her legs. Usually, the pains were worse in the morning, and less acute in the evening. They never stopped altogether. But this was a new pain. When she undressed she couldn't hold back a few groans. It was only when she lay down that the new pain went away, and only the old pains remained. Sometimes, just as sleep was overcoming her, she felt as if she were suspended between heaven and earth, floating to and fro without finding a bit of ground on which to plant her ailing feet. The feeling of heaviness was taken from her, and she floated in the air like a weightless object. Yet this brought her no sense of deliverance, but filled her with the dread of death and oblivion, because at that strange moment, when the pains in her legs completely disappeared, she did not know if she was still herself, so inseparable had she become from her pain in her own mind.

chapter four

In the morning, when the three friends left the dining room, Fichman came toward them, energetically turning the wheels of his chair, and Clara said to Mrs. Moscowitz: "Your boyfriend wants you." And indeed, Fichman beckoned her vigorously to follow him. She walked more slowly than usual due to the pain in her ankle, and he rode ahead of her. During the short distance between the dining room and the room in the men's wing he turned back several times to make sure that she was behind him. His face was grave and concerned, and it was almost possible to see a spark of intelligence in it. Even if she hadn't wanted to go with him, she wouldn't have dared to refuse: even at those moments when he looked like a chastised child, she couldn't rid herself of the sensation of hidden danger that he always aroused in her. His legs had been amputated, but he maneuvered his wheelchair with great agility and his hands were extremely strong. When they reached the door of the room, Fichman signaled her to stay where she was and he entered the room. It was Saturday morning and there were already visitors sitting in the room. She heard the voices of women and children. Fichman returned to the doorway and beckoned her to come inside.

Although she had never been in the room before, she knew immediately where to look for Kagan's bed. Her eyes fell on the head of the bed, on his face sunk into the pillow, paler than usual.

She approached the bed. There was a tube stuck in his forearm. One of the visitors gave her his chair, she thanked him with a sad smile for his courtesy, and Fichman pushed the chair close to the bed.

She sat down and Kagan slowly turned his face toward her in the hollow of the pillow and smiled at her with half-closed eyes.

"Yolanda," said Kagan softly, as if he were surprised to see her.

"What happened?"

"In night it was hard. Better to die," whispered Kagan. He barely moved his lips.

"And now?"

"Better. Only fever. Fever will pass. Pain not."

His white hair was disheveled and damp and his gray cheeks had sprouted a white stubble. On his face there was again the expression of incomprehension and resentment, just as when she had first encountered him in the corridor of the women's wing and their eyes had fleetingly met.

Beside the next bed sat the family of one of the patients. They had brought their small children with them and the children wandered about between the beds, approached the people lying in them and stared at their faces and their maimed limbs. When they came and stood next to Mrs. Moscowitz, leaning on the edge of Kagan's bed, he smiled at them, he even snapped his fingers to amuse them. But Fichman glared at them and chased them away with a flick of his hand as if he were chasing a bothersome fly. One of the adults who noticed this hurried to collect the children and seat them in their places, next to their grandfather's bed.

Kagan said again: "Yolanda."

She said to him in a whisper: "People have no sense. Why do they bring children here, to see us? It's not good for them. Only night-mares will come from it."

"How are you?" asked Kagan.

"The doctor said that soon they'll send me home," said Mrs. Moscowitz.

"When I feel better, I make from you beautiful picture," said Kagan.

"And I can never walk again, always only with the walker," she said.

"You must look after me that I don't do something silly," said Kagan, "otherwise they take off leg."

He held out his hand to her and left it suspended in the air until she understood and put her hand in his. His hand was as cold as the hand of a dead man. The chill passed into her body and spread through it rapidly. For the first time she saw at close quarters the distorted fingers, which tightened their grip on her hand, and the dark, crooked nails. Like worms his fingers crawled over her hand. Fichman, who was sitting next to her, suddenly whimpered: "Yolanda, Yolanda ... "

"He thinks I die now," said Kagan with a contemptuous snort.

"Who knows when I'll go home," said Mrs. Moscowitz, "perhaps already next week. The doctor didn't say."

Kagan's eyes half closed and his yellowish lashes fluttered, as if he was about to fall asleep. His hand dropped to the bed and Mrs. Moscowitz took her hand back. Fichman waved his hand at her to chase her away, as he had done with the children. She tried to rise from the chair but she couldn't. Fichman thumped her on the thigh with the back of his hand, to hurry her up. His impatience infected her, and she turned to the visitors: "Excuse me, perhaps someone can please to help."

The children's father came up to her, she held out her hands to him and he pulled hard until she was standing on her feet and supporting herself on the walker. She thanked the young man and he turned back to his family. As he walked away from her she saw him put his hands in his pockets and rub them hard against the lining.

Toward midday Mrs. Moscowitz went up to the nurse on duty at the station and asked her if she would let her use the telephone on the counter.

"Whatever next?" said the nurse. "Don't you know it's not allowed to phone from here? That's what you've got the public phones for."

"I can't walk so far. I haven't got the strength. And there are the bad pains, hardly I can stand."

"Because you don't walk enough," said the nurse. "You sit in the same place all the time without moving. And then you have to be lifted up from the chair. If you walked more you'd have more strength. And in physiotherapy you don't do what you're told either, you can't do anything, can you? So naturally you can't walk."

"They're sending me home. I must to phone my neighbor which has the key, to bring a cleaning woman to clean the apartment. So I can come home. Since nine months already the apartment is closed."

"I'm very sorry," said the nurse. "You can't phone from here. It's not allowed."

"That's not true," said Mrs. Moscowitz. "Many times my friends phone from here, it's only me you don't allow."

"You're allowed to take calls from here, but not to make outside calls," explained the nurse. "They're two different things."

"I can pay," suggested Mrs. Moscowitz.

"I'm telling you that I'm not allowed to do it, and you won't listen. Leave me alone, Yolanda. Ask Rosa. Let her give you permission to phone from here if she likes."

"I haven't got any more tokens left."

"You can buy some at the canteen tomorrow."

As on every Saturday morning, the rooms and corridor were crowded with visitors. Once she had liked these times, she had put on her best dresses, made up her face and fixed her hair, and walked up and down among the strangers so that they would see that she wasn't like the other patients, that she hadn't lost her dignity, that she belonged to their world and not this world of the dead, and that when she was cured she would go home and forget all about it, just like them when the visit was over. But now she no longer cared what the visitors thought of her, nor was she sure that any of them took any notice of her. And if one of them should touch her, he would wipe his hands in his trouser pockets, he couldn't wait to wash them with soap before they touched his wife and children. Now, as the time to go home approached, she felt more and more that this place was her real home.

Allegra had been told several times that she would have to leave the hospital, and then they had postponed sending her for a few months. Mrs. Moscowitz didn't know why they had kept on putting off the evil day. If only she knew, perhaps the knowledge might help her own case. Once she had played with the idea that when she recovered and went home, she would take Allegra to live with her. They would help each other and be like sisters to each other, sharing everything and reaping mutual benefits from the arrangement. And when the time came for Allegra to die, she would be by her side, hold her hand and say to her: Don't be afraid, don't be afraid. When she had told her friend about her plan, Allegra had smiled skeptically and said in her hoarse, tired voice: "My home will already be up there," and raised her eyes to the ceiling.

Mrs. Moscowitz also confided her plan to Clara. Later Allegra told her that Clara had warned her not to agree to Yolanda's proposal, because all she wanted was to make Allegra into a servant, and when she could no longer exploit her, she would turn her out into the street. In Clara's world there was no place for good faith or pure intentions.

On Sunday morning a thin woman dressed in black came and stood at the door of their room, next to Satana, and the head nurse pointed out Mrs. Moscowitz to her and disappeared into the corridor. The woman in black immediately approached Mrs. Moscowitz's bed. "Madame Rolanda?" she said and held out her hand. "Tanya Kagan, wife to Lazar. Glad to meet you. It's possible to speak a minute?"

Mrs. Moscowitz shook her hand. She felt the smooth, cool slender fingers gripping her hand tightly, as if to sqeeze out the last drop of warmth and vitality she possessed. After the visitor dropped her hand, Mrs. Moscowitz tried unsuccessfully to rise from the edge of her bed.

"Please to call someone to help me get up," explained Mrs. Moscowitz, "I am sick with the legs."

"I help," said Mrs. Kagan. She gripped her by the elbows and with great strength, almost lifting her in the air, hoisted her to her feet. The two women went out to the corridor and sat down. There was a moment of silence. Mrs. Moscowitz lowered her eyes. She sensed the woman scrutinizing her face and hair, the plain dressing-gown on her body. It was easy to guess what she was saying to herself. She could still feel the woman's astonishing strength in her elbows.

"Lazar told me about you," said the woman. "So good things, I am jealous. But really I am glad for him, you know. It's good there is someone normal here, to speak. He says only you two normal people here. And such I see too. This man Fichman which always follows him, definitely not normal, of course. And also others as well, I think. So, who can he have?"

"How does he feel?" asked Mrs. Moscowitz.

"Better," said the woman, "but not good." And she emphasized her words with a long silence and a penetrating stare.

104

Mrs. Moscowitz dared to look her straight in the face. A narrow face with two deep lines, like two dry creeks on a steep slope, running from the sides of the nose to the corners of the lips. Her eyes were small and brown, and her thick hair was braided in a heavy bun on her neck and drawn back severely at the sides, brown hair scattered with many silver threads, which from a distance made it look lighter than it really was.

"First thing," said the woman, "to return money you give for Lazar. How much?"

"Fifty shekels," said Mrs. Moscowitz, "but it's not important."

"Not important?" the woman said in a menacing tone, opened her purse and handed her a fifty-shekel note.

Mrs. Moscowitz made vague protesting noises for the sake of good manners, something between ignorance of the entire affair and a lofty superiority to anything as petty as money. But the woman would not be satisfied until she had taken the money from her hand.

"I must say to you, Madame Rolanda, that alcohol is forbidden for him. You know of this?"

"He told me."

"So why you gave money?"

"I didn't know what the money is for. He told me he needs it, and I gave it."

"It's forbidden to give him money! If he has money, he buys to drink. And bottle, why did you bring him, if you know this is forbidden for him?"

Mrs. Moscowitz was silent in her astonishment.

"Why, Madame Rolanda, why?"

"I never brought any bottle," said Mrs. Moscowitz.

"So who brought?"

"He told you that?—that I brought for him a bottle?"

"It's not true?" The woman tensed and fixed her small, interrogating eyes on Mrs. Moscowitz. "You didn't buy for him?"

Mrs. Moscowitz was silent.

"Tell me quick, I am in hurry," said the woman.

A feeling of power and pride filled Mrs. Moscowitz's heart. They were woman to woman now and the healthy one had no advantage over the sick one. She had become Kagan's accomplice and confidante, aiding and abetting him in his forbidden deed. Perhaps she had really done what the woman was accusing her of, perhaps she was really some kind of femme fatale.

"If you didn't bring bottle—who brought it?" asked the woman.

Mrs. Moscowitz looked into her face and smiled.

"You don't care they take off leg? If he drinks, gangrene finishes his leg." And she stared into Mrs. Moscowitz's eyes, to see the effect of her words on her. "If some other person brought, why you don't tell?"

"I don't speak to KGB," said Mrs. Moscowitz quietly.

The woman rose furiously from her seat and marched over to Satana at the nurses' station. She told her what had been said and Satana said loudly enough for Mrs. Moscowitz to hear:

"In any case we'll be rid of her soon and there'll be some peace and quiet here. The sooner the better for everyone. She's more trouble than she's worth . . . "

In the afternoon Seniora's two sons came to the hospital. Crushed and silent they sat next to Matilda Franco's bed. She had been closer to their mother than any of the other patients and she was the only one with whom they had exchanged a word when they came to visit. Now Matilda Franco tried to cheer them up, to draw them out—in Hebrew, Ladino, Turkish, but in vain.

Two big men, bowed under the weight of their grief, they had just risen from their mourning and they were inconsolable. They had large black skullcaps on their heads and their faces were unshaven as a sign of their bereavement—a coarse, dense stubble, black as pitch, covered their cheeks and only their eyes, demented with sorrow and despair, were blacker. The older, Albert, held a little suitcase on his knees, clasped it to his chest with both hands and wouldn't open his mouth. The younger, Victor, who was apparently more sociable than his brother, muttered something and sighed, and Albert grunted: "Shut up."

And once more they fell silent, looking at Matilda Franco with heartbroken, expectant looks. From the little she managed to get out of them it transpired that they had come to thank the doctors and nurses who had taken care of their mother and the roommates who had been with her in her last hours, but they didn't know how to do it, or where to find the doctors. So they clung to Matilda Franco and sat by her bedside as if rooted to the spot. Albert said nothing, but kept nodding his head. From time to time Victor, who found it harder to conquer his grief, took a handkerchief out of his pocket and blew his nose loudly, and his brother gave him an angry, rebuking look.

"It was like this," said Matilda Franco, "in the morning May-she-rest-in-peace went to wash. After a bit she didn't come out. And then she"—she pointed to Mrs. Moscowitz—"saw her there. Lying on the floor, next to the shower. Then she got a big fright, she came out and began to yell. Then Raffy ran right in and picked her up. She was already gone . . . "

While Matilda Franco was speaking the two men did not take their eyes off her, they sat there as if hypnotized. When she stopped, an expression of anguished, disappointed expectation returned to their faces. They sat and looked at her, waiting for her to continue. But there was no continuation, because the story was over.

"May-she-rest-in-peace was so good," added Matilda Franco in the attempt to do what little she could to appease their hunger, "always ready to help, a kind word for everyone. Everybody loved her. She helped me like my own mother. Seeing as I can't get out of bed because of the nails they put in me here"—she pointed to her hip—"she was always coming up to ask me if I wanted anything. She brought me everything I wanted. At night she slept hardly two hours, not a minute more. Early in the morning, when it's still dark, when everybody's sleeping, she's already awake—first thing she takes hold of the crochet hook and begins to work. Without any light, without seeing a thing. Just by the feeling in her fingers. What a saintly woman, May-she-rest-in-peace, a real saint."

They sat on, their eyes fixed questioningly on hers, waiting for more.

"And how much she loved you," said Matilda Franco, "too much. And she was only sorry for one thing all the time."

The two brothers shook their heads sadly, in impotent agreement.

"But it's not too late," she said and looked at them intently, to see if they understood her meaning. "And now go to her," she pointed to Mrs. Moscowitz's bed, "she saw her there at the last. She'll tell you."

Obediently they rose as one man, taking their chairs with them, and went to sit next to Mrs. Moscowitz's bed. Albert stood the suitcase on his knees again and clasped it in his arms, while his brother blew his nose in preparation for what he was about to hear. "Stop that, woman," growled Albert.

Mrs. Moscowitz saw their faces blackened by their beards, their thick brows and their eyes smoldering with the fire of their dark suffering, and took fright. Two big men, who looked to her like hired assasins, were sitting next to her bed and waiting for her to speak.

She didn't know what to say to them. Matilda Franco had already told them how she had found their mother lying dead in the bathroom, how she had screamed in horror. What more could she find to say? And if she did find something, perhaps they wouldn't like it, and who knows how they would react. There was something violent, something savage in the silent sorrow of their grief, as if they had made up their minds to revenge themselves on whoever had robbed them of their mother, whether man or god. In the end she found a way of appeasing them. She opened the drawer of the locker next to her bed, took out a crumpled, transparent plastic bag and drew forth the crocheted doily which Seniora had given her, spread it out before them and said: "This she gave me for a present. It's called crochet work. How beautiful it is! Everything she made, she made the most beautiful. All my life I'll keep it with love in my heart."

For a moment the two brothers sat still, astonished or stunned with grief, their eyes fixed on the cloth. Then Albert laid the suitcase flat on his knees, took a bunch of keys out of his pocket, selected the smallest key and opened the lock. It was crammed full of crocheted tablecloths, napkins and doilies, dozens of them, perhaps hundreds, neatly packed, folded one on top of the other. Mrs. Moscowitz gazed at the open suitcase and couldn't open her mouth, so unexpected was the sight. A long moment of silence fell on the three people, surrounding and enclosing them, as if they had been granted a glimpse of a secret not meant for human eyes. Albert bowed his head, raised the open suitcase to his chest, bent over and buried his face in the cloths. His shoulders shook. Victor blew his nose, sighed heavily, and this time his elder brother did not chastise him. Tears gathered in Mrs. Moscowitz's eyes.

"That's enough!" cried Matilda Franco from her bed. "What's the matter with you boys? Stop crying over your mother. You'd be better off doing what she was waiting for all the time. Go and get married and have children. And if there's a girl, you can call her Seniora for a memory of your mother."

The intimacy and fellowship of the tears gave Mrs. Moscowitz courage. "That's true," she said to them, "to be alone in life is no good. I myself remained alone, I know what it means."

Victor explained: "He already got married and divorced from his wife. It's only me who remained a bachelor."

Albert's voice choked inside the suitcase: "You shut your trap."

"If you want to give her soul a little joy, may she rest in peace, go and get married already and bring her grandchildren," said Matilda Franco. "Nothing will come of your crying, not children for sure."

Albert raised his head. His eyes were red, his cheeks wet. He looked in horror at the delicate crochet work, afraid that he had stained it forever with his tears. Then he shook his head and spread out his hands as if to express his helplessness. "I dunno what I'm going to do with all this," he said hoarsely.

"Sell it to the tourist shops," suggested Mrs. Moscowitz. "It's hand-made, you can get a lot of money for it."

Albert shook his head from side to side and Victor explained: "In the synagogue they told us to give it to poor people, or to the hospital, or for the soldiers in the army."

"Enough, enough!!" cried Matilda Franco. "Stop with those tablecloths already. Do something for her soul, May-she-rest-in-peace. Look how much she loved you and all the time she was eating her heart out that you don't get married. With the Ashkenazim," she turned to Mrs. Moscowitz, "they don't care if someone doesn't get married, they're even proud of it. But with us Sephardim, who's ever heard of a person not getting married?"

"After our mother," said Victor tearfully, "there isn't a woman in the whole world to suit a man as good as her."

"Shut up already, I'll kill you!" shouted Albert in a terrible voice that reverberated in the room and the corridor.

"Did you hear that?" cried Matilda Franco to Mrs. Moscowitz. "The oldest's forty-five and the other one's forty-two. And that's the way they talk!"

"It's the grief," explained Albert, "he doesn't know what he's saying." And he took the little lock out of his pocket, slipped it between the two rings and pressed it shut. Then he rose to his feet, and his brother followed suit.

"Missus," said Victor to Mrs. Moscowitz, "God give you health and strength for what you did for our mother."

And they each took their chair and resumed their places next to Matilda Franco, silent and waiting.

"Go home!" said Matilda Franco, "You're wasting your time."

"We'll come again," said Albert.

"No! Don't come! What do you want to hang round a hospital where there's only sick old people and invalids for? At least when May-she-rest-in-peace was alive you had a reason to come here every day, but now? It's not healthy for young people."

"We'll come to you, seeing as you was our mother's friend," said Victor.

"It's no good for you, believe me. But if you want to do a person a favor, then you can go and give regards to my daughter Rina."

She studied both of them and her eyes rested on Victor, the younger brother, whose face was more delicate, whose temper was better and whose heart was more open. "If you want," she said to him, "you can take her regards from me. Tell her to come on Monday, tell her I need her. I'll give you the address. Write!"

"Is there a phone?"

"No, don't phone! The phone's broken. You go talk to her yourself. See her for yourself. What's the matter with you, are you afraid or what?"

"If I tell him, he'll go," said Albert, "for the Mother's sake he'll do whatever you want."

A nurse came into the room to help one of the patients and asked the brothers to go outside for a while. Matilda Franco said to Victor: "Write quick, have you got something to write the address?"

"I don't need to write," said Victor, "I'll remember it by heart."

"If you don't write it down, you won't go," said Matilda Franco. "You wait outside now and come back when she's finished. You hear what I say? Wait and come back later!"

They left the room, and stood in the corridor looking up and down. Perhaps one of the doctors would appear at last, perhaps someone would tell them something they had not yet been told about their mother. Raffy passed down the corridor, holding a bundle of feces-soiled bedclothes, which he had just come from changing, under his arm. They turned to him and asked him where they could find the doctor. He replied with a question: "What's the problem?" From his reply they concluded that one of the doctors was finally before them. The young man with the childish body and the heavy face, an evasive look in his little eyes, stood uneasily next to them, holding the stinking bundle behind his back. But they were not offended by the smell. They explained that they wished to consult him as to how best they could express their gratitude to the hospital for the devoted care given to their mother. When they mentioned her name, Raffy told them that he was the one who had picked her up from the bathroom floor and carried her out in his arms. They trembled, caught him by his unoccupied hand, and begged him to sit down with them for a minute and tell them about it in as much detail as possible. Raffy, embarrassed and apologetic, mumbled that he had something urgent to do—and anyway, he had just told them everything there was to tell. But they hung onto his hand and implored him to tell them everything he remembered without holding anything back.

"Doctor, if you're busy now, just tell us when to come," begged Victor, "you tell us what to do."

And Albert added: "May the Lord bless you."

Fear fell on Raffy. His heart told him that he was heading for trouble, that his civility was spreading a trap at his feet. He looked around anxiously, scanning the corridor for someone to rescue him, but there was not a doctor or nurse in sight to come to his aid.

"In two, three weeks' time," he said, "come in three weeks' time and talk to the doctors."

"Thank you very much, doctor," said Albert, "may the Lord bless you."

They let go of his hand and he tucked his bundle back under his arm, said goodbye to them, and hurried off. Next to the nurses' station, before turning into the corridor of the men's wing, he glanced back and saw them. The younger brother, apparently insisting on trying his luck again, had turned back in the hope of finding someone who would satisfy their need on the spot, while the elder, holding the suitcase, was dragging his brother along the corridor by force to the exit from the ward, where they both finally disappeared into the darkness.

⟜

The next morning Kagan sat alone at his table in the dining room, wearing a burgundy-colored terry cloth robe. Clara said to her: "He's waiting for you. Aren't you going to go and sit next to him?" Mrs. Moscowitz hesitated for a moment, and Frieda growled: "What do you think, we'll be insulted if you go to him? Go ahead, enjoy yourself. It's only a pity his friend isn't here too."

She went up to him and sat down at his table. The dark burgundy of his new bathrobe emphasized the pallor of his shaven face.

"How are you, Lazar?" for the first time she called him by his first name. "How do you feel yourself?"

"Better," he replied, "it interests you?"

"Of course it interests me."

"After Saturday you didn't come to see me again."

"Once I came and from the distance I saw your wife in the room."

"Why didn't you come in? She wants to meet you. You should meet her, she's good woman."

"I already met her. On Sunday she came to shout at me that I'm giving you money and bringing you bottles, that you'll get gangrene and they'll cut off your leg."

He covered his eyes with his hands. His distorted fingers with their brown, crooked nails crawled over his face, over his eyes, his forehead, groping their way with their dark, blind tips.

"It doesn't matter," said Mrs. Moscowitz, "I can take it. But why did you tell her that I was bringing a bottle for you?"

"No, Yolanda, you don't understand!" He removed his hands from his eyes. "I tell her that I took from you fifty shekels. This is all. For her to give you back."

"Yes, she threw the money in my face." Mrs. Moscowitz studied his reaction. "And that—she brought it for you?" she asked and indicated the bathrobe.

"Yes. Is it beautiful?"

"Each to his taste," said Mrs. Moscowitz.

"What do I need it for, I don't know," said Kagan. "She says it's not nice all the time with pajama. In place like this, what's nice, what not nice, I don't know."

"You're hot, you're sweating," said Mrs. Moscowitz.

He took off the bathrobe and laid it on his knees.

"Don't drink, Lazar, please don't drink any more," said Mrs. Moscowitz.

"I know. When I drink I talk not nice," he said.

"No, not for me, for you," said Mrs. Moscowitz. "Soon I won't be here. They're sending me home."

He was stunned: "Sending home? When?"

"I already told you a few times and you didn't even hear."

He was quiet, reflecting.

"Where's Fichman?" she asked.

"He has some or other test."

"Is it him who brings you to drink?"

"How can he? He has legs?"

"Who brings it? Someone of the staff? Leon?"

"Why it matters?"

"For money Leon will do anything."

"Yolanda," said Kagan, "my Yolanda is leaving. How much time we have left?"

"I don't know. The doctor said soon. It can be days, it can be another week, two weeks."

"I must draw new picture from you quick," said Kagan, "so something remains."

"What's to draw?" asked Mrs. Moscowitz.

"Yolanda, what happened?"

"What you're seeing from me, it isn't really me."

"Why?"

"Everything goes wrong," she said. "There's no chance any more, like you said."

"Maybe you have depression," said Kagan and his eyes met hers in a sympathy and understanding she had not found in him up to now. "Yolanda, tell me if I can help you with something . . . "

"Lately, when I look in the mirror, I see that woman with those hairs that are falling on each other, and that face, with the wrinkles. Like you made her in that picture. You know her. Not me. And she isn't me. She's not normal. And little by little she's sending her thoughts into my head, what she remembers that once happened to her. And it's nothing to do from my life. It isn't Moscowitz Yolanda, believe me! It's something else. I'm so ashamed: such a not normal person! And I always like for a person to be the same like everybody else. No more and no less. At first I thought that she'll go away, but now I know that she'll never go away no more. There's no chance, like you said. Everything goes the same direction, and you can't move from it, until the end."

"This is depression, definite. You must ask for them to bring psychologist to helping you," suggested Kagan.

"And when I'm tired, and my leg it's hurting me, I don't know what belongs to me and what belongs to her. You think it's something psychological. No, no. This is something else. You don't believe these things, but I know how it began."

"Evil eye," said Kagan.

"Yes. You can laugh."

He laid his hand on hers. His fingers writhed on her clenched hand, which opened at his touch. Suddenly he laughed: "Yolanda, we make here our own Mayerling. You believe me?"

She was silent.

"You know Mayerling?"

"Of course, why not?"

"Why aren't you eating?" She heard the waitress's always irate voice behind them. "What are you waiting for? When are you going to finish? What's gotten into you today?"

"Take it away," said Mrs. Moscowitz. "Do me a favor. I can't look at it."

"Is that so? Does it disgust you?" asked the waitress. "What's so disgusting about this food? Nobody else complains about our food."

"Every day the same thing," said Mrs. Moscowitz.

"The same thing?" said the waitress. "Is that so? You want surprises? What, for example? What menu would her ladyship like to order?"

After the waitress left, Mrs. Moscowitz said: "They don't speak like that to anybody, only me. So much they hate me."

Kagan said: "After doctors' visit I come to take you to studio and draw you beautiful portrait."

She remained in her dressing gown and didn't go to the bathroom to make up her face. Her hair hadn't been dyed for a long time and the gray coming up at the roots was spreading. The gray areas seemed to her like places where the sick scalp had been exposed. When

Kagan came to take her to the room he called his studio, he was wearing the new bathrobe again. Fichman followed him, like a dog at the heels of its master, and she couldn't bear it.

"Will Fichman be there also?"

"Why not?" asked Kagan, "He won't be a nuisance."

"I don't want him," said Mrs. Moscowitz.

Kagan was momentarily at a loss, he looked first at her and then at Fichman, and in the end he said to him: "You go away now. Go to other place."

"Yolanda . . . " mumbled Fichman.

"Go away!" said Mrs. Moscowitz.

They moved off in the direction of the little room next to the physiotherapy room and Fichman stayed where he was, looking after them with a frozen expression on his face.

Kagan took the key out of his pajama pocket and opened the door, and they went inside. There was no sign of Raffy's belongings, of his presence or anyone else's. Kagan locked the door behind them. She sat down on the chair next to the bare table. Kagan looked at her for a moment and wheeled his chair into the corner where the angle seemed best to him.

"Sit so, that's right," he said.

He put the pad on his knees, turned the full pages under the cover and stroked the blank page with the same sensual caress that she remembered from before. And again she heard his rhythmic breathing, light as the breath of a sleeper, and the scratching of the pen on the paper. His eyes were concentrated on the page in front of him with only an occasional quick glance in her direction, as if to make sure that she was still there. She no longer felt the touch of his fingers on her face. From minute to minute he became more of a stranger to her, like the strange room in which they were sitting, like the strange light coming in through the window, like the beads of sweat breaking out on her upper lip, without her being able to raise her hand to wipe them away, like the strange body whose weight would one day defeat her. Just as she was a stranger to herself, just as the dead were strangers to each other.

Kagan turned under the page on which he had drawn, smoothed the new page, and glanced quickly at her. Her face must have fallen, for he smiled encouragingly and asked: "Tired?" And before she could answer: "No, no," he fixed his eyes on the page, his face took on the concentrated expression, and again the nib scratched the paper.

It had been a Wednesday, that day in December, a mild, cloudy winter day. Before leaving her apartment she had hesitated whether to close the door of the little kitchen balcony or to leave it open. After she had already locked the front door behind her, she decided to go back inside and close the balcony door, in case it rained. She went into the kitchen, and as she took hold of the handle to close the door she saw Mrs. Poldy standing at her window, in the next building, looking at her and laughing. Mrs. Poldy was wearing one of the dresses she made for herself out of bright pieces of cloth, a dress with a low neck and puffed sleeves, decorated with ribbons and bows, her long hair was dyed pitch black, hanging loose on her shoulders, and round her neck she wore chains and beads of every kind. Black paint was liberally smeared on her eyebrows and round her eyes, and there was a big black beauty spot decorating one of her cheeks. For some months Mrs. Poldy had not appeared at her window opposite Mrs. Moscowitz's kitchen balcony or telephoned her to tell her her troubles. She must have just returned from the hospital at Bat-Yam. Her face had never looked so terrible as when she laughed that morning, with her pouched lips painted blazing red. Mrs. Moscowitz pretended not to see her, closed the balcony door, went into the bedroom to fetch something, and just as she was heading for the front door, the telephone rang. She knew that it was Mrs. Poldy, and she went outside and locked the door. While she was standing on the landing the telephone went on ringing in her apartment.

She began descending the stairs, and the pains in her legs increased with every step. Her breath came heavily, interrupted by loud groans, which burst out of her and echoed in the stairwell. After every three or four stairs she stopped to rest and as always she asked herself why she did it, and as always she knew that there was no way back, since she had made an appointment at the hairdresser's and the taxi she had ordered would be arriving at any minute to wait for her opposite the building's entrance. On the third floor landing Mrs. Adler's door opened. Mrs. Adler often helped her, and Mrs. Moscowitz always left a key to her apartment with her, in case of need. Mrs. Adler heard her groans and brought a chair out for her. Mrs. Moscowitz sank into the chair, drank a little water from the glass offered her by her neighbor, sighed and pointed to her legs, the source of all her suffering, and said: "Like a thousand knives." The door of the next apartment on the landing opened and the hated Mrs. Horn appeared, a woolen scarf tied round her head to protect her ears from the cold. "What lovely hair you've got, Mrs. Moscowitz!" said Mrs. Horn. "What do you need all this for? If I had beautiful hair like yours I wouldn't go to the hairdresser at all."

"I asked you?" said Mrs. Moscowitz. "Why talk nonsense?"

Mrs. Horn laughed a brief, snorting laugh, to show that she wasn't insulted, smiled conspiratorially at Mrs. Adler and made a dismissive gesture with her hand. And she went on standing in her doorway, looking at Mrs. Moscowitz and nodding her head at her. Mrs. Moscowitz had hated her from the day she came to live in the building, though she couldn't find any logical reason for her hatred. Mrs. Horn always greeted her warmly, and she had often offered to help her with all kinds of things, but Mrs. Moscowitz had always recoiled from her and rejected her overtures with anger and suspicion. Now she could no longer bear Mrs. Horn's look and her nodding head in its woolen scarf, and she gripped her handbag and the plastic bag holding the various hair treatments, rose from the chair, thanked Mrs. Adler and moved toward the stairs. After she had gone down a few steps and the pain had begun to tear the groans from her throat again, she heard the taxi, which always came too early, hooting, and she hoped that someone would go and calm the driver down and ask him to wait a little longer. She looked back and saw that Mrs. Adler had gone inside and shut the door behind her, but that Mrs. Horn was still standing and watching her descend the stairs. And as she looked behind her, Mrs. Moscowitz's hand suddenly slipped from the railing on which she was leaning and she lost her balance. The second between the loss of balance and the fall and tumble downstairs was still vivid in her memory: an invisible hand had seized hold of her, lifted her and thrown her down with great force.

Someone outside in the corridor turned the handle of the door, and when it failed to open, knocked. Kagan raised his eyes from the drawing pad and gave her a questioning look. The knock was repeated. He wheeled himself to the door, unlocked it, and opened it. Fichman appeared in the doorway, smiling at them like a naughty child.

Kagan scolded him: "I told you to go, why do you come to be nuisance?"

Fichman tried to push his wheelchair into the room. Kagan's eyes implored Mrs. Moscowitz. "Maybe he comes in, poor man, he doesn't like to stay outside," he said.

"No," said Mrs. Moscowitz, "I can't. Believe me: I can't."

Kagan said to him: "Go away," and pushed his chair outside.

Fichman resisted but apparently without exerting all his strength, for Kagan succeeded in pushing him out of the room, after which he closed the door and locked it.

Kagan returned his chair to its previous place, and immediately started drawing again. It seemed to Mrs. Moscowitz that it was taking longer than the last time. She took a tissue out of her pocket and wiped the sweat off her face. Kagan broke the silence and said: "Today it will be beautiful for you. You won't cry for it again."

A muffled, rhythmic thudding began on the door, which grew into loud blows, accompanied by groans and sobs. Kagan cried: "What does he want of my life?" wheeled himself to the door and opened it. Fichman was in the act of aiming his head at the door, ready to butt it again, his forehead was bleeding and tears streamed from his eyes. When he saw them, he lowered his head and moaned. His chest quivered under the half-open pajama top.

"Why you don't go?" Kagan asked him and examined his face with concern, "What's wrong with you today?"

Fichman stayed where he was. "Impossible to work like this!" said Kagan and angrily shut the pad on his knees. Then he looked around as if searching for something, and wheeled himself up to Mrs. Moscowitz. Fichman pushed his chair into the room. "You want to see?" asked Kagan. "Soon it is finished."

"No, no need," said Mrs. Moscowitz, "perhaps another time."

"Why?" he asked in surprise. "Today it comes out good. I made it beautiful for you."

"It isn't me."

"How do you know if you don't see?"

"What you see from me isn't me."

"And what is you?" asked Kagan impatiently.

"I don't know any more," said Mrs. Moscowitz.

"Yolanda ..." mumbled Fichman, his eyes red.

They went out of the room and Kagan locked the door. Raffy was coming up the corridor toward them. "What happened?" he asked, when he saw Fichman's wounded forehead. "Did he fall?"

"He banged head on door," said Kagan. "So ... " and he made a butting movement.

Raffy pushed Fichman's chair to the nurses' station, and one of them took him to have his wound dressed. Kagan wheeled himself after them.

Mrs. Moscowitz said to Raffy: "I saw your brother. He's a good boy."

"Yes," said Raffy, "he's poor boy."

"Something is wrong with his leg?"

"Yes. He was born like that. But he walks fast. He's very strong for work," said Raffy. "He's strong boy. Stronger than me."

"He doesn't go to school?"

"No," said Raffy, "he hasn't got the sense. He's good boy but he hasn't got the sense for school. That's how he was born."

"Where are you sleeping now?"

"Downstairs."

"Is it a place where you can study there?"

He shrugged his shoulders without replying.

"I was in the room where were your things. Did they throw you out from there?"

"Yes," said Raffy. "It's not allowed to stay there any more."

"And your brother, he's also sleeping here at night?"

"Yes," said Raffy. "We're together downstairs."

"You know that I'm teacher for French? If you like, I'll teach you French. It's good to know French."

"Thank you very much," said Raffy. "There's not enough time for everything."

"You're a good person, Raffy. I wish I could do something for you."

He grinned in embarrassment and murmured his thanks.

"The most important is that a person wants to learn," said Mrs. Moscowitz, "and you've got brains in your head and a good heart also. I'm sure you'll be a famous doctor and help people."

"Thank you very much," said Raffy.

"I saw you once down there, in the garden," said Mrs. Moscowitz, "praying on the ground with your brother. It was so beautiful. A person who's believing in God is a good person."

"It's for my brother, poor boy," said Raffy. "I don't want to. Only my brother asks me."

"He's right," said Mrs. Moscowitz, "it's good to pray, good to believe in God. You don't believe in God?"

Raffy shrugged his shoulders.

"Tomorrow my father's coming to kill everybody, him too," cried Paula, who was sitting on one of the chairs lining the wall, and pointed at Raffy.

"Why do you speak like that? " asked Mrs. Moscowitz. "Raffy isn't a good person?"

"He'll kill the good ones too," said Paula, "and nobody will be left here, nobody."

"You're a wicked woman," said Mrs. Moscowitz.

"And what do you think, he won't kill you?" said Paula. "You too!"

Clara was in the room with her daughter. She was sitting on the edge of her bed and her daughter was packing her belongings into big plastic bags. Clara's face was gray. She had difficulty speaking and she didn't answer Mrs. Moscowitz when she asked what the matter was.

"They're taking her to an institution," growled Frieda in an ominous voice.

The daughter said: "They can't keep her here any longer. Believe me, we did everything possible."

Clara opened her mouth to say something, her shoulders and her hump shook, but her voice was inaudible.

The daughter said: "We found her the best place we could."

Matilda Franco called from her bed: "Any place is better than here. The people here are all bastards. They don't do nothing for us, they don't come when you call them, they don't care if the patients dry up with shouting. You'll be better off there!"

Mrs. Moscowitz went up to Clara and stroked her white hair. Clara raised eyes full of fear to her.

"Perhaps you'll be better off there?" said Mrs. Moscowitz in their language, and her voice failed her, because she didn't believe it herself.

And Clara, stunned, stretched up her neck, gathered all her strength, and said in a whisper: "I don't want to die, Yolanda. In those places they don't let you live."

"That's not true," said the daughter, who understood their language but spoke Hebrew, "who told you such nonsense?"

"I know," whispered Clara with a frozen face, "I know. They finish people off quickly there. They give them special pills to finish them off quick. To make room for other people."

"You'll be in a good place," said the daughter, "they don't do things like that."

"I want to live," whispered Clara to Mrs. Moscowitz, "to live a little longer."

Mrs. Moscowitz turned to her bed, sat down on it, took a tissue out of her bag and covered her eyes, which were filling with tears.

Clara's daughter said to her: "Don't be afraid. We'll see to it that they take good care of you. We know the directress and we'll come to see you every few days."

Frieda bemoaned her bitter fate to the daughter: "You see what they do to me!" she said to her in Hebrew. "We were all together. First Allegra went, now Clara goes, soon Yolanda will go, everybody leaves and only I'm left here alone, without anybody! Why do they keep me here? I don't want to stay without anybody."

"You're a fine one too, what kind of talk is that?" called Matilda Franco from her bed. "What do you mean there's nobody here? God forbid! What about us? Are we dead already? What are we, dogs?"

"You don't understand anything!" retorted Frieda's baritone.

"What I've already forgotten, you'll never know in your life," said Matilda Franco.

"I meant, friends who speak my language," said Frieda.

"Thank God we won't hear your language no more. Anyway I can't stand it: Eshta-beshta-meshta, all day and all night, my head dries up from it."

"I don't want to die," mumbled Clara, perhaps to her daughter, perhaps to herself, "I've still got a little time left."

In the end the two of them went out into the long corridor, the daughter laden with the plastic bags full of her mother's possessions, and Clara hobbling after her on her walker, with Frieda and Mrs. Moscowitz bringing up the rear. Peretz Kabiri broke into his single song in the men's corridor. Next to the entrance to the ward lobby they stopped, Mrs. Moscowitz bent down to the little hunchback, hugged her and kissed her, and Clara whispered in her ear, panting with the effort: "If you want to live, don't believe anybody."

Mrs. Moscowitz asked the daughter to write down the telephone number of the institution where Clara was going on a piece of paper. The daughter set the plastic bags on the floor, opened her handbag and removed a typed envelope from it. And while she was busy looking for a pen to copy down the number, Clara whispered to Mrs. Moscowitz: "What do you need it for? Who're you going to phone? I'll be in my grave already."

"*Ama—do mio,* love me for ever!" Peretz Kabiri's song echoed in the corridors.

Clara and her daughter turned into the entrance lobby. Clara on her walker, slower than she used to be, older than she used to be, and her daughter stopping every now and then to wait for her to catch up. Mrs. Moscowitz looked at them until they disappeared from sight, and only then did she realize that she would never see Clara again.

chapter five

During lunch Kagan asked for a loan again. He smiled and looked her straight in the eyes to see her reaction, as if he were testing her. She hesitated for a moment and said: "I want also to drink."

"Really?" Kagan was startled.

"What can happen?" said Mrs. Moscowitz. "If it makes people happy, let it make me happy too."

"We go in our room," said Kagan.

"But only us. Not him."

Kagan frowned at Fichman who was sitting next to him, absorbed in his food. "Why?" he asked in the end.

"I'm afraid from him."

"What's there to be afraid?" laughed Kagan. "He is like child. I love him like my child."

"And I don't love him," said Mrs. Moscowitz.

After leaving the dining room, she slipped a fifty-shekel note into his hand, went to her room and lay down for the afternoon rest. She closed her eyes and for a long time she couldn't fall asleep. The world was shrinking, receding, and there was nowhere to wait until the light went out. And if she allowed herself to be swept away in this emptiness, the memory would come back to haunt her like a dybbuk, the memory of the old hatred from the cold nights in that room, the sounds and voices that undermined her foundations, breached her walls, invaded her being, overpowered and plundered her. The coughing of the old woman, who buried her head under the blanket like a thief taking cover, in the futile hope that she would not be heard, would break out in a sharp staccato bark every few seconds, like a Satanic clock. And Elvira snoring and muttering in her sleep, on the mattress next to the old woman, and her sullen grumbling when she woke to the sound of baby Rosalia's crying, and her heavy footsteps dragging to the cradle, to calm the baby, to rock her and rock her endlessly. For hours baby Rosalia's crying would continue, and when Elvira fell asleep on her feet and the rocking stopped, the crying would grow louder and burst out of the hoarse little throat in a terrible threatening scream, and the rhythmic rocking of the cradle and the creaking of the floorboards under it would resume, and under cover of the noise the old woman's coughing would grow more prolonged, bold and free, taking advantage of the opportunity to gain a more lasting relief.

Every moment was robbing her of something that was hers, until there was nothing left, only the passionate hatred and the unquenchable thirst for revenge. She cursed them without stopping, moving her lips in the heat of her hatred, and she even cursed baby Rosalia, aiming her heart at a familiar, sympathetic deity that was present and would come to her aid.

She got out of bed and went to sit on the balcony. Beyond the balustrade stretched large lawns surrounded by hedges and poplars, and beyond that—soft hills dotted with one- and two-storied houses, rows of cypresses and citrus groves. The afternoon sun had just passed its zenith, there was no trace of a breeze to alleviate the heat, and the heavy silence was interrupted only by the rhythmic clicking of the shears in the hands of the boy, Raffy's brother, standing on a ladder and trimming the hedge to an even height. When he opened the big shears his elbows stood out from the sides of his body and he leaned forward, as if about to spread his wings, and when he closed the blades he straightened, lowering his elbows to the sound of the metallic click. This movement repeated itself at a regular tempo until the boy descended to the ground, moved the ladder, climbed it again, and went on with his work. When he climbed up and down the ladder he dragged his lame leg, but he did everything nimbly. From time to time he plucked the pruned twigs from the bushes with his fingers and threw them to the ground, and afterwards he raked them into piles at the foot of the hedge. He was utterly absorbed in his task, he never stopped to rest, never looked right or left. Suddenly her eyes were drawn back to the balcony, which ran the length of all the patients' rooms on the floor, and she saw Leon leaning against the balustrade a few yards away and looking at her, waiting silently for her to see him.

"Why aren't you in bed?" he asked.

"I'm resting here," said Mrs. Moscowitz, "I can't sleep."

"What's going to happen when you leave here, how are you going to manage alone at home?" asked Leon.

Mrs. Moscowitz said: "How was I always managing?"

"It'll be harder for you now, with the walker. And who'll help you to get up from your chair, when you can't call Leon?"

"Why are you asking?"

"I can help you," said Leon, "even though you hate me."

She looked at him suspiciously: "Why do you say that? You know it's not true."

"It doesn't matter," said Leon.

"How can you help?"

"I told you I'm leaving this job soon. Me and a few others from our profession are opening a special home for older people who can't manage on their own and need professional help. Something high class, with specialist doctors and first-rate conditions, in a nice place. No more than twenty, maximum thirty, people."

"That's an institution," said Mrs. Moscowitz. "I don't want to be in an institution."

"Then you'll need someone at home day and night. Can you afford it?"

"And to pay for a place like that I can afford? I suppose it will cost a lot of money, more than my pension."

"Sell your apartment," said Leon.

She laughed bitterly.

"What's the big deal?" asked Leon. "You'll have a new home. You can take a special room, on your own. You'll feel better there than at home. You won't lack for anything, you'll be waited on, you'll get physiotherapy, checkups from the best doctors, everything will be taken care of for you, and you'll have company, the highest standard—people from America and England and France, teachers from the university."

"And if I don't like there, where will I go back to?" asked Mrs. Moscowitz.

Leon came up to her and laid his hand on her shoulder. She felt the warmth of his body enveloping her face like steam, and it embarrassed her. He smiled. "Of course you'll like it! I'll be there!"

"I need my house," she said, "I'm not going anywhere."

"There comes a time when you can't stay at home any longer," said Leon, "you can't function any more. Even making a cup of tea is a big problem then. And you can't bathe yourself, and you can't get out of bed. Not even to call for help, for an ambulance. And then, like it or not, you land up in one of those institutions run by nonprofessional people, whose only aim is to take their patients' money and get rid of them as quickly as possible, to make room for some other poor bastard. Believe me, it's terrible. I've seen those places."

"It's better for me to take somebody to help me at home," said Mrs. Moscowitz.

"I can help you with that too. We've got high class helpers who take care of people in their homes, and I'll send you a professional, a woman you can rely on. Because you can't take just anyone into your home. I know cases of helpers ..."

"You said you're going into business with the father of your girl-friend," Mrs. Moscowitz reminded him, "which you're getting married to."

"In the meantime a few things have changed," said Leon.

"And you're not getting married to her?"

"No. She's not a serious woman."

She smiled and shook her head, and Leon burst out laughing: "You see, you don't believe me. You think I'm a liar, right? Admit I'm right."

She said nothing and went on smiling and shaking her head.

"Why do you think I'm a liar? Go on, Yolanda, tell me. When did I ever lie to you?"

"Every time you tell a different story," said Mrs. Moscowitz.

"You hate me, that's all there is to it," said Leon and he went on laughing.

"When I leave here, you'll get something from me that you'll see I don't hate you."

"Money again!" said Leon. "But I don't want your money. I only want to help you, and you won't let me. You want me to fix you up with something good?"

"We'll see," said Mrs. Moscowitz, "I have to think about it. First I should be at home, and then we'll see how it's going. Give me your telephone."

"It would be better for you to give me your phone number," said Leon, "and I'll get in touch with you after you leave."

Satana's voice rose in the corridor, calling Leon.

"Don't tell anyone what I said to you. It's confidential. Nobody must know before I leave my job here."

"Word of honor," said Mrs. Moscowitz, and Leon ran into the corridor.

Raffy's brother finished trimming the hedge to the left of the lawn and raked all the piles of pruned twigs and leaves into one big pile at the corner of the garden, dragged the ladder to the farther hedge, climbed the rungs and began pruning energetically, to a regular rhythm, with the same repetitive bowing and straightening movements, and Mrs. Moscowitz said to herself: He's an ugly backward Arab boy and I'm a French teacher with an apartment in north Tel Aviv, and his life is better than mine. This conclusion did not bring tears to her eyes or make her feel pity for herself or resentment at the way of the world, but only weariness and a desire to sleep. She went back to her room, got into bed and fell asleep at once.

—

At supper Kagan was again wearing the burgundy bathrobe his wife had brought him. His abundant white hair was combed smoothly back, his face was shaved and gave off an aroma of aftershave that she had never smelled on him before. Fichman had already finished eating and sat next to him with an expressionless face, ignoring her presence. At moments like these she sometimes thought that Fichman heard and understood everything and that he was pulling the wool over their eyes. Kagan's eyes laughed when he asked her why she was sad.

"There are bad pains in the leg," said Mrs. Moscowitz, "something new."

"It will be okay," he said, "everything will pass and everyone will be healthy." And in an intimate, seductive whisper he recited the verses that she already knew:

Mon enfant, ma soeur,
Songe à la douceur
D'aller là-bas vivre ensemble!
Aimer à loisir
Aimer et mourir
Au pays qui te ressemble!

There was something insulting in his freshness, his high spirits, his cheerful optimism, which seemed to her like a childish attempt to avoid sympathizing with her situation. She said: "Yesterday they took from here my friend Clara, to an institution. And she didn't want to go, she knows that over there she'll die right away. At the end, before she went, she said to me: If you want to live, don't believe anyone."

"Why to speak this macabre things, of people who go to die in institution? This is not good, to enter into such mentality. You know there is here clubroom? Well, so I don't know up to now. People play cards, chess, different things. Normal people, from other wards. There are here other normal people and we don't know. So I for example go now to play chess with woman from kibbutz, which I met there before. I saw how she plays. And I for long time have not played chess. Now we see what happened to my head. Why you don't come too? Good for morale. Cards you know?"

"No," said Mrs. Moscowitz, "I don't feel good."

"So!" said Kagan. "All comes from depression. You must to do something, to be with normal people and to finish with depression. You know where is club? Next to big hall of visitors."

"No, I don't want to," she said, "and it doesn't interest me to see the woman from the kibbutz who'll play chess with you."

Fichman suddenly pushed his wheelchair back from the table, rolled down the aisle, and left the dining room. Kagan followed him with his eyes and said: "Poor man, I don't know what eats him."

She hardly ate anything, waited for Kagan to finish drinking his tea, and the two of them left the dining room. When she parted from him, she wished him luck in his chess game, and went to sit next to Frieda and her family.

This time only Frieda's son-in-law had come with one of the children, because the other child was sick and his mother had stayed at home with him. Frieda told him about how they had taken Clara from her after she had already lost Allegra and that Yolanda too would be leaving her soon. Again she lamented the fact that she was being left on her own and complained about the doctors who would not let her go home at last. The son-in-law explained that doctors' orders were sacred to them, and that although they too were longing to have her at home with them, they would not endanger her health, perhaps even her life, in spite of the expense and the inconvenience of the daily trips to the hospital. "But nothing changes," said Frieda, "legs I'll never have again. And apart from that, everything is the same as it was. What are they waiting for?"

"Mother," said the son-in-law, "they know what they're doing. And we have to do as they say."

And what about Kagan's promise that they would get drunk together, by themselves, in that room? Hadn't she given him fifty shekels to buy the alcohol? And he hadn't even mentioned it. Every day he was a different person, with new attitudes and new qualities, and it was impossible to know who he really was. Would he give her back the money at least? Did he even remember that she had given it to him? Naturally it wasn't just a question of the money but mainly a question of honor. And in general, what was she to him?

Frieda's conversation with her son-in-law began to bore her and now Clara was no longer there to exchange glances with her and explain her interpretations and conclusions about human hypocrisy afterwards. Since she was sitting on a high chair, she did not require assistance to get up, and she began walking along the corridor. When she came to the end, the new pain in her ankle began to trouble her.

As she pushed her walker she tried to put the weight of her body on the other leg. Her legs were soon tired, and she paused to rest in the lobby. You have to walk a lot, the doctor had said, and she hardly walked at all. She decided to push on in spite of the pain. Next to the public telephones she stood still to rest again. The corner was dimly lit, and there was nobody there. She almost gave in to the temptation to sit down on one of the chairs next to the round table, but she was afraid that by now she wouldn't have the strength to get up, even from a high chair. On the closed window of the canteen there was a list of prices. She succeeded in reading it in spite of the semi-darkness. When Allegra was still with her, she had often sent her to buy a can of her favorite apple juice for her, as well as lemon-flavored wafers, and needless to say, she had never inquired about the price or counted the change, because she had relied on her friend's honesty. Since Allegra had gone, she hadn't tasted either the apple juice or the lemon-flavored wafers. Now she pined for them. How they would have refreshed her, cheered her spirits and strengthened her body! And she decided that the next day, when the canteen was open, she would come all the way again and buy herself apple juice and wafers.

She continued walking until she reached the entrance to the big visitors' lounge, whose two outer walls were made of glass. Beyond the glass the sun was setting, and in the lounge the fluorescent lights were already burning. Visitors were sitting in some of the armchairs, with patients she didn't know, and Peretz Kabiri was standing on his crutches next to a group of people who were sitting and talking to an old woman in a wheelchair and taking no notice of him. Mrs. Moscowitz turned right in the corridor opposite the visitors' lounge and reached a smaller room, both of whose double doors were open. She stood next to the doorway, her shoulder to the wall, and peered inside. There were people sitting at four of the tables, playing chess, and he was at the table farthest from the door. She saw him from the back, in his new burgundy bathrobe, his head bowed, his elbows on the table, his hands supporting his temples, and opposite him, in a wheelchair, the chess-player from the kibbutz, who kept turning her broad, square shoulders jerkily from side to side, appearing first on his right and then on his left, with her short thick neck, her cropped gray hair, and a cigarette between her lips.

Before the people sitting there could see her, she retreated from the door, turned her walker around, and began making her way back. The memory of the taste of the apple juice would not let her be. Her craving for it tormented her even more than the pain in her ankle and the weakness of her knees. If she had been at home, she could have phoned the grocer to send the delivery boy with a few cans of the juice and so have refreshed her parched throat immediately. The need grew so powerful, so urgent, that she felt her heart would fail her.

A tall, thin man on a walker and a woman carrying a small suitcase emerged from the visitors' lounge, with Peretz Kabiri on his crutches behind them, gabbling incoherently about the singing of "Hatikva" in the Acre jail, which he demonstrated, about Captain Cooper's batman, damn his soul, about the girls from the ATS and about the traitor, damn his soul to hell, who had ratted to the CID.

Mrs. Moscowitz stopped and waited for them to pass her. The thirst and the unaccustomed effort had weakened her heart. She went on walking, but when she reached the public telephones her strength failed and her legs refused to obey her. She decided to sit down on one of the chairs to rest. Next to the last telephone booth a bald head shone in the darkness—it was Fichman, lurking there to ambush her. When she saw him she started in panic and almost lost her balance. With the last of her strength she hung onto the walker and dropped at once into the nearest chair.

Now she strained her eyes to examine his face, trying to guess his intentions. His face was grave and enigmatic, and he sat in his wheelchair without moving. She started trembling, from weakness or fear. She tried to stand up but failed. The echoes of voices could be heard in the distance, from the visitors' lounge or the ward, but in their immediate vicinity silence reigned.

"What are you doing there?" she called out, to chase away her fear, for she knew he would not answer. "Go away, go away!" He sat still as a statue but his eyes looked straight into hers—small, half-closed eyes, full of hatred and obstinacy. For a long moment they sat facing each other in the dusk. Suddenly he pushed his wheels and passed nimbly through the narrow space between the telephones and the chair on which she was sitting. She looked after him and saw him reach the door of the visitors' lounge, where he turned right and disappeared from view. In the corridor she saw a man and a woman and a child coming toward her—Frieda's son-in-law, his son, and Satana, who wasn't wearing her nurse's uniform. Frieda's daughter and son-in-law often gave Satana a lift home in their car when she finished her evening shift. She overheard the son-in-law saying: "Good for you, Rosa, good for you." They walked past without noticing her. She called out to them: "Excuse me, perhaps you can help to get up?"

"Yolanda!" cried Frieda's son-in-law in astonishment, as if the telephone corner was the last place in the world where he would expect to find Mrs. Moscowitz. Satana went up to her, gripped her elbows and raised her to her feet.

"When she wants to, she can get up by herself," said Satana.

"I went to the telephone," said Mrs. Moscowitz, "and suddenly, the legs ... "

The three people had already gone.

When she reached the ward corridor, Leon saw her and he asked: "What's the matter with you, why are you so pale?"

"I'm terribly thirsty," said Mrs. Moscowitz, "I must quickly to drink."

She sat down in the corridor next to the door of her room and he brought her a cup of water, and after she drank it she asked for more and he went back and brought her another cup. He stood and looked at her as she drank and when she had emptied the second cup, she sighed and smiled at him in relief.

"I walked too much," she said, "and I tired myself."

"Where did you walk to?" asked Leon.

"To the visitors' lounge."

"That's not so far," said Leon, "that's right here. You don't walk enough, you're not used to walking any more."

The warmth of his body and his smell enveloped her pleasantly, and the affection she had once felt for him returned. She put her hand on his thick, sweating hairy forearm and looked into his face. "You're so strong," she said, "you give me strength. What would I do without Leon?"

He was silent and his eyes with their unfocused look looked her up and down with a faint, knowing smile, then he loosened his arm from her grip and said: "And what will you do without Leon?"

Paula approached them on her walker with a malicious expression on her face.

"No!" said Mrs. Moscowitz. "I don't want to hear what you're saying, go to your room."

"No one will remain alive," said Paula, "you'll all die like dogs."

"For shame," scolded Mrs. Moscowitz. "You were teacher once. This is how a teacher talks?"

"The teachers will die too," said Paula.

Leon laughed and went to sit at the nurses' station.

"By the way, perhaps you know what date it is today? I don't remember anything," said Paula.

Mrs. Moscowitz turned her face toward the television screen. Four people were sitting around a table and talking in Arabic. She often sat and watched the people on the screen, who spoke Arabic at this hour, examining their hairstyles, their faces, their clothes, their gestures, and wondering what kind of people they were, what kind of lives they led, until the picture blurred and her eyes closed. When she felt that she was falling asleep, she roused herself, opened her eyes, and looked through the glass walls at the opposite corridor of the men's wing, and then at the television set again, which was beginning to broadcast the Arabic news. Her head dropped but she forbade herself to fall asleep and shook her body to keep it awake. For a long time she struggled with the force drawing her into herself and just before eight o'clock she saw Fichman passing rapidly down the men's corridor on the other side of the glass partitions. A moment later Kagan too passed down the corridor.

chapter six

The next morning Kagan joined her at her breakfast table and said: "I am sick and tired from hospital. So long time not to see outside. As if there is no world. Where people are not seeing sky with stars, this is inferno. Lucky for you that you go soon."

"How was the chess yesterday?" asked Mrs. Moscowitz.

"Ha, was very good. But she more stronger. My head is already old. And also for long time I didn't play."

"She won?"

"Yes," said Kagan, "quick. Three times. And I not once."

Mrs. Moscowitz said: "This must be hard for you. You're used to having a good life from the women, that they do everything you want."

He laughed in surprise: "Why you say so? It's not true. This is compliment for me, but not true."

"You have the bottle?" asked Mrs. Moscowitz.

"Sure thing," said Kagan. "We go today in studio, after physiotherapy. I practice to walk with walker."

"Very good," she said. "You must be healthy, this is the most important."

"I will be healthy, Yolanda, I have now strong desire to be healthy, to leave inferno, to return to normal world."

"You said: Here will be our Mayerling," she reminded him.

"That was joke," said Kagan.

"Yes, I know," she said.

During the doctors' visit Mrs. Moscowitz complained about the pain in her ankle. Dr. Chen examined her ankle, pressed on a few places and asked if it hurt her, asked her to move it, and said that they would take an X-ray. Dr. Ziv, who was standing next to him, turned to Satana and whispered to her. The head nurse wrote something down on one of the pages attached to the board in her hand.

"Before you go home, we'll see about the problem with your ankle," said Dr. Chen, "we'll do everything possible."

"When am I going?" she asked.

"Soon," said the doctor.

"And when am I going?" thundered Frieda's baritone. "Why is everyone going and the only one to stay behind is me?"

After the doctors left, Mrs. Moscowitz went to the bathroom to meet her double in the mirror. The hair was flat and fading, and the gray at the roots was spreading. It was especially conspicuous at the hairline on the forehead. Rebellious wisps of hair stuck out in the most peculiar places. The face was even stranger to her than up to now. There was nothing in it to remind her of herself, its expression repelled her, all the tiny wrinkles at the corners of her lips and around her eyes, and the bigger wrinkles on her cheeks and chin looked to her like cracks on a fragile and precious vessel that had fallen and broken into bits, and which diligent hands had tried to piece together again, sticking bit to bit, fragment to fragment, but which no longer held a hint of what it had once been. When had the fall happened, when had the break occurred? The eyes too, from which a clear sky blue had not long ago looked out as from two narrow slits, were now lost under the collapse of the lids and it was hard to make them out. This alien reflection that had attached itself to her filled her with hatred and a desire to destroy.

At the appointed hour Kagan appeared in his new bathrobe. The dark burgundy color accentuated his eyes, which had remained youthful, as had his voice. The mood of optimistic serenity he had adopted over the past few days gave him an air of remote beauty. The drawing pad lay on his knees, and she didn't know if he meant to draw her again or if it was only an excuse for going to the room which he called his studio. The key was in his bathrobe pocket, they went inside and he locked the door. He smiled slyly at her, like an experienced man who was familiar with all the caprices, both open and hidden, of the female sex, and who could never be suprised at anything they did.

"How was the physiotherapy?" asked Mrs. Moscowitz.

"Very good. She works with me hard. Already I can walk with walker. Later I throw away walker too."

"With me she does nothing," said Mrs. Moscowitz. "Leg up, leg down. And after two minutes it's all over. She never gives me any massage. For the others she gives massage."

"Maybe for you there's nothing to do already. Leg will stay like now."

"Maybe. Who knows?"

"I have to walk like once, before accident," said Kagan and took the bottle out of his bathrobe. "I am not finished to live."

"Nobody can know what's waiting for him," said Mrs. Moscowitz.

The bottle was not full. He took a red plastic cup out of the pocket of his robe, opened the bottle, poured and offered her the cup. She looked at the liquid in the cup and said: "You drink too."

"Sure thing," said Kagan.

Gingerly she dipped the tip of her tongue in the drink and winced from the burning taste. She was used to the taste of the sweet wine served in the dining room on Friday nights.

Kagan laughed: "All at once to drink, Yolanda. Look." He raised the bottle to his mouth, took a swig and blew out his breath, as if to extinguish the fire in his throat. "So!" he said.

In two gulps she finished the liquor in the red plastic cup. At first she felt only the bitter taste of the alcohol but then a shudder ran through her body and her shoulders hunched. When she raised her head and opened her eyes she saw Kagan looking at her with the faint, curious smile of an experienced old hand. Gradually warmth spread through her chest, something tingled in her breasts. Her heartbeat accelerated pleasantly. Her legs began to lose their weight until she was almost insensible of the chair touching her thighs. Her feet scarcely touched the inner soles of her shoes, they did not feel the floor. She sometimes woke at night and felt like this, suspended between heaven and earth, drifting here and there like a weightless object without finding solid ground, and now this feeling was accompanied by one of exhilarating release. She held out the empty cup, Kagan filled it again, and this time she drank it down in one gulp. She shuddered and immediately recovered. An invisible hand began to rock her slowly and pleasurably to and fro, a gentle, loving maternal hand rocking her like a baby in a cradle. She felt no fear. Tremors of irresistible laughter began bubbling up inside her.

"Lazar, why you don't drink?" she heard her voice coming from a distance, a distorted voice she did not recognize.

"I already drank," said Kagan, "that's enough. No more."

"That's enough?" The laughter burst out of her, shaking her body. "You won't drink. You're afraid!"

He looked at her in amusement.

"Give me more!" demanded Mrs. Moscowitz.

"No, Yolanda, no more. You're not used."

She laughed loudly and her body writhed.

"Be quiet. They'll hear you outside," said Kagan.

"You're afraid!" she cried. "Give me more. I'm not afraid."

He poured her another little drink. She drank it immediately.

"More I don't give," said Kagan. "For today it's enough."

"What are you afraid from more—to die or your wife?" asked Mrs. Moscowitz and she went on laughing.

"If you don't keep quiet, I go," said Kagan.

She lowered her voice, but was unable to suppress her laughter. "I thought you knew to drink. I knew somebody that really knew to drink."

"Your husband."

"Correct. He was finishing such a bottle just like that! It was nothing for him."

"And after this he hit you with stick."

"Correct. With everything he went to the end. If to love—then with all the heart, with all the soul. If to hate—then with all the evil strength inside him. In any case I loved him. I never saw such a man. He loved me like a madman and he hated me like a madman. He wasn't afraid from anything. Not anything and not nobody, including God. That's how he was. Drink for me, Lazar."

"I don't want to drink so much. It's not good for me. I have to be healthy, to walk with my legs. Already I can walk with walker."

"One more drop," she laughed, "one teeny-weeny drop."

He took a little sip from the bottle, closed the lid and put it back under his bathrobe. "Enough, for today we finished to drink."

She looked at him and his figure was blurred. "You're afraid from your wife," she said. "And I have nothing to be afraid. Better to be alone, to do what you want, even some silly things. I feel so good, Lazar. I have more than what I need. Believe me, it's not good, a sick old man with a young wife. Nobody knows what the other person is thinking in his head. Impossible to go inside there and see, isn't it so? Even a husband and a wife. Each one has his own plan. And each one is more egoist than the other. A young woman is staying alone in the home, the husband goes to the hospital, far from the home. What will she do? She won't dream some dreams? She won't look to the side if somebody nice, somebody young, smiles for her?"

Kagan laughed: "You speak nonsense, Yolanda. You're drunk. I didn't think I'll ever see you drunk."

She began taking deep breaths. "I feel so good," she said, "I don't know where I am. Maybe I'm in the second world?" She breathed deeply and looked around with narrowed eyes, examining his blurred face, straining to see it clearly. She surveyed the walls of the room, the table and chair, the floor, as if she had woken up in a place where she had never been before. Her body was so light and relaxed and confident that she wanted to stand up like a normal person, to feel her legs, to see if any trace of the pain remained. With unaccustomed haste she rose from the chair and stood for a few seconds with her knees bent and her arms outspread, like a swimmer about to dive into the water, finding her balance. But when she tried to straighten her legs her head swam, and the giddiness spun her round as in a whirlpool, unsteadying her feet on the floor. For a moment she almost fell on her side, but the invisible maternal hand held her, set her hands on the arms of the chair, and lowered her body into it. She dropped onto the chair and heard her heart beating like a drum inside her body, which had become hollow, and she breathed in a lungful of air. Beads of perspiration chilled her forehead and her neck, broke out on her upper lip. Through the veil spread thinly over her eyes she saw Kagan looking at her from a distance, his blurred face grave. His voice said: "It's not good for you."

The void gaping in her body expanded, and the drumbeats inside it shook its sides, which grew thinner and thinner. She and the chair she was sitting on swayed from side to side, she felt as if she were about to be seasick. She closed her eyes and clung tightly to the chair. Some force broke out inside her, pounced on her heart and began to wring it. More than anything she wanted to cry. She didn't know what she had to cry about, because she felt no remorse or self-pity. But the tears were stronger than she was, like a physical necessity. They burst out of her eyes, streamed down her face, and she sat still, without moving a muscle, as if she were afraid of cutting this moment short. A sense of liberation and expansion carried her far away from herself, perhaps too far. It was the sensation closest to joy that she remembered feeling for many years.

A strange drowsiness overcame her and when she woke up and opened her eyes, the world had steadied around her and her body felt battered and bruised. Her head was so heavy that she could barely raise it. She saw Kagan sitting far away from her, his back to the door, one hand holding the open drawing pad at an angle on his thigh, and his other hand drawing with the fountain pen. His expression was stern and his eyes were concentrated on the page in front of him. For a long moment she looked at him without his being aware of it. When he raised his eyes to look at her, a brief smile flashed in them, but he immediately grew grave again and went on drawing. A dull pain pounded rhythmically in her temples and a weight pressed on her chest. He stopped drawing, held the page away from him and contemplated it. Then he shut the pad, and looked at her. And in his beautiful eyes, whose yellow lashes were no more now than a surmise or a distant memory, glittered a cruel smile, which was like to break her heart with love and insatiable longings.

"I'm so ashamed," she said and buried her face in her hands.

He didn't even approach her, to hold her hand and comfort her. "We must go, Yolanda. You can walk?"

With a tissue she took out of her dressing gown pocket she wiped her dry eyes. "I drank so much," she said in a wail.

"I didn't give you so much," said Kagan. "This is nothing. But you're not used." He looked at his watch. "You can stand?"

She rose from the chair and leaned on her walker. Her body hurt as if she had been savagely beaten, but her legs could carry her. She took a few steps and came up to him. "I can see the picture?"

He opened the pad and showed her. This time the figure was sketched with a few fine lines. The woman was lying slumped on the chair. Her head was lolling on her shoulder and her face was hidden. Only the folds of her chin, her slack, open lips, the tip of her nose, a single nostril and a wrinkled cheek were visible under the mop of hair. Her hands were hanging from either side of the chair with their fragile fingers slightly curled in. The open flaps of her gown revealed a thick knee which looked like the capital of a pillar whose base was a slipper. The other slipper was far from its fellow, peeping out from the hem of the gown. There was no life in this woman.

She was silent and he asked: "What do you say?"

"She isn't alive," said Mrs. Moscowitz.

Kagan laughed: "I call it 'Yolanda sleeping.'"

"This isn't sleeping, this is dead. This is how a dead person is looking."

He didn't reply, but looked at his drawing and smiled. Then he went out of the room, waited for her to follow him, and locked the door. Fichman could be seen retreating rapidly in the direction of the ward entrance, where he stopped next to the men's wing, lowered his round, bald head, and tightened his lips over his toothless mouth.

Kagan's face clouded. "I don't know what is matter with him," he said, "always he follows me and runs from me."

"I feel bad. I must go quickly to the bathroom," said Mrs. Moscowitz and turned into the women's wing.

As she walked along the corridor she tried to disguise her weakness, straighten her aching body as much as possible, and look her usual self. The fear that she would not reach the bathroom in time, or that it would be occupied, was stronger than the pain. Her eyes were fixed on the bar of the walker before her, and the rows of tiles beneath it, receding row after row. She saw no one and heard nothing. As she approached the bathroom she quickened her steps. It was unoccupied. She went inside, locked the door, bent over the basin and vomited. The strange bleat that escaped her lips sounded more like a cry of defiance than a sigh of relief. For a long time she went on standing there, her head bowed over the basin, panting as if after prolonged effort. She felt a little better. She washed her face, turned on the faucet as far as it would go and rinsed the basin in the strong jet of water until it was clean. In the absence of a towel, she raised the hem of her dressing gown and dried her face and hands with it.

She went to her room, lay down and closed her eyes. She was too weak to move. She did not fall asleep at once, but resting with her eyes closed made her feel better. For a long time she lay half awake, half asleep, before she sank into slumber. When she awoke, she was very thirsty. Slowly she turned onto her side and saw Allegra sitting on the next bed, which had remained empty all the time she was away, so thin that her body was lost in the gray dressing gown. Her sparse hair was even scantier and her narrow head seemed to have shrunk. She was sitting with her back bowed and from the wide sleeves of her gown her dark, emaciated arms emerged, their hands spread on her knees. Her eyes were fixed on the balcony outside the room and the expression on her face was calm and indifferent. Their eyes met, and Mrs. Moscowitz was afraid to open her mouth lest she drive the fleeting apparition away. She looked her straight in the eye and she could not tell if the calmness she exuded was that of great weariness or of repose. And then she pushed her body downwards, moved her legs sideways, and sat up on the edge of the bed. They sat there facing each other, and Mrs. Moscowitz looked at her without saying a word. Finally she stretched out her hands to hold those of her friend, as she had often done in the past, but Allegra drew back and put her hands behind her.

"Better not to touch. It's not healthy," she said. Her hoarse voice was weak and monotonous.

"Why?"

"My skin's opening all over. Everything goes right through into the flesh."

Mrs. Moscowitz looked at Allegra's thin arms and saw that the skin was full of sores. Had her skin become like a tattered old garment, its holes exposing to view the nakedness of the body inside, the living flesh which had been left without any protection?

"This is the first time I've ever heard of such a thing. Did the doctors tell you that?"

"No," said Allegra. "They don't have to tell me anything. I know for myself."

"Is it infectious? Is that what you mean?" asked Mrs. Moscowitz.

"No. Anybody can infect me. And then I'm lost."

"But I'm not sick. What can you get from me?"

"Everyone's sick," said Allegra. "Healthy people too."

Mrs. Moscowitz looked at her in dismay. "I don't understand," she said. She bent over and made an effort to get up.

"It's impossible to recognize you, you've changed so much," said Allegra.

"The hair?"

"Yes. You look older."

"I don't feel well," said Mrs. Moscowitz.

She stood up, pulled the walker toward her and crouched over it, waiting until she overcame her weakness.

"Where are you going?" asked Allegra.

"I have to get something to drink."

"Wait. Sit on the bed. I'll bring it for you."

"How can that be?" said Mrs. Moscowitz in astonishment. "I won't let you."

Allegra stood up: "Why not? Eveything will be the same as before. I can do all kinds of things that you want me to do for you."

"Have you got the strength?"

"Yes. Nothing's changed. I can walk."

And she took the glass from the locker next to her friend's bed, went to the bathroom and came back immediately. Mrs. Moscowitz sat down on her bed again, drank the water quickly, and remained thirsty.

"I have to go and phone Adela," said Allegra. "She doesn't know they brought me back here. She'll go over there for nothing. I don't want her to waste her strength. When I come back, I'll bring you apple juice from the canteen."

"I don't like to ask you," said Mrs. Moscowitz, "really I don't. And I don't even know what you went through all this time."

"Nothing," said Allegra. "I'm still alive."

"Did they give you blood?"

"Yes, they gave me blood," she stood facing her and smiled.

Mrs. Moscowitz undid the cloth bag, took out her purse, and held out the money to her, the price of the apple juice and her weekly retainer.

"Put it here," Allegra pointed to her locker, "and I'll take it."

Mrs. Moscowitz did as she requested, and Allegra took the money, counted it, put it in her dressing gown pocket and left the room.

Mrs. Moscowitz scanned the room and the patients lying in it, to make sure that this hadn't been a mirage. Allegra's bed was made and the possessions so familiar to her were lying on her friend's bed and on her locker. Frieda came into the room and thundered in a despairing baritone: "Where is she? Where is she? I heard that Allegra's come back!"

"She'll come soon," said Mrs. Moscowitz.

"You saw her?" asked Frieda.

"Yes."

"Everybody's seen her already, except me!" complained Frieda.

"She was here in the room."

"And I was sitting there all the time working on my tapestry without knowing a thing. I didn't know that she was coming. How could I know? Did you know before?"

"No."

"Ha! Thank God, my Allegra's come back to me," sighed Frieda. "What did she tell you?"

"Nothing," said Mrs. Moscowitz.

Frieda looked at her crossly, trying to guess what she was hiding from her. When Allegra returned Frieda went to meet her on her wheelchair: "My treasure!" she called. "How hard it was for me not knowing what was happening to you, if you were even alive, how I suffered! Ask Yolanda, day and night I never stopped thinking about you. How are you, how do you feel?"

"All right," said Allegra. "As usual."

And she placed a transparent pale green plastic bag containing a can of apple juice and a package of lemon-flavored wafers on Mrs. Moscowitz's locker. "That's my treat," she said, pointing to the wafers.

"I'm paying," said Mrs. Moscowitz.

"No. That's from me."

"Are you working for her again?" asked Frieda, outraged. "She's sending you to fetch and carry for her, after everything you've been through? You have to wait on her like a servant again?"

"Everything is the same as it used to be," said Allegra. "That's how I want it."

"Ha!" laughed Frieda. "All the time you weren't here, she was with her boyfriend. They eat together all the time. He comes to call her and they disappear for hours on end."

Mrs. Moscowitz opened the can of apple juice and drank avidly. Then she opened the packet of wafers, nibbled a couple and drank more juice. "That did me good, Allegra. I was so thirsty. God bless you. Take a few wafers. I haven't touched them."

"No thanks, I don't want any."

"She says he drew her picture," laughed Frieda.

"That's enough, Frieda," said Mrs. Moscowitz. "Don't talk nonsense."

Frieda came up to Allegra. "My treasure, how worried I was about you, how I suffered without you," she said and held out her hands to her.

"You mustn't touch me," said Allegra, "it's not good for me."

"Why, what happened?" asked Frieda in astonishment. "What did they do to you there?"

"They did what they had to," said Allegra. "That's why I'm here."

"Adela said they gave you blood," said Frieda.

"They gave me blood," said Allegra. "That's right. Everything Adela said is right."

"Ha!" thundered Frieda. "You can't imagine what she asked us to do. What papers she asked us to sign. If it wasn't for me, Yolanda would have signed!"

"I sent her to you," said Allegra. "I told her to tell you that I asked you sign the papers. I didn't think you'd object. I'm asking you now too. I owe her so much that even if I lived another hundred years I wouldn't be able to give her back even a fraction of it."

"They're sending Yolanda home," said Frieda.

Allegra looked at Mrs. Moscowitz questioningly.

"Yes, it's true. Soon I'll have to leave. That's what they want."

"And you still can't walk without the walker."

"I'll never walk again," said Mrs. Moscowitz. "The bones didn't knit properly, and they can't operate again."

"Go to another doctor," said Allegra. "There must be something they can do."

"And Adela?" Frieda suddenly asked. "What about her hands? Doesn't she touch you either?"

"When she treats me she wears rubber gloves, like the doctors," Allegra explained.

It was time for lunch, but Mrs. Moscowitz preferred to remain in the room. The apple juice and the wafers, she explained to Allegra, had satisfied her. Her friend said nothing but Mrs. Moscowitz thought that she could see disappointment in her face. So she decided to accompany them to the dining room. When they chose an unoccupied table, she hoped to sit with her back to the entrance, but the other two took the seats on that side of the table before she could get there, and she was left with no option but to sit down opposite them, facing the entrance to the hall. Frieda described how her heart had been broken by the way Clara had pleaded with her daughter not to be taken to the institution, she had been so shocked by what had been done to that poor woman, her family were her witnesses, they had seen her suffering and they couldn't console her. The whole night she hadn't slept a wink. Allegra listened to her and shook her head sympathetically, but Mrs. Moscowitz was constantly aware of Allegra's eyes scrutinizing her face. She looked apprehensively at the door, hoping he wouldn't come, that she wouldn't see him. The morning's events had already grown vague in her mind, like a bad dream whose details had been forgotten, but a bitter sediment of fear and shame remained.

Paula pushed her walker toward them, evidently intending to sit down at their table. This time Mrs. Moscowitz hoped that the woman would sit down beside her and there would be nowhere left for anyone else to sit. But Frieda waved her hands at her: "I don't want you sitting here!" she shouted at her, "Go somewhere else."

"Does the place belong to you?" asked Paula. "Have you got a title deed to it?"

"No, it belongs to your father," said Frieda, "I know. Go away!"

"*Like an arrow her doom flew past her: she too would die ...*" said Paula.

"She's cursing me!" cried Frieda. "Go there, witch!" She pointed to an empty table. "We don't want you next to us."

The waitress approached their table. "What do you want, Paula?" she asked. "You've finished eating, go back to your room."

"I haven't eaten yet," said Paula.

"Yes you have. I gave you your food myself. Now leave the room."

"That's not true," protested Paula. "I haven't eaten for a week. You've decided to starve me to death."

"Are you hungry?" asked the waitress.

"It isn't your food," said Paula. "Nothing here is yours, it all belongs to my father. All of you here are living on charity." All of a sudden her anger gave way to an expression of embarrassment and apprehension. "Excuse me, madame," she said to the waitress, "do you know me? My memory fails me. I don't remember anything. I'm not a human being any more." And she set off in search of somewhere else to sit, wandering like a lost soul among the tables.

Kagan entered the dining room, paused inside the door, put on his spectacles and looked around. His eyes met those of Mrs. Moscowitz and held them for a second. She dropped her eyes, and when she dared to raise them again he was still sitting in the doorway looking around the hall. In the end he wheeled his chair to one of the corner tables. When she saw that he wasn't coming to sit next to her, or to ask her to come and join him at another table, she relaxed. From where she was sitting she could see his back. There was no doubt that he had been looking for her in the dining room and there was no doubt that he had seen her—so why had he decided not to come up to her? Had the sight of her face reminded him of her revolting behavior that morning? A moment later Fichman came into the dining room, pushing his wheelchair forcefully along the aisles between the tables. He bumped into Paula's walker, thrusting it aside. Paula screamed in alarm. But for one of the nurses who was standing behind her, and who caught her arm in time, she would have fallen. Kagan turned his head and looked at Fichman, with an expression of disapproval and annoyance at having his peace disturbed. The nurse shouted at Fichman, pushed his chair backward to the door, turned it round and wheeled him out. Again Kagan's eyes met those of Mrs. Moscowitz, and this time it seemd to her that he smiled at her, a brief smile of grim amusement. She responded with a light, noncommittal nod.

Paula sat down at one of the tables, dazed. The waitress placed a glass of water in front of her but she didn't touch it. When she recovered, she took a sip of water and asked for food: "I haven't eaten for two days. All these parasites gorge without stopping and I have to go hungry. By the way, what date is it today?"

They finished eating. Frieda pushed her chair back and started wheeling it toward the door. Allegra rose too, but Mrs. Moscowitz asked her to sit with her a little longer. Allegra understood and sat down again across from her. When Frieda had moved away, Mrs. Moscowitz said: "Let's wait until he goes."

"Did you quarrel?" asked Allegra.

"No," said Mrs. Moscowitz, "but I behaved in such an ugly way that I'm ashamed to meet him."

"What did you do?"

"He gave me alcohol to drink and I talked nonsense. I was drunk. I made a fool of myself. At first he thought I was an aristocrat, and today I behaved like an old whore. I can't see him without thinking about it. I wish I would never see him again. While you were away I changed a lot," said Mrs. Moscowitz.

"And you stopped taking care of your beautiful hair," said Allegra sadly.

Mrs. Moscowitz's eyes were fixed on the entrance. At last she closed them, partly in relief and partly in pain.

"Has he gone?" asked Allegra.

"Yes."

In the corridor Adela came toward them, brisk and excited, her face flushed with heat and effort. She greeted Mrs. Moscowitz with a brief nod, and went into the room with Allegra. Mrs. Moscowitz followed them in and lay down on her bed for the afternoon rest. Adela took a little towel out of her bag and went to the bathroom. After a moment she returned, drying her wet hands, strode over to the corner of the room where the white screens were kept, and dragged two of them to Allegra's bed. This privacy too was new. Mrs. Moscowitz strained her ears to hear what they were whispering behind the screen, without success. Long, nerve-racking silences alternated with impatient voices. In the end she heard the quick whistle of the zipper, which sounded like a thin shriek: Adela had opened her big traveling bag. Then came the familiar sounds of the anointing of Allegra's body with baby oil, the slapping and the kneading, and moments of silence in which it was possible to imagine Adela's hands touching the flesh that it was forbidden to touch.

When the treatment was over Adela folded the screens and dragged them back to the corner of the room. Allegra lay in her gown, sweating and exhausted, her eyes closed. Adela sat down beside her, and wrote down what she whispered to her in a little notebook. Then she wrote out a check and Allegra opened her eyes and signed it. Finally Adela stood up, approached Mrs. Moscowitz's bed, and examined her face to see if she was sleeping.

"She says you're willing to sign."

"Yes," said Mrs. Moscowitz and sat up in bed.

Adela brought her bag and took out the typed documents, handed her a pen and showed her where to sign. Mrs. Moscowitz signed and lay back again.

"You won't be sorry," said Adela. Then she looked at Frieda's bed. "She's sleeping," she said in a disappointed voice. "She has to sign too," she said to Allegra. "Tell her not to make problems."

"She'll sign," said Allegra in a weak voice.

Adela went away and Allegra lay motionless with her eyes closed. Mrs. Moscowitz looked at her narrow tortured face, anointed like the rest of her body with the baby oil, at her dark, emaciated arms, whose dryness was still evident beneath the oily sheen. Allegra opened her eyes, turned her head and looked at her:

"What's wrong?" she asked.

"Nothing. We hardly had time to talk by ourselves in the dining room."

"Not now," Allegra requested, "after her massage I haven't got any strength left."

"Maybe it's not good for you?"

"I don't know."

Mrs. Moscowitz left her alone. Her head was heavy now and the muscles in her neck and shoulders hurt with every movement. Her body still remembered the morning's misadventures. Only a few hours had passed, and the shame and fear of Kagan had already dimmed and sunk with the joy and astonishment of Allegra's return, and her heart was given over once more to the sensations of the moment. The thirst bothered her again, vying with her wish to surrender to the paralysis spreading through her body. Two equally matched powers fought for the possession of her soul.

Raffy came into the room, wheeling a bed toward the empty place in the opposite row. She called him and held out the cup on her locker: "Do me a favor, Raffy," she said, "bring me water, I'm so thirsty and I can't get up."

He went to the bathroom and brought her water. "Thanks very much, you're a good person," she said to him, drank the water quickly, and sighed. He remained standing by her bed.

"How are you, Raffy?" she asked.

"All right," he said.

"And your brother?"

"Also all right."

"There are Arabs with good hearts too," said Mrs. Moscowitz. "It doesn't matter if a person is a Jew or an Arab, the main thing is he should have a good heart. You've got a good heart, and I'll always remember you."

He was silent, dropped his eyes and remained where he was. In the end he gathered his courage and said:

"That room . . . you still go there?"

"No, I'm never going there no more."

"It was very good for me to study there. Now I've got nowhere to go."

"Ask again," she suggested. "Maybe now they'll allow. Nobody's going there no more."

"Thank you very much."

"Raffy, please to bring me more water. I'm still thirsty."

He brought her more water.

When she woke up she was frightened for a few moments, because she didn't know where she was. It was the first time anything like this had happened to her. She went to the bathroom and washed her face. After drying it, she looked in the mirror and the face that looked back at her seemed familiar, domestic, sensible, no longer that of a crazy old woman who had strayed to strange places. She felt that something inside her had become impenetrable to the outside world, that it was protecting her, and she smiled at her reflection with a resigned, sober smile. Then she went into the corridor to sit next to Allegra. "I feel much better now," she said to her, as if in reply to an unasked question. Allegra too looked better, and her little eyes were as alert and inquisitive as ever. Allegra was drinking tea, and when Mrs. Moscowitz came to sit down beside her, she poured her a cup of tea from the trolley. After a while Kagan appeared at the end of the corridor, pushing a walker and advancing at a snail's pace, stopping to rest after every step. When he moved his bad leg and put his weight on it his face twisted in pain. Gradually he drew closer to the place where they were sitting, and when he paused to rest between steps, he nodded to Mrs. Moscowitz and a smile of pride appeared on his face. Mrs. Moscowitz murmured: "Bravo, bravo!" so that he wouldn't think she begrudged him his efforts to get well and return to the normal world.

When he moved away down the corridor, in the direction of the dining room, Allegra said to Mrs. Moscowitz: "He's certainly a good-looking man."

"Yes. And well educated too. He's a famous painter, he puts on exhibitions," said Mrs. Moscowitz, "but he's not a good person. He's only interested in one thing—him and him and him."

Kagan reached the end of the corridor, turned into the men's wing and disappeared from view. A few minutes later they heard his screams. The nurses ran in that direction.

"It's him," said Mrs. Moscowitz, "I'd know his voice in a thousand."

"He fell," said Allegra and stood up to go and see what had happened to him.

"No," said Mrs. Moscowitz, holding out her hand to stop the astonished Allegra and calling her back. "It's something else. I know exactly what it is."

She herself had no idea where her certainty, stronger than any eye-witness evidence, came from. But the knowledge was inside her, like an embryo in its mother's womb, waiting for the moment when it would be called upon to reveal itself. She couldn't understand what was happening to her. From the moment of her strange awakening from her afternoon sleep she felt that something had been sealed off inside her. Her feelings were detached from what was happening around her. A suspect calm had descended on her. Everything was happening at a great distance from her, as if she were still sleeping and her previous awakening had only been a dream. She felt nothing for Kagan and what had happened to him, she didn't care if he lived or died. Even Allegra had turned into one of the shadows inhabiting this place, a ghostly figure from the past, from whom she would soon part.

In the men's corridor, beyond the glass partitions, people hurried to and fro. Satana returned to the nurses' station and they heard her summoning the ambulance driver. Some of the women sitting on the chairs lining the wall asked the head nurse what had happened. She reacted with a grim silence and went back to the men's wing.

Frieda returned from the entrance to the ward, her face agitated and appalled. One of the patients from the men's wing had told her something terrible, she thundered in her deep voice, and gave Mrs. Moscowitz a penetrating, accusing look: "That lunatic, who follows him all the time, stabbed him in the stomach with a knife he stole from the kitchen. Now they're taking him to R. Hospital for an operation."

Mrs. Moscowitz smiled and nodded in confirmation of Frieda's story, and Allegra looked at her with concern.

"That's the kind of thing that happens in this hospital," said Frieda. "I'm afraid to stay here. There are a few more people here capable of doing the same thing. Why do they keep them here with us? Why don't they take them to the lunatic asylum?"

"Where's Fichman?" asked Mrs. Moscowitz.

"Who's Fichman? I didn't even know his name was Fichman," said Frieda contemptuously. "What am I, a friend of his? I suppose the police will come and take him away. The first time I saw him taking off his pajama in the dining room and hitting himself on the heart I knew he was a dangerous lunatic and I was afraid of him. And what about them—they didn't know? I suppose his family's got connections. That's the way it goes here. What's going to become of us? I don't want to stay here any more! When my family hears of this, they'll take me straight home. They won't let me stay here one day longer. I know them."

And then they saw Kagan being wheeled down the corridor of the men's wing on his bed to the elevators in the lobby. It was impossible to see his face through the glass partitions, but when the bed passed swiftly through the ray of light coming from the fixture in the corridor ceiling, the infusion bag hanging at his head suddenly caught fire and shone radiantly for a second, shone and faded away like a solitary passing star in a dark, starless sky.

When Frieda's family came to visit her, Mrs. Moscowitz and Allegra sat nearby, drinking tea and staring at the television screen. Frieda described to her daughter and son-in-law how the patient from Kagan's room had told her what had happened, how horrified she had been, how she had almost fainted, and how frightened she was of staying in the hospital. She pleaded with them to take her home with them that very evening. They tried to reassure her, and told her about their conversation with the head nurse, who had explained how it had happened, and assured them that measures had already been taken to prevent anything like that from happening in the future.

"And that lunatic's still wandering around here?" asked Frieda. "Who knows what he'll do next."

"No," said her son-in-law. "Tomorrow morning they're sending him to the lunatic asylum. In the meantime they've put him in a room by himself, and he can't get out of bed."

"And the police?" asked Frieda. "Why don't they call the police?"

"They notified the police and they're taking care of it," said her daughter, "and taking all kinds of steps to make sure that it doesn't happen again."

"What about a trial? Aren't they going to put him on trial?" asked Frieda.

"Of course they'll put him on trial," said her son-in-law. "Don't worry, they won't let him get away with it."

"I don't think I'll have a moment's peace until I'm at home again," said Frieda.

When her family rose to leave, Frieda burst into tears. Her daughter embraced her. "You take things too much to heart," said the daughter, "go to sleep and when you wake up in the morning you'll have forgotten all about it."

As they left they called the head nurse, who had completed her shift, and she joined them. Frieda looked after them until they disappeared at the end of the corridor and muttered to herself: "Why are they so frightened of taking me out of here? What can already happen to me at home?"

Two nurses were sitting behind the counter watching television, a few of the patients had already gone to their rooms to sleep. Without saying anything to Allegra, Mrs. Moscowitz stood up and began walking down the corridor. When she passed the door to their room she didn't go inside, but went on walking in the direction of the dining room. Allegra watched her with a worried, curious look. She had been behaving strangely all evening. Leon came out of one of the rooms in Mrs. Moscowitz's path. "I have to walk a lot," she said to him. She herself didn't understand what she was doing or what force was compelling her in that direction, but she sensed that it had to happen. She went on walking and when she reached the end of the corridor, she looked behind her and saw that only Allegra was watching her. She went up to the last, empty room which was always kept locked, pushed the handle down and went inside.

There was a dim light on in the room and he lay on the only bed, opposite the door. The room was empty but for the bed and the locker at its head. Mrs. Moscowitz pushed her walker into the room and closed the door behind her. He was awake, and when she entered he raised his head. She approached the bed and looked at him. His round, smooth face wore an expression of distant calm and his small, light-colored eyes shone with a quiet intelligence that she had seen there before. He clamped his lips between his toothless gums, as if to suppress some sudden impulse, and in the end he opened his mouth and whispered: "Yolanda, Yolanda . . . "

Something burst inside her, breaking down the wall that had enclosed her, and flooded her heart.

Under the sheet his legless body looked as small as a child's. She put out her hand and touched his shoulder. His body was warm and the pajama was damp with perspiration. She stroked his shoulder and he dropped his head to the pillow and closed his eyes, entrusting himself to her hands. Suddenly he began to hum something in a faint, plaintive whimper. Then he began to sing, a strange song without beginning or end, interrupted by long silences, in which it seemed to her that she could hear words in Yiddish. She felt that they weren't alone, that someone was watching them from somewhere, and she was seized by fear: the last room would close in on her and she would never be able to leave it again. She wanted to run away but on no account could she tear herself away from him and his strange song, which she thought he was singing in her honor. Suddenly his voice choked and he opened his eyes, looked at her, swallowed his saliva and whispered: "Yolanda." She removed her hand from his shoulder, leaned on her walker, and retreated to the door. When she opened the door he raised his head from the pillow and called again: "Yolanda. . . " and she went out and shut the door.

The corridor was already empty. Leon and two nurses were watching television. When they saw her, they stared in surprise. Leon called: "Why don't you go to bed?"

"I'm going now," said Mrs. Moscowitz.

Paula emerged from one of the rooms in a nightgown and came toward her. "Excuse me, madame," she said, "perhaps you know where the cloakrooms are here?"

Mrs. Moscowitz walked a few steps with her, showed her the entrance to her room and the corner to the left of the entrance.

"Thank you, madame," said Paula, "all the places are taken and I haven't got a bed to sleep in."

"That's enough now," called Leon and emerged from behind the counter. "Goodnight, Yolanda," he said, went up to Paula, put his hand on her back and guided her to her room. "That's enough talking."

"Excuse me, sir, "said Paula, "why are you interfering? Can't you see that I'm talking to the lady? Madame," she called, "madame, just a minute! Perhaps you know what time it is?"

Allegra was already sleeping, or perhaps she was lying with her eyes closed waiting for her to return. Mrs. Moscowitz sat down on the edge of her bed and looked at her. She was wide awake and knew that she would not be able to fall asleep. For a long time she sat like that. Allegra turned over and sighed. This sigh, which contained both complaint at her pain and resignation to it, was so familiar to Mrs. Moscowitz that she now felt the full force of the knowledge that Allegra had indeed returned and was lying next to her, as if this was their true meeting.

chapter seven

S he woke up early in the morning, and Allegra wasn't in her bed. Then she saw her coming out of the bathroom holding the little plastic basin the patients used for doing their laundry. She went to the balcony to hang it up to dry. Mrs. Moscowitz saw that her dressing gown and underwear, which she had hung on the chair next to her bed when she got undressed last night, were not in their place. When Allegra returned, Mrs. Moscowitz waved to let her know that she was awake, and smiled at her. Allegra hurried to the bathroom and returned with the plastic basin full of laundry, and again she went out onto the porch to hang it up. When her work was done, she came back and sat on her bed and rubbed her hands with cream.

"I wanted to get it done before the rest of them got up and took up all the space," said Allegra with satisfaction, "now it's already drying." And when she had finished rubbing the cream into her hands she stood up and went over to the wall closet and fetched clean underwear from Mrs. Moscowitz's shelf. "Which dressing gown do you want?" she asked.

Mrs. Moscowitz said: "Perhaps you shouldn't touch the soap."

"Why?" asked Allegra. "I use the cream you gave me and no harm's done."

"And the dirt on the clothes doesn't touch your hands?"

"Clothes aren't people."

"Thank you, dear Allegra, thank you for doing it for me."

"You pay me for that too," said Allegra, "everything's just like it used to be."

"The blue gown, please," said Mrs. Moscowitz.

Allegra brought her the dressing gown she had requested.

When the three friends passed the room at the end of the corridor on their way back from the dining room, Mrs. Moscowitz went up to the door and tried to open it. It wasn't locked. The room was empty. The bed was gone and there was nobody there.

"Would you mind telling me what you think you're doing there?" Satana pushed her way past them.

"I thought Fichman was in here," said Mrs. Moscowitz.

"There's no Fichman in this ward," said Satana and slammed the door of the room.

"Did they take him to the lunatic asylum?" asked Frieda.

"They'll take me to the lunatic asylum soon," said Satana and went on her way.

"I'm not afraid of her anymore," said Mrs. Moscowitz. "Now they're sending me home, what can she do to me?"

Before lunch Mrs. Moscowitz and Allegra went out to the balcony. Allegra took the laundry, which was already dry, down from the line, folded it up and went to put it away in the closet. When she returned, she sat down next to Mrs. Moscowitz and said:

"You've got such beautiful hair, why do you make war on it? Why shouldn't it be like it used to be?"

"Nothing will be like it used to be," said Mrs. Moscowitz.

"Because of him?" asked Allegra.

"It's funny: I don't even care what happens to him anymore, if he lives or dies, if I see him again or not, as if I'd never met him."

"What's your hair to blame?"

"He drew me," said Mrs. Moscowitz, "and according to the picture he drew I knew how he saw me. Like a witch, like a madwoman he saw me."

"Why?"

"While he was drawing me, Satana came into the room where we were sitting. 'How beautiful, Yolanda! How beautiful!' she said. And I knew what she was doing. From the first day I arrived here she's been doing it to me all the time."

"The evil eye?"

"Yes. She hates me. From the day the doctor said I had beautiful hair. She was standing next to him and she heard him say it. I saw her, her eyes. They were burning like fire, I swear to you. I didn't know then that she was in love with him. And he doesn't take any notice of her. You can tell her that too if you like, I don't care. I'm not afraid of her anymore," said Mrs. Moscowitz, carried away by the heat of her words, and immediately regretting it.

Allegra gazed reflectively at the lawn in front of the balcony without saying anything. Mrs. Moscowitz understood that in order to avoid unpleasantness they should discuss the matter now, thrash it out and get it off their chests.

"Why did you tell her that I invented the name Satana for her? Why did you go and tell her all that business about how she tried to kill me? What happened, Allegra? I couldn't understand it."

"Did she tell you that I told her?"

"Yes. She thought that I wouldn't be seeing you again."

Allegra looked at her with a certain perplexity. "What's there to understand? I had to tell her. What could I give her to make her agree to get them to keep me here? What else did I have to give her? I've got nowhere to go. In the winter it's impossible to live in the room where I used to live. Now I'm quiet in my mind. I know that I'll die here and not there, in that room, alone, like a rat. Now I haven't got any other home. This is my home, here. I'm used to it and I want to die here. I had to pay her something. What have I got to pay her with?"

"Did you tell her anything else?"

"About you?"

"About me or the others."

"No. There wasn't always anything to tell. But she wants to know everything. Everything interests her. I don't know why."

"I'm not cross with you, believe me," said Mrs. Moscowitz. "If you let me, I'd embrace you, to show you that I still love you like always and forgive you with all my heart. But I can't."

"Why should you be cross? What difference does it make to you? Soon you'll be going home. What will you have to do with Satana? What will you have to do with me? What will any of it matter to you? You'll live your own life."

"I'll never forget you," said Mrs. Moscowitz. "However long I've got left to live, I'll always think about you. I wanted so much for you to come and stay with me, for us to be together, and help each other, and I would be with you up to the last minute."

"There won't be enough time left."

Mrs. Moscowitz was stunned: "Do you know . . . when?"

Allegra did not reply. She said: "If you want to make me happy, do your hair like you used to."

"Really? You really want me to so much?"

"Yes. I want you to be like you used to."

"The hairdresser Pnina disappeared suddenly. Now there's another one, I don't know what she's like. I'll make an appointment with her on Thursday."

"In all my life no man ever loved me," said Allegra, and there was no note of bitterness or complaint in her voice. Her small, slanting eyes were veiled, there was a shadow of a smile on her face, as if she were surveying her life with longing, with wonder, with forgiveness: "I don't know what all this love is about. No man ever embraced me, or kissed me. Maybe only my father, when I was a baby. I don't even know what people feel. I've got all kinds of ideas about it but I'm sure that in real life it's different. Once I wanted to ask you to tell me about it, to describe it to me in detail, so I'd feel as if it had happened to me. Because you were married once. But I was shy. I didn't know what you'd think of me."

She spread out her hands as if to express incomprehension and resignation to her fate. "And don't think I was ugly or repulsive. On the contrary. People said I was pretty. It's a pity I haven't got my pictures here. Then you'd see. I'll ask Adela to bring them. There were boys who were interested in me, who wanted to know me, who asked me to go out with them. Not only in the old country, here in Israel too. But it was never possible, there was never time. My mother was already gone and my father was sick in bed at home. There was nobody to look after him. My brothers couldn't help. And they didn't want to either. One of them's an idiot who can't do anything. And the other one's got a family, and he was in jail most of the time anyway. He's a dangerous person. What choice did I have? I had to do everything. They always relied on me to do whatever had to be done. And that's how it went on, year after year. Life passed quickly. I lost my life. To this day I'm still a girl. And that's how I'll die, a girl."

"Girl or woman, you lose your life anyway," said Mrs. Moscowitz. "I'm going home to wait for death."

"Is that how you feel?" asked Allegra in surprise. "I thought you loved life."

"Lately I've begun to feel all kinds of things. I'm paying off an old debt."

"What for?"

"For wanting to live, for wanting to live so much. After my divorce I received French money from my husband. I changed it and I got a lot of our money for it. I took a room and looked for work. I wanted to meet new people, to rebuild my life, to begin again. And then my mother arrived with my younger sister, whose husband had abandoned her with a baby. They came back to town from the place where they'd been during the war. They had nothing. Only the rags they were wearing. They didn't have anywhere to sleep and they were hungry. Plain and simple. And there was nobody to help them. What choice did I have? The two of them with the baby moved in with me. They didn't even ask me. It was hard. And I was mean to them, to the baby too. Very mean. I couldn't invite friends to my room. I couldn't live with anyone. I didn't have a place of my own. I gave them to understand that they were ruining my life. There were nights when I couldn't fall asleep I was so full of anger and hate. I lay awake with their mattresses and the baby's cradle next to me. I heard them sleeping next to me and I couldn't sleep. I cursed them. Night after night I lay awake and cursed them. For ruining my life. I cursed them without a sound, with my lips, with all my heart and soul. I hated them so much, I was so desperate.

"Don't think I didn't know. I knew that one day I would pay for it. But I was still young, I believed in myself and I wanted to live so much. And after all, I didn't throw them out. It was my home, my money that paid the rent. I could have said to them: Find yourselves somewhere else, I have to live my life. Soon it will be too late for me. But I didn't say it. I knew they didn't have anywhere else. If they didn't sleep with me, they'd have to sleep in the streets and beg for charity. I began teaching French, I earned a little money giving private lessons to the families of high officials. I let them live in my room, eat my food. And at night when I couldn't sleep I cursed them in my heart, all night long I cursed them. I know how to curse. I didn't say anything to them. But they sensed it. They knew what I thought of them. I saw it in their eyes. And all the time they kept on asking me to forgive them. I couldn't bear to hear it. And when will I be forgiven? I have to pay for everything. When will it end? When will my forgiveness come?"

On Thursday afternoon Mrs. Moscowitz kept her promise to Allegra and made an appointment with the new hairdresser to have her hair done. When the hairdresser complimented her on the beauty of her hair and scolded her for neglecting it, her heart expanded with joy and pride. The hairdresser took several hours to do her hair, and Mrs. Moscowitz enjoyed the touch of her fingers as she washed it, the vigorous rubbing with the towel, the strokes of the comb and the friction of its teeth on her scalp, the way it tingled when she poured on the dye, the snapping of the scissors, the rolling of her hair on the rollers, the feeling of tightness, with every hair in its place, the long wait for it to dry, the warm wind blowing from the hairdryer when the rollers were loosened, the scratching of the hard bristles of the hairbrush and the erection of the structure, layer by layer, the smell of the spray on the completed hairdo. It was as if she were seeing her furniture and her kitchenware and personal belongings again after a long absence from home. After she had sentenced herself to realism and resignation and become reconciled to the melancholy figure in the mirror, she tasted once more the taste of the old illusion, now ridiculous even in her own eyes, that with the new hairdo everything would be different.

When the hairdresser had finished her work and received her fee, Mrs. Moscowitz went to the bathroom to look at herself in the mirror. It was strange to see once more the terrible contrast between the worn, wrinkled face and the dome of brown glassy hair. When she smiled into the mirror her blue eyes glittered at her from between their slits. She returned to her room and Allegra uttered a cry of admiration. The two of them sat down to drink the apple juice and eat the lemon-flavored wafers that Allegra had brought to celebrate the occasion.

The thirty days of mourning were not yet over when Seniora's sons came back to visit the hospital. Their beards had grown and become thick and dense, covering their faces and necks like black masks. They came into the room and walked straight over to Matilda Franco's bed. Albert, the elder brother, sat down on the unoccupied chair next to her and Victor stood behind him. For a long moment both of them looked at her in silence. Finally Victor said: "We've just been to visit the Mother in the cemetery."

Matilda Franco cried angrily: "What's the matter with you? Enough! Leave the cemetery and the Mother alone already and start living like human beings!"

They were silent. Albert smiled bitterly and nodded his head, as if he had anticipated these words in advance and had expected nothing better of her.

"What do you come here for?" asked Matilda Franco, "Haven't you got anything else to do? What is it with you two, hanging around sick people and old people and dead people all the time?"

"We have to speak to the doctor," said Victor, "he told us to come to him, and we don't know where to look for him."

"What have you got to speak to the doctor for? What can he do now? What do you want, for him to cure her, May-she-rest-in-peace? For him to bring her back to life?" asked Matilda Franco.

"We've got an appointment with him," said Victor. "We fixed it up with him to come and talk to him."

"So go and ask the nurse over there, she'll tell you where he is."

She said he's busy now, so we're waiting for him," said Victor, "he has to tell us what to do for . . . "

"Why don't you shut up?" growled Albert.

Paula came into the room. In her endless wandering through the rooms in search of her lost place, she arrived at Mrs. Moscowitz's bed, which happened to be empty. She sat on the bed, took off her slippers, and was about to lie down. Matilda Franco shouted at her: "That's not your bed! What are you lying down here for?"

"Pardon me, Madame," said Paula. "Does this place belong to you? Are you the manager here? Why are you interfering?"

"It's her bed," said Matlida Franco, "she's gone to the bathroom, she'll be back soon. Go to your own room."

"You're mistaken," said Paula. "This is actually my bed." And she laid her head on the pillow, stretched herself out on the bed and covered herself with the sheet. "I have to sleep a while," she said, "for five days I haven't slept a wink."

"Here she comes!" announced Matilda Franco.

Mrs. Moscowitz entered the room and started at the sight of the two big men in the masks of black hair.

"She's already lying in your bed," said Matilda Franco.

Mrs. Moscowitz shouted from the other end of the room: "Paula!" She hurried over to the bed as fast as she could, took hold of Paula, who already seemed to be sound asleep, and shook her. Paula opened her eyes and there was an expression of terrible suffering on her face. "Go to your room, to your own bed!" shouted Mrs. Moscowitz, "Why are you lying on other people's beds?"

"Madame," said Paula, "I don't know you but you seem like a nice woman. Why are you disturbing my sleep, after so many sleepless nights?"

"You're lying on my bed!"

"No, Madame, this is my bed. You can ask the management. If you like, you can ask for a bed and they'll give you one too. Please don't bother me." And she closed her eyes again with an expression of celestial serenity.

Mrs. Moscowitz turned her walker and went out to the corridor to ask for help. "Paula's in my bed!" she cried to Satana. "Get her out of there quickly!"

Next to the nurses' station stood Raffy, in his own clothes, and with him his brother, the child gardener, clutching a full, plastic carrying bag. Satana said to Raffy: "Go and get her out of her bed and after that you can go home. Tell your brother to wait here," and she pointed to the chairs lining the wall.

"Where's Leon?" asked Mrs. Moscowitz. "He knows how to get her out."

"I know too," said Raffy proudly.

Mrs. Moscowitz returned to the room with Raffy.

"Please to see that they change the sheets," she requested, "I can't lie on them now."

"Okay," promised Raffy. "I'll change them for you."

When Raffy went up to Mrs. Moscowitz's bed, Albert noticed him and recognized him immediately, although he was not in his hospital uniform. His face lit up, and he stood up and approached him: "Doctor! Doctor!"

"We were looking for you, you remember us? We belong to the late Seniora," said Victor, "we've got a meeting with you."

"Get up," said Raffy to Paula. "I'll take you to your bed, you come with me." He held out his hands, took hold of hers, and pulled. She resisted and freed her hands from his.

"Let me rest," she begged. "I haven't got the strength. I have to sleep a while."

"What doctor, which doctor!" said Matilda Franco. "What have you got to do with him?"

"Come with me," pleaded Raffy. "I take you to a better place." He took hold of her elbows and pulled her into a sitting position.

"What cruelty," said Paula, "dragging me out of bed in the middle of my sleep."

"This is the doctor that we've got a meeting with," explained Victor to Matilda Franco.

"Get up now," pleaded Raffy, "get up." In the end he succeeded in setting her on her feet and gave her the walker.

"Do you know that this place belongs to my father?" said Paula. "Do you know that he can throw you all out and get some order into this place at last? By the way, what time is it now?"

"Missus," said Victor to her, "the doctor is a good person. He helped our mother. . . . "

"Shut your mouth," growled Albert, "If you don't shut up I'll smash your face in."

"You're both as crazy as coots," said Matilda Franco.

Paula began walking and Raffy quickened his step, in order to leave the room before her and escape into the corridor. But Albert rose, got there before him and barred his way: "Doctor, just a minute . . . "

"What do you want of him?" said Matilda Franco. "Are you sick in your heads? That's not a doctor, that's an Arab."

"An Arab?" repeated Victor. "An Arab doctor?"

"What doctor? That's an Arab worker, he's a sanitary worker here."

"Leave him alone," called Victor to his brother. "He's not a doctor, just some Arab."

Albert took a step backwards, narrowed his eyes and examined Raffy. "Arab?" he muttered. "You're an Arab?"

Raffy admitted it with a nod.

"It's him who took May-she-rest-in-peace out of the bathroom after she fell there," said Matilda Franco.

"An Arab took our mother out?" growled Albert. "They let him touch our mother?"

And then a single, stunning blow landed on Raffy. He crumpled immediately and with the brief thud of his fall there was a scream from Mrs. Moscowitz, who collapsed onto her bed, and covered her mouth tightly with her hands to prevent the screams from coming out. Albert gave the body lying on the floor a powerful kick and shook it violently from side to side. "Who gave you permission to lay a finger on our mother?" groaned Albert, his voice hoarse, choked with pain and fury.

Matilda Franco was shouting: "Goddamn you, both of you, what have you done to him? He's a good boy, poor thing. Damn your souls to hell!"

"What are we going to do now?" whimpered Victor in terror.

"Shut up, woman," growled Albert and stood rooted to the spot, glaring furiously at the body lying at his feet.

The child gardener, who was waiting obediently for his brother to finish his work so that they could both go home, came to the door of the room, holding the big plastic bag in his hand, and peeped in. His eyes widened with panic and he hopped swiftly inside. He knelt down next to his brother, shook his shoulder to wake him and let out a shrill, terrible scream: "Raffik! Raffik!"

The body stirred slightly. Raffy, who was lying on his stomach, stretched his neck and raised his head slightly from the floor. Blood flowed from his chin. Immediately his head slumped again, and the bloodstain on the floor spread. The boy's hands began to shake, the plastic bag fell on its side and a dirty shirt tumbled out of it. He wailed and his distorted face was bathed in tears. "Raffik! Raffik!" he sobbed. Again he patted his brother's back to rouse him. His red eyes scanned the strange faces in the room. Then he hung his head, hunched his shoulders, covered his face with his big hands and began sobbing softly.

At the sound of the child's screams one of the nurses came into the room to take him away. When she saw Raffy lying on the floor with a pool of blood under his head, she ran into the corridor to fetch help.

Victor said: "Let's get out of here, this is going to end badly."

"Go on, woman, go!" growled Albert in contempt. "You're already wetting your pants."

Satana came running into the room, with Leon. She looked at the child sitting on the floor crying, at Raffy lying on his stomach, and then glanced at Albert standing behind him and Victor next to Matilda Franco's bed. Her narrow lips trembled with rage but she didn't say a word. She and Leon started toward Raffy but Albert clenched his fists, warning them away from his prey lying at his feet.

"Goddamn your souls to hell, you bastards!" shouted Matilda Franco, "You're not normal, you're sick in your heads. You belong in jail!"

"He's sorry," said Victor, "he didn't mean it."

"Will you shut up already?" groaned Albert.

A number of the patients who were sitting in the corridor tried to enter the room, to see what had happened. Satana hurried to the door and called one of the nurses to stand there and prevent them from coming in. She herself went out to the corridor and Leon, who remained in the room, sat down on one of the empty beds with a sad, helpless expression on his face.

There was a moment of silence. Nobody moved, nobody said a word. Only the sound of the television from the corridor and the sniffles of the crying boy and Albert's angry breathing were heard in the room. And from the soft hills on the horizon, from the cracked red soil, from the sleepy dirt roads, from the dark green patches of the orange groves, the dusty cypress avenues, the tiled roofs of the old houses, from the pine trees on the hillside—the dusky early evening light stole in through the back porch, a heavy sensuous light, saturated with the reddish haze of the end of a summer that refused to die, and covered the room in a half-transparent veil, obliterating details, wiping out facial features, freezing movements and silencing every whisper, until the place was no longer a hospital room but a temporary wayside station on an endless journey into the great night of oblivion.

Mrs. Moscowitz lay with her eyes closed and traveled far away. She arrived home. Her eyes passed over the little hall, the living room, the bedroom, the bathroom, taking stock of the furniture, the ornaments, the bric-a-brac, the carpets, the curtains, the pictures on the walls, and ticking them off one by one on an inner inventory, trying to see whether she could still remember all the little details after such a long time, checking the name of each item against its shape and place and the circumstances of its acquisition. Her possessions inspired in her a feeling of security, gave her back her sense of identity, stood like a wall between her and the alien world outside. She passed into the bedroom and the bed was unmade, the eiderdown in its new cover purchased for her by her neighbor, Mrs. Adler, not long before she fell, a pink cover with pale blue stripes, was pushed untidily against the wall, exactly as she had left it when she got out of bed in the morning, on that winter's day when she had set out for the hairdressing salon. She got undressed and lay down naked in her bed. In spite of the summer heat she covered herself with the thick eiderdown and its touch, at first cool and strange, merged little by little with the warmth of her body, caressing her groin, rising to her chest, enfolding her breasts, descending to her hips and thighs, flowing inside her, trying to quicken the dying flesh with new life. She felt a sharp tingling in her breasts. A faint foretaste of this feeling she had experienced before, when she was drunk, and there was no telling if what she felt was actual pleasure or only longing.

The man in charge of security in the hospital, a short fat pensioner in sandals, jeans and a bright, sleeveless T-shirt, with a revolver in his belt, came into the room accompanied by a muscular young man who worked in maintenance. After them came the doctor and the head nurse. The security officer and the muscular youth stationed themselves between Raffy and Albert, who dropped his hands to his sides and narrowed his eyes, as if assessing their strength. The security officer said: "Move," and thrust out his hand.

Albert said: "Don't touch me. I'll come with you."

Only then did Victor gather his courage to say to the security offi-cer and the tough guy with him: "He's a good person but nervous. We're a good family. Everybody knows us. You knew our mother, May-she-rest-in-peace. We're the same like her. We're not criminals. It's only because of the grief of losing the Mother, May-she-rest-in-peace, that he got nervous and hit the Arab harder than he should have."

"Idiot!" yelled Albert. "You don't understand anything! The Arab killed our mother. They're all to blame. All of them—" and he point-ed at all the people in the room, the head nurse and the doctor and the patients in their beds and especially at Matilda Franco. He began walking out of the room, but slowly, taking his time. The security officer drew his revolver and followed him out.

The doctor knelt down next to Raffy, turned him over gently and laid him on his back. His face was covered with blood. For a moment he opened his eyes and tried to move his head, but the pain was too much for him and he moaned softly.

Victor hurried out into the corridor after his brother and his two captors and called out to them: "The Arab opened his eyes, he moved his head. He's alive! Everything's all right, you can let Albert go!" But the three men went into the lobby and disappeared from view. He returned to the room and appealed to the doctor and the head nurse: "You don't know what a good man he is. What wouldn't he do to help people! You don't know the favors he does. He made a new basin and tap for washing hands at the synagogue too. For free. He didn't take a penny. For the sake of the mitzvah. He's not a criminal. He's sorry, he'll apologize. Tell them to let him go."

The doctor lifted Raffy up and set him on a chair. His head slumped onto his shoulder, his wounded chin bled onto his shirt. "Try to get up and walk," said the doctor. "We'll take you to the clinic. Okay?" Raffy opened his eyes, made an effort to say something, tried to nod his head. The doctor and Leon raised him to his feet and the child gardener who had been sitting on the floor all this time stood up too, stuffed the fallen shirt back into the plastic bag and again the shrill, terrible scream burst from his mouth: "Raffik! Raffik!"

"It's his brother," Satana explained to the doctor, "He works here as a gardener. They were supposed to go home for an Arab holiday."

The doctor and Leon supported Raffy under his armpits and led him slowly from the room. The child walked behind them crying.

One of the nurses brought a pail and a rag and wiped the blood-stain off the floor. Victor paced to and fro in the room, not knowing where to go or what to do. In the end he sat down on one of the chairs, buried his head in his hands and sighed again and again.

Allegra came and sat down on the edge of her bed. She called a number of times "Yolanda!" but there was no reply. Mrs. Moscowitz lay on her unchanged linen without moving or opening her eyes. When Satana came into the room and saw Victor she scowled: "What are you doing here?" she called. "Go home. You've done enough for today."

"Missus, I'm waiting for my brother," said Victor, "when will you let him go?"

"Go to the police. That's where you'll find your brother," said Satana.

"The police?" said Victor, flabbergasted. He sighed, stood up and began pacing the room again, slapping his thighs as he did so. "We wanted to do the hospital a favor, to bring a present in memory of the Mother, to honor the doctors and nurses, and that Arab spoiled everything," he cried in a tearful voice and walked out.

"Yolanda," said Allegra, "it's time to go and eat."

"What's wrong with her?" asked Satana. "Doesn't she feel well? Was she upset by what happened? If she hadn't made such a fuss about getting Paula out of her bed on the spot, Raffy would have gone home without any problems and nothing would have happened to him. That's how it is with people who think of nothing but themselves and have to get everything they want on the spot without any consideration for anybody."

"She's gone," said Allegra to Mrs. Moscowitz after the head nurse left the room, "You must get up to eat. Get up, please."

"I have to go home," Mrs. Moscowitz mumbled in her sleep.

"I'll bring you some tea," offered Allegra, "it'll give you strength." And she rose and returned soon afterward with a cup of tea in her hands.

Mrs. Moscowitz sat up on the edge of her bed, looking very tired. She sipped the tea slowly and asked: "Where did you get it?"

"There's an electric kettle in the nurses' room, and teabags and sugar," said Allegra.

"How come they let you in?"

"I asked," said Allegra.

"They wouldn't let me in if I asked."

Allegra smiled sadly and said nothing.

Leon came in and said to Mrs. Moscowitz: "You're wanted on the telephone."

"Somebody's calling me on the telephone?"

"Yes," said Leon, "somebody you know."

Nobody had ever phoned her in the hospital. When she reached the nurses' station, Satana held the receiver out to her with an expression of contempt. Kagan's voice, clear and youthful as usual, came through.

"Yolanda, how are you?"

"How are you yourself?" she asked in alarm. "What happened to you?"

"Okay. Today I got out of bed and already with walker. How about you?"

"As always. I was so worried for you, after what happened."

"I won't come back to your hospital, and you soon go home. Write my telephone number at home in Beersheba."

"A moment," said Mrs. Moscowitz and asked Satana, who was listening to the conversation, for a pen and paper. The head nurse handed them to her with a bored expression on her face.

He dictated the number and she said: "I'll give you my number at my home too."

"No, no need. You have my number. When you come home, you phone me up."

She couldn't understand why he insisted that she phone him: did he want to spare himself the money for the call? (She had long suspected him of stinginess.) Or perhaps his wife had a hand in it— perhaps this way it was easier for her to supervise his calls?

"Lazar, were you hurt bad? Did they operate? Did they give blood? I was afraid that he killed you."

"No, no. There was no danger. Something small. They put stitches and now they let wound heal. Soon they take out stitches. What about Fichman?"

"I think they took him from here. I don't see him. Look what he did to you, the lunatic . . . "

"Really this was drama. Poor Fichman. Who knows what happens with him now."

"We should have pity of him," Mrs. Moscowitz confirmed his words.

"Well, of course," said Kagan, "in general we should have pity of everybody. Now I must finish to speak. Here are more people waiting for telephone. Feel good, Yolanda, be healthy. It was good for me to meet you there."

"For me also, Lazar, for me also. Maybe one day I'll see you again."

"Maybe." said Kagan. "We'll speak again. Goodbye, Yolanda."

When she replaced the receiver her hand was shaking.

"What a beautiful new hairdo," said Satana.

"Thank you," said Mrs. Moscowitz with ostentatious coldness and cursed her in her heart, adding the special formula efficacious for removing the evil eye and casting it back on the caster.

She returned to her room and sank onto the edge of her bed, exhausted. "It was Kagan," she said to Allegra, "from R. Hospital. He's all right. He's already walking. He gave me his phone number at home, he asked me to phone him when I'm back at home."

"You see?" said Allegra. "You're glad that he phoned. And you said that you didn't care if he lived or died."

"He said it was good for him that he met me here," said Mrs. Moscowitz and covered her eyes with her hands.

chapter eight

One morning she woke up earlier than usual. She opened her eyes at once and turned her head to her friend's bed. Allegra was sitting on the edge of her bed, and her nightgown and sheets were covered with blood. A strangled scream burst from Mrs. Moscowitz's lips.

Allegra looked at her with her small eyes which slanted like those of a Chinese woman: "I got up in the night to make pee-pee," she whispered, "and it hurt so much here," she pointed to the bottom of her stomach, "as if I was being burned alive. And there was a lot of blood. I washed myself with water and I thought it was over. When I came back to bed, it gradually got better, but I went on bleeding without feeling it. What will they do to me now? Send me to R. Hospital again? I don't want to go there. It's not my place. I want to stay here until it's all over. Now it doesn't hurt, but I'm afraid to go and make pee-pee again. And I have to." This was the first time she had ever described her pains without the dismissive words: It's nothing, it's nothing.

The nurse who came in to wake the patients paused next to Allegra's bed, looked at the bloodstained nightgown and sheets, and went away. Another nurse came and changed the sheets without saying a word. Allegra remained in her bloodstained nightgown. She could no longer control herself and she went to the bathroom.

Mrs. Moscowitz got up and went and put her ear to the door. At first she couldn't hear anything. Then she heard Allegra's groans, like muffled echoes of the screams of pain she held suffocating inside her. The noise of water silenced her groans. For a long time there was a sound of water running in the basin and when it stopped, Allegra opened the door. She was pale, her eyes were red, and she leaned against the doorjamb, afraid to take another step. At last she began to walk, and every step was so agonizing that she almost collapsed. She raised the hem of her long gown, held her legs wide apart, her knees bent, and with a curious froglike hop she made her way groaning back to bed. Mrs. Moscowitz walked behind her and saw the blood dripping between her legs to the floor, marking her path from the bathroom to her bed. Allegra sat down on her bed, moaning softly, bowed her head and buried her face in her hands. Mrs. Moscowitz stood opposite her, leaning on her walker, and asked what she could do for her. Allegra whispered through her hands: "Phone Adela and ask her to come. You can use the nurses' telephone. Tell them it's for me."

Mrs. Moscowitz opened the drawer of her locker and took out a piece of paper and a ballpoint pen and wrote down the telephone number. To her relief, Leon, who had been on the night shift, was sitting at the nurses' station. With a tired face he listened to her request, took the piece of paper from her, dialed the number, and handed her the receiver. There was no reply from Adela's house. Mrs. Moscowitz asked him to try again, in case there had been some mistake, and he dialed the number once more, handing her the receiver with a disgruntled expression on his face. There was still no answer.

Allegra remained lying in her bloodstained nightgown, and her meal was brought to her in bed. During the doctor's daily visit he examined the source of the bleeding. She closed her eyes, as if refusing to hear the verdict, but the doctor said nothing. He conferred in whispers with Satana and the other nurse, then he continued on his round and finally left the room with the two nurses. Allegra opened her eyes. "She's sure to come," she said. "She always comes when I need her. Even from a distance she'll sense me calling her."

Mrs. Moscowitz felt her mind dimming. Her sight failed for a second and fear choked her throat. She looked around her in astonishment. What did all this have to do with her? She could no longer endure the painful intimacy, the bitter community of fate which dispossessed her of herself, which invaded her borders. Her solitary voice of old rose up from her depths, warning of danger, crying out for help. Something broke in her. She went to the bathroom, stood again in front of the mirror and saw hair that needed cutting, dying and combing, eyebrows that had to be plucked again. This slack, wrinkled mask expressed indifference and hard-heartedness. No sorrow from outside would breach this wall of dead flesh covering the original face. The suffering of others would not succeed in invading the new fortress, which was only ostensibly a patchwork of folds and furrows, hollows and swellings, layers randomly heaped up by the hand of time, but which had actually been created by a precise plan of defense. And only the eyes were the eyes of the bygone face, two strips of clear cool blue looking out of two narrow cracks, like a pair of faithful old guards appointed to protect her life and ensure that there would be no mercy in this war.

⟜

During the afternoon rest Adela appeared in the corridor, energetic and sweating. The nurses told her about Allegra's condition and she nodded her head and asked no questions, as if she had known it all in advance. Afterward she went into the patients' room, walked up to Allegra's bed, deposited her handbag and traveling bag on the floor at her feet, and sat down on the edge of the bed. For a while she spoke in whispers to Allegra, and then she turned her head for a moment and with a nod of her head greeted Mrs. Moscowitz, who nodded back. She put her arm around the sick woman's shoulders, helped her to get up, and went with her to the bathroom. Mrs. Moscowitz turned onto her side, with her back to Allegra's bed, and tried to fall asleep. Matilda Franco, whose plaster cast had been removed from her hips, came into the room on a walker, accompanying every step with a groan and a curse, until she reached her bed and fell onto it with a scream. Mrs. Moscowitz called out angrily: "Quiet! People are sleeping here, you can't see?"

Matilda Franco said with the last of her strength: "What's the matter with her, the fat cow. This is a hospital here, not a hotel."

"Quiet!" shouted Mrs. Moscowitz.

"You tell your mother to be quiet, you old witch!" said Matilda Franco. "And when you jabber all day long, eshta-beshta-meshta, and a person gets a hole in her head from it?"

Allegra and Adela emerged from the bathroom. Allegra was wrapped in a big towel, and Adela had her arm around her shoulders supporting her and holding the edges of the towel together. They reached the bed, and Adela opened the towel and spread it on the bed and Allegra lay on top of it. At first Adela covered her with the edges of the big towel and patted her lightly on her body. After that she spread the towel out again, helped Allegra to turn onto her stomach, took the bottle of baby oil out of her big bag and began to anoint her shoulders, back, and buttocks with it. Mrs. Moscowitz heard the familiar oily swish of the massage, and felt an urge to turn around and watch, as usual, but she refrained from doing so.

Perhaps she really was an old witch, she said to herself, only she didn't know it. Perhaps she really had such powers latent within her, but she had forgotten the ancient words that would wake them from their slumbers, summon them to strengthen her resistance, show her how to act. If only she could, for example, bundle up what was happening now behind her back and send it flying to the end of the world. If only she could be returned to herself by a miraculous shortcut, put back inside her walls, be like an island in a sea of loneliness and silence.

Despite herself, she turned onto her other side. The locker next to her bed hid Allegra's face from her eyes, and she was glad of it. Adela crouched over the naked, light brown body, thin as an adolescent girl's, rolled it slowly over on the towel until it was lying on its back. Ungloved, her fingers massaged the smooth, narrow thighs, the bony hips, the sunken belly and the small, barely perceptible breasts, the entire oiled, shining body. Allegra's ribs stuck out under her skin, her skinny arms lay stretched out on either side of the pillow with the hands protruding over the edges of the mattress, palms up, like a beggar's. Adela parted Allegra's thighs, poured oil onto her hand and anointed the sick woman's vagina. There was a hoarse, brief moan of pain and Allegra's whole body shuddered. The tips of Adela's fingers disappeared into the lips of the vagina, moving very gently to and fro. She poured a little more oil out of the bottle and massaged the place some more. As she did so, she put her face close to Allegra's and whispered something in her ear, and the sick woman laughed softly.

Adela finished her work. For a long time she dried her hands on the edge of the big towel, wiped the sweat from her face with the back of her wrist and smiled wordlessly. Then she picked up Allegra's blood-stained nightgown, folded it and left the room. Allegra lay without moving, her stomach rising and falling to the rhythm of her breathing. After a short rest, she shifted her body so that the locker no longer separated her face from Mrs. Moscowitz's, and smiled at her. Mrs. Moscowitz did not respond and Allegra's face fell. "It's better now," she said, "I won't bleed."

"For how long?" asked Mrs. Moscowitz. She herself was surprised by the dry, curt tone of her voice.

Allegra did not reply. She resumed her former position, covering her nakedness with a flap of the towel on which she was lying, and once more the locker hid her face. Adela returned with a clean night-gown. She put it down on the bed, took a little towel out of her bag, and went to the bathroom to wash her hands. When she came back, she sat down on the edge of Allegra's bed, and took a little notebook and a pen out of her handbag to write down the sick woman's requests. The hoarse, monotonous voice said: "Please bring me my old pictures. They're in a shoebox, on top of the wardrobe. I want to show Yolanda."

Mrs. Moscowitz went out of the room, crossed over to the nurses' station, asked where she could find Rosa and was told that the head nurse was busy. She sat down in the corridor to wait for her. She was impatient now to go home. It was a long time since she had felt so determined, so sure of a decision. The corridor was deserted. In the men's wing, beyond the glass partition, Peretz Kabiri could be heard pouring his heart out in a loud voice, and his familiar song rolled down the corridor like an evil omen: "*Ama—do mio*, love me for ever!" The head nurse was nowhere to be seen, and Mrs. Moscowitz, who didn't want to go back to her room, turned her walker in the direction of the exit. From the moment her decision was made, she felt that a new strength was making it easier for her to walk.

She passed the entrance to the ward and when she reached the tele-phone corner she went up to the canteen, bought a number of telephone tokens, a can of apple juice and a packet of lemon-flavored wafers, sat down at the round table across from the telephones and ate and drank to her heart's content. Then she stood up and contin-ued along the corridor until she reached the big visitors' lounge, passed it and turned right, to the games' room. At a few of the tables patients were sitting and playing various games, and at the table near-est the door sat the chess-player from the kibbutz, no longer in a wheelchair—there was a walker standing next to her. Her close-cropped head jerked from side to side on her square shoulders, and smoke from the cigarette stuck in the corner of her mouth rose into her face. Opposite her sat a thin, gray-haired man with thick spectacles, who bent his face toward the table to see the chess pieces and their positions on the board.

Mrs. Moscowitz went into the clubroom, passed between the tables, studied the faces of the players, and couldn't make up her mind where to sit. There was a comfortable silence in the room. The only sound was the clatter of the dice, snatches of laughter and occasional comments from the players. The late morning light coming in at the windows lent the players an air of confidence and relaxation. In an armchair in the corner sat a woman in a nurse's gown, who looked like a volunteer, reading a newspaper. Mrs. Moscowitz directed her walker toward a table where two men and a woman who looked less old and more cheerful than the others were sitting. She had scarcely asked their permission to join them before the volunteer came hurrying up, asked her name, introduced her to the people sitting at the table, who introduced themselves as well, helped her to sit down, explained the rules of the game of dominoes to her, and asked her to wait for the next round and watch the others in the meantime. She thus had an opportunity to examine them thoroughly. At close quarters they looked older and less cheerful than they had from the door, but they spoke Hebrew with the fluency of native speakers and behaved in every respect like people from the normal world. Her heart contracted inside her: the words "people from the normal world" suddenly echoed in her ears and woke from their slumbers moments of wounded feelings and longings that she tried to banish from her mind.

The game concluded in a victory for Batya, the woman in the wig sitting opposite her. Batya smiled with satisfaction and looked around her proudly. One of the men shuffled the black counters and dealt them out to the four players. Mrs. Moscowitz followed the example of the others and set the dominoes up in front of her, but when Batya said: "Your turn, Yolanda," she became confused and forgot what she was supposed to do. Instead of examining her counters to see how many dots they had on them, she had been looking around at the players and congratulating herself on being one of them, normal like them. The happiness of participating in their game prevented her from concentrating on the game itself.

Yosef, one of the two men sitting next to her, leaned toward her and looked at her dominoes. "Here, you've got it," he said, and he took one of her dominoes and placed it on the table next to the pieces that had been played by the others. "Do you understand?" asked Yosef. Mrs. Moscowitz nodded her head. This friendly intimacy was highly agreeable to her. They continued the game until David, the other man at the table, looked at his watch and asked them to stop for a minute. "The news," he said and took a small transistor radio from his wheelchair, set it on the table, and switched it on. They listened to the news, and other people at the nearby tables, as well as the volunteer, pricked up their ears and listened too.

Mrs. Moscowitz took the opportunity of the break in the game to study her fellow players some more. David, a short, broad man with a swarthy, Eastern complexion, who still had a lot of black threads left in his curly hair and his moustache, was in her opinion the handsomer of the two. He rested his cheek on his hand, his elbow propped on the table. His dark eyes still preserved a flicker of vitality. He had broad, thick-fingered hands, like a worker's. Yosef, taller and thinner, was bald, with sparse white hair fringing his temples and the back of his neck. He was older than David, his eyes were small and bleary and as he listened to the news he closed them. His hands were white and delicate, with big, dark spots on them. His fingers were long and slender, almost transparent. Batya was a small woman with a lively, optimistic expression, who wore, for religious or other reasons, a wig. When the news was over, David switched off the radio and returned it to his wheelchair.

"Your turn, Yolanda," said David.

In the corridor of the women's wing sat Frieda, an expression of ostentatious sadness on her face. When she saw Mrs. Moscowitz, she called out to her, a note of stern moral rebuke in her masculine voice: "Where have you been? Don't you know what happened? Clara's dead!"

"Clara?" asked Mrs. Moscowitz in astonishment.

"My daughter phoned me, she heard it from Clara's daughter!" rasped Frieda, proud and jealous of her unique position as the source of information.

"I forgot about Clara," said Mrs. Moscowitz, without sorrow, "I forgot her completely."

"You forgot?" Frieda was silenced, flabbergasted, but soon returned to the attack. Her voice rasped again, emphatic and threatening: "She died yesterday! In the institution! She stopped eating! They took her to the hospital! They fed her by force, with a tube! They sent her back to the institution! And she wouldn't touch her food again! They couldn't make her! She wouldn't get out of bed! She didn't want to live . . . "

Dr. Chen walked down the corridor and paused at the nurses' station. Mrs. Moscowitz hurried to him while Frieda was still talking to her.

"Good morning, Doctor, excuse me please," she said to him.

"Yes, Yolanda, what do you want?"

"To go home, I want to go home," she said quickly. Out of the corner of her eye she caught Frieda's wrathful look as she wheeled herself closer to listen to her conversation with the doctor.

"Certainly!" he said. "It really is time."

"When?" asked Mrs. Moscowitz.

"You're in such a hurry to leave us?"

"I must to return to the normal world."

"You're right," said the doctor. "I'm glad you've changed your mind. I remember you were afraid to go home."

"I feel better. I walk a lot, to have strength in the legs."

"We'll give you another examination, and if everything's all right, you might go home before the end of the week."

"Also I want to go home!" cried Frieda, who had returned to her place by the wall. "You don't know that I want to go home? Why don't you let me go too? When comes my turn?"

The doctor didn't answer Frieda, and when Mrs. Moscowitz thanked him and turned back to their room, she cried: "Maybe also I'll stop eating until I die!"

Allegra was sitting on her bed in her big gray dressing gown. "Did you hear what happened?" she asked. "Poor Clara."

"I know."

"I feel all right now," said Allegra. "I did the laundry. You didn't have much." And she pointed to the porch, where the laundry was hanging out to dry.

"No need," said Mrs. Moscowitz, "in a few days' time I'm going home."

She undid the bag hanging on the walker, took out her purse and went over to Allegra's locker in order to put some money on it. Allegra closed her eyes and waved her open hand in a gesture of protest and adamant refusal. Mrs. Moscowitz put her purse back in the bag and tied it to the walker. There was a prolonged silence, which Allegra broke by saying:

"Forgive me that you had to see me like that."

"At home I'll forget everything."

"Once you said that you'd never forget me as long as you live," said Allegra in astonishment.

"I have to forget. Otherwise I won't have the strength to go on living."

"Once you said that we would both live together in your house, that we would help one another like sisters," said Allegra, and her hoarse, weak, monotonous voice was innocent of reproach or any other feeling, as if she was reminiscing to herself. "You stayed here so long, that my time's over. Once you said that you wanted to be by my side when the last moment comes, that you would hold my hand, that I wouldn't be alone in the room with it."

"That isn't going to work out," said Mrs. Moscowitz.

"Once you loved me. And now you don't any more. But that's the way it should be. I'm not alive any more. You have to forget the dead. You're right. You don't owe me anything. I'm not complaining: you were good to me, much more than I deserve."

"I have to be strong," said Mrs. Moscowitz. "You've got Adela. I've got nobody. I have to look after myself."

She went over to the wall closet, opened one of the doors, inspected the summer and winter clothes hanging on the hangers, the underwear folded on the shelf, and wondered how she was going to take home all the possessions that had accumulated over the many months of her stay. Some of the things had been bought for her by one of the nurses, some by Leon, and she had rewarded them with tips and by pretending to trust them; sometimes they forgot to bring her a receipt, sometimes the receipts looked suspicious. She had no doubt that they were in cahoots with the merchants to cheat her, but she knew that she had to keep quiet and resign herself. This time too she would need Leon's help, and she would ask him to buy her a suitcase.

At lunch she sat at an empty table, not far from the table where Frieda and Allegra were sitting. From time to time she caught them looking at her. Frieda talked and Allegra listened to her with a weary expression. It was easy to guess that Frieda was running her down, to make Allegra hate her. But all this belonged to the past. All her thoughts were now devoted to anticipating the salvation of forgetfulness. Even the usual tastelessness of the food now served to remind her of her remoteness from this place, of the impending moment when she would set out on her journey of return to herself.

She pushed her tray aside and gazed toward the glass wall overlooking the hospital entrance. From where she was sitting she could see only the tops of the pine trees on the steep hill next to the road leading into the hospital. The midday sun glared in her eyes, some of the big sliding windows had been opened and a light breeze blew from the pine grove, passed through the dining room and caressed her face. Paula shuffled along the aisle between the tables on her walker, her chin hanging on her neck, her lips moving ceaselessly and her voice inaudible. Every few steps she stopped, raised her head with its stringy gray hair pulled behind her ears, her eyes narrowed behind the thick lenses of her glasses, her face severe, and scanned the hall, looking for her lost place. Mrs. Moscowitz looked at her and called her wordlessly to come and sit at her table. Paula immediately obeyed the summons, aimed the walker in her direction and sat down opposite her. "That's my food," she said at once and drew Mrs. Moscowitz's tray toward her, picked up the spoon and began to eat.

Mrs. Moscowitz watched her. Slowly Paula raised the spoon of cold soup to her mouth, blew on it, pursing her lips, swallowed silently, and then repeated the performance, taking care to wipe her mouth on her sleeve after every spoonful. After that she dug into the boiled vegetables and the remains of the chicken.

The waitress said to Mrs. Moscowitz: "What are you giving her your food for? She's already eaten three lunches today."

"Let her enjoy herself," said Mrs. Moscowitz, "I can't eat it."

"You'll cook yourself better food at home," said the waitress.

"It's my food," said Paula.

"Where's your father?" asked Mrs. Moscowitz. "When will he come?"

"Do I know you?" asked Paula suspiciously.

"Always you say: He'll come, he'll come, and he doesn't come."

Paula laid her knife and fork down on the tray and looked at her. Through the thick lenses of her glasses her eyes looked like two dead fish. Her lips tightened over her false teeth, dislodged them and returned them to their place, but not before she had run her tongue over them to get rid of the crumbs of food.

"I don't remember anything. Not the day, not the hour and not the date," said Paula.

"Your father will never come."

"Excuse me, Madame, you look like a very nice woman," said Paula. "Do I know you?" And she stood up to leave the table.

Mrs. Moscowitz said to her: "Sit!"

The sound of Frieda's manly laughter rose from her friends' table. Mrs. Moscowitz glanced in their direction and saw that they were watching her.

"What will your father do here when he comes? Tell me!"

Paula stared at her in silence.

"You don't know?" asked Mrs. Moscowitz.

Paula smiled and made an effort to focus her eyes on her. Her lips parted to say something, but she immediately regretted it, looked around, leaned over the table, put her head close to Mrs. Moscowitz and whispered confidentially: "Once I was a human being." And she shook her head nervously. Then she put her hand over her thick glasses and bowed her head.

"They'll die?" asked Mrs. Moscowitz. "Everyone will die?"

Paula looked at her and the two dead fish behind her thick spectacle lenses began to move as if they were floating on light, invisible waves.

"They'll die like dogs?" asked Mrs. Moscowitz.

"I'm tired now. I'm in a hurry. I have to go. By the way, what's the time?"

"Your father won't come," said Mrs. Moscowitz. "You haven't got one. He can't be alive when you're so old. Your father's dead a long time ago."

"Do you know me?"

Paula got up, gripped her walker, shuffled into the aisle between the tables, looked around, and went to sit at an unoccupied table. The dining room was already almost empty. Paula banged on the table and shouted at the top of her voice: "Will someone bring me food at last?"

—

When Mrs. Moscowitz entered the room, she saw Allegra coming in from the porch with the basin of dry washing. She went over to the wall closet, and setting the basin down on the floor, opened Mrs. Moscowitz's door, folding each item and putting it away on the shelf. The dressing gown she hung on a hanger. Again and again Allegra bent over the basin and straightened up again, and to the observer she looked as if she were praying to some domestic god that had revealed itself to her in the closet. Then she took the empty basin to return it to its place in the bathroom. When she came back and got into bed for the afternoon rest, Mrs. Moscowitz said to her: "Thank you very much. You don't need to do any more."

She took her purse out of her bag, looked through the bank notes and came to the conclusion that she didn't have enough for her preparations to return home. She would have to ask Leon or one of the nurses to cash a check for her at the bank in the village and take something for their trouble. This is what she always had done during her long stay in the hospital. She put the bag under her pillow and lay down to rest. But all her thoughts were now concentrated on preparing to leave the hospital, on the shopping and chores she would have to do when she went back to live alone in her apartment. Afraid that she might forget something, she sat up once more, took a notebook and a pen out of the drawer of her locker, and began to write a list of the tasks ahead. When she raised her eyes from the notebook she saw that Allegra was looking at her. Their eyes met and Allegra closed hers, averting her face on the pillow, and turning her narrow, almost bald cranium toward Mrs. Moscowitz. But Allegra's look, which had touched her for the fraction of a second, clung to her and would not let her be; it knocked on her walls, peeped through the cracks, stole in like a thief, a look that held the shadow of a smile, of resignation or gratuitous compassion, like the look of those who have given up all hope of love.

Mrs. Moscowitz could not bear this look and she got up and went out onto the balcony. There were no chairs there, so she stood next to the balustrade, closed her eyes and let them gradually grow accustomed to the blinding light. The broad lawns with the hedges and the slender poplar trees rising from them at regular intervals came slowly into view. Beyond these was a landscape of low hills, with a water tower and little houses huddled at its feet, and patches of citrus groves and stripes of roads and rows of trees and plots of bare land, glittering like metal, as far as the last mountain range on the horizon, dissolving and disappearing into the haze. There was nobody to be seen in all this expanse, no movement disturbed its rest. The noise of traffic on the main road, a distant, monotonous hum, erupted occasionally in the splutter of a grumbling engine, and subsided again. She brought her eyes back to the garden. Something was stirring there underneath the skin of the slumbering afternoon, in the invisible shivering of the grass, in the dancing of the light on the leaves, in the hot, transparent, shimmering vapors rising from the ground.

"Yolanda," she heard Leon's voice behind her shoulder. Her heart missed a beat, and when she recovered she felt ashamed of the way she was standing there, as if she wanted to jump and had been caught red-handed.

"Why do you do that," she said breathlessly, "come up so quiet from behind the back and give someone a fright? You could give a person a heart attack."

He laughed, pleased with his trick. "Why aren't you resting?"

"In a few more days I'm going home."

"I know."

"I need you."

"Wait, I'll fetch a chair."

He went into the room and returned with two chairs hanging from his thick, strong hairy arms. They sat down facing the railing.

"I'll miss seeing you here," said Leon, "because for me you're something special, not like the other patients."

"I need a suitcase to take all my things and money from the bank also. I'll give you a check."

"And you won't miss me, you won't feel homesick for Leon?"

"When can you go for me? It's urgent."

"Tomorrow morning. Okay? What size suitcase?"

She showed him the size she needed with her hands, and he took one of them and held it. She liked feeling his fingers damp with sweat closing on her hand, the warmth of his face close to hers, his familiar, particular smell. His whole bearish body exuded health and strength.

"You're a handsome fellow," she said, "but you're so fat. Why don't you make a diet?"

"Plenty of women like me the way I am," said Leon. "Why should I change? I'm happy like I am."

He let go of her hand, rose from the chair, stood behind her, put his hand on the nape of her neck and began stroking her and massaging her shoulders. The touch of his hand sent a shiver through her body, and she didn't know if it was of pleasure or of fear. "What can I do? I like mature women," whispered Leon very close to her face. His breath, warm and intoxicating, filled her ear, slid over her cheek and neck down to her shoulder and chest. "And they like me. Because I know how to make a woman feel good. If she's good to me, she gets something good back from me. I know how to make her feel young and beautiful and desirable."

"Leon, stop it," said Mrs. Moscowitz. "You're making fun again. Please to behave."

"I'm not joking," whispered Leon. "I'm making you a proposition. I'll come to your house, if you want. I'll come once, and you'll see what I mean."

"I'm ashamed for you," said Mrs. Moscowitz, "for you and for me."

"Don't you deserve to be happy, to feel young?" whispered Leon, and he sat down next to her again. This time he didn't look as if he were suppressing laughter. He sounded completely serious. "What's there to be ashamed of?" he said. "It's normal. Don't you love me?"

"Yes," said Mrs. Moscowitz softly and shuddered at the sound of her voice, "I love you."

"You won't be sorry." He stood up. "Give me the check and I'll get you everything you need."

Mrs. Moscowitz looked at her walker and gasped: the bag that she took with her wherever she went was not hanging in its usual place. She had forgotten it underneath her pillow, abandoned it there for all this time. And again she felt the strange calm of certain knowledge waiting for the moment of its manifestation in reality. Detached from what was happening around her, as if half asleep, she felt that she was nothing but a plaything in the hands of distant forces and this passivity filled her with confidence and strength. She rose from her chair and Leon followed her into the room. Allegra was sitting on the edge of her bed and when she saw her she avoided her eyes with a look of pain and anxiety on her face. Mrs. Moscowitz sat on the edge of her bed, pulled the bag out from under her pillow, and took out her checkbook. She wrote a check, her hand trembling with anger and anticipation, and gave it to Leon. He glanced at it, put it in his wallet, put the wallet into his back trouser pocket, and went out.

Mrs. Moscowitz immediately emptied her purse, spread the notes out on her bed and counted them. Then she raised her eyes from the money lying on the bed to Allegra's face, and gave her a reproachful look. Allegra looked back at her and nodded her head, as if she were reading her thoughts.

"There's a fifty missing," said Mrs. Moscowitz softly, as if speaking to herself, or to her money.

Allegra's little eyes narrowed, and she stared at her appraisingly, as if wondering how far she would go.

"I wanted to give it to you and you refused. Now it's missing," she said to Allegra and pointed to the incriminating evidence lying on the bed. She put her money back in the purse, tied the bag to the walker, took her toilet bag and went to the bathroom.

After a long time she emerged with her hair combed, perfumed and heavily made-up. She paused at the wall closet, removed the green dress, stained because of Allegra, from its hanger, and standing next to her bed changed into it. One of the nurses came into the room, went up to Frieda's bed and helped her into her wheelchair. As she was turning toward another patient, the nurse's eye fell on Mrs. Moscowitz, splendid in her gleaming green dress, her face alarming in its heavy makeup. "Yolanda!" she cried and a laugh of surprise escaped her lips.

"What's so funny?" inquired Mrs. Moscowitz.

"It's not funny, it's enough to scare a person to death to look at you!" cried Matilda Franco.

"I wasn't talking to you," said Mrs. Moscowitz. "It's underneath my dignity to talk to you."

"Some dignity!" Matilda Franco laughed bitterly. "Walking around all dressed up with her face painted like an old whore from the time of Abdul Hameed!"

Mrs. Moscowitz fixed her with her eyes and muttered something under her breath.

"Now she's cursing me, damn her!" said Matilda Franco. "You see? You're all my witnesses that she's cursing me, the old witch. May all her curses be on her own head, please God, amen!"

The nurse said: "That's enough now. Quiet. Stop cursing."

"Don't take any notice, Yolanda," whispered Allegra, who had not yet despaired of regaining the favor of bygone days, in her hoarse, monotonous voice. "It suits you, really. Everyone can see how young and beautiful you look."

Mrs. Moscowitz went out into the corridor. A woman's scream of pain rose from one of the rooms, repeated over and over with animal obstinacy. None of the nurses got up to go to the screaming woman. Mrs. Moscowitz was seized with anger at the sound of this scream trying to undermine her walls. She longed to be alone, to hear silence, to be absorbed by the empty stillness.

"Oho!" a hated voice jarred on her ears and her body recoiled. "How glamorous you look, Yolanda! Are you going to look for men?" asked the head nurse behind her shoulder, examining her from top to toe and smiling in malicious enjoyment.

She knew that she now looked almost like her neighbor, the crazy Mrs. Poldy, and she didn't care—she only knew that she had to be different from all the others, because she still had her strength, and the creatures around her, both patients and nurses, were nothing but shadows trying to draw her in so that she would disintegrate with them. She left the ward, and her legs, ready for any effort, stepped behind the walker and led her as if of their own accord to the canteen. The woman behind the counter had already cleared away the cardboard boxes prior to closing the shutter. At the sight of Mrs. Moscowitz's new face she grunted something, asked her what she wanted, placed the can of apple juice and the package of lemon-flavored wafers on the counter and took the money, looking at her out of the corner of her eye with suspicion and vindictive enjoyment. Mrs. Moscowitz sat down at the round table next to the public telephones. Before she opened the can of juice and the package of wafers, she caught sight of a man in a wheelchair squeezed into the last telephone booth in the row. All she could see of him were his hunched, pajama-clad shoulders and a bit of the nape of his neck. His abundant, combed-back white hair reached his pajama collar. Her heart stopped beating, as if paralyzed by the shock of the surprise. Pain and longing engulfed her. She craned her head as far as she could to try to see even a little of his face, but the side of his cheek was hidden by the telephone receiver. She saw the back of his hand holding the telephone, but the tips of his fingers and his nails were hidden from her. He spoke in a whisper. She couldn't even hear what language he was speaking, but the possibility that it was Kagan put every other thought out of her mind.

She felt as if something hitherto experienced only in dreams was happening to her: something similar to those encounters with a loved one who has died many years ago, met at an unexpected time and place, in perfectly ordinary circumstances. Like a cheat caught out, he excuses himself on the grounds that he never died at all, and was reported to be dead by mistake—but the chill of his reserve, his undisguised annoyance at the chance meeting, his pressing need to get somewhere for some urgent reason he refuses to reveal, his avoidance of any promise to stay in touch, of any explicit agreement to meet again, even if only one more time, the shadow of anxiety clouding his face, his shifty looks, his indifferent expression, the fog of vagueness surrounding his words; all these things make it evident that he is no longer himself and can no longer do as he wishes, as if he were subject to some secret power which has left nothing of his old self in him, but only preserved his old shape, like a shell, as a barrier against the hand of time, a disguise to cover up his treachery.

She hadn't touched the apple juice and the wafers on the table in front of her, so intently was she watching the figure squeezed into the telephone booth. And the man apparently sensed her eyes on him, for suddenly he turned his head and faced her.

Often the dead reveal themselves to their loved ones not in a dream, but in the shape of a passerby in the street, a stranger momentarily clad in their form. Here is his face, here his stature, his gait, all of him stands before you. And even if this is not the first time you have experienced the mirage whose end is known, and always the same, your heart is drawn again and again to the horizon of the dream, it can't resist the force compelling it to try another angle of vision, to hurry to the place and the moment, not to miss the split second of the disappearance, when the stranger parts from the host and vanishes like a spy into the crowd.

The man's long, narrow face, with its thick, wild black eyebrows, its narrow lips and pointed chin, looked at her in surprise. A little skullcap, crocheted from brown and yellow thread, was fastened to his hair with a lady's hairpin, and his ears were enormous. He turned his face aside again, leaned forward into the telephone booth, so that even the back of his neck with the long straight hair falling over it was no longer visible.

Lazar couldn't possibly be dead! her heart told her. From the bag hanging on her walker she took out her notebook, removed a few telephone tokens from her purse, and went up to the booth nearest the table. She turned the pages of the notebook until she found the number he had dictated to her when they last spoke, picked up the receiver, inserted a couple of tokens into the slot, dialed the number and waited. After the last click of the dial the earphone was silent— not an empty mechanical silence but a tense, mute stillness, as if the distance were holding its breath. She called: Hallo! Hallo! and there was no reply. Her heart told her that somebody was listening to her there and refusing to answer. In the end she gave up and dialed again. This time, the signal rang with a clear, definite sound in her ears and a sudden fear fell on her: perhaps something had really happened to him. On the other end of the line somebody picked up the receiver and a woman's voice, one she well remembered, called: "Hallo!" Mrs. Moscowitz covered the mouthpiece with her hand and waited. The woman raised her voice and called: "Hallo! Hello? Lazar? Lazar!" and added a few words in their language. Mrs. Moscowitz slowly replaced the receiver. The man in the wheelchair was still whispering into the telephone in the last booth.

She returned to the round table, picked up the can of juice and the package of wafers and ate and drank with relish. The chilliness of the tart-tasting drink was agreeable to her throat, dry from excitement. He wasn't yet at home. So his recovery had not been as swift as he anticipated. Why did this please her no less than the knowledge that he wasn't dead? She nibbled a few of the wafers and when she was satisfied, she put the package away in the bag hanging on her walker and finished off the apple juice.

The man in the last booth sighed. He replaced the receiver, wheeled his chair backward out of the telephone booth and moved toward her. Although there was enough space for him to pass by between Mrs. Moscowitz's chair and the row of telephones, he stopped his chair in front of her and presented her with a full view of his ugly face. She couldn't bear the sight of him. Immediately, she stood up and directed her walker out of the telephone corner, turned left and continued to the visitors' lounge. He followed on her heels. Next to the entrance to the lounge she turned her head and saw him stop not far behind her. He took a comb out of his pajama pocket, and removing his skullcap with its hairpin, he ran the comb through his hair, from his brow to the nape of his neck. After replacing the skullcap and putting the comb back in his pocket, he smiled at her with his narrow lips.

At the back of the visitors' hall Peretz Kabiri was brandishing his crutch and repeating snatches of his muddled memoirs in a loud voice to a handful of patients and visitors. He roundly abused the enemies of Israel and began to sing "*Amado mio*." The ugly man came closer to her and whispered something. She ignored him, turned right and proceeded to the games' room. From the door she saw that the group from the morning wasn't there, only Yosef was sitting and playing cards by himself. She went up to him, and he looked up at her in astonishment:

"Ha! Shalom!" he called. And after a brief pause he added: "You're so dolled up!"

The man in the wheelchair entered the room too, and approached their table.

"I can sit down?"

"Of course."

"You're playing alone," she said, in a tone that conveyed a mixture of surprise and disapproval.

"Patience," whispered the ugly man in a barely audible voice.

"Where is everybody?" asked Mrs. Moscowitz.

Yosef shrugged his shoulders. His thin, almost transparent fingers took a card from the top of the pack, and his eyes scanned the cards laid out in rows in front of him.

"In Europe," said Mrs. Moscowitz, "there are women who know how to tell somebody's whole life from the cards. You believe such things?"

Yosef smiled at the card in his hand without answering. Out of the corner of her eye Mrs. Moscowitz saw the chess-player from the kibbutz sitting alone in her regular place next to the door, the cigarette smoke rising from the ashtray into her face. She was staring at Mrs. Moscowitz and clapping her hands and laughing.

"Nonsense!" snorted the ugly man. "Nonsense!"

"I believe," said Mrs. Moscowitz. "And also curses and the evil eye I believe. I saw it myself from my own life."

Yosef raised his bleary eyes from the cards and examined her: "You certainly look different today. I didn't recognize you at first."

"Purim," whispered the ugly man.

"Amanda?" asked Yosef.

"Yolanda," said Mrs. Moscowitz.

"Right," said Yosef. "Do you know each other?" he asked. "Yolanda—Wolf."

She and the ugly man nodded at each other. Wolf's thin lips smiled at her. He knitted his wild, black brows and whispered: "Excuse me for talking like this. My voice is gone."

"In a few days I'm going home," said Mrs. Moscowitz to Yosef. "I'm sick and tired already from being here."

The ugly man laughed softly.

"I have to go home," said Mrs. Moscowitz.

"Forgive me for saying so," said Yosef apologetically, "but it really is too much." He patted his face to explain his meaning.

"It makes me feel good," said Mrs. Moscowitz. "I do it for myself, not for somebody else."

The ugly man laughed soundlessly again.

Mrs. Moscowitz said: "Today a woman who's going to die stole from my purse fifty shekels. For what does a person who's going to die need money?"

"To put in his shroud," whispered the ugly man.

Yosef gathered the cards laid out in front of him into a pile and shuffled them rapidly.

"And I always helped her," said Mrs. Moscowitz. "I gave her everything what she needed, I was so pitying the poor woman, I really loved her. Now she steals."

"Do you know how to play rummy?" asked Yosef.

"Once I knew. Now I forget. Just tell me how, and I can play immediately."

He explained the rules of the game to her.

"Your friends that were here this morning, why didn't they come now?" asked Mrs. Moscowitz.

Yosef examined the cards fanned out in his hand, moved one of them to another place, frowned, moved another one, and in the end took one out and put it down face-up on the table. Then he looked at her with his expressionless eyes, over the reading glasses halfway down his nose: "I don't know," he replied, and paused. "I don't know them," he said in the end. The ugly man took a card from the pack.

"I thought you were always playing together," said Mrs. Moscowitz.

"Your turn, Yolanda," said Yosef.

"He knows me," whispered the ugly man. "We're in the same room, our beds are next to each other."

"Why does he talk like that?" Mrs. Moscowitz asked Yosef.

"Surgery," whispered the ugly man and ran his finger over his throat.

In her eagerness to win she fumbled over arranging her hand and fanning it out. She took a card from the pack and her fingers put it immediately and automatically in the right place in her hand. A shiver of fear and delight ran through her. Her heart pounded, as if she were gambling for her life. She felt that her hands were obeying orders from above and that she didn't understand what she was doing. She looked at the two men, whose eyes were fixed on their cards, and had no doubt that she would beat them. With trembling fingers she picked up the cards they discarded and replaced them with cards of her own. After a while she displayed her hand, and they stared at the cards in amazement. The ugly man laughed his hollow, gasping laugh and his eyes scrutinized her from underneath his wild, dark brows, as if he suspected her of cheating. Yosef also displayed his cards to show them that he was missing only one card to complete his hand. Then he gathered up the cards, and shuffled them in all kinds of different ways, with astonishing dexterity. He suggested they play another round. But Mrs. Moscowitz was content with her victory and her renewed faith in her powers. She shook her head. A pleasant tiredness descended on her. She would gladly have gone on sitting there and resting for a while, but she could no longer endure the sight of the ugly man and the way he never took his eyes off her. She looked at her watch and rose to her feet.

"It's already late, " she said, "soon it's supper."

Yosef went on shuffling the cards.

When she left the games' room she noticed that the ugly man was following her in his wheelchair. Not far from the telephone booths she stole a look back and he was still following her. She stopped and waited for him to catch up with her.

"Why are you following me?" she asked.

His lips mumbled something.

"I can't hear. I can't hear what you speak."

He pointed to his throat and spread out his hands to indicate that he was unable to raise his voice. She bent toward him on the walker.

"What do you want?" she asked sharply.

"I've never seen anything like it before," he whispered.

"What you have never seen?"

"A woman so . . . a face with all that powder and paint. It makes my heart beat to see it."

"You should be ashamed, a man with a yarmulke. You're not afraid from God?"

"I've been a widower for seventeen years," said the ugly man, "seventeen years alone."

"So why are you following me?"

"Maybe we can sit together for a while, talk. There's nothing wrong with talking, is there?"

She straightened up and turned her back on him, took a few steps and turned her head again. He was still following her.

"How do you think you look like?" she asked him. "Tell me."

"They say that any man, as long as he isn't a monkey, is good-looking enough," he whispered.

"Thanks for the compliment," said Mrs. Moscowitz.

He laughed voicelessly and his face lit up. Perhaps he interpreted her sarcasm as deliberate provocation, and his confidence grew: "I bet you had a lot of men in your life."

"And you, how many women you had? Also a lot?"

"Only one," his face grew grave. "Only one my whole life. And now, for seventeen years already, alone, always alone."

"I don't believe in God. I do what I want. You're not afraid?"

His thick black brows knitted, and his long, narrow, sharp-chinned face looked at her curiously.

"You didn't see how I won at the cards? I don't know this game. Never before have I played cards. For the first time in my life."

"I don't care," whispered the ugly man, pulled the hairpin out of his hair, took off the skullcap and put it in his pajama pocket. "There," he smiled, "you see? I'm not afraid."

"Please to leave me alone," said Mrs. Moscowitz firmly and politely. "Stop following me. I can't look at you."

He took the comb out of his pocket and ran it through his hair several times, from his brow to the nape of his neck.

"In any case in a few days I'm going home," she added.

"So am I," said the ugly man. "Where do you live?"

She did not reply.

"How old do you think I am?" he asked.

"I'm not interested."

"Less than it looks." He parted his lips with his thumb and finger, "All mine," he whispered, "no bridges, not one false tooth. All mine. Have a look."

"You don't know me, maybe I've got a husband. How can you talk to me like that?"

He shook his head from side to side. "A married woman doesn't walk around like that," he whispered.

"I'm not alone," said Mrs. Moscowitz. "I've got somebody. Please to leave me alone now."

In the ward corridor the patients sat along the wall, looking at the children's program on television. Two nurses standing behind the counter giggled loudly behind her back. Frieda gave her a wrathful look as she passed, and growled something in Allegra's ear, who was sitting next to her with her hands around her empty red cup. Mrs. Moscowitz went into the bathroom and stood in front of the mirror to examine her face. Sweat had spoiled the makeup in a number of places, and she went into the room and fetched her toilet bag. Looking in the bathroom mirror she wiped off the makeup melted by sweat with a tissue, dusted her face with a heavy layer of powder, renewed the eyeshadow on her eyelids, blackened the arches of her eyebrows and the tips of the lashes peeping out of the folds of flesh, brushed orange-pink rouge onto her cheeks, and smeared her lips with blazing red. Then she fixed her hair, splashed cologne onto her palms, applied it to the back of her ears and her neck, rubbed her hands together and raised them to her nose to breathe in the scent. Finally she examined her reflection again and smiled in satisfaction.

chapter nine

The next morning, when Mrs. Moscowitz woke up, Allegra's bed was stained with blood again. The memory of her new identity flashed through her mind and instantly curbed the old impulse to get up and go to the sick woman. She saw her lying and crying quietly, and she knew that she was crying not only from pain but also from shame. Mrs. Moscowitz pulled her bag out from under her pillow, tied it to her walker and went to the bathroom. On her way she took care not to tread on the bloodstains blackening on the floor between Allegra's bed and the bathroom, and also not to put the legs of the walker on them.

When she returned to the room the head nurse was already standing next to Allegra's bed. She said: "Is Adela coming today? We have to talk to her. We'll have to see what to do about you. I'm very sorry. We can't have this every night. This isn't the place for you. You need somewhere suitable."

"It's a pity it wasn't all over long ago," said Allegra in her permanently hoarse voice. "When they took me over there. It would have been better to get it over. What do I need this for?"

Rosa instructed one of the nurses to fetch a clean nightgown and clean sheets for Allegra and to wash the bloodstains from the floor.

"You're going for an examination at R. Hospital today," said the head nurse to Mrs. Moscowitz. "I'll tell you when it's time for them to take you."

"When am I going home?"

"If the tests are okay, you're going tomorrow," said Rosa. "You've been here over nine months. Isn't it enough for you?"

"I want to go too."

"Congratulations!" said Rosa. "And do me a favor and don't go to the examination the way you were walking round here yesterday with all that stuff on your face, like some ... I don't want to say what."

"Like an old whore," said Matilda Franco.

"Thank you very much for your help," said Rosa.

Mrs. Moscowitz wanted to curse Rosa and Matilda Franco, but she could not find the necessary passion to empower the words. Glumly she put on her dressing gown and went to the dining room, where she sat down at one of the empty tables. She began to suspect that money had been stolen from her purse again, and she undid the bag on the walker, opened her purse, and counted her money. All her calculations led to the conclusion that twenty shekels were missing. The bag with the purse inside it had been under her pillow all night, even when she got out of bed to go to the bathroom she had taken it with her. So how had Allegra succeeding in getting to it? Mrs. Moscowitz did not exert herself to find a solution—the discovery itself was enough for her. It alerted her mind, filled her with energy, gave her back her feeling of power.

Leon brought the suitcase that he had bought for her and counted the money he had taken out of the bank. She rewarded him handsomely for his trouble and didn't even glance at the receipt. He looked at the money she put in his hand, smiled, put it into his pocket, and said as usual: "You know I don't do it for the money. Because for me you're something special."

"I know," said Mrs. Moscowitz, "I believe you. You're something special for me too, Leon."

The presence of the other patients in the room did not deter her from putting out her hand and stroking his sweaty cheek. At the touch of her hand he closed his eyes and stood still, and she felt that the moist warmth sticking to her hand transmitted something of his strength and vitality to her.

"It's a pity you didn't work yesterday evening," she took her hand from his face. "You didn't see me how I did my face," said Mrs. Moscowitz, "everybody was annoyed from it."

Leon laughed: "Why did you do it?"

"So they should know I'm not afraid from anything."

Allegra sat up slowly in bed, tried to stand, and was defeated by pain. For a moment she sat with her face in her hands and then she tried to get up again. A moan of pain escaped her as she stood on her feet at last, bent over, her legs wide apart and her hands supporting her hips. Leon went up and asked her what the matter was.

"I need to make pee-pee," groaned Allegra.

"Lie down, I'll bring you a bedpan," offered Leon.

"No," said Allegra, "I don't want."

She raised the hem of her gown to her knees and began hobbling to the bathroom.

Leon watched Allegra as she took a small step, stopped, examined the floor behind her, and took another step, and when she was out of hearing he whispered: "This isn't the right place for her."

"She bleeds down there a lot after she goes. And now her blood will be all over the floor again," said Mrs. Moscowitz, "I can't stand to see it."

Allegra went into the bathroom.

"Tell me: what does she want to live for like this?" continued Mrs. Moscowitz. "Wouldn't it be better for her if she died long ago?"

"What happened? You used to love her so much. You were always together and she did all kinds of things for you."

"I thought she was good, that she loved me. Now she steals from me money. Even in the night, when I'm sleeping with my purse under the pillow, she steals."

Leon frowned and said: "I don't believe it."

"Yes. It's true. Why does she take it? A person who's going to die, for what she needs money?"

"You thought I stole from you too," said Leon. "You think I don't know? We're the same kind, I know all your thoughts. I can read them like a newspaper."

Mrs. Moscowitz was silent.

"I'm going with you to the examination," said Leon. "Are you pleased?"

"Of course I'm pleased. You fixed it for me."

"No. I didn't even know about it. Rosa just told me now."

"Rosa?" said Mrs. Moscowitz in surprise. "What, she didn't know I'll be pleased from it? Always she only does bad to me."

"Why do you say that? It's not true. Rosa's okay."

"Once I was calling her 'Satana.' Now I think it's a compliment for her."

He laughed. "If you like," he said, "I'll help you to pack your case."

Rosa called Leon to say that the taxi to take them to R. Hospital had been ordered. Mrs. Moscowitz went to the bathroom to fix her face, but Allegra had locked herself in there, and judging by the noise of the water she was washing away her blood. Mrs. Moscowitz was obliged to content herself with the little mirror of her powder compact. Leon went to fetch the wheelchair.

Rosa came into the room and saw her smearing the cream on her face.

"I told you not to paint your face like yesterday when you go for the examination!" she scolded her. "This is a hospital, not a brothel!"

"It's only face cream, just a little face cream," said Mrs. Moscowitz calmly and smiled sweetly. "Don't worry." And she muttered something under her breath.

"You think you can frighten me with your curses too?" said Rosa. "Not me! You can curse as much as you like. Satana isn't afraid of curses!"

When Leon returned Mrs. Moscowitz sat down in the wheelchair and he wheeled her rapidly along the hospital corridors and down the ramps next to the stairs. They emerged from a side entrance. She found herself in the little garden with the white chairs and tables and the furled umbrellas. When he wheeled her down the steep concrete path crossing the middle of the garden, she said: "Not so fast, Leon."

He slowed down and said: "You said you weren't afraid of anything."

"Who does this place belong to? Who sits here?" asked Mrs. Moscowitz.

"The patients from the ward down here," said Leon. "Why?"

"In this place Rosa once wanted to kill me," said Mrs. Moscowitz.

"What do you mean?"

"Truly! A few days after I came I went out here with my wheelchair, and she came suddenly behind my back, without I should see her, and pushed my chair as hard as she could. I rolled down to the bottom until I fell with the chair on top of me."

Leon burst out laughing.

"I know you don't believe me. But it really happened."

"Why? Why did she want to kill you?"

"You don't understand? Right away she sensed that me and her too, like you said, are the same kind. And she didn't want me here."

From the little garden Leon wheeled her onto the driveway leading from the main road to the front entrance of the hospital, where he put on the brakes of the wheelchair, sat down on a stone next to her, rested his forehead on his hand, his elbow propped on his knee, and was silent. The pine grove at the side of the road protected them from the dazzling sunlight. Mrs. Moscowitz took off her dark glasses, wiped them with a tissue, and looked at Leon, who suddenly stood up and took off his sweaty white hospital gown, revealing a short-sleeved undershirt. Then he sat down on the stone again, put the folded gown on his thighs, propped his elbow on his knee again, and rested his forehead on the back of his hand. The edge of the undershirt rode up and revealed his big, hairy stomach, shining with sweat, bulging over the belt of his trousers. From time to time he looked up at the road to see if the taxi was coming, glanced at his watch and lowered his head again. She knew these moments when his mood would suddenly change for no apparent reason, and he would sink into a gloomy silence. She knew that at such moments it was best to maintain a distance.

In the end Leon broke the silence and muttered: "Why doesn't he come?" and he got up, draped the gown over his shoulders, and strode to the road, where he stood staring straight ahead. She saw him in profile, his hand shading his eyes, his round face strained as if with pain, because of the sun beating down on it, and his belly bulging between his undershirt and his trousers. Her heart contracted with love for him.

After a while he returned and wheeled her to the road. The taxi drove up and stopped next to them. Leon opened the back door and held out his hands to Mrs. Moscowitz, and she took hold of them, rose from her chair, and walked over to the taxi with him, where he put his arm around her shoulders and helped her to get in and sit down. He quickly folded the wheelchair, took it around to the back of the car and put it into the trunk. Then he slammed the back door, opened the front door and sat down next to the driver. She had hoped he would sit next to her.

The driver, who apparently knew Leon, tried to start up a conversation with him, but Leon responded with impatient grunts and the driver left him alone. The taxi turned onto the main road. Mrs. Moscowitz looked at the scenery on the sides of the road and felt nothing of what she had expected to feel at her first encounter with the outside world, after being secluded for so long. Nothing caught her eye, roused her interest, reminded her of forgotten things. For the moment she could see only Leon's back, his big shoulders, his thick neck and the curls of black hair on his shoulders, peeping out of the top of his sweat-soaked undershirt. His smell and the warmth of his body filled the interior of the car. Her experience told her that she couldn't rely on him, that she couldn't trust anybody, but the voice of her heart was stronger, and it told her that Leon was her ally, the agent of the power which had taken her under its protection.

"Put on the news," said Leon.

The driver turned on the radio. The announcer's voice made her feel sleepy. The heat and humidity and Leon's smell all made her feel sleepy, and again she experienced the urge to sink inside herself. Again she felt the ground slipping from under her feet, as if she were hanging suspended between heaven and earth, weightless, and even the pain, her constant companion, disappeared. Her head dropped onto her chest and when Leon woke her up at the entrance to R. Hospital, she was bathed in sweat and her mind was in a daze. He helped her out of the taxi and into the wheelchair, wheeled her into the entrance lobby and stopped at the elevators. She took a tissue out of her handbag and wiped her face.

"You want something to drink?" asked Leon.

"Yes. Please. I forgot how the summer is. Where we are we don't feel the heat."

"You'll feel homesick for us," said Leon. "Why are you in such a hurry to leave?"

"For the normal life," said Mrs. Moscowitz.

"Nothing's going to be normal any more. What do you want to drink?"

"Apple juice, please. Take money," she opened her handbag.

"No need. I'm treating you. There's a vending machine here. I don't know if they've got apple juice."

"I want to treat you," said Mrs. Moscowitz and held out her purse.

He took the purse, opened it and looked inside. "Just so you don't say afterwards that I stole your money, like you say now about Allegra."

"You don't believe she stole from me?"

"Old people always think someone is stealing from them."

"I'm not like them. I'm not senile."

He left her next to the elevators and went over to the vending machine in the corner of the hall. She followed him with her eyes. She was still dazed from her snooze in the taxi. She didn't care what happened to her. Other people came and stood next to her, waiting for the elevator. Leon returned and gave her her purse, together with a can of juice and a straw. "Drink, it'll do you good," he said. The elevator door opened and they were swallowed up inside it, together with the rest of the people. On the right floor they got out and Leon wheeled her down one of the corridors to the doctor's room. There he parked the wheelchair while he went to the office to deal with the forms. Mrs. Moscowitz remembered this ward from the time when she was operated on and hospitalized there, before being transferred to G. Hospital for rehabilitation, but she didn't recognize any of the patients or nurses who passed her in the corridor. She opened the can, slowly sucked up the tart drink she liked so much, and her spirits revived.

From the end of the corridor a man in a wheelchair came toward her. She caught her breath, afraid of being drawn into the spell of the mirage again, and the heartbreak at its end. She stopped drinking and fixed her eyes on the fair face, the smooth, abundant hair combed back from the brow, the burgundy-colored terry cloth bathrobe. Why did his appearance here come as such a surprise to her? After she had called his home she herself had concluded that he was still in R. Hospital. And why was there no joy in her heart to see him?

"Yolanda!" the clear, youthful voice reverberated in the corridor. He stopped in front of her and smiled, with no appearance of surprise, as if he had planned this meeting himself. He was unshaven and the stubble of white hair added to his usual pallor, and slightly blurred the outlines of his face. She had forgotten how handsome his face was, the unusual shape of his eyes with their light brown irises and golden lashes, she had forgotten, too, the feeling of strangeness and the anxiety they always aroused in her.

"What are you doing here?"

"I came for an examination. Tomorrow I go home. How are you, Lazar?"

He wheeled himself closer until his chair touched hers and took both her hands in his, which were as cold as a dead man's. "I don't go home yet," he said, "there are problems. My wound doesn't close."

"That's what Fichman did."

"No, this was nonsense. But wound in leg, from accident."

She lowered her eyes and saw his terrible fingernails, and they reminded her of the moments of shame and fear. "What will become of you?" she asked.

He closed his eyes, smiled dreamily and whispered with passion:

> O Mort, vieux capitaine, il est temps! levons l'ancre!
> Ce pays nous ennuie, o Mort! Appareillons!

"Again you're drinking?" asked Mrs. Moscowitz.

He was silent.

"The truth, Lazar."

He nodded his head and his face grew serious: "Sometimes. Only teeny little drop."

"Here too somebody's bringing you."

"There's always somebody to do favor."

He took his hands back.

"How come they left you here?" asked Mrs. Moscowitz. "Why didn't they bring you back?"

"Ha!" he laughed. "I was lucky. Director fixed it for me."

"You didn't want to go back there?"

"Definitely no! Inferno such as that is not for me! Again to see everybody so ugly, half-dead, half-abnormal, all the time screaming day and night and smell of kaka everywhere. This is not my world, Yolanda. How can I exist there? Here is something different. Here are also young people, even soldiers."

"There are normal people there too," said Mrs. Moscowitz. "I met in the games' room some Israeli people playing cards together, speaking about the news. Like people outside."

"You know something about Fichman?" inquired Kagan.

"No," said Mrs. Moscowitz.

"Where is he? What did they do to him?"

"Why should you worry for him? After what he did."

He kept quiet, looked into her face for a moment, and said: "Now you go to live alone?"

"Yes," said Mrs. Moscowitz, "I like to live alone. I feel strong, I'm not afraid."

He smiled in disbelief. "You have my telephone at home," he said. "Give me ring."

"When are you going home?"

"I don't know," said Kagan. "No change in condition."

"If you drink, the wound doesn't close. You must stop. Why can't you have the strength not to touch the bottle no more?"

"No, it does nothing, believe me. Doctors know nothing."

"Perhaps you want to die."

"Really, I'm embarrassed. . . . Maybe you can help me."

"What do you want?"

"Maybe you have twenty shekel for me. I need it urgent. Next week I send it back by post."

"I haven't got any money here," said Mrs. Moscowitz. "I didn't bring."

"Maybe fifteen?"

"I really haven't got. I didn't bring money. This Leon bought for me," she indicated the can of juice and sucked up what was left.

"How about ten?" mumbled Kagan.

To her relief she saw Leon returning. He came up to them, and after greeting Kagan and asking him how he was, he said to Mrs. Moscowitz: "We have to go in now."

"You have my telephone," said Kagan.

"Yes."

"It was good to see you," he said to her, took both her hands in his again, raised them to his lips and kissed them.

Leon pushed the wheelchair and Kagan called after them:

"Yolanda!"

She turned her head and he waved his hand and smiled. But when their eyes met, his smile vanished and was replaced by a look of incomprehension and resentment, like the expression she had seen there when she first set eyes on him being wheeled down the corridor to the physiotherapy room. She knew that she would never see him again.

In the taxi taking them back to G. Hospital, Leon sat next to her, and after a long silence he said: "You still love him."

"I don't know. Not like once," said Mrs. Moscowitz.

"I saw how he kissed your hands," said Leon sulkily.

She examined his face to see if he was making fun of her again, but his expression was serious, and his protruding, unfocused eyes were angry and suspicious.

"Why do you mention it?"

"You don't know what's good for you," said Leon.

"He's an artist, something special," said Mrs. Moscowitz.

"And I'm not special?"

She said nothing, and felt his eyes on her, demanding an answer.

"I still don't know when you're making fun and when speaking serious," she said in the end.

"He won't make you feel young and beautiful," said Leon.

"What will happen to him?"

"They'll take off his leg," said Leon, "and after that they'll probably take the other one off too."

"Here also somebody brings him to drink," said Mrs. Moscowitz.

"It makes no difference. Even without drinking he'll lose his leg. He's a goner."

She laid the back of her hand on Leon's warm, sweaty cheek and he didn't pull away.

"Never to lose your dignity, Leon," she said to him. "Dignity is the most important thing. More important than to be rich, or handsome or educated."

He turned his face and looked at her in surprise.

"A man without dignity," said Mrs. Moscowitz, "you can't really love."

The taxi turned onto the drive leading to the main entrance of G. Hospital, and the spacious plaza, flooded by the midday sun, was revealed in all its dazzling splendor. It was deserted. The checkered gray and dark red tiles, like a gigantic chessboard, shone and steamed, making the transparent air above them shimmer. Between the edges of the plaza and the lawns the tall, slender poplars stood motionless, not casting a scrap of shade. A few cars sweltered in the parking lot, next to a low wall covered with crimson bougainvillea. The cruel beauty of the plaza and the blazing sun oppressed Mrs. Moscowitz. Now she began to believe in the reality of the parting and her return the next day to her home in Tel Aviv. The wheelchair crossed the checkered tiles, ascending from one level to the next on the ramps installed alongside the steps, and Leon whistled a nervous tune behind her back.

The chilly air of the main entrance lobby roused her from the pleasant passivity and the sense of security that Leon's proximity gave her. When they emerged from the elevator on the floor of her ward, she was assailed by the pervasive stench that Kagan had called the smell of kaka. Now she felt that her walls were not strong enough to withstand it. In the room Adela was sitting on the edge of Allegra's bed. The sick woman lay in her dressing gown, her eyes closed, her face and arms gleaming with the oil of the massage. When Leon wheeled Mrs. Moscowitz up to the walker next to her bed, Adela looked up and gave her a smile of complicity.

"You're going home," she said in their language.

"Tomorrow morning," said Mrs. Moscowitz.

"I wish you luck."

"Thank you very much."

Leon helped her up and set the walker in front of her.

"I'll give you my phone number. You can never know," said Adela. She took a piece of paper out of her bag and studied it for a moment, tore off the half with writing on it, set the blank half on the bag on her knees, and wrote rapidly. Handing the paper to Mrs. Moscowitz, she took an address book out of her bag and asked: "What's your phone number and address?"

Mrs. Moscowitz told her and she wrote them down. Leon stood to one side, watching. Adela turned to Allegra again, and Mrs. Moscowitz picked up her towel and went to the bathroom. Leon followed her, and instead of going out into the corridor, he came into the bathroom with her.

"What business have you got with that woman?" he asked.

"Nothing," said Mrs. Moscowitz. "She wants my telephone. Why not?"

"Are you trying to be funny or don't you realize that she's got her eye on you? You're her next victim. She'll stick to you like she stuck to Allegra and you'll finish up the same way Allegra did."

"I don't owe her anything."

"You don't know her. She'll come and give you her stupid massages, she'll tell you how much she loves you, how much she cares about you. She'll say she only wants to help you, for free, you don't have to give her a penny, for love, and in the end you'll sign all kinds of papers without knowing what you're signing, and that'll be the end of you."

"I'm not senile," said Mrs. Moscowitz.

"She knows how to get round people. She's got crooked lawyers, and by the time the police get proof of what she's up to and stick her in jail, you'll be left with nothing, no home, no money, no nothing. She'll push you into some dirty hole of an institution to die there and you'll still thank her for it."

"I'm not afraid. I can look after myself."

"All I can do is warn you. Do what you think fit. But one thing I have to know: are you going to go with me, who can really help you?

She's not a nurse, she doesn't know how to look after people, she's not qualified. Look what she did to Allegra!"

"I'm not in Allegra's position, thank God."

"Allegra wasn't always like that either. She wants Allegra to die, to get what she left her."

"Allegra hasn't got anything. So what can she leave?" said Mrs. Moscowitz.

He scrutinized her face, as if to discover her hidden intentions: "Do you believe in me? Are you going with me?"

"Yes," said Mrs. Moscowitz. "I believe."

He stroked the nape of her neck. "You won't be sorry. Nobody'll give you what you'll get from me."

When he left she washed her hands, dried them and examined the naked face reflected in the mirror. The color of her hair would be black, she decided, no longer brown; the makeup base lighter, almost white; the lipstick, the rouge, the eye shadow, the eyebrow pencil more emphatic. She narrowed her eyes, trying to imagine the overall impression, and felt that she had made the right decision.

She walked out onto the balcony, leaned on the balustrade and looked out at the garden. The lawn lay limp and exhausted and in the trees and bushes too not a breath of life stirred. Like ghostly sentries fallen asleep at their posts the poplars stood motionless at regular intervals along the hedge separating the two worlds. Why hadn't she given Kagan money to buy alcohol? This question now awoke in her apprehension and concern. Kagan's face as he begged for fifteen shekels, for ten, rose before her eyes and refused to go away. He had looked at her appraisingly. He had asked her to test her, not because he really needed her help. Hadn't he said himself: There's always somebody to do favor. Suddenly she realized that she had failed the test. And he was no longer contemptible in her eyes. Her resentment at his eagerness to stay in R. Hospital, far away from her, turned into an acknowledgement of the fact that he did not value her above her true worth. And once more she longed to have him by her side, to share his life and go with him to the end of the road.

Back in the room Adela was packing her things in her traveling bag. She bent over Allegra's bed, whispered something in her ear, held her face next to hers and stroked her cheek for a long time. Finally she kissed her on the forehead, stood up, wiped her eyes, and went on her way. Mrs. Moscowitz took off the gown in which she had traveled to the examination, sprayed herself with eau de cologne, and put on a fresh dressing gown.

"She's a good woman," whispered Allegra, "maybe she'll help you too."

"I don't need her," said Mrs. Moscowitz.

"She's going to arrange for my grave and headstone too. Everything."

Mrs. Moscowitz was silent.

"You should have your hair done again," said Allegra.

"I know."

"I never took your money," said Allegra.

"I don't want to talk about it. Tomorrow, after I leave here, I want to forget everything. Forget I was ever here at all."

After lunch Mrs. Moscowitz did not return to the room to rest, but went to phone her neighbor, Mrs. Adler. She had already made out a list of the most essential groceries and vegetables, seeing that she would be leaving the hospital on Friday and there was no knowing when she would arrive home. There was always a key to her flat with Mrs. Adler, and when the delivery boys came from the shops, she would be able to receive the food and put anything that needed to be kept cold into the fridge. Mrs. Adler expressed her happiness at the news that Mrs. Moscowitz was coming home, and asked her to wait a minute while she fetched a piece of paper. Mrs. Moscowitz put on her reading glasses and heard her neighbor's voice in the distance saying: "Moscowitz is coming home tomorrow." And her husband's voice replying: "Really? I thought she was never going to get out of there."

After dictating the shopping list to her, Mrs. Moscowitz thanked Mrs. Adler for her trouble and said goodbye. Then she went to the canteen, bought a can of apple juice and sat down to quench her thirst. As she drank she checked her notebook to see what other arrangements she had to make in preparation for her homecoming. And suddenly she saw the ugly Wolf approaching her in his wheel-chair. He peered at her hesitantly for a moment and then smiled all over his long, narrow face.

"Is it you?" whispered Wolf. "Where's all that?" he tapped his face with his fingers: "All bare?"

"Don't you like it?" said Mrs. Moscowitz.

"Yesterday it was better," he whispered. He knitted his wild eye-brows, closed his eyes and shook his head to express the powerful impression her appearance had made on him the day before.

"So we won't get married," said Mrs. Moscowitz.

Wolf blew out his voiceless laughter. "Where were you all day? I looked all over for you. In the games room they said you might come maybe. They were waiting for you for rummy."

"I haven't got time. Tomorrow I'm going home."

"I know."

"Did you come to phone?" asked Mrs. Moscowitz.

"No," whispered Wolf. "Just passing the time."

Slowly she sipped the apple juice, with her eyes fixed on his ugly face, his crocheted yellow-and-brown skullcap fastened with a hair-pin, his enormous, hairy ears. Her revulsion and hatred revived some of the strength which she feared had deserted her.

"Now everyone is supposed to rest in the bed," she said.

"I can't rest," he whispered. "Ever since I saw you yesterday, I can't rest."

She stood up and walked away and he followed her in his wheel-chair. When she reached the visitors' lounge and turned in the direction of the games' room, he called: "There's nobody there! Only the woman in the wig who was playing rummy this morning."

Batya was sitting at one of the tables in the games' room writing a letter. When Mrs. Moscowitz approached the table she closed the writing pad and greeted her with a smile. "Where were you this morning?" she asked. "We played rummy. Yosef said that yesterday you won." And after a short pause she added: "And that you were all powdered and painted. Something special. I was sorry I missed it."

"Today I had an examination at R. Hospital. Tomorrow I'm going home."

"Tomorrow already? What a shame! We've hardly had a chance to get to know each other."

Wolf, who had already taken his place at the table, whispered: "Why don't we have a game now?"

"No," said Batya. "I'm not in the mood. How did the examination go?"

"All right," said Mrs. Moscowitz. "If they let me go home, it means everything's all right."

"What's all right is all right, and what isn't all right—isn't all right," whispered Wolf.

"The doctors don't always know. I've got no faith left in doctors anymore," said Batya. "Only today I read in the newspaper about something terrible that happened in America. They brought a dead man to the cemetery and suddenly they heard a voice coming from one of the graves not far away. Someone shouted: Help! Get me out of here! I'm alive! They went right over to the grave and opened it, they opened the coffin—it was a gentile cemetery—and they found a living person with his eyes open. His nails and his hair were this long. And he lay there like that without food or water. It's lucky they heard him. They removed him from the coffin, took him home to his family, and to this day he's alive and well."

Wolf laughed breathily: "No, that's not true. I read the article too. That's not the way it was."

Batya protested: "That's what it said in the newspaper I read. I'm not responsible for what you read."

"It wasn't in an old grave. It was the man they were bringing for burial. When they let down the coffin, he began to shout that he was alive. And true enough, when they opened up the coffin they saw that he wasn't dead. The doctors made a mistake, or else they mixed him up with somebody else in the hospital where he was. They gave him a strong injection and he was so fast asleep that he didn't know what was happening to him. Until he woke up in the grave. If they'd filled it up he wouldn't have had any air to breathe and he would have suffocated to death anyway. "

"So how did his hair and fingernails grow so long? It takes time, no?" Batya defended her version.

"There was nothing in the paper about hair and nails. But it's a well-known fact that people's hair and nails go on growing after they're dead."

"What paper do you read?" asked Batya.

"The same one you do," whispered Wolf.

"It's a pity I threw my paper away, I would have showed you," said Batya.

"Jews don't bury in a coffin?" asked Mrs. Moscowitz anxiously.

"Of course not!" said Wolf in astonishment. "You didn't know?"

"They put in the ground just like that?"

"No good?" Wolf laughed his breathy laugh.

"And if someone asks special, if they write it in their will with a lawyer?" inquired Mrs. Moscowitz.

"It's the law," whispered Wolf. "A Jew is a Jew."

"What difference does it make, with a coffin or without one?" asked Batya.

"How is it possible, with all the animals, the worms, the insects, all kinds of different things, in the dirt, without respect?"

"When the dead rise it'll be easier for the Jews to get out, without a coffin," whispered Wolf, and it was hard to tell if he was serious or joking.

Batya looked at her watch. She took her writing pad and pen and said goodbye. Mrs. Moscowitz too rose to her feet, but Wolf rasped angrily: "Sit a minute. Why do you run away from me all the time? Can't you talk to a person for a bit?"

"Soon I have the hairdresser."

"It's the rest period now. They won't let the hairdresser in. Sit!" commanded Wolf voicelessly.

She sat down. "I have to get different things ready too," said Mrs. Moscowitz.

"If it was somebody else you would stay. You think I don't know?"

"What do you want?"

"Tell me, madam, what kind of world are we living in? People see a man choking with suffering and misery and loneliness and nobody cares? On the contrary, they run away from him as if he's got leprosy. What are we, animals? Not Jews? Take me, for instance, seventeen years a widower, alone in the house like a dog. The children left the country. Both of them. First one then the other. I hardly know my grandchildren. Once a year, two years, they come to visit for a week. We've grown apart. If I had a daughter, maybe everything would be different. Girls take more of an interest. And from the friends and relations nobody's left either. They're all dead. There's a new crowd in the synagogue, strangers I don't get on with. So what's going to become of me in the years I've still got left, God willing, to live?

"The worst is at home. I need a wife. The right wife, nice to look at, to be with. And there isn't one. Seventeen years and nothing. It never works out. I can't find anyone. Only all kinds of nurses and house-keepers who think of nothing but money, property, who want to get into my will, for me to leave them my money. Seventeen years without a woman. I'll never get used to it. How much more can I take?"

"Why do you say this to me?"

"Because you're right for me."

"But you're not right for me."

"Why not? What's not right? The only one right for you is a star from Hollywood? You don't know me, how do you know that I'm not right?"

"I want to be alone," said Mrs. Moscowitz. "I'm not going to get married now."

His thin lips and pointed chin trembled: "Why? Why? Why be alone? I don't understand! Why not two together? In the grave you'll lie alone. I'm a healthy man. After I get out of this chair, I'll manage without any problems. And you're with a walker. It's better together."

"I also can walk without a walker," said Mrs. Moscowitz. "I can do everything."

"And what about pity? You haven't got any pity?" asked Wolf, and his bleary eyes narrowed in rage under his wild black brows. "Can't you see that I'm like that man shouting from the grave? He was lucky, people heard and let him out. Nobody hears me. I haven't even got a voice to shout out loud and make them hear me. I have to stay down there and choke. You understand what I'm saying?"

"Go to an old people's home. There's company there, you can find someone," suggested Mrs. Moscowitz.

"Why should I go to an old people's home? I've got a home. I'm not old yet. I only look old, because I've been a widower seventeen years and I can't get used to being without a woman. I've got a house, I've got means, I can get as much help as I need and live like a human being. If only I had the right woman. I haven't finished my life yet that I should go to an old people's home and wait there for the end. I love my house, my neighborhood, my synagogue. I love life. What kind of people are there in an old people's home? What kind of women? I need a woman ... a woman for a man. I still have thoughts about women.... You know what I mean? I'm not past it. I'm still like a young man. For a religious man like me to live without a wife is a sin, a real sin. Terrible things go through my head. About young women. Even little girls. You hear? Little girls! I'm ashamed of myself. I'm ashamed I'm saying this to you now. But I'm sure you understand. I need the right woman to be by my side and get my life back on the right track again. It's no good for me to be alone and think about it all the time. The evil instinct takes advantage of the situation. If a man's hungry all the time, what else does he think about but food?"

"I'm not religious," said Mrs. Moscowitz. "The opposite. Yesterday I already told you that I don't believe in God. Now I have to go for the hairdresser."

He looked at her suspiciously: "Wait a minute. Just tell me the truth: why did you go around like that with the powder and paint on your face and with that dress, if you didn't want somebody to come? It isn't like an invitation? So what's it for then, who's it for?"

"Not for you," she said and rose to her feet.

"And when I was talking on the telephone, you kept looking at me all the time, as if you were sending a signal. I saw."

His ugliness and the whisper that lent his words an imaginary intimacy filled her heart with uncontrollable hatred and revulsion: "From the back I thought you were somebody else, a handsome man that I know."

"Handsome! Handsome! Who cares about handsome? What are we, children? Who said a man has to be handsome? A woman doesn't look for handsomeness in a man. Not a decent woman anyway."

"I look."

"The nerve to say such a thing! A woman of your age. What kind of a way is that to talk?"

She walked away from the table.

"And there's nothing handsome about me? Nothing?"

"Yes. Only your hair. It's for that I thought you were somebody else."

He took the comb out of his pajama pocket and ran it through his hair. "Have you got somebody here?" he asked.

"I told you already yesterday I've got somebody. It's only for him I'm making my face."

"Please tell me who," whispered Wolf. "Is it somebody from here?"

"Better you should be afraid from him. He can be mean."

"You're mean too," sighed Wolf, "the way you talk. You haven't got a Jewish heart. Seeing you is bad for me. I'm glad you're leaving tomorrow."

⟡

Opposite the nurses' station sat Frieda, her deep voice filling the corridor, howling and quieting and howling again, like an animal struggling with its slaughterers. When Mrs. Moscowitz passed her she fixed her with an accusing stare, her eyes red from crying. "They're all liars!" roared the masculine woman. "The whole world are liars!" Mrs. Moscowitz entered the room and saw that Allegra's bed was gone. Frieda came in after her.

"She fell asleep and never woke up again," groaned Frieda, "it was all over in a second. I was the first to see it. She never slept like that. They couldn't wake her up. I knew at once that it wouldn't help. I didn't have the heart to look at her, she was so beautiful. When they lifted her from the bed she looked just like a girl, like a little girl." And again she let out a howl. Then she said: "I know it. It's my turn next. If they don't take me away from here it's going to happen to me. But they don't want me at home. They're liars. They're all liars. The whole world are liars. Everyone looks out for himself. And they think I don't understand. They lie to me all the time and they think I believe them. They don't care how I feel. All that's important is them. Their comfort, their convenience. Until my time comes and they'll be rid of me and get their hands on all the money and the property. That's what interests them. If they wanted to they could take a doctor and a nurse to look after me at home. But they're too stingy. Here it's cheap, and they don't have to see me next to them all the time. They don't have to hear my misery. You think I don't understand? I knew all the time, I just put on an act. Out of respect for myself, respect for them. So people wouldn't know what they're really like."

Mrs. Moscowitz went out to sit in the corridor and wait for the hairdresser. The tea trolley passed, and the Ethiopian nurse Shulamith poured the tea into red plastic cups and gave it to the women sitting along the wall.

"This is my last day here," said Mrs. Moscowitz, "the last time for you to give me tea."

"You remember when you couldn't get up by yourself from the chair?" said Shulamith.

"Now it's much better," said Mrs. Moscowitz, "soon I can walk without the walker too."

"Only I'm like a doll in a stroller," groaned Frieda.

After drinking her tea, Mrs. Moscowitz got up and walked down the corridor in the direction of the dining room. In front of the door of the last room she looked around and tried the handle. The room was not locked and she went inside and shut the door behind her. The room was dark. When her eyes got used to the darkness, she saw the bed standing next to the wall and a figure lying on it. There was a walker standing next to the bed. She did not dare go any closer, but remained leaning with her back against the door, and strained her eyes to see who was lying on the bed. The figure rose and sat on the edge of the bed. A brief scream escaped Mrs. Moscowitz, and her hand groped for the light switch next to the door. When she turned on the light she saw Paula shading her thick glasses with her hand, to protect her eyes from the dazzling light.

"How cruel," said Paula, "chasing me out wherever I go. Why don't you let me rest? For three days and three nights I haven't slept a wink."

There were big black bloodstains on the bedsheets.

"What are you doing here?" asked Mrs. Moscowitz.

"Do I know you?" asked Paula.

"This is a bad place. Go to your own bed, in your own room."

"This is my room, Madame, and this is my bed. And I have to lie down for a while. My bones hurt very much and I'm tired. You look like a nice woman. Try to understand me."

"I'll bring you to your bed," said Mrs. Moscowitz.

"*My crime is very grave,*" said Paula.

"This bed was belonging to a woman who died."

"Not now. The class is waiting. Please be quiet," said Paula. "I don't remember anything." She closed her eyes and moaned softly as if in some nagging pain.

"This is her blood, that woman who died," said Mrs. Moscowitz.

"*Beautiful she was unto death, that woman,*" said Paula.

"She had a disease in her blood."

"*Forgive me, God, my crime is very grave,*" said Paula.

"God forgot you," said Mrs. Moscowitz, "he doesn't remember us. He doesn't hear what you say."

"*Forgive me, God,*" cried Paula, "*my crime is very grave. Beautiful she was unto death, that woman, unto sin . . .*"

"It's not good to touch that blood."

"Nothing's left. Everything's gone," said Paula. "My memory fails me. Once I was a human being, do you believe me?"

"I know. You were teacher. I too was teacher. French teacher. You know French?"

"French?" said Paula wonderingly. "Do I know French?"

"Come outside. It's not allowed to be here," said Mrs. Moscowitz.

Paula lay back on the bed. "This is my bed. Nobody's going to take it away from me. I'm entitled to a bed too."

"It's not allowed to be here."

"How can such a thing be possible? Years and years without a moment's rest, without tasting a bite of food, without a drop of water?"

The hairdresser was due to arrive at any minute and Mrs. Moscowitz left Paula lying on the bed, went out and closed the door behind her. But after a while she saw Paula emerging from the room, leaving the door open, and shuffling behind her walker, stopping from time to time to peer suspiciously into one of the rooms, advancing toward the row of women sitting on the chairs along the wall and coming to a halt opposite Matilda Franco.

"Excuse me, Madame, what date is it today?" asked Paula.

"That's the most urgent thing you have to know now?" said Matlida Franco. "Except for the date you already remember everything?"

"I don't know anything," said Paula, "I'm not a human being."

"Good morning!" cheered Matilda Franco. "You finally found out!"

Mrs. Moscowitz went into the bathroom with the hairdresser and shampooed her hair. Then she sat on the chair next to her bed and undid the towel wrapped around her head like a turban. The hairdresser put the bag containing the tools of her trade on the bed and gave Mrs. Moscowitz a mirror so that she could watch her at work.

"Today I want it black," said Mrs. Moscowitz.

"Black?"

"Yes, the most black. Have you got?"

"All right," said the hairdresser disapprovingly. "I'm not saying anything. I've got black. If that's what you want, you can have black."

"What's the matter with black?" asked Mrs. Moscowitz.

"For you, brown's better."

"And I want black. I'm fed up from brown, brown all the time. Give me the pitchiest black which you've got."

Her hand holding the mirror suddenly shifted and she saw the empty wall behind her, where Allegra's bed had previously stood, Allegra who would never see her pitch black hair, her new face, who would never again whisper in her hoarse voice: "It suits you like that, Yolanda, it suits you better." The weariness of the long, exhausting day suddenly intensified and fell upon her body, weighing like a heavy stone on her shoulders, turning her into a toy in the hands of the strange, disapproving woman, to whom she had entrusted her most precious possession. Her eyes closed, her hand holding the mirror dropped to her thighs, her head slumped onto her chest, and before she fell asleep she felt the hairdresser gently removing the mirror from her hand, and placing her head firmly in the position she required.

The sweetish smell of the spray and the hot air blowing from the hair dryer onto her face and scalp woke her up. She opened her eyes and knew that she had been asleep for a long time. The hairdresser completed her work and held up the mirror, but Mrs. Moscowitz averted her eyes from it. More than anything else she wanted now to be alone, to undergo the transformation undisturbed. She therefore hurried to pay the hairdresser her fee and send her on her way. Then she took her toilet bag and went to the bathroom. With a feeling of satisfaction she contemplated her hair. Now all that remained was to bring her face into line with the requirements of the new black hairdo. For a long time she stayed in the bathroom, and when she came out her face looked almost like her neighbor Mrs. Poldy's. Her forehead and face were covered with a heavy layer of white powder, her lips were painted bright red, there were orange spots on her cheekbones, dark blue eye shadow around her eyes, and her eyebrows were drawn in a bold, black arch, not too narrow. She went to the wall closet and took out the green dress which had been stained because of Allegra. After buttoning all the buttons from the neck to the hem, she went straight out onto the porch.

Evening was drawing in, the sprinklers were revolving in the garden and glints of water and light danced on the lawn. Life streamed between the blades of grass. Bearlike, lazy and langorous, something sprawled on the lawn, reveling in the splashing water and the last rays of the sun, abandoning itself to the caresses of each moment as it passed and gave way to the moment following it. Soon it would slowly stretch itself, unashamed of its nakedness. Its presence stirred inside her like a savage infant, dangerous and beloved. Her whole body sensed its nearness. For a moment she was seized by an impulse to jump off the balcony in her green dress and be united with it. But she would never be able to climb onto the low wall and lift her leg over the iron railing on top of it. She raised her eyes to the poplars growing along the hedge—the ancient guardians of the garden, who had woken from their afternoon siesta. The trees waved their branches in a friendly salute—their leaves ceaselessly trembling and changing their color: pale green, silver gray, pale green, silver gray—and told her that she had been approved.

When it was time for supper she returned to the room and Matilda Franco, coming in from the corridor, saw her and stopped in her tracks. For a long moment she stood in silence, glaring at Mrs. Moscowitz with astonished indignation, and when she recovered she cried loudly: "Come on, everybody! Come and see her! Now she's gone and got herself up as the Angel of Death!" She spat on the floor, and muttered a curse in her language.

"What's this, what's gotten into you?" asked Leon when she passed him in the corridor on her way to the dining room.

"Where's Rosa? I want her to see me like this too."

"Rosa's been hurt in a car crash," said Leon, "she won't be coming back to work for a few days."

"In the legs?" asked Mrs. Moscowitz.

"Yes," said Leon in surprise. "How did you know?"

She smiled and continued on her way, and Leon watched her with suspicion and concern. The mocking looks, the nurses' comments and the waitress' sarcastic questions all confirmed her belief in her power and her secret uniqueness. She sat alone at one of the tables in the corner of the dining room, and this time the food of which she was so heartily sick tasted delicious. Frieda came into the dining room. Her daughter was pushing her wheelchair and her son-in-law walked behind her. From the doorway they surveyed the hall until their eyes fell on Mrs. Moscowitz's table. They approached her, looked at her for a moment as if they couldn't believe their eyes, and without saying a word parked the wheelchair opposite Mrs. Moscowitz and sat down on either side of her. Frieda covered her mouth with her hand.

"She doesn't want to eat," said her daughter.

"Maybe she wants to be fed with a tube," said her son-in-law.

"Tomorrow Yolanda's going home," wailed Frieda in her deep voice, "only I haven't got a home. You took away my home! You took away my life!"

"That's not true, Mother," said the son-in-law, "we want you at home with us, but the doctors won't allow it."

"You pay them to keep me here!" said Frieda. "You think I don't know? I know your whole plan. I'm changing my will. There's a lawyer who'll do it for me. I know where to find him. You'll get nothing from me."

The waitress put the tray in front of her, and she pushed it furiously to the end of the table. "I'm not eating. From today I'm not eating anything. Until I die. Better to be like Yolanda, alone, without a family. Who needs a family of snakes?"

"The doctor promised to release you in a few weeks' time," said her daughter.

"That's a lie!" shouted Frieda. "You say that all the time. You buried me here and here you want to leave me until the end."

"I promise you, Mother. Look, Yolanda can hear. She's our witness."

"Yolanda won't be here tomorrow. Look what she did to herself, she's so happy she's going home."

"You have to eat," said the son-in-law. "If you don't eat, they'll feed you by force, they'll stick a tube in you, they won't have any choice."

"Nobody will force me to eat. I'll finish myself off like Clara. The quicker the better. After I write a new will. Get out of my house. It's not your house. It's registered in my name. Go and find another house, at your own expense. You've got all the money your father left you. It's my house, I want to rent it, I need the money. Get out, quick!"

"Allegra's death's affected her," said her daughter.

"I'm not poor like Allegra!" sobbed Frieda. "I can afford to live at home in my own house for years and years with a private doctor and a nurse day and night. I don't need your favors. You want to see me die here like a dog."

"You don't understand," said the son-in-law.

"I understand everything!" thundered Frieda. "She was a good girl. She loved me. You put the whole thing into her head, how to get rid of me and take everything I've got. All you can think about is money. However much you've got it's not enough. You need it for cards, for trips abroad, for the stock exchange you need it. All you know is how to lose money and waste. A person like you should be put in prison."

"Perhaps you can persuade her to eat," the daughter appealed to Mrs. Moscowitz. "Explain the situation to her, that we're doing everything possible."

"I'm already on my way home," said Mrs. Moscowitz. "I'm already not from here."

She stood up and crossed the dining room, and as she walked she heard Frieda's baritone behind her back: "I haven't got anybody to talk to here any more. Now she's going too. I haven't got anybody left."

Mrs. Moscowitz passed down the corridor. Next to the nurses' station stood Leon, watching her with suspicion and resentment: "You want me to help you pack now?" he asked.

"Later," she said, "now I have to go somewhere. I'm expected. Soon I'll be back."

In the games' room Yosef, David and Batya were sitting and playing dominoes. She went up to their table and once they had recognized her and recovered from their astonishment, Batya could not control her laughter. Yosef said: "Quiet, quiet, it's not nice to laugh."

David, the Eastern man whose eyes were full of life and who still had plenty of black hair on his curly head and in his moustache, asked with a smile: "Is it a special occasion?"

"Yes," said Mrs. Moscowitz, "tomorrow I'm going home. I came to say goodbye. It was a pleasure to meet you."

"Will you play with us?" asked Yosef.

"No, I'm in a hurry, I have to put all my things in the suitcase."

Out of the corner of her eye she saw the ugly Wolf sitting in his wheelchair at the other end of the room, reading a newspaper. He raised his head and looked at her. At first it seemed as if he did not recognize her and was only looking out of curiosity, but suddenly his wild brows knitted and his expression grew angry. She turned away and left the games' room and she knew that he was following her. Next to the visitors' lounge she stopped and turned round. He came up to her and whispered:

"I told you I didn't want to see you. Why did you come?"

"I can go here where I like," said Mrs. Moscowitz, "this is a public place."

"Hussy, hussy," he breathed, "I shouldn't see such things. Look what you've done to your face. Women like this one sees in hell. You're walking round like that on purpose to provoke."

"Nobody has to look."

"What woman would dare to walk around like that in a place with people," he covered his eyes with his hand. "You're like ... I don't want to say the word. Hussy, get out of my sight! Out of my memory too—not to see and not to think!"

She walked on in the direction of the visitors' lounge and heard him whispering behind her. Next to the entrance to the hall she turned around again and he was beside her, his eyebrows quivering with rage: "Have pity on me, madam. I'm begging you. Please don't let me see you any more. I told you about myself. I'm a religious Jew. Understand: I shouldn't see such things. Why are you laughing? What are you so happy about? A man chokes on his suffering and misery and you smile. I have to look after my health."

She walked away from him and entered the visitors' lounge. The red glow of twilight suffused the long glass wall, filtered into the hall and mingled with the white fluorescent lights. Patients sat with their visitors in pairs and little groups, talking softly or in silence, and Peretz Kabiri stood in the middle of the room and held forth: "Don't be sorry that I'm leaving here tomorrow. I've got all kinds of things to arrange. It won't take long, I'll be back soon. And we'll be together again and have some fun! And you'll still hear lots of stories from me about the war against the Nazi, may his name and memory be blotted out, and what we did in Eretz, Israel, and how we trounced the foreign invader and chased him out forever and ever." And in conclusion he threw back his head and burst into song: "*Ama—do mio,* love me for ever. . . . "

chapter ten

Mrs. Moscowitz sank into an armchair, breathed deeply and tried to steady her pounding heart. She was very thirsty and she didn't have the strength to get up and go to the fridge. The sound of the ambulance crew's footsteps descending the stairs grew fainter. They had carried her up to the fourth floor in a chair, past all her neighbors' apartments. A few of the doors had opened a crack for a stealthy peek at the spectacle, and some of them had opened wide to welcome her in her passage from floor to floor. Most forthcoming of all had been Mrs. Horn, who came out onto the landing, the woolen scarf wrapped round her head in the middle of summer, to protect her ears, and announced in her nasal whine: "How wonderful! Mrs. Moscowitz has come home! How are you? Oho! This I've never seen before. A pity I haven't got people to drag me on a chair up to my apartment. For me too it's no joke to climb the stairs, believe me. Sometimes I stand there in the middle and think: Oy, I can't get home already. And how wonderful you look, Mrs. Moscowitz. Really, much better than before."

Before she disappeared from sight around the bend in the stairs, Mrs. Moscowitz saw the spiteful smile in her evil eyes.

Her apartment was shrouded in gloom. The windows, the blinds and the big balcony were closed and they protected the interior from the glare of the sun. In another hour or two the room would be so stifling that she would have to open them. Her dress was soaked in sweat from the journey. In the hospital she had not suffered at all from the heat of the summer, a light breeze had blown continuously through the rooms and corridors, and they had sometimes had to close the balcony doors. A loud ring shattered the silence in the room, and then another one. It took a few seconds before she remembered that it was the telephone in the hall. The ringing went on and on, she tried to get up from the armchair but failed. The chair turned out to be lower than she had remembered. Again and again she exerted herself but she could not get up. The telephone went on ringing insistently, but it was not the need to answer it that worried her—it was the fear that she was trapped in the armchair with no one to rescue her. The ringing stopped and the room filled with the sound of her own breathing. Again she gripped the arms in her hands, pushed down hard with all the force of her rage and despair, and rose from the seat of the chair. Little by little she straightened herself. For a moment she teetered, then quickly grabbed hold of her walker.

The bed in the bedroom was made. The cleaning woman called in by Mrs. Adler had not left a trace of that winter day when Mrs. Moscowitz had set out for the hairdresser and fallen down the stairs. When she entered the kitchen, the phone rang again. She returned to the hall and picked up the receiver. As she had guessed, it was Mrs. Poldy from the building next door.

"I phoned before and you didn't answer me," said Mrs. Poldy. "If you open the kitchen door you can see me."

"I just got in. I didn't have a chance to move yet."

"I saw how they brought you in the ambulance."

"Are you still standing all the time by the window?" asked Mrs. Moscowitz.

"He won't let me out from the house. He locks me in with the key," said Mrs. Poldy.

"I wasn't at home for a long time."

"I phoned lots of times and there was no answer."

"I was in the hospital, almost a year."

"Me too," said Mrs. Poldy, "he put me in Bat-Yam again. I only got out last week."

"I have to go now to arrange my things in the house," said Mrs. Moscowitz. "I didn't get a chance even to change my dress."

"Go and open the kitchen door. I'm waiting."

Mrs. Moscowitz put the receiver down on the shelf, went to the kitchen, opened the door to the little kitchen balcony, and saw her standing at the window, painted like a doll with her long black hair falling onto her bare shoulders, wearing a shiny black slip decorated with bright ribbons, chains and beads around her neck.

When Mrs. Poldy saw her, she waved the telephone receiver at her. Mrs. Moscowitz returned to the hall, took the phone and set it on the table, and sat down on a chair opposite the kitchen balcony, so that they could see each other.

"He hits me something terrible," said Mrs. Poldy. "A few days ago he tried to kill me again. At the last minute he stopped, I was already half here, half there."

"I still didn't get a chance to drink a glass of water from the minute I came in," said Mrs. Moscowitz, and tapped her hand on her chest to show that she was feeling faint. She herself didn't understand where she got the patience for this woman from, and why she didn't cut short the annoying phone conversations in Hebrew.

"All the time he tells me: Crazy, crazy. In the hospital at Bat-Yam the doctor himself said it's only a mental depression disease. Either I want to die and I can't do anything, or I want to live. And when I want to live my blood's getting hot and I'm getting a little crazy, because I feel happy in my heart and I want to do all kinds of different things. For this you lock a person up in the house? And if there's a fire? Who'll take me out?"

251

"He loves you," said Mrs. Moscowitz, "he's a good man. His life he gives for you."

"I know," said Mrs. Poldy sadly, "but he's not for me. He's old. He doesn't know to dance. And me, only to dance and sing all day long. And his family—so common. People from the street. With us at home we wouldn't talk to such people. You should never marry somebody from a common family. All my troubles in life are only from this."

There was a ring at the door.

"There's somebody at the door," said Mrs. Moscowitz. "Feel well, Mrs. Poldy."

"You always say Mrs. Poldy. My name's not Poldy. He's Poldy. I'm Betty. Say Betty."

Mrs. Moscowitz hung up the phone, rose without difficulty from the chair and went to open the door. Mrs. Adler came in, went into the kitchen and opened the refrigerator. She showed her the food she had bought for her the day before, and gave her the bills. Mrs. Moscowitz wanted to pay her at once, but Mrs. Adler said: "What's the rush? That's what's going to stop me from sleeping at night?" But Mrs. Moscowitz insisted on paying her debt immediately. She got out a pen and a piece of paper to add it up, and Mrs. Adler added the cleaning woman's wages and the price of the stamps for the mail which the good neighbor had collected for her and sent to the hospital—mainly bank statements, bills and requests for donations from various charities. Mrs. Moscowitz paid her and thanked her for her trouble, and Mrs. Adler inquired about the state of her health, asked her how she was going to manage alone at home, and as usual offered her help whenever it might be needed.

After she had left, Mrs. Moscowitz went into her bedroom, selected a dressing gown from the wardrobe, and changed her clothes. Then she went into the bathroom to examine her appearance in the mirror. Sweat had marred the light makeup she had put on in honor of her return home, but the black hairdo was unharmed. With tissues she wiped off the remains of the eye shadow, eyebrow pencil and lipstick, washed her hands and face and dried them well. On the shelf under the mirror, in its usual place, stood the old pot of face cream, and Mrs. Moscowitz smoothed it over her face and rubbed it in with the tips of her fingers. Beads of sweat broke out on top of the cream, and she patted them lightly with a tissue—and a pleasant coolness enveloped her face. She went into the kitchen, where she practiced maneuvering the walker in the narrow space between the table and the fridge, sink and stove, and again she saw Mrs. Poldy standing at the window and waving to her. She closed the door to the little balcony, found the bag of fresh coffee Mrs. Adler had bought for her, and brewed herself a cup of coffee the way she used to like it. But the taste was strange to her palate, acrid as soot, and she spat the dregs left in her mouth into the sink and rinsed her throat with water. She had never kept tea in the house, but in the hospital she had grown accustomed to its taste.

Again she went into the bedroom, meaning to unpack the suitcase and bags she had brought with her from the hospital, but she could not bring herself to touch them, as if they were not hers, as if they had been contaminated by contact with others. She pushed them into a corner of the room, turned down the covers of her bed, threw the eiderdown quilt that had remained there since winter onto the floor, and lay down to rest.

When she awoke she didn't know what time it was or how long she had been asleep. The clock on the bedside table had stopped many months ago, and her wristwatch had been out of order for years and served as an ornament only. The closed apartment was stiflingly hot, her body, nightgown and sheet were drenched with sweat. For a long time she lay in a stupor, her limbs sprawled out, without moving.

Voices from outside filtered into the room. Someone was practicing the trumpet. Someone else had turned the radio or television on as loud as it would go and the sound reverberated in the inner courtyard.

A dull, rhythmic tremor thudded inside the room over and over again, as if someone was pounding on the wall behind her head with his fists. She sat up in bed and tried to get up. After several vain attempts she succeeded in getting to her feet, put a dressing gown over her sweaty nightdress, and went to open the windows and the balcony doors. Now the noises from outside burst in far more loudly than before. The trumpet blasts tried to drown out the thunderous voice of the radio or television announcer, to the accompaniment of a terrible din of music.

There was a huge Persian lilac in the courtyard, its roots, so she imagined, watered by the sewage, and its branches spreading opposite the blinds of her balcony. And now, as she opened the slats, the branches of the hated tree poked through them. It had been a long time since she had last laboriously clipped them with her kitchen scissors. She peered through the slits and examined the windows of the other apartments overlooking the courtyard, in the hope of discovering where the noise was coming from, but she couldn't see anything in the dim interiors, and some of the windows were hidden by the branches of the tree. The sounds hammered in her head, rushed around her like squalling winds. She didn't know where to turn, she couldn't find a place for herself in her own house.

She dragged one of the balcony chairs into the bathroom and showered sitting down, the way she had been taught in the hospital. When she emerged, feeling fresher, it was already evening. She hadn't had anything to eat since morning, so she went to the kitchen, prepared something and sat down to eat. In the hospital she had always known the time by the big electric clock in the corridor and by the regular daily routine. Now this question occupied her mind. The apartment was dark. She put on the light, turned on the television, dragged one of the kitchen chairs into the living room, afraid to sit in the low armchair, and sat down to watch. Based on the Hebrew program, she guessed that it was between eight and nine o'clock. But she couldn't hear. The cacaphony of sounds bursting in from outside—especially the screaming of the singers and the din of the instruments accompanying them, which prevailed over all the other sounds—stunned her, filled her with hatred and furious rage. She stood up, went out to the balcony, and shouted:

"Quiet! Quiet! Shut the radio! What happens here?"

She couldn't believe that it was her voice shouting, she didn't know this voice. Through the slats she saw people standing up in the windows and on the balconies of the apartments opposite her, raising their heads and staring at the building from which the shouts had come. She didn't budge, in order not to reveal her presence on the balcony, and waited until they returned to their places. The trumpet blasts stopped, but the other noises continued unabated. Her telephone began to ring. She went back inside and picked up the phone.

Mrs. Poldy said: "That was you who shouted 'Quiet,' right?"

"It's impossible to sit in the house like this," said Mrs. Moscowitz, "a person can go crazy."

"Open the kitchen door and you'll see me in the window," said Mrs. Poldy.

"I don't feel well."

"I don't mind at all the noise from outside. It makes me happy. I've got nothing to do, and he won't let me go out from the house. So I look in the window what people are doing and hear their music. I want noise. Quiet will be in the grave. Did you see my cats? He won't let me go to them, and all the time they're waiting for me. Now Poldy speaks." Her husband took the receiver from her: "Hello Mrs. Moscowitz, how are you, welcome, good wishes for health, all the time like this. Day and night, the noise more and more worse. To shout quiet, no use. I phone up police, here come policemen, it gets quiet hardly one day, then such noise again. Nothing can help. All from young peoples coming here for pay rent. They listen their music the most loud there is, hours and hours. Only Betty like to listen such noise. Before, I go, excuse, to the bathroom, Betty make light on balcony, open everything and dance there like Valkyrie, in petticoat, for everybody to see. These days Betty so bad. Last week she make fire in the house. The neighbors call fire department. Now half kitchen black. Finish with gas in house. Now only electricity. What happens next?"

"She's sick," said Mrs. Moscowitz.

"Of course," said Poldy. "What to do? To kill? Betty my wife. Now begins news, goodbye." He hung up the phone.

In the bedroom, at the head of her bed, she put her ear to the wall and listened to the terrible din and the rhythmic pounding that had been making her room shake all afternoon. She went out onto the landing, where the sounds were strong and sharp, filling the stairwell with their echoes. On the doormat in front of the door next to hers stood a pair of shabby gym shoes and leaning against the wall next to it a plastic bag full of garbage, leaking a murky liquid that trickled in a thin line to the top of the stairs, and dripped onto the step below. She pressed the bell. She rang twice with no answer and it was only after the third ring that the door opened, the noise blaring out, and a slight young man with tousled hair, dressed in nothing but a pair of shorts stood in the doorway, blinking as if he had just woken up, and asked her what she wanted.

"The noise," said Mrs. Moscowitz. "I can't stand anymore to hear such noise. So loud. Please to make softer."

"The music?"

"I am here," she pointed to the door of her apartment, "behind the wall. A sick woman."

"They said nobody lived there," said the youth and looked at her suspiciously.

He looked about twenty, his tousled hair was black and there was a somewhat confused expression on his face. He was a new tenant.

She had known the previous tenant, a somber, lonely woman of about forty, who persistently ignored her greetings on the few occasions when they met on the landing. Behind his shoulders she could see the apartment, which had orginally been built to the same plan as her own, but had been changed beyond recognition: the wall dividing the bedroom from the big room had been torn down, and so had the wall and the double doors between the room and the balcony. The whole apartment had been turned into one big room, barely furnished, dark but for the pool of white light which a single electric bulb on the ceiling shed on to the bare floor. A cushion lay there and next to it a huge bottle of some fizzy drink and scattered newspapers. There was no girl in the apartment, or anything to indicate the presence of one.

"Who said?"

He shrugged his shoulders and said nothing.

"I was in the hospital a long time," said Mrs. Moscowitz.

"Okay, okay," said the young man.

She returned to her apartment and sat down in front of the television again. The Friday night entertainment program began. The din of the music from the apartment next door had diminished, but not disappeared, and it continued as a background to the voices coming from the television set. Now too she found it difficult to concentrate on watching the program, since the noise in the background reminded her of the young man lying on the floor of the next-door flat, which had been transformed into a big, dark, empty room. She could not shake off the apprehension which all this inspired in her.

Little by little her rage subsided and her nerves calmed. A light, fresh breeze came from the sea and blew through the room. Sitting on the kitchen chair for so long at a time was uncomfortable. She decided to risk the armchair again, the one she always sat in to watch television. She pulled the cushion from the back of the other armchair and laid it on the seat to make it higher. Now she began to feel that she had really come home. The entertainment program came to an end and a movie began. After a few minutes she realized that she would not be able to follow the plot. Her eyes grew tired of deciphering the rapidly changing Hebrew subtitles. The sounds behind her bedroom wall had died away, and she heard the young man slam his front door and lock it. He was apparently going out to enjoy himself.

It was late and the noise outside grew faint and distant. Her timetable was completely out of joint. Despite her long nap in the afternoon her body was sending her signals of tiredness and confusion: the long months in the hospital had accustomed her to going to bed early. And now she had suddenly returned to her old routine. There was nothing left for her to do but wait for Mrs. Poldy's screams. It was nearly midnight, the hour when Mrs. Poldy struggled to leave the house and her husband beat her and forced her to swallow the pills that tranquilized and sedated her. This happened every night when Mrs. Poldy was at home. The monotonous hum of the air conditioners was more clearly audible now, a few houses away she heard the sounds of a party, snatches of conversation and loud bursts of laughter and music of the kind which had previously shaken the wall behind her bed. From the direction of the boulevard she heard the roar of the automobiles whizzing past and sometimes shouts of laughter. Police or ambulance sirens wailed in distant streets, and from time to time the dreadful screech of a motorcycle shattered the deepening silence of the night.

Before long Mrs. Poldy began screaming: "Police! Police! He's killing me! I want to go outside! Please to come quick! He's killing me!" Her screams were quickly smothered and this was Mrs. Moscowitz's signal that the time had come for her to go to bed. She switched off the television and went out onto the balcony. In some of the apartments across the courtyard the lights were already off, and in others the bluish shadows of television screens flickered. A baby's crying broke out suddenly from somewhere, his mother's voice was heard trying to soothe him and put him to sleep, and after a while the crying stopped. On the top-floor balcony three couples were playing cards. She tried to close the slats in order to move the sliding blind, but the branches of the tree were stuck in the slits between them. She pushed them back with her fingers but they poked through again. She gave up and went to the bedroom, rolled up the window shade and looked outside. Above the roofs hung a strip of black sky, empty and opaque. No stars, thought Mrs. Moscowitz, years and years without a star to be seen.

—

Most of the hours of the day she passed in sleep. She would never have imagined that she could need so much sleep, both night and day. And the more she slept, the lighter her sleep became, the more vulnerable to noise. At daybreak the birds on the Persian lilac would begin to utter their strange cries outside her open window. Industrious, early rising housewives, full of murderous energy, would greet the sunrise with the dull, explosive thuds of their carpet-beaters. The morning news on the radio would blare out everywhere. The second-hand goods dealer would already be driving round the streets, his loudspeaker announcing: "Alte zachen!" The banging of hammers, the whine of an electric drill and the thunder of falling bricks rose from the latest apartment building to be renovated. All day the music went on, and in the afternoon voices from the television joined the chorus. Had it always been like this, and she had forgotten, or had something happened during the long months of her absence, something that had opened the way to this assault? It would often take Mrs. Moscowitz an hour or more to fall asleep, and then her sleep would not last long, because some new noise would erupt and wake her up. Sometimes she would go out to the balcony and shout "Quiet!" but by now the neighbors ignored her shout, and they didn't even look out of their windows or balconies to see who was shouting. Only Mrs. Poldy, vigilant at her window, like her own private Providence, would immediately telephone to announce that she had heard the shout and to complain of her troubles. As she cooked her meals, washed the dishes, and did her laundry, Mrs. Moscowitz felt tired and drowsy, even though she spent most of the day sleeping.

One day before Rosh Hashanah she could no longer restrain herself and she telephoned the hospital. When they put her through to the ward one of the nurses answered, and at the sound of her voice Mrs. Moscowitz cried joyfully: "Suzie! How are you? This is Yolanda speaking."

"How can I help you?" asked Suzie.

"How is everybody? How are things at the hospital?"

"All right," said Suzie. "Who do you want to speak to?"

"How's Rosa? Did she come back to work yet?" asked Mrs. Moscowitz.

"Yes," said the nurse, "shall I give her a message?"

"No. Maybe Leon is there?"

"No, he's working nights. What do you want?"

"What about Frieda, is she still in the hospital?"

"Yes. She's in physiotherapy now. I haven't got time to talk. I've got work to do."

"Please tell everybody Happy New Year from me," requested Mrs. Moscowitz.

"Happy New Year," said the nurse and hung up.

For a long time Mrs. Moscowitz went on sitting next to the phone, trying to work out what had happened to her, where the connection was between herself and the Yolanda who had been in the hospital. All that remained of the hospital Yolanda was packed in the suitcase and the big plastic bags she had pushed into a corner on the day of her homecoming. She still shrank from touching them. But

260

the messengers of that place, which had vanished too quickly, were knocking on her memory, crowding forward and standing in front of her like old aquaintances who had returned from a long journey, transmitting the image of that Yolanda to her. Something had triggered the stilled mechanism into motion and now it was working and there was no stopping it. Like the branches of the sewage tree growing and twining between the slats of the blind and invading the balcony, her previous incarnation was stretching out its arms to embrace her new being as if nothing had happened in the meantime.

Sounds of pruning and digging from the courtyard disturbed her siesta. She got out of bed, slipped on a dressing gown and went out to the balcony, where she peered through the slats. She couldn't see anything, but she had no doubt that the noise was coming from there. She shouted: "Quiet!" and a boy moved and came into sight, leaning on the handle of his hoe, looking up to the fourth floor, shading his eyes with his hand from the glare of the sun and seeking the source of the shout. At once she called out: "Raffy!" pushed her hand through the slats and waved, to show him where she was. His brother too appeared from somewhere, holding the huge pruning shears. Standing next to Raffy he too looked at the hand waving out of the balcony blind. Now there was no doubt left in her heart. "Raffy, is it you?" cried Mrs. Moscowitz. The boy did not react. "I'm Yolanda!" she cried. "You remember me?"

One of the neighbors from the opposite building shouted: "Quiet! Quiet!" and she knew that someone was mimicking her.

The two figures disappeared from her angle of vision and again she heard the sounds of their work in the yard. Mrs. Moscowitz returned to her bedroom and got into bed but she knew that now she would never fall asleep. Her heart pounded from the intensity of the surprise, joy and perhaps also anxiety at such a coincidence. She remembered how she had withdrawn into herself as she lay on her hospital bed on that distant day and imagined her homecoming, imagined how she would lie naked in bed, pull her eiderdown over her, in spite of the summer heat, and the touch of the eiderdown would be strange at first and little by little it would merge with the warmth of her body, caress the folds of her stomach and envelop her breasts, and stream inside her, quickening the dead flesh into new life. The intoxication which would flood her body then, and she would not know if it was actual pleasure or only longing.

The telephone rang. Mrs. Poldy said: "It was you that was shouting before and talking to people, right? Are they making a noise for you? Sit in the kitchen, then you'll see me."

"I'm tired, I want to sleep," said Mrs. Moscowitz, "I was in the bed."

"I heard you shouting," said Mrs. Poldy. "Why don't you put air condition in? Then it can be closed and cold the whole day for you in the house, like us."

"You know I'm sick with the legs. I'm not allowed. It gives rheumatism."

"Poldy likes the air condition, so it can be closed and cold the whole house. I don't like it. I want everything open, I like noise, for it to be hot, to be plenty of people outside. He says: you're crazy. Now he wants to send me in Bat-Yam again. He doesn't want me in the house. He's got a woman. I know he has."

When the conversation was over, Mrs. Moscowitz got a can of apple juice from the refrigerator and sat down at the kitchen table. From the balcony door she saw Mrs. Poldy opening the window and calling affectionately to the cats by the rubbish bins. She heard her young neighbor talking in an aggressive voice to somebody on the landing. Mrs. Moscowitz got up, went to the front door and peeped through the peephole. The young neighbor was standing there and arguing with Raffy. She went into her bedroom, slipped on her dressing gown and opened the door. They both looked at her and Raffy lowered his eyes. He was naked from the waist up, bathed in sweat, his short pants were sweat-stained too, and he was holding the handle of a mop with the pail and cloth at his feet.

The young neighbor said to him: "Show me your papers."

Raffy pulled a wallet from his back pocket, extracted a shabby document from it and handed it to the young man, who examined it for a moment with an expert air and gave it back to Raffy.

"What do you want from him?" said Mrs. Moscowitz.

"What do you bring Arabs to work here for? One day he'll take out a knife and kill somebody."

"He's a good person. I know him a long time."

"How do you know him? He only began working here this week," the young man said in a hectoring voice.

"I know him from somewhere. I know what I'm talking. Leave him alone!"

"I'll speak to the house committee."

"So will I speak to them to let him work here," said Mrs. Moscowitz.

"It's not healthy for him to hang around here anyway," said the young man. "A few days ago they beat up an Arab who was working on a building site in Ibn Gvirol Street. He went to buy himself a cold drink in a shop and they nearly killed him."

Raffy's brother came hopping up the stairs to stand beside him, panting for breath, his little eyes darting anxiously between Raffy and the neighbor.

"Who's he?" the neighbor asked Raffy.

"It's his brother," said Mrs. Moscowitz.

"Why are you answering for him?"

"He's my brother," said Raffy. "He's the gardener here."

The neighbor grimaced and raised his eyebrows in an expression of despair, turned his back on them and went down the stairs. Raffy's brother asked him something in Arabic, and Raffy muttered briefly in reply, pulled the cloth out of the bucket, wrung it, and wrapped it round the bar of the mop, as if to declare his desire to get on with his work and end the incident.

"Raffy, how are you? It's a long time I haven't seen you," said Mrs. Moscowitz.

"I don't know you, lady," he said. "I never saw you before."

"In G. Hospital, where you worked there, you don't remember Yolanda, that always helped you?"

"I never worked in hospital. Maybe it was somebody else," the boy insisted, and his eyes avoided hers.

For a moment a doubt crept into her heart. Was her memory deceiving her? Perhaps she had imagined it all, perhaps the memory of some other woman was invading her again with ghosts from an imaginary past which had never existed. The brother said something in Arabic again—she remembered his crooked mouth too—and her confidence in the lucidity of her mind came back to her. The doors of the other apartments on the landing had opened and the neighbors stood watching and listening.

"What happened? Why don't you want to remember?" asked Mrs. Moscowitz, raising her voice so the neighbors would hear. "You know I only want what's good for you. I know you from my hospital, you worked there, and I know what a good person you are. How much you like to help everybody. Soon you'll go to learn at the university and definite you'll succeed, because you're a clever boy. I can tell, I was teacher. And you'll be a good doctor, and help sick people. Everybody will love you and you'll get respect."

A tremor suddenly passed over the boy's big face, which was too old for his years, and he bowed his head. She saw that there were tears in his eyes. The mop slipped from his hand and fell against the railing. He turned away quickly and went to stand next to the fuse box, his face to the wall, with his right hand covering his cheek. His sweaty shoulders shook with the strain of his effort to control himself. His brother limped up to him, took hold of his arm and said in his strange, piping voice: "Raffik, Raffik." It was clear which of them was the stronger.

Mrs. Moscowitz said to Raffy: "Come in, I'll give you to drink."

He hurried into her apartment with his brother limping behind him. She led them to the kitchen, and put a bottle of cold water and two glasses on the table. Raffy sat down, wiped his eyes with the back of his arm, and averted his face from her. Then he poured water into the glasses for himself and his brother and they drank in silence. In the end he said: "Thank you very much, lady."

"Why do you say this to me, Raffy?" asked Mrs. Moscowitz. "You don't want to remember me from the hospital? Are you angry at me?"

"I never worked in hospital," he said. "I clean the stairs and my brother he works in the garden. I never saw you before. All the time you say to me Raffy, and it's not my name."

"Maybe you want to do something for me? I'll pay you. Every week, when you're coming to do the stairs, to take my garbage down to the bin, because I can't go down from the house. You know what I have with the legs." And she mentioned a sum of money.

"I can do your whole house," offered Raffy. "The whole place will be clean. You'll see that I work good."

"I've got a woman to clean," said Mrs. Moscowitz. "For years and years already she's coming to me."

"Okay."

"But every week when you're coming here for the stairs, come to me and I give you the garbage to take down."

"Thank you very much," said Raffy. "Is there any today?"

He and his brother stood up. She showed him the garbage pail and he took out the plastic bag. He and his brother were ready to leave, but she asked him to wait a moment, until she brought him his money. When she returned with the money in her hand, she said to him: "Never mind, Raffy. The cleaning work isn't a dirty work. Even the garbage isn't dirty. There are only dirty people and clean people, in their heart, in their soul. You're a clean person. That's what matters."

"Thank you very much," said Raffy and went out onto the landing holding the garbage bag, and his eyes though now dry, still avoided hers.

"One more thing I want," said Mrs. Moscowitz. "Come with me a minute."

He put the bag full of garbage down next to the wall, under the fuse box, and followed her back into the apartment, with his brother trailing behind him. She went out onto the balcony and showed him the branches of the Persian lilac which had grown inside and become tangled up with the slats of the blind.

"I can't cut. Before I did it with the scissors. Now they can't cut, it's too strong. Maybe you can do it with your big scissors?"

Raffy said something to his brother in Arabic, and the child went out onto the landing.

"This tree is no good, it's growing from the drains. It's not healthy. The best is to chop it all down. Nobody needs it. It can only make dirt and give diseases. Why not to chop it all down?"

He spread out his hands to indicate that the project was out of his jurisdiction. "Only if they say so from the building," he said. "It's not our work. We can do it, but only if they tell us from the building."

His brother returned with the shears, went up to the balcony blind and clipped the invading branches. Then he climbed rapidly up a ladder which he dragged up from the corner of the balcony and cut off the farther, thicker branches too. Now she could close the slats, push the blinds apart and open up most of the front of her balcony.

After they had left the apartment, she peered through the peephole again and saw Raffy carrying the garbage bag down the stairs. After a while he returned and began vigorously washing the floor of the landing in front of her door and the steps leading down from it, until he reached the landing below and disappeared from her view. In the courtyard the sounds of pruning and hoeing rose again. She went out onto the balcony and saw Raffy's brother raking up the pruned branches and the uprooted thorns and weeds, and heaping them beside the fence of the next building. Raffy, his work apparently done, joined his brother in the yard. The two of them filled big red plastic bags with the branches and carried them round the corner of the building. When they had cleared away all the heaps, Raffy turned on the faucet in the courtyard, bent down next to it, cupped the water in his hand and poured it over his head and shoulders, washed his face, his arms and armpits, chest and stomach, held his feet under the jet of water and rubbed them with his hands. His brother sat on the ground and watched. When Raffy had finished washing himself, he turned off the faucet and his brother stood up and hopped out of view to the front of the building, came back with a plastic bag, took out a towel and handed it to him. Raffy dried himself all over, and when he had finished he hung the towel over his shoulder and raised his head, his eyes narrowed against the glare. After scanning the facades of the buildings around the courtyard, he stood sideways next to the tree trunk, took off his short trousers leaving only his underpants. From the plastic bag he pulled out a pair of jeans and quickly put them on, slipped into a shirt, and pushed his feet into his sandals. Then he began pushing his brother toward the faucet, but the child slipped out of his grasp. Perhaps he was trying to persuade him to wash, but without any success. Raffy burst out laughing, trying again and again to propel his brother to the faucet, while the boy eluded him, making faces and laughing too, in a high, broken voice. The sound of their laughter reverberated in the courtyard. Mrs. Moscowitz stood and watched them for a long time from her balcony, through the open slats of the blind, as they laughed and romped like a couple of little children. For a moment it seemed to her that there was something malevolent about this laughter. From the windows and balconies of the opposite building too she saw a number of people looking down on them. Raffy and his brother looked up at her balcony. She couldn't tell if they saw her or not, but in any case they went on laughing. Mrs. Moscowitz wondered if they were laughing at her.

In the end they picked up their bundles and tools and left the courtyard, and she went back inside the apartment, which had become emptier and more exposed to the outside. The afternoon attack of noise began to flood the house.

chapter eleven

fortnight or so later, toward midday, there was a long ring at the door. By the time she rose to her feet and went to the door, the ring was repeated, this time more firmly. In the doorway stood Adela, her handbag hanging on her shoulder and a large plastic bag in her hand. A strong smell of sour sweat mingled with cigarette smoke and traffic fumes entered with her. She went straight to the kitchen, took a few covered glass dishes and a little saucepan out of the plastic bag and placed them on the table. Then she took the bottle of cold water out of the fridge and poured some into a glass, lit a cigarette and looked around for an ashtray. Since there was no ashtray in the apartment, she used a glass saucer that she found in the kitchen cupboard.

"Were you sleeping when I rang the doorbell?" Adela asked.

"Yes," said Mrs. Moscowitz.

"At this hour?"

"I feel tired all the time and I have to sleep. There aren't enough hours in the day and night for me to sleep as much as I need."

"It's not healthy. You'll get bedsores. Your body will stop functioning. You won't be able to move at all. Do you want to die?"

"If death comes, it comes," said Mrs. Moscowitz. "I'm not afraid."

"What's the matter with you?" Adela upbraided her. "The last time I saw you in the hospital you were so strong and happy."

"This tiredness is sucking my blood," said Mrs. Moscowitz.

"Appetite?" asked Adela.

"Not much."

"We'll have lunch together. I brought some food I prepared, the way we like it."

Adela stood up and went to the stove, lit one of the gas burners, turned the flame down to the minimum and put the little saucepan on it to heat up the meatballs in tomato sauce it contained. Then she opened one of the cupboards, took out one of Mrs. Moscowitz's saucepans and emptied the stuffed peppers and braised vegetables from the glass dishes into it. She added a little water, set it on the burner, and lit the flame under it. She did all this quickly and confidently, like a member of the household who was familiar with every corner of the kitchen and knew what each of its little cupboards contained. She remained standing next to the gas stove, watching to see that the food didn't burn, stirring and adding water from time to time.

"Why didn't you phone before you came?" asked Mrs. Moscowitz.

"I knew you'd say no."

"I'm glad you came."

Adela set the table for two, lit herself another cigarette and waited for the food to heat up.

"You ought to have help," said Adela behind the screen of the cigarette smoke. "A woman to come and clean the house, do your shopping and cook for you."

"I've got a cleaning woman who comes once a week. I get the groceries delivered. That's enough for me. I can manage."

Adela turned off one of the burners, and slid a stuffed pepper onto each of their plates. "Good appetite!" she said.

"I've got a surprise for you after lunch," said Adela. She watched Mrs. Moscowitz eating. "You see, you've got an appetite."

"It's very tasty," said Mrs. Moscowitz. "Like the food in the old days."

They finished the stuffed peppers and Adela served the meatballs with the braised vegetables.

"You shouldn't have worked so hard for me," said Mrs. Moscowitz.

"Why not? It's my pleasure. I had to be in Tel Aviv anyway, and I thought to myself: I'd better go and visit Yolanda, see how she's getting on. You promised me you'd keep in touch, remember?"

"Yes. Leon shouted at me afterwards for giving you my address."

"Naturally," said Adela. "He's afraid it'll get in the way of his business."

"What business?"

"You don't know? He's got a partner, a crooked lawyer who pretends to be a rabbi, with a hat and a beard, and they keep their eye out for patients leaving the hospital who haven't got a family. They go and visit them at home, frighten them with all kinds of stories about how dangerous it is to live alone, and persuade them to sign their apartments over to them and move into an institution they're connected with. And they don't understand what they're signing, the poor old things, they don't know what's waiting for them. I knew a woman who was there, poor thing, she died after a few months. They treat them like animals. They starve them. They leave them in their dirt, they even beat them. They're just waiting for them to die and free their beds for the next victims. What can the poor women do? They've got nothing left, nowhere to go back to. All they can do is beg for mercy, and they've got no mercy. They're only interested in one thing: money. They haven't even got doctors and nurses. Nothing. That's your Leon. A lot of people fell into his trap. Soon he'll be caught together with his partner and thrown into jail. But until then, how many poor innocent victims will end their lives in hell?"

"He knows how to say all kinds of sweet things, pay a woman compliments, promise to make her young again. . . . " Mrs. Moscowitz smiled.

"He's a disgusting person, how could a woman stand to be with him?"

Mrs. Moscowitz was silent.

"Don't you agree?" asked Adela.

They finished their meal. Adela piled the dishes in the sink, cleaned the table, and said: "Now we'll have coffee."

"I can't drink coffee any more," said Mrs. Moscowitz, "I don't like the taste."

"No wonder you want to sleep all the time. I'll make us real coffee. You'll see that you'll like it."

Right away she found the package of coffee where it had been lying ever since the day of Mrs. Moscowitz's return, opened it and sniffed. The smell apparently satisfied her. Then she found the coffee pot, boiled up the coffee with sugar, poured it out, took the cups and the saucer that served her as an ashtray into the living room and sat down on the sofa. Mrs. Moscowitz sat opposite her, on the armchair with the raised seat, and drank the coffee which tasted strange but good. Adela lit a cigarette, set her big handbag on her knees, opened it and took out a crumpled envelope.

"The last time I saw her, the day before she died, she asked me to bring the photos from her room and give them to you, so you'll have something to remember her by," said Adela. She took a bundle of photographs out of the envelope, put them on the table before Mrs. Moscowitz and contemplated her in silence, smoking and waiting for her to look at them. Mrs. Moscowitz picked up the photographs. They were old, some of them faded and worn.

Allegra at about twenty, tall and thin in a short-sleeved, light-colored dress that emphasized her swarthy complexion. Her dark hair curly and abundant, and her eyes, slanting almost like a Chinese woman's, smiling in wonder, her high cheekbones lending an air of austerity and mystery to her face.

"So beautiful," said Mrs. Moscowitz.

Allegra as a girl of about fifteen, between two other girls with their arms around her shoulders, in a park in the old country, in a little snapshot too blurred to make out the features on her face. Allegra in her forties, beginning to look as she did at the end of her life, her hair less curly, cut shorter, her face rounder but still smooth, and her eyes asking a question.

"If you agree," said Adela, "I'd like you to give me this photo that I'm particularly fond of. I haven't got a single picture of her."

Mrs. Moscowitz looked at the picture a little longer before parting with it, and then put it on the table in front of Adela. Adela said: "You can see how good she was."

"And beautiful," said Mrs. Moscowitz.

Allegra at about thirty, standing next to a thin man of about sixty in a suit and tie, sitting in an armchair. He was half bald, and his narrow moustache was drawn like a line over his lip. Her hand rested on his shoulder, barely touching, as if she were afraid of burdening him. And on the other side of the armchair, two younger men, one of them, the one nearest the chair, resembling Allegra, with the same good looks.

Adela said: "That's her sick father she looked after all her life, and those are her two brothers when they were young." Her finger, with its black-rimmed nail, rested on the photograph. "This is the idiot," she pointed to the handsomer of the two, "and this is Marco, the criminal."

Mrs. Moscowitz couldn't get enough of looking at Allegra, at the black of her eyes and hair still preserved in this family photograph, at the bright smile on her face, a serene, innocent smile, at the long neck turning toward the armchair, at the hand lying gently on her father's shoulder.

"He's taking me to court," said Adela, "but I'm not afraid of him. With me everything's in order, everything's honest and aboveboard. He'll lose and pay the cost of the lawyer and the trial as well. You signed for me too. She told you about me. You saw yourself what I did for her. It didn't matter to me if it was day or night. Whenever she needed me I came right away, up to the end. I kept her alive with my baths and massages. Her body stayed young. Even at the end, when she had sores all over. The whole body, the woman's place too, you know? You wouldn't have believed it if you saw it. All so young and beautiful. Up to the end. And I made the funeral arrangements, the stone, everything. That's how she wanted it."

Allegra as a little girl, her curls falling on her forehead, in a dark school pinafore, holding a doll in her arms, looking down at it with motherly concern.

The telephone rang, and Adela got up to answer it. Mrs. Moscowitz guessed who it was. She heard Adela say: "I'm a friend of hers. Just a minute, I'll call her."

"You should have seen how they jumped when they saw me on the balcony," said Mrs. Poldy. "They love me so much. I gave them nice things to eat from the house."

"I have now a visitor," said Mrs. Moscowitz.

"I saw her when you sat in the kitchen," said Mrs. Poldy. "You ate together. She's in your house a long time already."

"Goodbye Mrs. Poldy. I talk to you later. Now I have to go to my visitor."

"And I have to go to my cats, and I can't get out from the house. Can you hear them calling to me? Bet—ty, Bet—ty . . . "

"Goodbye . . . "

"Poldy's got a girlfriend . . . "

Mrs. Moscowitz hung up and went back into the living room.

"A friend of yours?" asked Adela.

"A neighbor. Not right up here," Mrs. Moscowitz tapped her temple.

"Have you got pains?" asked Adela.

"Pains I'm already used to, but I feel weak, and terribly tired all the time. I haven't got the strength to hold my body together. Maybe your massages would help?"

"What a question. Your blood would begin to flow, your body would wake up, you'll begin to feel alive."

"Will you do it now?"

"It's not good after eating."

"When?"

"I can come and give you a massage one day, just to show you what it's like," said Adela, "but the effects won't last long. You should think about regular treatments. For that we need to make an agreement between us."

"Like with Allegra?"

"Yes," said Adela, "think about it. If you're interested we can discuss the details later."

Allegra between the ages of fifty and sixty, looking as she did at the hospital. Photographed from the shoulders up, her hair beginning to go gray, short and combed behind her ears. Her face expressing impotent insult. There was no knowing why the photograph had been taken, but her eyes, looking away from the camera, expressed resentment at the occasion, as if she had been talked into it against her will.

"Haven't you got anything to say?" asked Adela. "I'm going to wash the dishes, and in the meantime you can think about my proposition."

"The apartment and everything?" asked Mrs. Moscowitz.

"Think about it," said Adela, "decide whether it's worth your while."

She went briskly into the kitchen and immediately there was a sound of running water and a clatter of pots and dishes in the sink.

After a while she returned to the living room, wiping her hands on the kitchen towel. "You'll get the strength back in your legs," she said, "you won't need the walker, you'll be able to go down the stairs, go outside."

Adela finally left with the promise that she would be in touch soon, and Mrs. Moscowitz took the bundle of photographs and went to lie down. On her bed she examined them one by one and picked out the best. For a long time she gazed at the picture in which Allegra's eyes were turned aside in a protest which contained both the innocence of a child and the willingness to resign herself to the worst of all. Mrs. Moscowitz's eyes closed, and her hand dropped to the bed. Effortlessly she conjured up in her memory Allegra as she had once been revealed to her in her imagination—standing in the last room with her back to the wall and her hands covering her nakedness, and for the moment when light came in from the corridor, between the opening and closing of the door, her face was illuminated and her head with its halo of short, thin stubble, and her narrow eyes were dazzled by the light and turned away to the dark side of the room.

When Mrs. Moscowitz woke up late in the afternoon, she felt that the sleep had done her good. The tiredness was gone, her body felt stronger and the trumpet blasts and other noises erupting outside and crashing into her apartment did not madden her as they had before. She showered, put on a clean gown and sat down in the kitchen to make herself coffee in the same way as Adela had prepared it. The phone rang. Through the open balcony door she saw Mrs. Poldy standing at her window, waving the telephone receiver at her.

"Every day, before he goes out, he wants to take me outside to see my cats and go for a walk in the street," said Mrs. Poldy, "only if I wear old women's clothes. Why I should wear old women's clothes?

I'm ashamed. Everybody likes my clothes except for him. What about his girlfriends? He tells them too to wear old women's clothes? Now Poldy speaks." Mr. Poldy's voice came over the line: "How are you, Mrs. Moscowitz, I hope fine. What Betty does today? She take everything in fridgidaire and throw down for cats. The eggs, the freezed meat, the vegetables, the margarine, everything there is. Nothing is left in house to eat. All rubbish in yard. I come home, here comes the neighbors to shout me: Look what Betty done today, how she throw off the balcony. I go myself to clean up there. This I have to, isn't it so? So many cats down there, not only ours. From all places. Drag pieces in yard. Everything go to rubbish. Dirt like this you can't bring home."

"Maybe it's doing her good to go out a bit?" said Mrs. Moscowitz. "Her blood is hot. She can't stay shut up all the time in the house."

"I say Betty: In morning, before my work, we can go for walk in the street, going to rubbish, to see cats she love so much, but please— to dress normal. How I'm walking with Betty in the street and Betty with petticoat, all the body outside, and rags on head? Even when Betty in the house, people coming in their window to look and showing with the hand and laughing. We have no respect for ourself? But Betty say: No clothes for old lady. I ask you: Normal clothes is for old lady?"

"I can talk to her?" suggested Mrs. Moscowitz.

"Now Betty on balcony, talk to cats. One minute."

He put the receiver down, and Mrs. Moscowitz heard his footsteps receding and his voice coaxing his wife to leave the cats and come and talk to Mrs. Moscowitz.

"Did you tell him to say about his girlfriends?" inquired Mrs. Poldy. "He says he goes to work. He's a pensioner! What work is there for pensioner? All day he's with girls and I'm in the house, the door locked three times, impossible to go out, I've got nothing to do.

Even a healthy person gets sick from this and I'm suffering already with disease of mental depression. . . . "

"He'll go every day outside with you, but with the clothes he's telling you," said Mrs. Moscowitz.

"Like an old woman? I'm ashamed."

"You're young? You're old! We're the same age. I wear such clothes like you do?"

"We're not the same age. I'm not old," said Mrs. Poldy. "I'm just fatter than you, because of eating all the time, I can't stop, from being always in the house shut up with nothing to do. Soon I'm going on a diet."

"A thousand times you said you're going on a diet, and nothing happened."

"The clothes are too small for me," said Mrs. Poldy, "now I really am going on a diet. Tomorrow I start in the morning."

"You haven't got some big clothes?" asked Mrs. Moscowitz. "I'll give you. I've got good things. If it fits me, it can fit you too. Will you wear it?"

"If it's pretty," said Mrs. Poldy. "Aren't you afraid it'll get ruined from me?"

"Never mind. I already don't wear it. I can't go out from the house. Be grateful for your legs are good, you've got the strength to go outside, you've got a good man who's taking you for a walk."

"Is it old women's things that you give?"

"Tell him to come to the phone, I tell him to come and get," said Mrs. Moscowitz.

"You see?" said Mr. Poldy. "There's nobody to talk. Betty bad and bad."

"I'm giving her a dress of mine that suits for her and she'll wear it when you go outside in the street. She promised me. Come and get it."

"Thank you very much, Mrs. Moscowitz. I come in few more minutes."

She hung up the phone and went into the bedroom to the suitcase she had pushed into the corner and left untouched since the day of her return from the hospital. For a moment she hesitated but she quickly recovered, pulled the suitcase towards her and opened it. Dresses and gowns and underwear were folded on top of each other, just as Leon had packed them on her last evening. She lifted the edges of a number of garments until she found the dress she had chosen for Mrs. Poldy, the grass green dress with the unremovable stain. She pulled it out and threw it on the bed, closed the suitcase again and put it back in the corner. Then she folded the dress and waited for Mr. Poldy to arrive.

They had never been in her house, and she had never visited them. Up to now she had never spoken to either of them face to face. Only on the phone. Years ago they had come to live in the building next door, on the fourth floor, in the apartment opposite hers. One day, when Mrs. Moscowitz went out to hang up her washing on the clothesline outside her kitchen balcony, Mrs. Poldy saw her from her window, called to her and asked her for her telephone number, and immediately called her up on the phone. Ever since then she had spoken to her almost daily, sometimes several times a day, and her husband, who had at first apologized to Mrs. Moscowitz for his wife making a nuisance of herself on the telephone, sometimes took part in the conversations too. In those days Mrs. Poldy was still allowed to leave the house, and Mrs. Moscowitz sometimes saw her walking in the courtyard with her long hair hanging loose on her shoulders and down her back, in her strange garments, shouting with laughter and playing with the cats next to the rubbish bins.

He rang the bell discreetly and when she opened it he shook her hand. At the sight of the walker his face took on expression of disappointment and dismay. "It's not for always," said Mr. Poldy, "only for beginning."

"Soon it will be a year," said Mrs. Moscowitz.

He was a slight man with a rather delicate face, bifocal glasses, and thin white hair combed severely back from the dome of his head, which was glistening with sweat, to the nape of his neck. He fanned his face with his hand. "In my house air condition," he said.

"No good for my legs," said Mrs. Moscowitz.

Politely she offered him a seat, and he thanked her politely and excused his refusal: "Betty by herself in house."

She showed him the dress and he admired its beauty: "It's not a charity? So dear thing. Maybe I pay?"

"No. It's a present. I don't need."

"Thanks very much, Mrs. Moscowitz. I want plenty times to buy clothes, I can pay, but Betty say: For old lady. There's nobody can talk to her. Now comes new thing: I going to girls. Pensioner, in my age? Funny joke, no? I have job half-day, accounts in firm Sanitary Imports, King George Street. Pension today not enough. All the time in office. Definite never to go out the room, so much work. Girls! I only love Betty, Betty my wife for all the life. Excuse for Betty bothering all day."

"I love her too," said Mrs. Moscowitz, "just like a little girl. She's got the soul of a little girl."

"Betty sick. She not know what good, what bad," said Mr. Poldy. "Every foods in frigidaire she throw to cats. Only yesterday I go in supermarket. Like dream all the life for Betty, like hallucinate."

"She's sick, the poor thing," said Mrs. Moscowitz, "lucky for her that you're a good person."

"I always love Betty and Betty never to loving me back. From beginning Betty say: Poldy not right, not know to dancing, she good family and me from common peoples. So why Betty's marry me? I take by force? Mrs. Moscowitz, when no luck, the life like hell."

The next day the phone rang early in the morning and woke her from her sleep. Mrs. Poldy was standing in the window, wearing the green dress, waving happily. Mr. Poldy spoke on the phone: "Mrs. Moscowitz, good morning. Thanks very much on nice dress. Everything fit tip-top, but buttons on top Betty won't close. All the body outside and not even bra. How I can go outside together?"

"Call her, I speak to her."

"Mrs. Moscowitz!" cried Mrs. Poldy over the phone. "Thank you very much! Did you see how good it fits? This is a dress to go dancing, I know. Is it really a present for me?"

"Yes," said Mrs. Moscowitz, "because I love you and I want for everybody to see how beautiful you are. But why without a brassiere? You need the brassiere, it's better with a brassiere."

"No," said Mrs. Poldy, "I don't need. Everything sits tight from the dress."

"So close the buttons. It's not nice for people to see everything."

"They can't see! Only a little in the middle."

"Now it's the latest fashion to close the buttons to the top," said Mrs. Moscowitz. "So the young girls are doing."

Mrs. Poldy was silent for a minute. In the end she said: "I'm closing two, all right?"

Mr. Poldy took the receiver: "If Betty closing two, then I go out together in the yard."

A little later Mrs. Moscowitz saw them strolling arm-in-arm in the courtyard, proceeding slowly along the paved path leading to the corner with the garbage bins. Mrs. Poldy had indeed put on a lot of weight, and the dress was too tight on her fat body. She was far shorter than Mrs. Moscowitz, and the hem trailed on the ground. When they approached the garbage bins, she freed her arm from her husband's and hurried forward to look for her cats, uttering cries of joy. Her husband stood at a little distance on the paved path, anxiously surveying the buildings surrounding the courtyard.

Allegra's profile at about forty. Her pointed nose sticking out defiantly from the gentle harmony of her face. This was the only photograph in the entire bundle in which she was wearing earrings and lipstick. And again the photograph with her father and two brothers. Her eyes looked straight at the camera and the smile on her face was unlike anything Mrs. Moscowitz had seen in all the time they had spent together in the hospital. Allegra in her last years, in a small snapshot, sitting on a folding chair, perhaps in her house, her hair sparse and short already, her eyes narrowed in an effort to see something far away and her lips parted, as if about to whisper in her permanently hoarse voice: It's nothing, nothing.

Early that evening Mrs. Moscowitz sat down to phone Kagan's home in Beersheba. For a moment her finger hesitated on the dial, in case his wife should answer the phone. She decided that this time too she would hang up the minute she heard her voice. His wife did answer, but Mrs. Moscowitz was surprised to hear herself saying confidently:

"Mrs. Kagan? Hello, I was with your husband in G. Hospital. I'm phoning to ask how is he. He's already home?"

"No, he's still in hospital. This is Rolanda?"

"Yes," said Mrs. Moscowitz. "How is he?"

"No good, Rolanda, no good. They took off leg."

Mrs. Moscowitz said nothing and thought: This is the moment to hang up.

Mrs. Kagan said: "You don't know this is going to happen?"

"When did they take off?" asked Mrs. Moscowitz.

"Last week."

"How is the condition now?"

"They think gangrene finished. Now is question if doctors right or wrong."

"From the drinking?"

"Doctors in hospital say not only from this. But friend of our, doctor, says different. I understand something too, I think. I told you this will happen, you remember? In R. Hospital also somebody brought him bottle. Now that Lazar sees what comes from it, maybe he stops."

"I didn't bring him a bottle," said Mrs. Moscowitz.

"You gave him money," said Mrs. Kagan. "It's the same thing. But now we don't talk of this. Maybe now everything will be different. Well, and how are you? You can walk?"

"Only with the walker. All the time alone in the house, it's very hard."

"Wouldn't it be better some place with people, old-folks' home?"

"There it's worse. G. Hospital is better."

"Be well, Rolanda. Tomorrow I go to Lazar. I'll tell him we spoke. He'll be happy, of course, you phoned. He has your phone number?"

Mrs. Moscowitz gave her her phone number. "When will he come home?" she asked.

"I don't know," said Mrs. Kagan, "maybe in another week. We'll keep touch. He'll want to talk to you, of course. In all G. Hospital he loved only you, except that poor not-normal man, Fichman. It will be good for him to talk with you. He had bad shock after operation, now he gets in depression from everything. It's pity you can't go to him."

After replacing the receiver, Mrs. Moscowitz went on sitting on the stool next to the telephone. She wondered why this sad news didn't really touch her heart. The more she examined herself, the clearer it became to her that her account with Kagan was settled. So the relationship had been nothing but a contest. His victory had seemed assured, and now he had been beaten and fallen. His situation was no better than hers, and even worse. After the operation he was less Kagan than he had been before. Now they were equals. She didn't gloat, but she had a strong sense of justice being done. Could it be possible that the longings she frequently felt for him stemmed simply from her need to know the results of the competition between them, to see justice done?

She remembered his boasts that he would soon be walking around in the normal world on two healthy legs, like everybody else, and his insulting arrogance, as if he were a temporary guest who had landed up by mistake among the living dead of G. Hospital, which he compared to hell. How pathetic it seemed now, his pretense that their sentence did not apply to him, that he did not belong to this world of the dead, but to the other world waiting for him outside. He knew the truth. The failure was planted inside him and he cultivated it lovingly, fortified the self-destruction that was as strong in him as the lust for life. From the outset he was no less dead than the other dead stirring around him, no less dead than she was herself. At their last meeting in R. Hospital, it was very obvious that he had surrendered, he had even given up the pretense. She no longer regretted that she had closed her ears to his pleas for money. She had no part in his fate. And Leon had said: They'll take off his other leg too. If that happened, he would be confined to a wheelchair. And could there be any doubt as to the superiority of someone who walked with a walker over someone confined to a wheelchair?

~

The days were getting shorter, and in the daytime the heat and humidity were no longer oppressive. At night she would cover herself with a woolen blanket and soon it would be time for the eiderdown. The house was closing in on itself and the sounds from outside were growing weaker. The noise and the heat no longer disturbed her sleep. Most of the hours of the day she spent in bed, and now again her sleep did not assuage her unbounded weariness.

One evening, when she was drowsing in front of the television, the phone rang. It was Leon. At first she didn't recognize his voice. He was surprised, perhaps insulted:

"Yolanda, have you forgotten me already?"

"We never spoke on the phone," said Mrs. Moscowitz, "the voice is different on the phone. You're talking from the hospital?"

"Yes," said Leon.

"You're working the night?"

"Yes, I'm working nights. I wanted to know how you're getting on? How do you feel? And how're you managing? What's it like being independent after so long?"

"I forgot already that I was in the hospital," said Mrs. Moscowitz. "So much time passed. How are you?"

"I couldn't get in touch. I had personal problems."

"You don't owe me anything."

"What do you mean? Isn't there something between us?" said Leon.

"I don't know," said Mrs. Moscowitz. "But it's nice of you that you phoned, that you didn't forget me. You've got plenty patients, not only me."

"Don't you love me any more?" asked Leon.

"Now you're talking to me like to the girls you're catching with your phones in the night."

"Are you laughing at me? Yolanda, I've got something for you. You remember we talked about it? I want to see you. I can come and visit you at home tomorrow."

"What time?"

"Round nine o'clock."

"No, I'm still sleeping. I get up late," said Mrs. Moscowitz.

"Ten?"

"No, that's still too early for me."

"I can't make it later. I have to be back at the hospital at noon."

"Never mind. Come another time. When it'll be convenient."

"I have to bring someone with me, to explain the conditions to you."

"What conditions?"

"I fixed up a place for you."

"I don't need any place. I'm happy at home."

"But we spoke about it. I relied on you. Now I've given my word for you."

"Leon," pleaded Mrs. Moscowitz, "you were good to me and I have a good memory from you. Now I'm living in my own world."

"We have to talk," said Leon. "I can't explain the problems to you over the phone. You don't understand how dangerous it is for you in your condition to live alone at home. I'm worried about you, don't you understand? You're not just anyone for me, you're Yolanda! You know how I feel about you. When do you get up in the morning?"

"Not before eleven."

"I'll come with somebody who'll explain the situation to you."

"A lawyer?"

There was a short silence on the other end, and then Leon said: "Has Adela been talking to you? Has she gotten to you already?"

"Leon," said Mrs. Moscowitz, "I'm staying at home. I'm not going anywhere. If you come, please to come by yourself. I'll be glad to see you. But in my situation, I can't receive people that I don't know."

Leon said goodbye in a surly tone and for a moment her heart contracted. On her last evening at the hospital he had helped her to pack and refused to accept money for it. She had embraced him and kissed him on the cheek, she was sure that she had found a kindred spirit in him. Now she was inclined to believe Adela that he was a disgusting person and she was sorry that she had spoken to him politely and said that she would be glad to see him.

A few days later he appeared on her doorstep without having notified her that he was coming. At first she was happy to see his bearish figure, his round face and dark, bulging eyes with their unfocused look. Afterward, when he tried to shower her with signs of affection and caresses, she pushed him away firmly and said: "I'm already not Yolanda. Now I'm Mrs. Moscowitz."

"Yes," said Leon and looked at her with ostentatious sadness, "you've really changed. You've turned into an old woman. What happened to you? In the hospital you were much younger and better looking. On the last evening, with the black hair and made-up face, you were an attractive woman. Remember? You wanted Rosa to see how beautiful you were. Now your hair's gray, your face is gray. Why are you neglecting yourself? Aren't you happy at home?"

They sat down on either side of the table in the living room and she asked: "Where is your lawyer hiding?"

"You really believe Adela's stories? She's trying to make trouble between us, don't you understand? You remember I warned you that she would get to you. You fell into her trap and you don't know how deep you fell."

"I didn't promise Adela nothing, word of honor," said Mrs. Moscowitz. "I want for her to come here and take care of me to the end, and arrange everything afterwards too, and I'll leave her what she's entitled, whatever we agree."

"How long do you think you can go on staying at home like this? One day you won't be able to get out of bed without help, you won't be able to wash yourself, to make a cup of tea. You won't be strong anymore. And if something happens to you, in the middle of the night, and you're all alone, what will you do? Shout for the neighbors?"

"I've got good neighbors," said Mrs. Moscowitz.

"You think I want to make money out of you. You don't believe me that I'm really worried about you, out of friendship, that I love you. You always thought I was a thief, that I was dirty. You think I don't know? I've been working with old people long enough to know all the crazy ideas they've got in their heads. But I fixed up a fantastic place for you. You don't have to promise me a thing. Just come with me to see the place, the people, the staff. See for yourself. You'll live like a queen over there. Here you can't even go out in the street, see people, see a bit of life. It's like a cage, a prison. How can you live like this?"

"I like it."

"I see she really got to you," said Leon. "You hate me. Just like you loved Allegra and then you began to hate her and said she was stealing from you. You don't know what's good for you. Who helped you all the time in the hospital? Adela? Who did you call when you needed something? Is there anybody else who gave you what I gave?"

He stood up, went round to the back of her chair, and began massaging her neck and shoulders. She pushed him away and shouted: "I don't allow! Stop it!"

"You hate whoever loves you."

"Go away, Leon. What's in the memory—stays there. Don't spoil it. Now everything's different."

"On the day of the examination at R. Hospital, you said we had a deal. That was a promise. I trusted you. I committed myself for you in the new place. I paid for you. You can't tell me now, a couple of months later, that everything's different just because that liar Adela got to you. And for your information, Allegra's brothers are taking Adela to court, for cheating her and taking everything away from her. When she's sitting in jail there'll be nobody to come here and kiss your ass and turn you against people. You'll be all alone."

"I like to be alone. I'm used to it all my life."

"You don't read the newspapers, you don't listen to the radio? You don't know what's going on today. Every night burglars break into old people's houses, beat them up, kill them and take everything they've got."

"I've got a special door, guaranteed, you can't open," said Mrs. Moscowitz.

"Don't make me laugh, Yolanda. The door doesn't exist that they can't open. There isn't a lock they can't break. Today there are special tools that break into every door quietly and quickly, without the neighbors hearing. And you're high up, on the top floor, they can climb on the roof and get in through the balcony or the window. It's a joke to them. These aren't ordinary burglars I'm talking about, these are people who have to buy drugs. Nothing stops them, they've got no pity for old people. They gag them and tie them up, beat them, break their bones, kill them, until they give them their money and precious things. And afterwards the old people lie there dying in terrible pain and nobody knows. Even if they're not dead already they haven't got the strength to get up, to get free, to phone up, to shout. None of the neighbors knows anything. It's a crime to leave a weak old person alone in the house when he can't even run away from these gangsters.

"They know everything about the old people who live alone. They know what their condition is, when they go to bed, when they can break in without them knowing. I'm sorry, but you don't know what kind of world you're living in. You don't know what's good for you. I'm not trying to talk you in. You're a lost case. Adela's got you in her pocket. You've already signed the papers her lawyer drew up for her. But you should know that the whole thing's illegal. The police are on to her already. You can change your mind, your signature isn't binding. Just like Allegra's signature won't do Adela and her partner no good neither."

"I didn't sign nothing," said Mrs. Moscowitz.

"Lucky for you. Maybe there's still hope for you, if you start using your brains. Do what you want. If you hate me and don't believe me, go with somebody else. So long as you don't stay at home alone. That's the worst. I know you don't want me. Even what I paid there for you I won't get back from you. What do you care about that stupid Leon, who believed what you told him, who trusted your word, who thought there was something special between us? You can throw him away when you think you don't need him anymore. But you don't have to think about me. You just think about how to save yourself. And if you want me to help you, I'll always come. I'll do what I can. Like I always helped you in the hospital."

"You're a good person, Leon. I'm not saying you're not. And really you helped me a lot. But my life is different now, not the same like it was in the hospital."

He rose wordlessly from the sofa and went to the door. Then he came back into the room and said coldly: "You know where to find me. Even after what you've done to me, I'll always be ready to help you. Because I still love you. I haven't changed. I'm still the same Leon I always was."

For a long time after he was gone his voice went on echoing in the room. The affection she bore him in her heart came back to life, and with it the fear of the shadow that always accompanied him, and sometimes covered him completely, the shadow reflected in his shifting moods, his lies, his acting, his joking and his long silences. There was something dubious and suspect, something appealing and touching in all his actions and behavior. She knew that she must not put her property, her fate, into his hands, but she also knew that she would never find a soul as close to hers as Leon's again. No circle had closed with her homecoming. Her life in the hospital would not let her be. Like the advance guard of an invading army its messengers kept arriving to fill the void she had sought to maintain in her new life, besieging the house, eroding the independence and security she had hoped to find in it. And bringing up the rear the memories flooded in.

More and more now she found herself thinking about her life in the hospital, the nurses and the doctors, the women in her room. And not only about Allegra—whose pictures lay on her bedside table, where night after night she studied them before she fell asleep, as if trying to read a book whose language she did not know—but also about Kagan and her attempts to come close to him, and about the crazy Fichman, about Seniora and Clara who had died, about her hated enemies, the head nurse Rosa and Matilda Franco, and poor Frieda and muddled Paula, and the friendly group in the games' room, and even about the ugly Wolf who had forced his attentions on her, and the hairdresser who had done her hair and given her back her self-respect. Perhaps these had actually been the best days of her life?

Would she ever go back there? If she did go back, it would all be different from the first time. Perhaps, like Allegra, she would arrive there toward the end, dreading being sent home to die alone—not to die alone, only not alone. Leon had reached out to her from there, and she had rejected his outstretched hand. She knew she had done the right thing, but the pain of parting from G. Hospital prevented her from coming to terms with her decision.

chapter twelve

On Saturday afternoon her sleep was suddenly cut short. It seemed to her that a sudden noise had woken her, but the house was closed and quiet. She sat up in bed. People began shouting outside. She put on her dressing gown and went out to the kitchen balcony. Mrs. Poldy was lying in the courtyard, in the green dress, her face on the paved path and a bloodstain spreading around her head. A number of neighbors hurried to the scene, and the youngest of them, in a dark blue tracksuit, shouted to his wife to phone for an ambulance at once. More neighbors, some of them from the adjacent buildings, came running up and surrounded Mrs. Poldy. Mrs. Horn, her head wrapped in the scarf which permanently protected her sensitive ears, elbowed her way through them and cried in her whining voice: "Oy, what's happened! Oy, poor thing! Oy, I can't look at it! I shouldn't see such things!"

"She jumped from their balcony," said the young man in the tracksuit. "I was going to throw out the garbage," he said and indicated the empty pail in his hand, "and when I was standing there, next to the bins, I suddenly saw her in the air, falling onto the branches of the tree, breaking them and crash! onto the ground."

The neighbors raised their eyes to the fourth floor. Mr. Poldy stood between the two halves of the open blind, his hands gripping the railing, looking curiously at the crowd gathered below, as if it had nothing to do with him.

"He's in shock," said one of the neighbors.

"Somebody should go to him, stay with him till the doctor comes," said the youth in the tracksuit but nobody broke away from the circle.

"Maybe he pushed her off?" said Mrs. Horn with a horrified expression on her face.

"I didn't see him," said the neighbor in the tracksuit, "I don't know."

"She was always screaming," wailed Mrs. Horn, "that he was hitting her, that he wanted to kill her."

"What are you talking nonsense for?" a woman from the building next door scolded her. "She was sick," she said and tapped her forehead, "he couldn't control her."

"She was friends with Mrs. Moscowitz," cried Mrs. Horn in a tearful voice, hinting perhaps at some possible guilt, "they were always talking to each other on the telephone."

Now they all raised their eyes to Mrs. Moscowitz's apartment, to the kitchen balcony where she was standing, and examined her face. She averted her eyes from them, raised her head and looked at Mr. Poldy. He felt her eyes on him and turned his face to her. The sunlight glinted on the lenses of his glasses and his eyes were invisible behind them. He looked like a blind man.

Two paramedics from the ambulance crew came into the yard. One of them went straight up to Mrs. Poldy to see if she was breathing, looked at his friend and shook his head. They moved the neighbors away from the body toward the garbage bins. The wailing of a siren rose in the air, came closer and stopped. Three policemen came running up the paved path, bent over Mrs. Poldy and consulted in low voices. The young man in the tracksuit showed them the balcony where Mr. Poldy was standing and looking down at the courtyard. One of the policemen photographed Mrs. Poldy from different angles while the second wrote down what the third, who appeared to be in charge, told him. The paramedics stood to one side and waited until the policeman in charge said something to them. Then they went out into the street and came back carrying a stretcher, lifted Mrs. Poldy onto it and took her out of the yard.

For a while longer the neighbors stood and talked, occasionally looking up at Mr. Poldy, who never moved from his place on the balcony and whose expression of polite curiosity did not change. In the end they turned away and went home. Mrs. Moscowitz saw Mr. Poldy retreat from the railing, slide the middle blind along its runner until it joined up with the ones on either side of it, and turn down the slats on the whole balcony. After that the blinds in the rest of the apartment came down one after the other. For a long time she went on looking at Mrs. Poldy's blood staining the path on the way to her cats.

During the course of the evening she looked again and again at the apartment opposite her kitchen balcony but she could see no light there. It was impossible to tell if Mr. Poldy had gone out or if he was sitting alone in the dark.

She dozed off in front of the television and before midnight, at the hour when Mrs. Poldy's screams usually rose from the building next door, the telephone rang and startled her into wakefulness. She stood up to answer, but before she reached the phone it stopped ringing. She turned off the television and the light in the living room and went into the bedroom. The telephone rang again. She went over and picked up the receiver. There was no sound. She cried: "Hello! Hello! Who is it?" but there was no reply. She replaced the receiver, went into the kitchen and opened the balcony door. Mr. Poldy's apartment still was in darkness.

She got into bed and picked up Allegra's photographs, but was unable to concentrate her thoughts on them. Her ears were constantly on the alert for the telephone to ring. Finally she switched off the light next to her bed but she couldn't fall asleep. For a long time she lay with her eyes open, then she got up, went into the kitchen, boiled water and made herself a cup of tea. She believed in its power to calm her nerves. Taking her time, she drank the hot beverage and tried to distract her thoughts from the horrors of the day. When she was finished, she looked again at Mr. Poldy's dark flat and went back to bed. Half asleep, she started up at the ringing of the telephone. She got out of bed, and picked up the receiver. She pressed the earpiece to her ear and heard the sound of breathing. "Hello!" she cried. "Who is it? Mr. Poldy, it's you? Why don't you speak?" Pants of laughter were audible on the other end of the line. "Who's there? Hello! What do you want?" cried Mrs. Moscowitz. Then she went on listening silently and a few moments later the line went dead. This time she did not hang up, but left the receiver lying on the phone directory shelf.

When she lay down again in bed she heard the continuous dial tone coming from the earpiece of the telephone. Now she remembered what Leon had said about the gangsters who broke into the homes of old people living alone, and she got up and went to check if the door was properly locked and barred. She looked through the peephole too, and it was dark. She pressed the switch next to the door that turned on the light in the stairwell. There was nobody there. She went back to bed. The sound of the dial tone went on cutting through the silence, sharp and final as a verdict. Usually she slept with the door between the bedroom and the hall open. Now it occurred to her to close the door, so that she wouldn't hear the nerve-racking whine of the telephone. But when the bedroom door was open, she could see the front door from her bed, and if she saw a point of light in the darkness coming from the peephole, she would know that someone was on their way up the stairs. So she decided to leave the bedroom door open. Suddenly the dial tone turned into the staccato buzz of the engaged signal, and she didn't know what that meant. There were still several hours before daybreak and relief.

Her weariness overcame her and her eyes closed, but the persistent hum of the telephone kept tearing the web of sleep as it began to weave and she woke up and stared at the door from her bed. She hoped that the phone would not ring again at this hour, and she got out of bed to replace the receiver. When she lay down once more and switched off the light, a point of light appeared in the peephole. She got up, trying not to make any noise with her slippers and the legs of the walker, approached the door and looked through the peephole. There was nobody there, no sound of footsteps on the stairs, or of a door opening or closing on the landing. But after a while she saw her neighbor leaping up the stairs in the running shoes that he always took off and left outside his door. When he reached the last step before the landing he stopped, bent down and unlaced his shoes. When he straightened up, he took a key ring out of his pocket, stepped up to the landing, and disappeared from view.

She heard him open the door, close it and lock it from inside. The light went off in the stairwell. She went back to bed and listened to the sounds coming from the other side of the wall, feeling reassured by his presence. He moved something in his apartment and the thud of bare heels crossed the floor tiles. Then she heard music playing softly, accompanied from time to time by the young man humming. She imagined that he was in bed with the radio playing next to him. The sounds flowed into her ears and at last her exhausted body began to savor the taste of rest.

A telephone rang and jolted her out of her sleep. By the time she got out of bed it had stopped ringing and the neighbor's voice answered from behind the wall. She couldn't catch the words but from the tone of his voice it sounded to her like a conversation between lovers. The light of daybreak began to filter into the apartment, coloring the room a pale gray. The telephone conversation on the other side of the wall came to an end. She knew she would not be able to fall asleep again. Her throat was dry. She got up and went to the kitchen to make herself another cup of tea. While she waited for the water to boil she went out onto the kitchen balcony. The chilly night air sent a shiver through her body. She looked down at the paved path. The light outside was already bright enough to prove the truth of the bloodstain. Suddenly two people ran into the courtyard, as if fleeing their pursuers, reached the garbage bins, and rapidly and with a terrible grating noise dragged the black plastic bins over the paved path and the bloodstain, disappearing abruptly from view. In Poldy's apartment nothing stirred.

Later that morning she called Adela's house several times without getting a reply. When the doorbell rang, she hoped that the energetic helper had heard her call, as she had often done with Allegra, and come hurrying to her aid. She looked through the peephole and saw a policeman. She undid the locks and bolts but left the chain on, and opened the door a crack. The policeman displayed his ID and she closed the door, loosened the chain, and let him in. The policeman sat down on the sofa, facing her, took off his hat and put it down beside him, then took a metal board with papers clipped to it from his briefcase. He was an Eastern man of about forty, tall and rather handsome. His inquiries as to the state of her health, her daily routine, the details of her past and her relationships with other people gave her a feeling of reassurance. He made notes on the clipboard, occasionally asked her to enlarge on one or another question, and looked at her with a kind, sympathetic, concerned expression in his eyes. She was just about to tell him about the distressing night she had spent, when he began asking her about Mrs. Poldy.

"Did you see her fall?" he asked.

"No," said Mrs. Moscowitz, "when I went out to look, she lay already on the ground, poor thing, and there was blood from the head."

"How did you know when to go out and look?"

"The people shouted outside."

"And her husband was on their balcony?"

"Yes."

"What did he do?"

"He looked down, he wasn't understanding what happened."

"How do you know he didn't understand what happened?"

"He looked like a person which had a shock. He stood there without moving."

"Did he see you?"

"I don't know," said Mrs. Moscowitz. Now she began to guess at the intention behind his questions.

"He didn't look at you?"

"He picked up the head, but I don't know if he saw me."

"You were friends, weren't you?"

"I was having pity of her, that she was such a poor thing. She was sick."

"And her husband suffered from it too," said the policeman, "living like that can get a person down."

"Of course. He was good to her, he was loving her."

"The neighbors often heard her shouting that he wanted to kill her."

"She was sick. He was holding her so she shouldn't go out from the house, so she should take the pills for sleeping, and she didn't want."

"Did he tell you how hard it was for him?"

"He wanted that I should influence her to be good."

"You would meet."

"No, we talked only on the phone. She was telephoning all the time, few times a day, and sometimes he took from her the phone and said something. He was asking me to tell her she should be good."

"Did you talk to them on Saturday, before it happened?"

"No."

"And Friday?"

"She rang up and talked, like always. Nothing special."

"And her husband, what did he say?"

"He didn't speak. Only she. Always the same thing, about her cats that she's loving them so much, and they love her. All the time she wanted to go and to see them in the rubbish. Maybe she jumped there to go to the cats. She was sick, she didn't know what she's doing."

"But sometimes her husband came to your house," said the policeman and studied her face to see the effect of his words.

"One time he came. I gave a dress for her, so they can go together outside. She was putting on funny things, and he was ashamed. She was sick."

"And he came back afterwards to return the dress?"

"No. I gave it a present for her. The dress remained to her. With this dress she jumped at the end."

"You only met her husband alone once?" asked the policeman.

"Yes. I never was together with them. Only talking on the phone. Years and years she was standing at the window and I saw her from the kitchen and she was speaking."

"And did you ever go to their house?"

"No, never."

"And when her husband came to fetch the dress, he stayed a while, you spoke to each other, no?"

"He didn't sit down even. He took the dress and went. He said: I must go. I don't want to leave her alone."

"But when he went to work, he left her alone in the house anyway."

"Correct. But in the afternoon her condition was becoming worse. Her blood was becoming hot."

"Some people think he pushed her. Poor man, it's understandable. How long can you go on living like that," said the policeman.

"I know who's saying this. Mrs. Horn, my neighbor downstairs. She's a wicked woman, she thinks everybody is the same like she is. And she also told you he was coming to me, I know. She always looks out from the door to see who's going to who."

"You didn't want people to know that he came to visit you? Was it a secret?"

"I have no secret. I told you everything."

"Perhaps there's something you forgot to tell me. What did she say to you about him? How did he treat her?"

"She said different nonsense. She was sick with the head."

"People heard her shouting that he had somebody, that he had a girlfriend he went to," said the policeman.

A complacent smile suddenly illuminated Mrs. Moscowitz's face. She remembered her meeting with Kagan's wife in the hospital and now, as then, she felt a glow of pleasure at the thought: Maybe I really am a femme fatale?

"You see," said the policeman, "you've remembered something else."

"Mrs. Horn told you this also, that me and Poldy? . . . "

"It's so many years since you got divorced, and all those years you've been alone, without a man. There's nothing wrong with it. Why not? He's a nice guy, isn't he?"

"I understand," said Mrs. Moscowitz, "he killed her for to marry me. And maybe the both of us were making the plan together? So we'll go to prison—what can we do? Twenty years already we're neighbors, why only now? Isn't it a pity of all the time we wasted?"

"And he didn't have some other woman? He didn't confide in you? And her, she never said anything to you about it?"

"Go to his work. Sanitary Imports Company, King George Street, ask them. . . . "

"You know where he worked? Have you ever been there?"

"No, he told me . . . "

"When?"

"When he came to take the dress."

"Why did he tell you that? You couldn't go there in your condition."

"No, I can't go out from the house. I can't go down the stair."

The policeman looked at her for a moment in silence and smiled. "I'm here to help," he said finally, "not to do anyone any harm. You say you loved her. I'm sure you'd like to know exactly how she died."

"Yes. I'm telling everything what I know. Every word the truth. If he killed her, he should go to hell. But I don't believe. That's all. Where is he now? In the house you can't see somebody."

"Do you want to talk to him?"

"Why not? It hurts me the heart for her and for him. Where is he? Did you see him?"

"He hasn't spoken to you since it happened?"

"No, I told you already. When you came here I thought you're coming for something else."

He put the clipboard down next to him on the sofa. "What did you think?" he asked.

"In the night, someone was ringing me all the time on the phone, and when I'm picking it up there's nothing. And at the end there was a noise of a person laughing quiet. I didn't sleep all the night."

"When was this?" asked the policeman, sitting up and putting the clipboard on his knees, but not writing anything yet.

"The last night," said Mrs. Moscowitz.

"And before last night, did it ever happen before?"

"No."

"Maybe it was him, her husband?"

"For what he should do it?"

"You know him so well, that you know what he might do and might not do?"

"The whole night I didn't sleep and I had a terrible fear."

"What were you afraid of?"

"Maybe somebody wants to know that I'm alone in the house and afterwards he'll break inside here and kill me to take my things. I know what they're doing to old people which lives alone. It's people from the drugs which aren't afraid from anything. And where's the police?"

"Don't open the door to anyone that you don't know. Not even with the chain. Look through the hole in the door, and if you don't know the person—don't open."

"But they've got different things for opening every door."

He stood up and went over to the front door. "Has anybody got a key to this door?"

"No," said Mrs. Moscowitz.

"Not even the husband of the woman who was killed?"

"I see you don't believe me one single thing I'm telling you."

"Okay. Look, breaking into a door like this would take time and make a lot of noise. They don't like messing with this kind of thing. Do you know how to phone the police? I'll write the number down for you. If anyone really tries to break in, just call this number and they'll be here right away. And if you happen to remember anything you forgot to tell me about what we were discussing before, call this number too and ask for me. I may come again soon to have a chat with you," said the policeman. He handed her a piece of paper and and put on his hat.

"And what about if somebody's phoning again in the night and not speaking? I should call the police?"

"If the phone calls are repeated, get in touch with me in the morning at the number I gave you. Don't lose the note."

Before he left, Mrs. Moscowitz asked him: "Where's Poldy, he's not at home?"

The policeman smiled at her politely, said goodbye and shut the door behind him.

After he had gone, she went out onto the kitchen balcony and looked at the closed apartment opposite, at the courtyard and the paved path. The policeman came into the yard, walked down the path, looked at the bloodstain for a moment and then raised his eyes to Poldy's apartment and Mrs. Moscowitz's kitchen balcony. She waved to him but he ignored her salutation. He went on to the garbage bins, where he looked up again at Poldy's apartment, and then walked around the corner of the building and disappeared from view.

―

Mrs. Moscowitz tried to telephone Adela several times without getting an answer. Her impatience turned to anger at the helper who had been deceiving her with her glib tongue, coveting her property and not answering her when she was in trouble. She had no appetite, she couldn't bear the sight of food. Even though she had hardly slept a wink the night before, that afternoon she couldn't fall asleep. She got out of bed and wandered around the apartment, looking for somewhere to settle but not finding anyplace comfortable. The pain in her ankle came back to trouble her. She sat down next to the telephone and phoned G. Hospital. The head nurse of the ward answered the phone.

"Rosa!" called Mrs. Moscowitz joyfully. "How are you? How do you feel?"

"Who's speaking?" asked Rosa.

"Yolanda!"

"Who?"

"Yolanda! You don't remember me?"

"What do you want?"

"Before I was leaving the hospital you had an accident and I couldn't say goodbye. So now you're feeling all right?"

304

"Thank you for your concern."

"How is everybody? Is everything in the ward the same? It's a pity I can't come to visit. All day I'm at home with the walker. With the stair it's impossible. . . . "

"Is there anybody you want to talk to?"

"Is Leon there?"

"No, he worked the night shift."

"I was happy in the hospital," said Mrs. Moscowitz, "happier than now."

"Everyone's got their own troubles," said Rosa. "I've got work to do. What do you want?"

After hanging up she went to the bathroom. Her new face looked at her from the mirror. Her hair which had grown and turned gray, was rolled up into a bun and secured with plain hairpins. Her skin did not seem more wrinkled than it had been in the hospital, but the way her hair was pulled back behind her head stressed her sagging cheeks and the folds in her neck. The slits of her eyes had grown narrower. The almost lashless lids were pink, and the pouches under the eyes were netted with tiny, purplish red veins. But the narrow strips of blue looking out of the slits of her eyes were as clean and clear as ever, refusing to take part in her tiredness, her sleeplessness, the pains that had come back to her ankle, her growing sense that the world around her was emptying out. Her eyes of old scorned her fears.

Late that afternoon Adela answered the phone at last.

"I've been phoning you all day and you're never there. Where have you been? I need you!" said Mrs. Moscowitz.

"I'll be there tomorrow morning," said Adela. "I was working, I wasn't home all day. Why are you so nervous, what happened?"

"Not over the phone," said Mrs. Moscowitz.

"Did Leon come to see you?"

"I'll tell you when you come."

"Have you thought about what we discussed?" asked Adela. "Do you agree to our arrangement?"

"We'll discuss it tomorrow. My leg hurts me too, at the ankle. I can't stand. It only stops hurting in bed."

"I'll take care of everything and you'll be fine. But first I have to know if you want me to work with you. Should I bring the papers?"

"Yes, bring them. But come by yourself, without the lawyer," said Mrs. Moscowitz.

"Who said anything about a lawyer? Did I mention a lawyer? Has Leon been telling you lies about me? Did I bring a lawyer to Allegra? Everything was open and aboveboard, right? It'll be the same with you. Just between the two of us. We trust each other. We're like two friends, sisters, or mother and daughter. I haven't got a mother. You'll be like my mother. That's how I'll look after you and take care of you."

"I wanted you to come today, to stay with me a bit, because there are problems. But now I suppose it's too late for you."

"I've just this minute come home," said Adela. "I'm tired and I've got a lot of things to do in the house."

"I'm afraid of the night," said Mrs. Moscowitz. "More than that I can't say over the phone."

❦

If only there had been a noise from the neighbor's apartment, it would have been easier for her to wait for the night. Every few minutes she went into the bedroom and pressed her ear to the wall, but she couldn't hear anything. All the sounds from outside too died down as evening fell. The neighbors from the building on the other side of the courtyard retreated into their apartments from the winter's chill and pulled the blinds down behind them. At night, when she stood on the big balcony and looked out through the slats there was no sign of life in those apartments now, no way of knowing if the lights were burning, if the television was on. And against the blinds of her own balcony the naked sewage tree fawned, shaking its thin, leafless branches like sick arms at the starless sky.

Just before ten o'clock the phone rang while she was sleeping in her armchair opposite the television. So deep was her sleep that when she woke up she thought for a moment that it was Mrs. Poldy phoning her again. But immediately afterwards she remembered, and when she picked up the phone she expected to hear the nerve-racking silence of the night before.

"Who's there?" said a deep, hoarse male voice in her mother tongue. "Who's speaking?"

"Who are you?" replied Mrs. Moscowitz in the same language.

There was a short silence and the hoarse voice said: "You're Yolanda." She didn't reply and he called: "Hello! Yolanda!"

"Where do you know the name Yolanda from?" asked Mrs. Moscowitz.

"I know you from G. Hospital," said the man. "I had someone there I used to visit and I saw you lots of times. You don't know me."

"What do you want?"

"To tell you to be careful, to watch out for yourself and not do anything stupid. To listen to good people who want to help you and not to go with crooks who'll take everything you've got and won't give you a place where you can live with dignity."

"What's your name?"

"You don't know my name. You don't know me. I've never spoken to you."

"I can't speak to a person who won't tell me his name. I'm hanging up."

"Did you know Allegra Levy?"

"Yes. She was my friend."

"It so happens I was a neighbor of hers in Ramle. The house next door. I knew her from way back. She could have gone on living for

307

years. Someone saw to it that she died quickly, to get their hands on her property. You know who. A criminal woman, who cheats sick old people, separates them from their families and makes trouble between them and their relations, so they'll be completely dependent on her. And she gets them to sign papers that they don't understand what's written there and takes over their lives. They trust her and do everything she tells them. And when she's got them in her pocket she begins to give them all kinds of things that instead of helping them to get over their sicknesses, finish them off. And all to get her hands on the inheritance. Now it's all come out and the police are investigating. I thought it was my duty to tell you before it's too late. I saw you there, that you're a good woman and you were a friend of Allegra Levy's. But out of naiveté, apparently, you agreed to sign that crook's papers against the family."

"Allegra herself asked me to sign. I didn't want to, I only did it for Allegra."

"She was already under her thumb by then," said the man, "she had to do everything that crook told her. It'll happen to you too, if you let her get her hands on you."

"She was good to Allegra," said Mrs. Moscowitz, "I saw how she came to look after her, how she did everything for her."

"That's what you think. It was all an act. Ask the doctors and nurses at G. Hospital, they'll tell you what she did to her. Today it's all come out. If they knew then, they wouldn't have let that woman in."

"Why don't you tell me your name?"

"I don't want to get involved, to get called for a witness to go to the police and the court to tell what I know. I haven't got the time for it. I only wanted to warn you, because I used to see you all the time when I came to visit in the hospital, you gave the impression of a good woman, and we come from the same country, we speak the same language. I'm sorry for you. Be careful of that criminal. And you'd better be careful of Allegra Levy's brother too. He's got a terrible temper. He's looking for you now because of your signature on those papers. He wants you to sign a declaration in front of lawyers that the criminal put pressure on you to sign and you didn't even read what was written there."

"But that isn't true," said Mrs. Moscowitz.

"Your friend, Frieda Bakal, already did it. There's one more signature, of Clara Hershkowitz who died. But it's enough if two of Allegra Levy's friends cancel their signature. You see, Yolanda, how that criminal's already gotten you into trouble, even before she did anything for you."

There was a worrying contradiction between the politeness of his words and the coarseness of his hoarse voice, as well as the way he pronounced her first name, in the tone of someone scolding a disobedient dog.

"Did you phone me last night too?" asked Mrs. Moscowitz.

"No, why? Did somebody talk to you about it yesterday?"

"I'll have to think about what you've told me," said Mrs. Moscowitz diplomatically.

"That's what I phoned you for, Yolanda. Good night."

She lay in bed and even when drowsiness began to take hold of her, she still kept her ears pricked up in the silence. Suddenly she was roused from her sleep with a start by a kind of bang followed by the steady, monotonous chugging of an engine. She stood up and went to the door, put on the light in the stairwell and peered through the peephole. There was nobody there, the noise was coming from another direction—the kitchen. She went into the kitchen, switched on the light and heard the motor of the refrigerator, which had begun to run. She didn't remember having heard this chugging before. For a long time she stood next to the refrigerator and listened anxiously to the noise. Suddenly the engine coughed and the refrigerator shuddered and was silent. As if the demon had departed from it.

She went back to bed and lay in the dark with her eyes open, dazed with weariness, and not a chance of sleep. A point of light appeared in the peephole of the front door and she roused herself from the stupor into which she had sunk. She did not get up, but went on listening to the silence from her bed, waiting for the sound of footsteps or a door opening and closing in one of the apartments. The point of light went out and then she heard someone trying to insert a key into the lock of her door. For a moment her heart froze, but she immediately collected herself and got up to make her way to the door without putting on the light. Slowly she advanced in the darkness, careful not to make a noise. The attempts to insert the key in the keyhole continued. When she was next to the door, she put the light on in the stairwell, pressed her eye to the peephole and saw the face of her young neighbor, distorted by the lens. He retreated from the door, leaned against the railing, closed his eyes and swayed unsteadily on his feet, as if trying to recover his balance. And again he approached the door and tried to insert the key into the keyhole. Suddenly he raised his head, stared glassily at the door, closed his eyes and mumbled to himself: "Ha, ha, sorry," and immediately turned aside and disappeared from view. Mrs. Moscowitz heard him scratching at the door of his apartment until he succeeded in fitting the key into the keyhole. In the end he opened his door and slammed it with a bang that reverberated in the stairwell.

From the other side of the wall loud music burst forth accompanied by a rhythmic pounding that shook the building. She had never enjoyed music and singing, not even in her youth when she swayed in the arms of her partner to the strains of a dance band. But now she welcomed the savage sounds bursting into her bedroom, assailing her bed, pouncing on her body.

Someone in one of the apartments shouted "Quiet!" but the noises drowned out his voice. They went on invading her body, filling her as if she were their sound box. Strange and cruel they ran riot inside her, fighting for a place in her body, for her memory, for the stifled sighing of her heart. Like a mighty pulse bursting from the bowels of the earth, the rhythmic shaking continued unabated, uniting with the beating of her heart, with the tempo of her breathing, and bearing her to the limits of time, to no-place, and slowly returned her to the loneliness of the body, lamenting the death of the flesh.

A fist pounded violently on the door of the next-door apartment. Mr. Adler's voice shouted: "Quiet! It's three o'clock at night! What's going on here?"

Immediately silence fell. A pleasant lassitude spread through Mrs. Moscowitz's limbs and her heart was at peace and grateful for the consolation of surrender and the sweetness of passivity, as if she had been given a foretaste of the final mortification.

"What nerve!" cried Mr. Adler. "If it starts again, I'm calling the police!" And she heard his footsteps descending the stairs.

Late the next morning Adela rang the doorbell and woke her from her sleep.

"Yesterday you were in such a panic," said Adela as she went to the kitchen to put down the cooked dishes she had brought with her. "Today we're going to spend a lot of time together. I've got plenty of time."

"A lot of things have happened since the last time you were here," said Mrs. Moscowitz.

"You can tell me later. Come, you're still half-asleep. I'll give you a bath," said Adela. She looked at her for a moment and asked: "What do you need such long hair for? First of all I'll cut it for you."

"Do you know how?"

"Of course."

She took a pair of scissors out of her bag, went into the bathroom and brought a comb and a big towel, seated Mrs. Moscowitz on a chair in the kitchen, draped the towel around her shoulders and began to cut her hair. The floor around the chair was soon covered with her shorn tresses, and she didn't even have a mirror to see what kind of a haircut Adela was giving her.

"Not too short," requested Mrs. Moscowitz.

"We won't talk now," said Adela, "we'll keep quiet."

When she had finished her work, she shook out the towel on the kitchen balcony, swept the cut hair into a pile, gathered it up in her hands and threw it into the garbage pail. She led her into the bathroom, where the electric heater was already on. Mrs. Moscowitz examined the short haircut in the mirror and kept quiet, in obedience to Adela's instructions. "You'll see what it looks like after the shampoo," said the masseuse.

Adela adjusted the temperature of the water, rinsed out the tub, put in the plug and began to fill it up. Mrs. Moscowitz pointed to the shower stall and explained: "No, not here. I take a shower, on a chair, like they taught me in the hospital."

Adela put her finger on her lips to silence her and smiled. She went out to the living room and returned with a blue plastic container without a label on it, poured some grayish green salt into the bath, crouched down and stirred it with her hand until it dissolved. Then she took the walker out of the room and shut the door. She moved the chair from the shower to the side of the bath and helped Mrs. Moscowitz out of her dressing gown and nightgown. And while the bathtub was filling up, she seated her naked on the chair and gently stroked her shoulders, neck and arms. Mrs. Moscowitz put her arms around Adela's waist and buried her head in her bosom. The smell of Adela's body saturated her breath, a female smell, warm and strong, which clung to the brown corduroy dress she was wearing and mingled with the sourness of her sweat and the cigarette smoke and the bus fumes, the smell of the world, the smell of life.

Adela turned off the faucet, dipped her hand into the bathtub and once more checked the heat of the water, which was steaming. She helped her to rise from the chair, and Mrs. Moscowitz swung her healthy leg over the side of the tub and dipped it in the water, but was unable to bend her bad leg to the required degree. Adela held her under the armpits and raised her body until she was able to put her other leg too into the tub. Then she gradually lowered her into the bath and Mrs. Moscowitz let out a cry of surprise, since the water was far hotter than her feet had guessed. When she was lying in the water, Adela laid her hand on Mrs. Moscowitz's forehead and passed it over her eyes to close them. Sweat broke out on her forehead and her upper lip and poured down her face. She nearly swooned and was no longer able to distinguish between her body and the water encompassing it. Adela's hand supported her neck, raised her head and shampooed her hair. She massaged her scalp with her fingertips and then cupped the bathwater in her hands and rinsed her hair well.

Adela raised her back into a sitting position, gripped her by the armpits and stood her on her feet. Mrs. Moscowitz opened her eyes and saw the helper looking at her expressionlessly, a big towel draped over her shoulder, as she held her by the arm, bent down and helped her to lift her legs over the side of the tub and set them on the floor, wrapped her in the towel, put her arms around her and patted her all over her body. Then Adela unwrapped the towel, seated her on the chair and rubbed her hair with it, knelt down in front of her and dried her feet. After that she stood up again, combed Mrs. Moscowitz's hair, wrapped a towel around her head, and dressed her in her bathrobe. She took the little scissors from the shelf under the mirror, cut her toenails and removed the lumps of calloused skin from her toes and the soles of her feet.

"Wait here for a minute," Adela broke her long silence, "I want to heat the room."

She went out and shut the bathroom door behind her. Mrs. Moscowitz felt weak, she breathed heavily and her heart pounded.

The bathroom began spinning around, and the chair lost its grip on the floor. Adela came back and raised her from the chair, but Mrs. Moscowitz fell limply into her arms. She seated her on the chair again and supported her there until she recovered from her faintness. Then she led her to her bed and helped her to lie down. She slipped her arms out of the sleeves of the bathrobe, spread the two halves out on either side of her body, and helped her to turn over and lie on her stomach.

Mrs. Moscowitz knew that Adela was now taking the baby oil out of her bag, opening the bottle and pouring oil into the palm of her hand. The first oily contact sent a shiver down her spine. Then Adela's hands began to massage her shoulders, her arms and her back, rubbing and slapping her flesh. Her thumbs pressed hard, in a circular motion, on various points on her hips and hurt her. Adela added more oil to her palm and massaged her buttocks, pinching the soft falls of flesh and shaking them briskly. The masseuse's fingers slid down her thighs, increasing their pressure more and more, ploughing furrows of heat down them. Her skin burned with the friction but the heat did not penetrate her flesh. Adela helped her to turn over and lie on her back. Mrs. Moscowitz closed her eyes. Then Adela began to anoint her chest with oil. She took each breast in her hands and gently massaged it and the chest beneath it. Mrs. Moscowitz heard her panting rhythmically, with a machine like sound, and felt the expelled air on her stomach. The energy and skill invested in the massage were evident, but there wasn't a drop of love in it to wake the flesh from the sleep of death that was conquering it. Mrs. Moscowitz remembered how she used to massage Allegra, how she would snuggle up to the sick woman and whisper funny things in her ear, and there was no knowing what they were. She even remembered what Adela had said about Allegra's body, that until the last it had preserved its youthful appearance, even in the most private parts. Adela's oily hands, which had finished massaging her stomach, gradually parted her legs, stroked her vagina, reached for her buttocks, stroked them and returned to her groin. Something inside her was drawing her to sink into drowsiness and give her body into Adela's hands, but the sound of the rhythmic, mechanical panting kept her eyes open watching the woman sitting on the edge of her bed. She saw her forehead frowning with effort, her face like the face of a drudge, bending over the lower abdomen which her hands were massaging, and her large bosom rising and falling with the rhythm of her breathing, full of strength and determination. Fear crept into Mrs. Moscowitz's heart, fear of this strong woman and suspicion of her hidden plans, and at the same time she knew that she would cling to her and would not let her leave her, whatever conditions she laid down. Adela sensed her look, raised her eyes to her and grunted: "Is it nice?"

Mrs. Moscowitz nodded her head and made herself smile gratefully.

Adela stood up, bent over her, buried her face in the angle between her shoulder and her neck and kissed her. Then she sat down again, and once more she crouched over Mrs. Moscowitz's stomach and stuck her thumbs into her groin, pushing them in and out, tightening and letting go, and with a circular motion her hands descended to her knees, anointed them with oil and rubbed them gently before passing on to her calves and ankles, her feet and her toes.

Finally Adela rose to her feet, gathered up the sides of the bathrobe and slipped Mrs. Moscowitz's arms into the sleeves. Wrapping the robe around her body she tied the belt, covered her with the blanket and said: "Now close your eyes and rest. When the food's ready, get up and we'll eat together and have a talk. And then you'll be able to tell me all the the things you wanted to tell me, too." She kissed her on the forehead, drew the blanket up to her shoulders and left the room.

Mrs. Moscowitz felt as if Adela's hands were still rubbing her aching, tormented, weary body, burning it like fire. She decided that when she told Adela about the telephone calls of the last two nights, she would not mention what the anonymous caller had said about the nature of her treatments. But nevertheless she would ask her, casually, as if by the way, what that gray green salt was that she had poured into the bathwater from the blue plastic box without a label.

—

Adela woke her from her slumbers. The kitchen was full of the smell of food heating up on the stove. Mrs. Moscowitz sipped the soup eagerly and as she did so she told Adela about Mrs. Poldy's death and about the night of the nerve-racking silent telephone calls and the anonymous caller last night, how he had spoken about Allegra's brother who was looking for her in order to force her to withdraw her signature from Adela's documents.

"Don't you understand?" asked Adela incredulously. "Leon's behind it all! He wants to frighten you. It's him who phoned you up and didn't say anything, to make you lose your confidence, to think people were after you, so you'd be afraid to stay at home, and in the end you'd give in and go to that place where he wants to throw you."

"In the hospital, at night, Leon really did phone all kinds of places, he would talk to all kinds of girls and say rude things to them. That's how he passed the time when he was on night duty," said Mrs. Moscowitz.

"He did the same thing on Saturday night," said Adela.

"And I know he was there in the hospital on Saturday night. I spoke to the hospital and Rosa told me."

"Why did you ask about him?"

"I asked about everybody. I was bored. You weren't at home. I wanted to talk to somebody. I was homesick for the hospital, for my friends there, for everybody. I called them up."

"What do you want to phone the hospital for? It's no good for you. Forget it and everything you saw there. You have to get well,

to live like a normal human being. You'll be able to walk, to go outside, to see people. Of course, you can do what you want and talk to
whoever you want," said Adela, "it's none of my business. But be
careful of Leon, that's my advice. For your own good, don't talk to
him. He can take advantage of it and use it against you afterward. If
he phones you, don't answer and hang up. Don't have anything to do
with him. It's not healthy. He's a friend of Marco's, Allegra's gangster
brother. They help each other, like between criminals. And who do
you think spoke to you last night? Don't you understand? It was
Marco himself. He's walking around free now, but not for long. Soon
he'll be back where he belongs, in jail. Together with Leon. He won't
be able to do you any harm. The police tail him everywhere."

"He said that Frieda had already canceled her signature and signed
a statement against you."

Adela burst out laughing. "Call her and ask her," she suggested,
and she stood up and went to the telephone, as if to bring it to the
kitchen.

"There's no need," said Mrs. Moscowitz. "I believe you."

"He and Leon collaborated to scare you, two nights in a row. Leon
thought that after a couple of nights like that, you'd come running to
him to save you. You've got nothing to fear, Yolanda, neither of them
will be free for long. They tried to threaten me too. I went to the
police and they told me that they were already keeping an eye on
them. You're not the first. It's the end for them. They can't do you any
harm. What else did Marco say about me? Didn't he tell you that I
poison people, that I kill them so that I can get my hands on their
property, like I did to Allegra?"

"He talked about my signature on Allegra's papers," said Mrs.
Moscowitz.

"Are you sorry that you signed for Allegra?"

"No."

"Do you want to sign an agreement with me, for yourself?"

"Yes," said Mrs. Moscowitz, "I've decided to go with you."

"You see the appetite you've got now, after the bath and the massage? Don't you feel stronger? In a minute we'll see if you can walk without the walker."

"Not today," requested Mrs. Moscowtiz, "I'm a little tired after these last nights. I didn't sleep much."

"Come to the living room," said Adela after they had finished eating. "I'll make coffee, and I've brought a nice cake too, that I baked specially for you, like in the old country."

Mrs. Moscowitz sat down in the armchair in the living room, and Adela put the papers down in front of her. "In the meantime, read what it says here. It's not complicated and it's in our language. Know what you're signing. I'm going to make coffee."

When Adela came back with the coffee and the slices of cake, she asked her: "Have you read it?"

"Yes," said Mrs. Moscowitz, "I wrote what I had to write and I signed. But I've got a request. It's written here what you have to do after I die, about the burial and the gravestone. I also want them to bury me in a coffin, not to throw me into the ground. I can't stand it. It makes me nervous to think about it. Only in a coffin."

"All right," said Adela. "You want us to write it in the agreement?"

"What for? Can I come and complain to you, if you don't do what I ask? Just promise me."

"I promise," said Adela.

"Even if according to the Jewish religion it's forbidden in a coffin."

"Don't worry," said Adela. "They'll do what I tell them."

They drank their coffee, and Mrs. Moscowitz praised the cake. Adela said: "Have you seen how pretty your hair is now? How it suits you? It's much healthier like this."

Adela went into the kitchen to wash the dishes and clear the table, and Mrs. Moscowitz sat next to her and knew that soon she would go away and leave her alone in the apartment. And what did it hold in store for her, the night that was already beginning to turn her windows gray? She couldn't bring herself to ask Adela to stay with her tonight and lie next to her and quiet her sleep, even though the request did not seem excessive to her, now that she had transferred all her property to Adela after she died.

At their next meeting—Adela explained to her—she would bring a lawyer who would ask her to sign a will drawn up in accordance with the agreement between them. She would let her know in advance when they were coming so that she would be able to prepare herself and dress suitably for the occasion. Before they said goodbye, Adela embraced her warmly and kissed her, and Mrs. Moscowitz thanked her for all her trouble. When she was alone, she put on the light in the room, which had grown dark, and it seemed to her that the light was dimmer than usual, as if the electric current had grown weaker. The apartment had become alien to her and she felt resentment against Adela, who knew how to guess all her needs, for not having offered of her own free will to sleep with her tonight. Was the swindle beginning already?

She sat down next to the telephone and dialed Kagan's number in Beersheba. His wife answered.

"Rolanda?" She recognized her voice immediately. "How are you? Lazar is already home. I call him. One moment."

Kagan's voice came over the line, feeble and gloomy. "How are you, Yolanda? What are you doing?"

"I'm at home," said Mrs. Moscowitz, "what about you? How do you feel?"

"You know they took leg off."

"Yes."

"Life is very hard. All the time there are pains. Also leg they took off hurts. This is paradox, but really so. What remains?"

"They'll give a prosthesis?" inquired Mrs. Moscowitz.

"What was missing when I was healthy?" said Kagan. "Everything was okay and life was fine. Suddenly accident from bus. Why does this happen to me? All is question of one second. I cross before or bus comes afterward, and nothing happens. But of course, I fall on exact same second when comes bus. And so all my life is ruined. What remains, Yolanda, what remains?"

"And I can't go out from the house with my legs. I can't go down the stair. Just like in prison, all the time alone in the house."

"But I was healthy man, with two legs walking, with strength, with ambition. What now? Nothing. Everything finished, and poor Tanya she has to give me everything, help me with crutches, listen how I cry to her, how I am angry. You know, I'm crying also. So much it hurts, so much I want already to die."

"Maybe this is only some depression that will pass, and you'll manage with the prosthesis, you'll do everything you want," said Mrs. Moscowitz.

"Phoo! I don't take prosthesis. I am aesthetic man. You forgot, Yolanda? I can't put such thing on my body. Better even crutches than prosthesis. I'll never leave house again, so nobody can see me without my leg."

"I had one neighbor," said Mrs. Moscowitz, "a crazy woman, who was ringing me on the telephone all day. On Saturday she threw herself off from the balcony, fourth floor, and died on the spot. Sometimes I'm thinking maybe she'll suddenly telephone and speak her nonsense. So much I want to hear her. And I've got nobody to talk anymore. The worst is to be alone. Thank God you've got a good wife and friends come . . . "

"No," said Kagan, "I don't want to come anybody, to see my state, to pity for me, to say poor man, without leg. This I can't. Body is whole thing, you understand? When something taken off, this is disgusting.

Now I am disgusting, Yolanda. Maybe this is really depression. But if depression or illusion—then better depression. What remains to do? Day and night I think and think only one thing—about one second then on road, one second that caught me so tight and impossible to get out any more. One more time and one more time I fall in same second, fall and fall until comes end. When will end come?"

"You don't paint?" asked Mrs. Moscowitz. "Maybe it's good for you to paint?"

"I can't," said Kagan, "with no joy in heart, is no energy. Impossible to work. Nothing is worth something. Nothing is good. Everything goes down, down and down. Just yesterday we looked with Tanya at my pad from G. Hospital. You remember? I made with pen sketches from you. There was one sketch there, 'Yolanda sleeping.' Tanya says it's beautiful, it's one of the best of mine. I looked and I thought: This isn't mine. This somebody else did. I can never draw like this again.

"We had good time, you remember? Really it wasn't so bad. And I said: Inferno. I didn't know what I'm saying. After every hell is another hell, but even more deeper down, even more bad. And I don't know when it ends.

"It's pity we can't meet one more time. I can't go there and you can't come here. I'll never see you again, I suppose. It was good for me to be with you there. You're good person, Yolanda. I'm not. Many times I wasn't good. Not nice. So much hope I had, so much egoism, I didn't think if it hurts you, if you're suffering, I said different things that afterwards I forgot. Today I remember. When we looked yesterday at 'Yolanda sleeping,' I thought about this. You were good to me, Yolanda. Really good friend. Forgive me that I wasn't good to you."

"I never met such a person before," said Mrs. Moscowitz, "I myself know nothing. Even a newspaper I don't read or listen to the radio, as if I'm not on the world. And even though I'm French teacher,

I didn't know what those things were that you said to me from the books in French and different other things too. I'm a simple woman, and I never had a chance to learn in my life. But in my heart I felt what you were, something special, which you meet once in the life. Everything was coming for me too late, everything was lost for me. And you were like a king for me. It was good for me to meet you, Lazar. It was good for me to be there with you together. Many times I'm thinking about you and I'll never forget you. I wish the depression leaves you and you'll feel better, and you'll begin to live normal, you'll begin again to paint. It's so important for a person to have something to do in the life."

"Nothing will be normal again, Yolanda. It won't be better," said Kagan, "only more and more bad. I told you: after every hell comes one more hell, even worse. In my heart is no hope. Only one thing: for end to come, to come quick. And until then, who will help me? 'O Satan, prends pitié de ma longue misère!' You remember, Yolanda?"

—

Once a week Raffy came to clean the stairwell and Mrs. Moscowitz would wait for him to ring her doorbell. Every Thursday, before he cleaned the stairs, she would take him into the kitchen and seat him at the table, give him a drink of water, inquire after his health and the health of his brother, who worked in the gardens of the surrounding buildings, and try again and again to get him to admit that he had worked at G. Hospital and that he remembered her—without success. Then Raffy would take the garbage bag out of the pail and carry it down to the bins in the yard. At the end of every month she would pay him for his trouble.

This Thursday Mrs. Moscowitz waited for Raffy's ring and it didn't come. From time to time she opened the door and saw that the stairs hadn't been cleaned. The day darkened and she still kept her ears pricked for a sound from the stairwell, hoping he might yet turn up. When she heard her neighbor opening and closing his door, she hurried out onto the landing. The neighbor locked his door and turned toward the stairs. She called him:

"Excuse me, he doesn't work today, the Arab boy?"

"I haven't seen him. They've got a curfew there. They can't get out," said the young neighbor.

"When will he come?"

"I don't know. What do you need them for?"

"Every Thursday he's coming to take my rubbish," said Mrs. Moscowitz, "to take down to the bins. Because I can't go myself." She pointed to the walker. "Now he didn't come. The rubbish is full."

"Do you want me to take it for you?"

"I'm embarrassed to ask," said Mrs. Moscowitz.

"I don't mind," he said, followed her into the kitchen and took the bag out of the pail.

"I'll pay you," offered Mrs. Moscowitz. The young man burst out laughing. "Why not?" she asked. She accompanied him to the landing. "When I saw he didn't come," she explained, "I thought maybe people hit him in the street. I know him a long time. He was working in the hospital where I was. He's a good boy. He helped me a lot. Everybody he helped. Over there too they hit him. Some crazy person took him and hit him for nothing, and the boy didn't do nothing to him. After that, he wasn't coming any more to work in the hospital. Now I owe him money for a month."

"Don't feel so sorry for them," said the young man. "They get what they deserve." And he hurried down the stairs.

"Thank you, thank you very much," she managed to call after him before he disappeared from view.

In the middle of the night she woke up suddenly and it seemed to her that the ringing of the telephone had jolted her out of her sleep.

But everything was still and the telephone was silent, just as it had been silent all evening and all the day before. She tried to fall asleep again but she couldn't. When her eyes closed she felt dozens of pairs of oily hands rubbing her body, cutting, burning stinging stripes into it. She got up and went into the kitchen to make herself a cup of tea, and while she waited for the water to boil, she went into the living room and opened the door to the balcony. The gust of cold air stopped her breath. The thick woolen dressing gown she was wearing over her nightgown suddenly felt as light and airy as a cobweb. She raised the collar of her gown, drew it together under her chin, and went out onto the balcony.

The silence outside, like the anguish of the void, deafened her ears. Never had she heard such a silence before. She moved the middle blind aside and its grating on the runner momentarily tore the skin of the silence, which immediately settled and closed in again. No stir in the air shook the naked branches of the sewage tree, which spread their twisted fingers in front of her. In the buildings around her all the apartments were dark and their blinds were down. For a long time now things had been sucked out of her world into another world, another time, and everything was emptying out around her, emptying more and more until she would be imprisoned in a transparent bubble of emptiness, naked and destitute.

The kettle whistled in the kitchen. At first a low growling which quickly increased and grew higher and sharper, like a whine of pain, shriller and shriller, piercing the heart of the night, rising higher and becoming so thin that no sound remained in it but for a rasping breath, a loud whisper, wounded and desperate, as if the earth had opened its mouth and silently sobbed.

She knew that she alone heard it, that in the whole world only she was left, all by herself on this sick, abandoned, grieving earth. When she raised her eyes she saw above the roofs of the houses a strip of sky as clear as black glass, and strewn with stars. At long last—Mrs. Moscowitz breathed a sigh of relief—who could remember when there had been any stars here.

Like glittering eyes they shone above her, like pure, eternally young eyes, contemplating themselves in an infinitude of love, and redeeming nothing with their gaze.

A NOTE ON THE AUTHOR

Yehoshua Kenaz writes in Hebrew and is the author of several novels and story collections. He was born in Israel in 1937 and lives in Tel Aviv where he works on the editorial staff of the daily newspaper *Ha'aretz*. He studied at the Hebrew University and later at the Sorbonne and is also a literary and theater critic and translator of French classics. A novel, *After the Holidays,* is his only other work to be published in English. A collection of four of his novellas, *Musical Moment,* will be published by Steerforth Press in 1995.

A NOTE ON THE BOOK

The text for this book was composed by Steerforth Press using a digital version of Sabon, a typeface designed by Jan Tschichold and first cut and cast at the Stempel Foundry in 1964. The book was printed on acid free papers and bound by Quebecor Printing~Book Press Inc. of North Brattleboro, Vermont.